# THE OBITUARY ARRIVES AT TWO O'CLOCK

## Shizuko Natsuki

BALLANTINE BOOKS • NEW YORK

Originally published in Japanese as *Fuho Wa Gogo Niji Ni Todoku* by Bungeishunju Ltd., Tokyo. Copyright © 1983 by Shizuko Natsuki.

Library of Congress Catalog Card Number: 88-91978

ISBN 0-345-35237-8

Manufactured in the United States of America

First American Edition: November 1988

He was peering into the night, looking for the house, when he suddenly braked the car. There, standing in the middle of the road all by itself was a child's tricycle. He felt a wave of fear wash over him. He could not see any suspicious movement, so making up his mind, he finally stepped out of the car and hurried over to the tricycle and threw it over toward the van. There was no moon and the road was wrapped in a mantle of darkness. He started back to the car only to stop again, fear seizing his heart with its icy talons. There, no more than two or three yards off, was the shadow of a man. He seemed to be wearing a black windbreaker with a hood, and dark glasses. They stood in silence.

"Who . . . who are you?"

# 1

# A Voice in the Night

IT HAD BEEN WET AND OVERCAST ALL AUTUMN, but this particular day a low-pressure front had swept over the country, bringing with it especially high winds and heavy rainfall. As night fell the winds dropped, but the cold rain showed no sign of letting up.

Kōsuke Ōkita had arrived back home three minutes earlier and had only paused to loosen his tie before settling back in an armchair and lighting a cigarette. The low-pressure front had brought a touch of winter with it and a chill was in the air. The room had been left empty all day, but it was still only the beginning of October and it shouldn't be this cold.

He was sitting in a living room *cum* dressing room adjacent to the master bedroom at the back of the house. The house, in the Kinuta area of Tokyo, was very quiet, and Tome, the old lady who worked as a live-in maid, wouldn't disturb him unless he called her for something. He had eaten his dinner out, and when he arrived home he told her he wouldn't be needing anything else, so he guessed that she had retired to her own room. His wife Shimako had gone to visit her mother at Chigasaki in Kanagawa Prefecture three days earlier and still hadn't come

1

back. She was not very strong and suffered from low blood pressure, and as they had no children, she often found excuses to stay with her parents. Kōsuke usually let her go, especially recently, as his company was not doing very well and he found it less trouble if she wasn't around. He could hear some faint rock music every now and again and guessed that it must be Hideo Naitō, the young man who lodged with them. For many years Hideo's father had worked for Kōsuke's father, who had been a nursery gardener, and when Hideo graduated from high school, his father asked Kōsuke to give him a job in his company, Wakashiba Landscaping, Inc. Of course, Kōsuke was more than willing to employ the boy, and as Hideo's family lived a long way from Tokyo, he also offered to put him up in his home. Hideo had a stubborn streak, but usually he was a quiet young man, and when Kōsuke came home, he would turn down his stereo or TV so as not to disturb him. This was especially true since the summer, when things started to go wrong at the company and Kōsuke had become very irritable.

Kōsuke silently gazed out the window at the dark garden. After a while the music stopped and all he could hear was the sound of the rain beating on the eaves of the house. He was thinking about his difficulties at work and trying to decide how to pay all the bills, but his thoughts just chased each other around in his head and he was getting nowhere.

He stood up with a heavy sigh, and finally taking off his jacket, he hung it up in the wardrobe. As he walked across the room, he caught sight of himself in the mirror on the dressing table; he had a well-defined, strong-looking face, but the worry about his company made him look much older than his thirty-nine years.

At that moment the telephone in the bedroom next door rang. He glanced over at the digital clock on the desk and saw that it was 10:17, then hurried to the phone, which was on the bedside table. He picked up the receiver, and as he put it to his ear he heard the buzz that meant the call was from a pay phone.

"Hello," said a woman's deep voice. "Is that Mr. Watanabe?"

"No, you must have the wrong number."

"What?" the woman said in surprise. "That's not Mr. Watanabe?"

"No, I'm afraid not."

"Isn't that 416-329X?"

"No, this is 327X."

"Ohh . . ." It was almost a cry of misery. "I'm sorry. I must have dialed the wrong number; you see I can't see very well." Her voice was very deep and she had a trace of an accent that he couldn't identify.

"That's all right," Kōsuke said after a pause, and started to hang up.

"Just a minute . . ." the woman said hurriedly. Kōsuke put the phone back to his ear. "I don't quite know how to say this, but I don't suppose you could be kind enough to phone Mr. Watanabe for me, could you? You see, I haven't any more coins and there aren't any shops open near here. I can't see very well and . . ." Her breathing was very ragged and she sounded as if she were in pain.

"That's okay, what did you say his number was?"

"416-329X."

Kōsuke looked around for something to write it down on, but unfortunately there was nothing at hand. "And it is a Mr. Watanabe, isn't it?"

"Yes, and my name is Takeshita."

"Okay, Ms. Takeshita, and what message would you like me to pass on?"

"I . . . I'm in a phone booth next to a large church and I'd like him to come and pick me up."

"Where is the church?"

"Let me see . . . I turned off a large main road, it's a very deserted area."

"What's the name of the road? What area are you in now?"

"I'm not sure, it was a difficult name. . . ." She seemed to be trying to remember and her breathing sounded very labored.

"Isn't it written down anywhere nearby?"

"Just a minute, I'll go and have a look."

She went away for so long that Kōsuke was worried that the line would go dead. He half regretted having agreed to telephone this Mr. Watanabe, but he couldn't hang up now. The woman finally came back on the line.

"Himonya."

"What? Did you say Himonya?"

"Yes, I'm in a phone booth next to a big white church with a neon cross on the top. Please help me, you see, I'm in trouble, I—"

The line suddenly went dead; her three minutes had obviously run out.

Kōsuke put the phone down and a few moments later the bell chimed again briefly. He guessed from this that the maid had been listening to his call from the extension in the kitchen and had hung up after him.

Tome was a distant relative of Shimako's, and as she didn't have any close family, she had come to live with the Ōkitas nine years ago. She was sixty-six years old but was very fit and rarely even caught a cold. She was a great help to Shimako, who often felt poorly, and Kōsuke's only complaint was that she had a habit of listening in on his phone calls. He had confronted her with it once and she had desisted for a while, but recently she seemed to have fallen back into her old ways. Although it was annoying to know that someone was listening in on his calls, she wasn't doing any harm, so he decided to let it pass.

He picked up the phone again and dialed the number that the woman had given him; it was the same as his own except for the last two digits. It soon stopped ringing.

"Hello, is that Mr. Watanabe's house?"

"No, my name is Yamaoka." It was a woman's voice.

"That's strange. . . ." He checked the number, but there was no mistake.

"You don't know a woman named Takeshita then? She speaks with a country accent and has bad eyesight."

"No, I don't." The woman sounded a little irritated.

Ōkita apologized and hung up. He thought that he must have gotten the last two numbers backward and redialed the number. This time a man answered.

"Hello, is that Mr. Watanabe?"

"No, it is not."

He checked the number, but once again there was no mistake—yet this man had also never heard of anyone called Takeshita. Kōsuke didn't know what to do; he realized now that he should have written the number down when the woman gave it to him, but unfortunately no pencil and paper had been handy. Even if he had heard the number correctly to begin with, he had probably forgotten it when he asked her name and the location of the phone booth she was in. The more he thought about it, the more confused he became, and in the end he couldn't even be sure he had gotten the exchange right. He dialed three more times, changing various numbers, but one call had no answer and the other two had never heard of a Ms. Takeshita. He looked at his watch and saw that it was almost eleven o'clock.

"I can't do any more," he said to himself, and dropped the phone back on the hook. He decided to take a bath and went to the next room to change. He started to draw the curtains and paused as he looked out at the heavy rain falling on the darkened garden. Suddenly he had a vision of the woman standing in a cold phone booth, waiting for someone who would never come. He had gotten the impression from the woman's accent that she was from the country somewhere and she had mentioned bad eyesight. Perhaps she was almost blind and had dialed the phone by touch; that would explain why she had made a mistake. He guessed that she was newly arrived from the country and was phoning a friend or relative to come and help her.

No. Maybe it was something even worse. What was she saying when the phone went dead? "Please help me, you see, I am in trouble. . . ." She had spoken very slowly and her breathing had sounded very strained; quite possibly she had had an accident or was sick. Once again he pictured her standing in the cold phone booth in the rain waiting for someone who would never come because he had failed to pass on her message; then he closed the curtains and took off his tie.

He told himself he shouldn't worry so much, he had already done more to help a stranger than most people would do. She'd probably give up soon and find her own way home or find somewhere to get some change. If by some chance she got through to him again, he could just tell her what happened and find out more about the trouble she was in.

He hung his tie over the back of a chair and lit a cigarette. He found his thoughts going back to the vision of a lonely phone booth on a dark street in the rain. He had heard that there were all kinds of hoax calls these days, but for some reason he didn't think that this was one of them. The woman had sounded too convincing and her voice had a ring of desperation to it that would be hard to fake.

What was it she had said? A large white church in Himonya? He knew the area a little and thought he knew this church. He looked at his watch—it was nine minutes past eleven—then he put his cigarette out and stood up.

Kōsuke halfheartedly opened the drawer that he kept his pajamas in.

The woman on the phone had said she couldn't see very well. That one fact had stuck in his mind and awoke painful memories that he would rather have left undisturbed.

I wonder if she's still in the phone booth, he thought.

He closed the drawer without removing his pajamas, then went to the closet and took out a windbreaker.

I'll just go and have a look; it's not far and it's better than spending the night worrying about her.

He slipped the jacket around his shoulders and left the room. As he walked through the kitchen Tome looked out from her room; she was wearing a woolen gown over her clothes.

"Are you going out again?" she asked. He always got the impression that she was checking up on his movements, perhaps because she was related to Shimako. If she had been listening in on his call, she might remember the number the woman had given him. But then her memory was not all that good, and anyway she'd probably resent his asking.

"Yes," he replied shortly, and unlocked the door. It was still raining outside and was colder than ever. He got the car from the garage, which was built next to the porch, and drove through the narrow, twisting streets that the Setagaya area of Tokyo is so notorious for.

There were a lot of small woods in the area around Kinuta Park which belonged to the nursery gardeners that the area was famous for. Kōsuke's father had been a gardener, too, but after graduating from college, Kōsuke had gone to work for a large firm of landscapers. Upon the death of his father in 1972, the year before the oil crisis rocked the Japanese economy, Kōsuke left the company to start Wakashiba Landscaping, Inc. It was a small company, employing only about thirty people, and most of their work involved small jobs brought to them by large construction companies or private people who wanted their gardens landscaped. Since the end of the previous year, however, the company had been given over wholly to the construction of a golf course. . . .

Kōsuke found his thoughts returning to the problems at work. He turned left into Meguro Avenue and the volume of traffic dropped slightly. All the shops had closed their shutters and the only lights to be seen were those at the numerous used-car lots.

The woman had said that she turned off a large road. Well, that could only be Meguro Avenue, and if he remembered correctly, there was a very large, impressive church up one of the roads to the right. He signaled and turned right, and as he did so he looked at the clock in the dashboard; it was 11:31. Only about fifteen minutes had passed since he left home, but it was quite a while since the woman had phoned. He wondered if she'd still be there; if not, the whole episode would have been a colossal waste of time.

As soon as he turned into the side road it became unbelievably deserted; there were no cars or pedestrians, nothing to see but the cold glow of the streetlights and the illuminated net of a golf practice range in the distance. The lights only served to make the houses look darker; anyone who got lost here would feel depressed, let alone a woman with bad eyesight.

He drove along watching both sides carefully; there was a junction up ahead and the occasional car drove across it. He had not gone five hundred yards before he realized this was not the road he wanted. He turned left at the next corner then left again into the next road; he continued in this fashion for three or more streets until he saw a large illuminated cross shining through the night. This was also a very desolate road, lined on both sides by the walls of a school and a warehouse. The sidewalk was bordered by a row of scraggly trees, and in the place of shops there were a few vending machines, their lights glowing dismally in the rain. Finally, on the left, he saw the large white church that the woman had described, just as he remembered it, with a large cross perched on top of the pointed roof, and opposite that there was a phone booth. Heaving a sigh of relief, he parked the car and walked over to the booth. It was surrounded by Himalayan cedars and the light inside shone brightly. He looked in, but there was no sign of anyone. He pulled open the heavy door and walked in; nobody was there, but a suggestion of perfume lingered in the air, which could only mean that the woman had been there until quite recently. He saw a floral handkerchief next to the phone, and when he picked it up he noticed it felt quite damp. There was a note under the handkerchief, written in pencil on a piece of paper that looked like the page of a diary. The note was also damp, and he could almost visualize her repeatedly stepping out into the rain, looking to see if anyone was coming to pick her up.

The writing was very faint and he had to hold it up to the light to read it.

*Watanabe,*
*I will be waiting at the coffee bar Eri. Please come*
*and pick me up there.*

*Takeshita*

Kōsuke frowned and looked at his watch; it was 11:42. More than an hour had passed since she had phoned. He could tell from the signature that the note was from the same woman; she obviously believed he had passed on her message, but an hour is a long time to wait, especially in a phone booth on a cold wet night. She must have been frozen to the bone and gone to wait for her friend at the coffee bar, leaving the note to say where she had gone. He picked up the note and went back to his car. The coffee bar could not be far away; it was probably just around the corner somewhere.

He started to drive slowly down the road again, but contrary to his expectations, it was a long time before he found it. He had finally gone two roads to the east, on the very outskirts of Himonya, before he saw the red sign of the coffee bar. It was a much bigger place than he had visualized, glass-fronted and with a red sunshade protruding out over the road. He walked in and looked around the dark interior; there was a bar and four box seats. There were several customers, but as far as he could see none were single women.

"Good evening," said the waitress.

Kōsuke closed the door behind him and went up to the bar. "Excuse me, but a woman didn't come here on her own, did she?" he asked. The waitress looked over at the man behind the bar questioningly.

"How old was she?"

Kōsuke was stuck for an answer for a minute.

"I'm not sure; all I know is that she can't see very well."

The waitress looked at the man behind the counter again, and this time he nodded and answered, "A woman in a black raincoat came in about twenty minutes ago and ordered a hot lemon juice. She left just a few minutes ago."

"Did she telephone anyone while she was here?"

"Yes, she used that phone over there, but I don't think she got through." He nodded toward the pay phone on the counter. "She seemed to be waiting for someone, but then she obviously gave up and left."

Kōsuke left the shop and looked left and right, but there was nobody in sight, just the rain beating on the empty sidewalk.

# 2

# The Tanzawa Country Club

THURSDAY, OCTOBER 7.

Kōsuke woke at 6:40 and started to think about the problems that awaited him that day. Today he would go and visit the head office of the Tanzawa Country Club. He had been thinking about it since the previous day and had finally made up his mind. The only way he could hope to get through the present crisis was to persuade the Tanzawa C.C. to pay their bills. He thought about Seiji Nasuno, the president of the club, and found himself starting to lose his temper, but he took a deep breath and forced himself to remain calm. He knew there was nothing to be gained by antagonizing him.

He got out of bed and drew the curtains. It was a lovely day, the sun was shining in a clear, blue autumn sky, and it was hard to imagine the rain of the night before. The bushes and trees in the garden all sparkled gaily as the sun hit the raindrops on their leaves.

Going next door to the dressing room, he noticed a red matchbox with the name Eri written on it lying on the table beside a crushed scrap of paper and a floral handkerchief, and the events of the night before came back to him. The man behind the bar had told him that the woman had been very slim and in her thirties, but that when she had made a phone call she had seemed to have trouble dialing; he thought something was wrong with her sight.

Kōsuke had picked up the matches from the bar to light a cigarette and then left. He drove around the area for a while but couldn't find a trace of anyone matching the woman's description, so he finally just gave up and went home. It was almost 12:30 before he reached his house.

I wonder if she got home all right, he thought to himself, still worrying slightly. He dropped the letter and handkerchief in the wastepaper basket and started to change.

When he walked into the kitchen, the maid Tome looked at him inquiringly.

"Your wife telephoned after you went out last night."

"Oh."

"Yes, she says she's feeling much better and will be coming back to Tokyo today."

When Shimako first started to feel unwell and visit her parents regularly, he had worried about her and always telephoned to ask how she was, but recently he didn't bother.

He finished the breakfast that Tome had prepared for him and then left for work. His company was housed in a small two-story building he had built on the fields that his father had used when he was a nursery gardener, and there was a large open area behind it that was used to store their stock of trees and plants before they were used on a job. It wasn't far from the house, which was the same one that his father had built, although Kōsuke had added to it quite a lot when he first married.

He arrived in the office a little before nine and sat watching the clock impatiently until ten, when, he had heard, Nasuno usually put in an appearance. He rang the head office of the Tanzawa Country Club in Kōjimachi and the switchboard operator put him through to Mr. Nasuno's secretary.

"I'm sorry, but I am afraid that Mr. Nasuno hasn't arrived yet."

She sounded a little tense and Kōsuke guessed that this

was because he had had a violent argument with Nasuno in his office a few days before.

"Did he say he'd be going anywhere else this morning?"

"No, I'm expecting him in any minute. Shall I have him phone you when he arrives?"

"No, that's okay, I'll call again later, thank you." Kōsuke knew that Nasuno was trying to avoid paying for the work Kōsuke had done on the golf course, and even if he asked Nasuno to phone back, he doubted that he would. At 10:30, he tried the number again.

"I'm very sorry, but I am afraid that he still hasn't arrived," the secretary said in an efficient voice. " . . . No, we are expecting him here this morning."

Kōsuke thought for a few moments. "Is the vice-president there then?"

"No, Mr. Kawai is at the course this morning."

"What, Ichihara?"

"No, Tanzawa."

Nasuno and Kawai owned two golf clubs, the Uchibō Country Club at Ichihara city in Chiba Prefecture and the Tanzawa Country Club in Kanagawa Prefecture. Nasuno was the president of both, while Kawai held the position of both vice-president and chairman of the board. The two men were a complete contrast to each other; whereas Nasuno was the epitome of a successful businessman, very clever and very sharp, Kawai was a fat man with sleepy-looking eyes, and you could never tell what he was thinking. Although Kōsuke hadn't had much to do with him personally, he had heard that he was a reasonable man and he made up his mind to go to see him. He learned that Kawai was scheduled to be at the Tanzawa Country Club until noon, so leaving a message as to his whereabouts, he left the office.

He drove down the ring road until he got to the Tōmei expressway, then he turned right and headed west out of the city. Although he was the president of his own company, it was only a small company and he couldn't justify the expense of a chauffeur. He had been to the club numerous times during the construction to oversee the work, so he knew the road well. The expressway was crowded, but the cars were moving, and it wasn't long before he was driving down the Atsugi exit ramp. The roadside was covered with signs advertising country clubs, as the area between the Atsugi and Hatano interchanges was filled with them. Most of them had been built during the boom years in the early seventies and the area had reached saturation point. As a result, new clubs rarely managed to receive planning permission. The Tanzawa Country Club was an exception; it received permission in 1979 and had provisionally opened in July of 1982.

It was about two and a half years ago, in the spring of 1980, that one of Kōsuke's friends from college introduced him to Nasuno. His first impression had been of an able, honest entrepreneur, and when he was offered a large job in the summer of that year, he could hardly believe his luck.

"As you know," Nasuno had said in his shrewd fashion, "when making a golf course, the owner usually hires a large contractor to deal with every aspect of the construction, and they either deal with the landscaping themselves or subcontract it to a major landscape gardener. We did the same when we made the Uchibō club, but this time I want to make a course that stands out from the others. I particularly like gardening myself, and I thought that if we were to plant a large number of flowering shrubs, it would help to make our course famous. So I want to separate the landscaping from the rest of the construction and would like to offer the job to you. I know there are any number of large landscape gardeners, but I like you and feel that you'd do a good job, so what do you say?"

Kōsuke didn't even have to think before accepting. Until then he had only done the gardens of private houses or small construction sites, and with the current depression he didn't even get as much of that as he would have liked. On top of that, with the new regulations for the construction of golf courses, there were now only a few made every year. It would be a real coup for a small company like his to receive such a contract.

He started work in June of '81 with a budget of three hundred and fifty million yen, and it was six months before he became suspicious of Nasuno's intentions. When making a golf course, the contractor first prepares the land and then the landscape gardener moves in and plants the trees, which in the Tokyo area usually consist of pine, zelkova, and numerous flowering shrubs. This generally takes quite a while as it is difficult to collect such a large number of trees at one time, but once it is finished, the turf is planted. The greens take a lot of care to shape, and when they are almost ready, the designer comes and gives detailed instructions concerning the gradient. The work was to be done over the course of a year and Kōsuke was to receive payments on a monthly basis. According to the agreement, Wakashiba Landscaping, Inc. was to receive ten percent in advance, five percent per month, and the final thirty percent upon completion of the work. However, the payments only came regularly for the first three months. The design had been left up to another small company, and as each hole was finished, the designer would come and give his okay before work was started on the next. There were no problems at first, but then suddenly he started finding fault with everything.

"You should move the green five yards to the left."

"That bunker should be moved forward another twenty yards."

It was easy enough to say, but it meant hours of extra work. If the designer said that he did not like the surface of the green or that the gradient was wrong, all the turf had to be lifted and relaid. Every time the designer made a claim against Wakashiba, Nasuno would make a deduction from the amount that he paid them that month, sometimes paying as little as half of the agreed amount. This was all well and good for him, but Kōsuke had to pay for the changes as well as paying for the work on the other greens, and when the next month came around, the designer would simply make another claim and Nasuno would postpone payment even longer.

Despite his loss of income, Kōsuke still had to pay the nursery gardeners for the turf and trees that he used and also had to pay the laborers he employed. A large project like a golf course required between forty and fifty workers a day, and, needless to say, these had to be paid on a daily basis. In order to pay all his overhead, he was forced to borrow from the bank, and as time passed, the interest on these loans only served to make things worse.

He was about halfway through the job when he began to realize that Nasuno had planned it this way from the beginning. The designer's company was connected to Nasuno and he had obviously been told to find fault with the greens so that Nasuno could delay payment. In July, after the construction was finished, Kōsuke's worst fears came true. By this time Nasuno was sixty-five million yen in arrears, and when the designer came up with a whole new batch of complaints, Nasuno announced that instead of paying the remaining thirty percent that was due to Kōsuke, he would only pay fifteen. Kōsuke had followed the plans faithfully and had all the records to prove it, so if he were to sue Nasuno, he would most probably win, but he knew that the company would not be able to stay solvent until the case came to court. Kōsuke forced himself to remain calm, and after the provisional opening he spent two weeks remaking everything to the designer's latest plan. However, it was no good; Nasuno continued to make claims against the work and refused to pay the almost one hundred and twenty million that remained outstanding.

Kōsuke had heard many stories of large contractors who had been forced to accept membership certificates from golf clubs that they had constructed in lieu of payment and in some cases were even forced to take over the running of the clubs themselves. He had also heard of major landscape gardeners who only accepted work from contractors and refused to work directly for the golf clubs in order to avoid being stuck in the same situation that Kōsuke was in now. When he realized that Nasuno had been setting him up from the very beginning, Kōsuke became furious. He had had a violent argument with Nasuno the previous Friday, but it did not do any good—his land, his house, and everything he owned was mortgaged, and payment on the loans was due soon. If the Tanzawa Country Club did not pay him what they owed soon, there was no way that his company could avoid bankruptcy. He had a very short temper, but this time he told himself that he must control himself and beg them to pay him.

He drove through the town of Atsugi, then leaving the

main road, he turned into a narrow asphalt road that led up into the mountains. Finally the clubhouse came into view, silhouetted against the clear blue sky in a grove of ginkgo trees, and Kōsuke realized that it must look very beautiful to anyone for whom it did not hold the same connotations it held for him.

There were two or three other cars in the parking lot when he arrived, but the interior of the clubhouse was very quiet. As he walked by the locker room on his way to the office he looked over in surprise to see a girl walk out. She was wearing white culottes and she also stopped in surprise when she saw him.

"Kōsuke!" Chiharu Nasuno said, her voice echoing her surprise and enthusiasm. The two stood looking at each other in silence for a few moments. Chiharu was twenty-four, about five foot three inches tall, and had a well-proportioned figure. She was wearing a blue-striped sports shirt, white culottes, and golf shoes. She appeared to have been on her way to the green when he met her.

"Is there something going on here today?" Kōsuke asked with a smile.

"No, I just thought that I would do a practice round here this morning. I'm halfway through at the moment," Chiharu replied, returning his smile. She was very beautiful and had a real sportswoman's figure.

"You must have started early then. What do you think of the course?"

"Well, the grass is still a little young, but the drainage seems to be good; yesterday's rain did not have any effect on my play today. The fairways are nice and big, too. On the whole I think that it is a good, open course." She knew that he had made the course and there was a certain amount of flattery in her speech. "That pine tree on the seventh hole keeps you from seeing the green from the tee, which makes it a really difficult shot."

During the period between the provisional opening and the real opening the course is closed to the general members except for one round each on the opening day; the grass is still young and bumps and ditches tend to form in the green if it is used too much. This period is mostly given over to the outfitting of the clubhouse, although the owners or staff at the club occasionally play a round, more to test the course than anything. Chiharu was one of these; her father was the president of the club and she had worked at his other course at Uchibō since leaving college.

"How is your game these days?" Kōsuke asked.

"My shot is okay, but my approach and putting still leave something to be desired." Chiharu's eyes dropped to the glove on her left hand for a moment, then she looked up again. "Are you here on business?"

"Yes, I've come to see Mr. Kawai."

"My father isn't here today."

"Yes, I know, he wasn't in the office when I left either."

"I haven't seen him since yesterday," she said with a smile. Her smile faded and she dropped her eyes to the ground again; she knew that Kōsuke and her father were not on friendly terms, and this caused her a lot of anguish.

"Are you here on your own today?" Kōsuke said to change the subject.

"Yes, I always do a round at the Uchibō club before I start work, but it's closed today, so I came over here."

"You're very eager."

"I started late, so I've got to work hard to catch up."

When she was in college, she had been very keen on tennis. It was probably a reaction to the fact that her father owned a golf club, but she refused to have anything to do with the game until she tried it once in her fourth year, and then before she knew what had happened, she was hooked on it. After she graduated she had gone to work for the caddie master at her father's club at Uchibō, and in her spare time she was taking lessons from the head coach.

Kōsuke had heard this story from her about two years previously. It was shortly after Nasuno had first suggested that Kōsuke do the work on the Tanzawa course and he had invited him down to the Uchibō course so he could see what kind of club it was. Despite the fact that Nasuno was the president of a golf club, he very rarely played himself, and he had had Chiharu play for him. After that, Kōsuke would always phone Chiharu if he was in the area to invite her out for a meal, and when they separated, they would usually arrange to play a round together at another course. When the Uchibō club was closed, Chiharu would often call him at his office and arrange to meet him downtown later on. They had been meeting each other once or twice a month for two years, and sometimes when they did not meet for a while, Kōsuke would find himself gripped by an overwhelming desire to talk to her. Ever since he had met her, he had felt a new emotion grow in him, but he was not yet aware of just what that emotion was or, rather, was scared to face up to it. Of course he had never spoken to her about the trouble he was having with her father, and now that things had come to a head, he had avoided meeting her so much.

"Are you going to practice some more?"

"Yes, I've still got half a round to go."

"Off you go then."

Kōsuke was about to go, but the look in her eye held him back.

"May I still phone you?" she asked seriously.

"Of course. I'll call you, too."

"Okay, I'll talk to you then."

He stood and watched as she trotted down the steps toward the green. Meeting her like this had brought a strange feeling of contentment and awakened an ache of longing within him.

He walked up to the office door and knocked. Although the club still had not had its official opening, the interior of the clubhouse was virtually finished and several people were working there full-time. There was no answer, so he opened the door and walked in. The office was very large and was fully fitted out with desks and filing cabinets; at the back a man was talking on the telephone. There was nobody else in the room, and when the man saw Kōsuke, he nodded in a friendly manner. Kōsuke had been in and out of the office a lot during the work there and knew most of the employees by sight. The managing director's room was at the end of the corridor on the other side of the room, and Kōsuke walked purposefully toward it. As he did so, the man put his hand over the receiver of the phone and called out, but Kōsuke ignored him. The door was partway open when he reached it, but he paused for a moment to force himself to calm down. He knew that he had a short temper, but he told himself that no matter what the other man might say, he was to just beg him very humbly to pay what he owed; there was no other way to save his company. He thought of Chiharu for a moment and felt himself calm down.

He lifted his hand to knock, but as he did so he heard a voice from inside.

"Come on, Kawai, we want an explanation." The voice sounded very angry and Kōsuke let his hand drop to his side again. "You can't honestly have thought that we'd accept this without any explanation. Suppose you tell us why you are deferring repayment of our guaranty money for another five years without discussing it with us first."

"I am sorry, but we are quite within our rights as set down in the club rules." The silky, mocking voice could only belong to Kawai. Kōsuke could picture him sitting there like some huge, fat bear, his sleepy eyes slipping away whenever someone tried to meet his gaze. "I've got the rules of the Uchibō club here and it says in section three, article nine: 'The membership guaranty money shall be deposited with the company, interest free for a period of ten years from the official opening of said club. However, in the case of a natural disaster or any other situation beyond the control of the management, said period may be extended at the discretion of the board of directors. . . .' So as you see, this decision was reached only after a full meeting of the board of directors."

Now Kōsuke understood what it was all about. In Japan, more than eighty percent of the golf clubs took guaranty money from the new members and kept this money to use as they liked for a set period after which, if the member wanted to leave, it would be refunded. Uchibō C.C. would have been open for ten years come September and the guaranty money was due to be refunded, but Kōsuke had heard that the deposit had been extended.

"That's all well and good, but what we want to know is the reason why you won't refund the money." This time it was a different voice; apparently more than one person was in there with Kawai.

"It was all set down in the letter we sent to the members," Kawai continued in the same slick tone. "After consideration of the financial situation the money was needed in order to pay for improvements in the club's facilities and—"

"Just who are you trying to kid? You know as well as I do that the bottom has fallen out of the market, and that if you started to refund the guaranty money, a majority of the members would ask for theirs back and you wouldn't be able to pay. Come on, admit it."

"When I joined at the opening in 1972, the minimum price was one and a half million, but now you can pick up a membership for as little as five or six hundred thousand. Suppose you tell us why it is so cheap."

"Admittedly the course is not very good, but that's not all. You sold too many memberships and on top of that you allow too many visitors in; no matter how often I phone, I'm never able to book a game. It's not surprising that people get fed up and sell their memberships, and that brings the price way down."

Apparently, at least three men were in the room with Kawai; one was nervous and logical while the other two were threatening.

"How many members are there in the Uchibō club?"

"Four thousand—no, a little more than that, perhaps."

"Don't give us that, it's more like ten thousand!"

"That's not true, but I'm afraid it has been decided not to make the member list public."

"That's very convenient; any honest club would publish its member list without a second thought."

"You can say that again; you could make any amount of money from a golf course as long as you're not too particular about your methods. There's no law that limits the number of members or how much guaranty money is charged. It's not even necessary to publish a membership list, so members can't even do anything to protect themselves."

"That's not all. If the market for memberships goes up, no one wants their money back, and if the market drops, you just hold a meeting to decide to extend the deposit period. You can't lose—whatever happens, you don't have to pay back any of the money you have collected.''

"We are not just after our own money," the nervous-sounding man said. "This is a social problem. Let's say that there are eight thousand members altogether and that they have each paid one and a half million; that makes a total of twelve billion yen. If as you say you can't pay it back, perhaps you should explain to us just where it has all disappeared to.''

"I don't think that I have to explain that to you here, although it will be made quite clear at the next stockholders meeting."

"Do you really mean that?''

"How are you going to explain the disappearance of three billion yen?''

"What?''

"There's an anonymous letter going around, haven't you heard about it?''

"What do you mean? What is it about?'' Kawai sounded uneasy for the first time.

"It says that there are thirty billion yen missing from the accounts of the Uchibō club and it claims that you and Nasuno used the money for your own ends. All the stockholders received a copy shortly after you refused to return our deposits.''

"That is a complete fabrication," Kawai said with a chuckle, making an effort to sound friendly. "But how can you fight against rumors if you don't know who's making them.''

"Anyway, we intend to overrule your decision to extend the period of deposit, even if it means taking you to court.''

"We're quite prepared to follow you anywhere you go until we get to the truth of the matter.''

"You're advertising for members at the Tanzawa Country Club at the moment, so it won't sound very good if this becomes public knowledge.''

"Uchibō and Tanzawa are completely separate companies,'' Kawai said weakly, and the other three laughed sarcastically.

"Don't be ridiculous. The executives and directors are the same for both, so what's separate about them?"

Kōsuke had heard that some of the members of the Uchibō Country Club were complaining about the extension of the deposit period, but he had also heard that they were a minority. In a club like the Uchibō where the member list was not made public, it was difficult for the members to form a united front and most of them just gave up. He had read about similar cases in a magazine: even if the members went to court and won, they usually didn't get enough to cover their legal fees. In most cases the clubs dealt out of court with the members who made a fuss and the other members never did get their money.

Listening to the voices in the room, Kōsuke felt his worst fears realized. There is no more variety to be found in business methods than in golf clubs in Japan. Of the approximately one thousand three hundred and forty clubs in the country, some are honest, friendly societies while others are little more than con games. Whereas some stick to the ideal of one hundred members per hole, others will enroll anywhere up to ten or twenty thousand members on an eighteen-hole course, and as a result the value of the membership to the first category continues to rise while that of the second soon drops below face value. During the boom years of the late sixties anything would sell, but now members looked for quality for their money.

Nasuno and Kawai's club was obviously one of the second variety, and Kōsuke thought about how he had been set up from the beginning. The whole world seemed to go black and he staggered slightly, but for some reason, at the same moment he saw an image of Chiharu in his mind's eye.

# 3

# The Body in the Mud

SEIJI NASUNO LIVED IN OH-OKAYAMA, A QUIET residential area of the Meguro ward of Tokyo set on a slight hill in a quarter of an acre of heavily wooded land. All the houses in the area are surrounded by stone walls and lush gardens and his was no exception. Nasuno had bought it about twenty years before he started the golf course, while he was still dealing in real estate. It had a curved driveway about six feet wide and thirty yards long that led up from the road to the house; the branches of the trees on either side arched over it to form a roof. The drive was paved with stone, but this had gotten a little old, so at the end of September Nasuno arranged to have it torn up and resurfaced with granite.

The workers removed the old surface and relaid the foundations on the fifth of October. Unfortunately, however, that afternoon it started to rain, so they covered the new concrete with tarpaulins and laid out some planks to walk on before going home. The next day it was still wet, and in the afternoon a low-pressure front moved over the country, causing it to rain even harder. On the seventh it finally stopped and it was a lovely clear day, so a little before noon the three workers came to see how their concrete was doing.

They slowly made their way up the drive, pulling off the tarpaulins as they went. Both sides of the drive were lined by large trees, which made the garden seem more like a small forest. They were about halfway up the curved driveway and one of the workers was just pulling a tarpaulin to one side when he suddenly stopped and peered into the trees.

"Hey, come and look at this," he shouted excitedly. "There's someone lying down in here!"

His two friends hurried over to join him and saw a pair of legs encased in light brown trousers and brown shoes sticking out of the low bamboo and weeds. The man was lying facedown with a wet handkerchief plastered to his head. The eldest of the three men went around to the man's head, and after a glance over to his friends for encouragement he carefully picked up a corner of the handkerchief. The sight that met his eyes was enough to cause him to drop it and have one of the others rush up the planks to the house.

When this worker arrived at the house, he found Nasuno's wife, Hisae, at home alone. As soon as she heard that there was a man in a brown-checked suit lying in the garden, she thought of her husband, who had not come home the previous evening, and she rushed out of the house and followed the man down to the spot where the body lay. Judging from the clothes and the build, she was almost sure it was in fact her husband lying there in the weeds, but she was too scared to remove the handkerchief and confirm her suspicions. Instead she hurried back to the house and telephoned the Himonya police station.

Ten policemen, including plainclothes, forensic, and uniformed men, arrived within ten minutes. Detective Inspector Momozaki and the forensic man in his blue overalls squatted down on either side of the body. Momozaki removed the handkerchief so they were able to see the man's hair and part of his face. The man had black hair but was fairly bald in the front. The area from his forehead to his right temple was dark purple and there was a large wound there. Blood had congealed around the wound, but most of it had been washed away by the rain the night before. Rigor mortis was quite advanced and Momozaki guessed that the man had been dead for about twelve hours.

"I am sorry, but could you check that this actually is your husband?" one of the policemen asked, and helped Hisae over to the body. Momozaki turned the body over and she was able to see the face. It had the same profile and the shape, but it was a strange gray color and the irises of the eyes were half hidden by the eyelids. The face with its terrible wound seemed to capture the horror of the man's final moment and Hisae gave a small scream.

"Yes, that is my husband," she managed to say weakly.

The police cordoned off the driveway, and a half hour later thirty more police from the central police department arrived with a scream of sirens. The investigation now got under way in earnest with some of them checking the area around the body while others started a door-to-door inquiry.

Detective Inspector Momozaki started to interview Hisae in a small reception room next to the front door. Seiji Nasuno was fifty-six, Hisae was fifty-one, and they had two daughters; one was married to a doctor and lived in Yokohama and the other still lived at home.

"Yes, her name is Chiharu. She went to the Tanzawa Country Club early this morning and is probably still there."

The head office of the Tanzawa Country Club had already been informed of the tragedy, and when Momozaki heard about Chiharu, he had one of his men contact the golf course, too.

"What time did your husband leave the house this morning?" Momozaki was a very soft-spoken man in his midforties.

"No . . . I mean, he did not come home last night," Hisae answered, biting her lip. She was an elegant-looking woman, although the knit dress she was wearing was not in the height of fashion. Her face was deathly pale and she was trembling violently.

"Oh, did he go away somewhere?"

"Yes, I suppose he probably went somewhere on business."

"So that means that the last time he was in the house was yesterday morning, does it?"

"Yes, his chauffeur came to pick him up at nine-thirty as usual."

"Did he go to the office?"

"Yes."

"And he did not tell you that he was not going to be coming home last night?"

"No, but that happens sometimes. He has all kinds of commitments at the office." Although she said this, she obviously did not believe it herself.

Momozaki had half guessed that Nasuno had not returned the previous night, as a brief examination of the body seemed to indicate that he had been dead for at least twelve hours. Although the body was found at his home, did that mean that he was murdered there or that his body was moved there later?

"Does that mean that no one used that path until the workmen came at around noon and found the body?"

"No, Chiharu went out at about seven-thirty, as I said earlier; she had gone to the Tanzawa club."

Hisae explained that although Nasuno had a chauffeur-driven car, Chiharu had a car that she drove herself and kept in a garage next to the house. However, as she could not use the driveway while it was being repaired, she had parked it in the street and walked down to it in the morning.

"So she went past that spot then?"

"Yes, she can't have noticed anything. I suppose that the same goes for Aoki."

"Who is Aoki?"

"My husband's chauffeur; he came at nine-thirty this morning as usual."

"What? So he did not know where your husband was going either?"

"That's the impression I got when I told him that my husband had not come home; he just assumed that he would be going to the company directly. Actually, this kind of thing happens three or four times a month. . . ." Her emotions finally broke through her control, and burying her face in her hands, she started to cry.

"So that means that the only people to have gone down the driveway this morning before the workmen arrived were your daughter, Chiharu, and the chauffeur Aoki."

"Yes, I think so. I haven't been out yet myself."

"And what about last night, who went along there last night?"

Driven by Momozaki's question, Hisae forced her feelings back under control and tried to think back on the previous night.

"Chiharu came home at about seven-thirty; it rained all day yesterday, so the members all left early." She explained that Chiharu worked at a golf club in Chiba Prefecture. "I went out for a short while at about four o'clock, but apart from that we had no visitors yesterday."

"How about the telephone?"

"No, I don't recall having any phone calls." That would mean that Nasuno had stayed out without even phoning to explain. "I do remember, though, that at about twelve o'clock the dogs in the neighborhood made a terrible row. Chiharu and I remarked on it at the time. Just what time did my husband die?" she asked, turning her tearstained face toward him.

"We can't be quite sure at the present moment, but we think that he was attacked at about midnight last night."

"Attacked?"

"Yes, he was hit on the head with a blunt object twice. We have not been able to find the murder weapon yet, but it would appear to have been a steel pipe or something similar."

Hisae turned away and closed her eyes in pain.

"Did your husband ever mention anything about being threatened or blackmailed recently?"

"No, I haven't—"

At that moment there was a disturbance at the front door, and opening the door to the room, Momozaki saw two men take off their shoes and approach them. One of them was thirty-five or thirty-six and was wearing a navy-blue suit; the other was a short, fat man with graying hair.

"I was horrified to hear the news," the young man said, and at the same instant Hisae cried out, "Oh, Mr. Kinumura . . ." and staggered toward him. Seeing a friendly face, she allowed herself to slacken the control she had been keeping over her emotions.

The man she had called Kinumura obviously did not know what to say and just stood biting his lip and patting her on the shoulder. He was of medium height and build, with no excess fat on him, and the steel-rimmed glasses he wore gave him an intellectual look.

"My name is Kinumura. I am in charge of sales for the Tanzawa club," he said, as soon as he found out who Momozaki was. "This is Mr. Nasuno's chauffeur, Aoki," he added, indicating the older man. "We hurried over as soon as we heard the news. I wondered if I could be of any assistance; you see, I was with Mr. Nasuno until quite late last night."

Momozaki looked at the business card he had been given. It said: CAMELLIA LTD. *Tōru Kinumura. Managing Director.*

"We are involved with collecting members for the Tanzawa Country Club. Although it's ostensibly a separate company, there are only twenty of us and we are really just the sales section of the club working under a different name," he said candidly, adding that the company's address was in the Akasaka area of Tokyo.

Now that he knew who Kinumura was, Momozaki decided to hear what he had to say.

"Last night Mr. Nasuno and I were entertaining a couple of clients. They were old friends of Mr. Nasuno's who run a wedding hall and they had agreed to take out a corporate membership. First we went to a restaurant in Akasaka, and after we left there at about eight o'clock we went on to a couple of bars in Ginza. We left the second bar, called Gaka, at a little before eleven and then we all split up to go home."

Aoki had driven them all as far as the first bar in Ginza, but Nasuno had told him that he could go home after that.

"Mr. Nasuno generally told me that I could leave when he went drinking, he did not like to think that he was keeping someone waiting and also he often had other places to go afterward." He looked over at Hisae and realized that he had said more than he ought.

"So, you say that you left the Gaka at a little before eleven?"

"Yes, we ordered three cars at about ten-forty, but it was ten-fifty before we got word that they had arrived," answered Kinumura. "As you know, at around eleven o'clock in Ginza, Dentsu Road is packed with hired cars waiting to pick up their passengers and it sometimes takes quite a while to find the car you are looking for. Several of the hostesses and waiters from the bar went with Mr. Nasuno and the others to help find their cars, but I had parked my own car nearby, so I said good-bye to them outside the bar." Kinumura seemed to be reliving the moment and he stood there gazing into space. He did not seem to realize that he had just admitted that he had committed a parking offense and driven under the influence of alcohol, but Momozaki decided that this was not the time to remark on it.

"Did Mr. Nasuno say that he was going to visit anywhere else on his way home?"

"No, I assumed that he was coming straight back here."

"So what time would you say that he finally left Ginza then?"

"It could not have been before ten past eleven at the earliest, and it takes a long time to get out of Dentsu Road at that time as it is so crowded."

On the evening of the seventh, Seiji Nasuno's body was taken to a university hospital for an autopsy. The results were sent to the investigation headquarters that had been set up at the Himonya police station.

Death was caused by two heavy blows to the front of the skull by a blunt instrument such as a length of steel pipe. The murder weapon was yet to be found, but the people on the investigation team thought that it might have been a golf club. There was no reason for them to think this other than the fact that Nasuno had been the owner of a golf club, but the medics agreed that the wound could easily have been caused by such a weapon. The time of death was set as being between ten and twelve o'clock, but after questioning the staff of the Gaka and the driver of the car that brought him home, the police were able to narrow this down to between eleven-forty and twelve o'clock.

The hostesses said that he got to his car in Dentsu Road at a little after eleven and he then told his driver to take him directly to his house in Oh-okayama. Usually he would tell the driver to drive right up to the front door, but as he was having the driveway resurfaced, he told him to park in front of the gate. They arrived at eleven-forty and the driver had gotten out with an umbrella and gone around to open his door, but Nasuno just waved him away. The overhanging trees on either side of the drive would keep him dry on his way to the house. He left the driver and marched away over the planks with a firm step, and that was the last the driver saw of him.

If the police were to believe the driver, Nasuno had been attacked as he walked up the planks toward the house and was then dragged off into the bushes. They checked all the tarpaulins that had been laid under the planks and sure enough they found traces of blood on one of them. He should have lost a much greater amount of blood than the traces would seem to indicate, but this had no doubt been washed away by the heavy rain that had continued to fall until about two A.M. The time that the driver said that he last saw Nasuno also coincided with the time that Hisae said that she had heard the dogs barking, but the police decided to leave a twenty-minute margin just in case.

Nasuno's wallet, containing his credit cards, about one hundred and fifty thousand yen in cash, and his wristwatch, which cost about two million yen when new, had been left on the body, so it would not appear that the crime had been committed for robbery. This, together with the fact that the murderer had covered the head with a handkerchief, would seem to indicate that the murderer had known his victim. As a result the investigation was narrowed down to someone who had a motive to kill the victim and who also knew that the driveway to the house was under construction.

"I first met Nasuno fourteen or fifteen years ago when I was running a hotel and parking lot in Chiba city. We were both in the same business, and although we were completely different types, we got on very well and decided to start a golf course together.''

Risaburō Kawai was sitting in the executive office of the Tanzawa Country Club in the Kōjimachi area of Tokyo answering the detective's questions. At fifty-three, Kawai was three years younger than Nasuno and he was so fat that he spilled out of his leather-covered chair. Since it had been decided that the murder had probably been committed by someone who knew the victim, the police were focusing on his contacts at work and his female relationships.

"I take it that you are referring to the Uchibō club in Ichihara.''

"Yes. That was back in 1972 at the peak of the golf boom. It was much cheaper to build then, only about one hundred million per hole, and it was much easier to attract members, too. The last ten years have gone very well and for that reason we decided to start the Tanzawa club.''

"Do I take it that the Tanzawa club is the same as the Uchibō club; you and Mr. Nasuno put up half the money each?''

"Yes, more or less, although there are several other small investors, too.''

"Mr. Nasuno was the president while you were merely the vice-president; does this reflect a difference in the amount you both invested?''

"No, not at all. We both invested approximately the same amount. It's just that I prefer not to have the responsibility of being the president. Anyway, I'm the chairman of the board as well.''

Most golf clubs have a board of trustees whose job it is to try to make the club run smoothly. Although a famous person is sometimes asked to take the position of chairman, more often than not it is filled by the president or someone nominated by him.

"Nasuno dealt with finding members for the club and I think it would be true to say that he was the president in more than just name. His sudden death has really put me in a nasty position, and I am at my wit's end.'' He put his hand to his forehead and heaved a heavy sigh.

"Do you have any idea who might have had a motive

to murder Mr. Nasuno? I realize that there may be things about your company that you would not like to become known, but we need any clues we can get."

"There is nothing about our company that would cause anyone to do anything like that. Oh, yes, there was some trouble over the way that Wakashiba Landscaping did their job."

"Wakashiba Landscaping?"

"Yes, they laid the turf at the Tanzawa club." Kawai looked over at a photograph hanging on the opposite wall. It showed him, Nasuno, and a foreign golfer on a golf course somewhere all smiling at the camera.

"What kind of trouble exactly?"

There were three detectives altogether, but the two younger ones sat back on the sofa and left the actual questioning to Inspector Momozaki from the Himonya station.

"Well, they did a bad job and obviously we told them to do it again; however, no matter how many times we told them, they could not get it right. That did not stop them from demanding payment as if they had done everything correctly. I realize that they are a small company and probably find it hard to make ends meet, but we had no guarantee that they would not just leave the job as it was if we paid them, so Nasuno decided to withhold payment until the designer gave the okay."

"So it was Mr. Nasuno who dealt with these negotiations, was it?"

"Yes, it was Nasuno who decided that he wanted to use that company to begin with and I had absolutely nothing to do with it. However, the boss of the company is a young guy in his late thirties called Ōkita and he has a really short temper. Why, only last Friday he had a terrible row with Nasuno in this very office and yesterday he came all the way out to the golf course to talk to me. I tried to explain the situation to him, but I don't know. . . ."

The wrinkles in the corner of his eyes deepened slightly as he gave a wry smile. One of the detectives took out a notebook and wrote "Ōkita—Wakashiba Landscaping."

"You said that it was Nasuno who decided to use Wakashiba Landscaping; was there any reason for this in particular?"

"Oh, Ōkita had been to college with Kinumura, the man in charge of all the membership sales for the club and he first introduced them to each other. Kinumura and Nasuno were very close, you know, and he could probably tell you more than me."

Kawai's comment seemed to have some hidden meaning, but he did not expand on it; he just turned slightly and looked toward the window where the bright sun was flooding into the room.

Camellia Ltd., the company that was responsible for the membership sales for the Tanzawa club, was situated on the second floor of a small building near the Tameike intersection in downtown Tokyo. There was a large sign outside showing the company's name and there were several posters of various golf courses taped to the window.

Inside there were about twenty desks, but when two detectives from the Himonya police station arrived at a little before noon on the eighth, only about half of them were in use, and the majority of these were taken by female workers. The two detectives stood at the door for a short while watching the scene with interest.

All the women in the office were rather overdressed and were holding telephones to their ears. They were going through lists of names with their left hands while they used their right hands to dial. When they got through to a switchboard at the other end of the line, they spoke in a bored, offhand tone, but as soon as they were connected to the person they wanted to speak to, their voices rose about an octave and became very sexy.

"Hello, is that Mr. Tanaka? I am Junko from the Tanzawa Country Club, which had its provisional opening in July. How is your game these days? . . . Oh, really? The Tanzawa Country Club is only about one hour from the city center and I am pleased to say that everybody who has seen it has been absolutely delighted with it. . . . Yes, that's right, I would like to tell you more about it in person if you can spare the time. It wouldn't take very long. . . ."

All of the girls were young and beautiful, and to listen to them, it was hard to believe that the owner of the golf course in question had been murdered a mere two days before. Eventually the woman who had met them when they first arrived came back and led them through to a small office at the back. As soon as they walked in Kinumura stood up to greet them. He was wearing a dark blue suit as usual, although today he also wore a black tie and looked rather haggard; the strain of the previous day seemed to be getting to him.

"I am sorry to disturb you," Momozaki said as he walked in.

"Not at all. In fact, your timing couldn't have been better. I will be going to Mr. Nasuno's house this afternoon, so I would not have been here to see you."

"Yes, the wake is to be held tonight, isn't it?"

"That's right, and we have also got to make preparations for the funeral tomorrow." Kinumura lowered his bloodshot eyes.

"Is that how you go about recruiting?" the other detective asked, nodding toward the other room.

"Yes, if the customer sounds interested, one of the girls will go and see him in person. We also use direct mail, and if someone is recommended to us, one of the male staff will go and talk to him. There are all kinds of techniques," Kinumura said in a crisp tone.

"I see; it must be very difficult to try to sell several thousand memberships at a price of several million yen each during a depression like we are having now."

"Yes, we're looking for a total of two thousand two hundred members for the Tanzawa club, but we're not the only people selling them. We've asked several companies to sell them, and in fact, most of the sales will come from there. However, we are the sole agent and our main job consists of keeping an eye on the other dealers."

Momozaki listened to the girls talking on the telephone with obvious enjoyment as he continued his questioning. "I hear that this is the third sales campaign you're working on at the moment."

"Yes, we got nearly all the members that we wanted during the pre-opening enrollment and the provisional opening enrollment, but we still need a few more to bring us up to strength. The head office is in a real turmoil after the murder, but I thought that it would be best if I were to just keep going as if nothing had happened. I feel sure that that is what Mr. Nasuno himself would have wanted," Kinumura said, looking strangely defiant.

A girl walked into the office with a trayful of tea and then left again after she had passed it around.

"Excuse me for asking, Mr. Kinumura, but how long have you been involved in this type of work?"

"It must be getting on to twelve years now. I was the site foreman for a small company that was involved in the construction of the Uchibō course, and one day I ran into Mr. Nasuno when he came to inspect the job. We hit it off from the very beginning, and one day he said that his was a new company that needed all the able people it could get and asked me if I would be interested in joining. He put me in the sales department and later, when he formed a separate agency to represent the club, I went to work there. In those days before the oil crisis, it was really easy to find members. I did so well, in fact, that when he started Camellia, he put me in charge."

"Was Mr. Nasuno the president of this company, too?"

"No, not directly, but it is a subsidiary of the Tanzawa Country Club."

However, there were no other executive offices and it was fairly obvious to the detectives that Kinumura dealt with all the actual day-to-day running of the business.

"You were very close to Mr. Nasuno both at work and socially, and we wondered if you had any idea who could have had a grudge against him."

"Yes, actually there is someone," he said with a determined look. "His name is Noboru Kuretani. He's a small shareholder in the Tanzawa club and Mr. Nasuno used to see quite a lot of him. He has a company that runs a type of publishing racket. He brings out a magazine called *Economic Growth* each month that has absolutely no real content and only exists for the money they can force industry to pay for advertising in it."

"Yes, we know the type," said the younger detective.

"He is very friendly with one of the bosses in the Takafuji gang and that is why he manages to blackmail large companies into advertising in his magazine. The gang manages to find out all kinds of inside information and the companies never know what kind of smear campaign they might have to go through if they refused to pay.''

The Takafuji gang was the major gang in the eastern part of Japan.

''I wonder why a man like Nasuno would know someone like that?'' the younger detective said, then he remembered that he had heard somewhere that most of the new golf clubs had connections with the mob.

''Well, Mr. Nasuno tried his hand at all kinds of things before he started the golf club at Uchibō, and I suppose that they got to know each other in those days. Their relationship certainly goes back to long before I first met Mr. Nasuno. Whenever Kuretani was short of money, he used to get Mr. Nasuno to withdraw the money from the club and give it to him. Also he used to introduce various people he met through his magazine and persuade them to become members, although whenever he did, he would take an outrageous amount of commission.''

''I think I get the general idea.''

''It was all right as long as they were friends, but I always worried about what would happen if they ever fell out.''

''I see,'' the detective said, and wrote down the address of Kuretani's office in the Daikanyama area. ''Oh, yes, incidentally, does the name of your company refer to anything in particular?''

''No, not really, it's just that there are a considerable number of camellias and other flowering shrubs at the Tanzawa course and we thought it would be appropriate.''

''Oh, yes, I almost forgot, I wanted to talk to you about the man who dealt with the landscaping of the Tanzawa course.''

Although the detective had sounded almost offhand, Kinumura realized that this was the main reason for their visit and frowned slightly.

''I believe that you and Kōsuke Ōkita went to college together and that in fact it was you who introduced him to Mr. Nasuno.''

''Yes, that is correct.'' Kinumura took a deep breath before replying, and it was obvious to the detectives that he knew about the trouble between the two men. ''Ōkita was three years older than I, but we were in the ski club together and we also continued to meet after we graduated at the O.B. get-togethers.''

''When exactly did you introduce him to Mr. Nasuno?''

''It was before work was started on the Tanzawa course. Mr. Nasuno said that he wanted to separate the landscaping from the rest of the job and that he was looking for a suitable company. I thought that it was a golden opportunity for Ōkita, so I introduced them to each other.'' He seemed to regret having done so now and lapsed into silence, frowning.

''Did Mr. Nasuno like him and offer him the job?''

''Yes.''

''But later there was trouble about the payment?'' the detective prompted. Kinumura did not answer immediately but sat gazing into the bottom of his teacup, then took a sip and put it slowly back down on the desk.

''I think they were both right in their own ways. As far as Mr. Nasuno was concerned, he did not want to pay until the designer was quite satisfied with the work—no matter how many times it had to be redone. For his part, Ōkita insisted that he had done the job according to the plans and demanded to be paid for what he had done. I must admit that designers do tend to say rather strange things at times, and being something of an artist, their way of looking at things is not always quite the same as that of the man on the job.''

''We heard that there is almost one hundred and twenty million yen outstanding and that recently Ōkita had violent arguments with Mr. Nasuno. He even forced his way into the office at Tanzawa to try to demand payment from Mr. Kawai.''

''As I said, I think that they both had valid arguments, but I wasn't involved personally, so I can't really give an opinion. I think it's a pity, however, that Mr. Nasuno refused to pay the outstanding money until the job was finished,'' Kinumura said, looking truly pained. ''I think that Mr. Nasuno was worried that if he did, Ōkita might stop work altogether. I told him several times that Ōkita was not that kind of man, but when it came to business, Mr. Nasuno would not listen to anyone.'' He seemed about to say something else, but then he broke off for a moment. "However, I don't think that Ōkita would ever attack him physically; it was not in his character. He is not a violent person."

# 4

# Motive and Opportunity

A MEETING TO DISCUSS THE DAY'S INVESTIGA-
tion was held at seven o'clock that evening in the investigation headquarters at the Himonya police station.

The police thought that it was safe to say that the murder was not the work of someone unconnected to the victim. It seemed likely that it was done out of anger or by
someone who stood to gain by Nasuno's death and that
whoever it was, he or she knew that Nasuno's driveway
was under construction and decided to make use of the
fact. A day and a half had passed since the body was
discovered, and as a result of their inquiries, the detectives
had already come up with a list of possible suspects.

"The vice-president of the Tanzawa Country Club, Risaburō Kawai, and Nasuno also founded the Uchibō Country Club ten years ago, and although there are several other
small stockholders, between them they held two-thirds of
the stock in each club," said the detective who had been
charged with investigating the golf-club side of the case.
"Looking into the background of the two clubs, I have
found all kinds of rumors about the Uchibō club. Although the accepted number of players for a club that size
is between eighteen and twenty-two hundred, it has been

rumored that the true number of members is in excess of eight thousand, although this number is a well-kept secret. As the final price of the membership was one and a half million yen this means that they managed to collect at least twelve billion yen, and now that it is due to be refundable they have unilaterally extended the deposit period for another five years. This has caused a lot of unrest among the members, who, on several occasions, had heated arguments with Kawai and Nasuno. Considering the amount of money involved, I think that it may be worth our checking out the relationship between Nasuno and Kawai.''

According to Kawai, at the time of the murder he was already in bed asleep at his house in Kamiogi. His family all agreed with this, but there was nobody else who could vouch for his alibi. So far the investigations had found that Kawai had two mistresses. One worked in a bar in Akasaka and the other in Ginza, but they also had alibis for the time in question.

"At the moment our main suspect would seem to be the president of Wakashiba Landscaping, Kōsuke Ōkita."

As he spoke, a ripple of excitement spread around the room. They had heard about the situation between Ōkita and Nasuno during their inquiries, but they still had not talked to Ōkita in person. With a major suspect in a murder case, they liked to check out everything else before attempting to interview the subject.

The following morning two detectives went to visit Kōsuke's house in Kinuta. Although it was Saturday, they knew that Kōsuke's company worked a six-day week and that he would not be there. They found Kōsuke's wife, Shimako, and the maid, Tome Yazawa, alone in the house, the lodger, Hideo Naitō, also being at work.

Shimako was a very beautiful woman of thirty-four, tall and slim, although her skin had a slightly unhealthy pallor and her eyes were somewhat slanted, which gave her a cold look.

"I am afraid I was not in Tokyo on the sixth," she answered the younger detective's question in a firm, high voice. "I was staying at my parents' house in Chigasaki from the third until the seventh. I often feel poorly when the seasons change and go down there to recuperate. My mother and sister live there alone and they are always happy to see me. No, my husband did not tell me anything in particular about the night of the sixth. I think that he said that he worked until about ten o'clock.''

She also denied any knowledge of the discord between Kōsuke and Nasuno.

''I am sorry, but I am afraid that my husband very rarely mentions anything to do with business after he comes home,'' she said, shaking her head slightly.

Tome was interviewed in another room. She was a short woman of sixty-six with her hair pulled back into a severe bun. At first she didn't seem to understand why the police were there.

''Let me see, the sixth . . .''

''Last Wednesday, the day when we had all that rain.''

''Oh, yes, I remember now, it was a cold evening.'' It finally came back to her. ''The missus was away and the boss did not come home until about ten o'clock and then he went out again a little while later.''

''About what time was this?''

''A little after eleven, I think; he had a phone call first, from a woman, I think.'' She whispered the last part so she would not be overheard by Shimako in the other room.

''Did you answer the phone?''

''No, when I heard it ring I hurried out to the kitchen to answer it, but when I got there, the boss had already taken it in the bedroom. They were already talking so I hung up immediately—I don't like to listen in to other people's conversations, you know.'' She smiled slightly, showing a flash of silver teeth. ''After that he telephoned somewhere else and then went out wearing a sports jacket. It must have been about eleven-fifteen when he went out in the car . . . No, he did not tell me where he was going.''

Upon hearing that Kōsuke had gone out at around the same time that Nasuno was murdered, the investigation team became very excited, and after getting as much detail as possible from Tome, they set off to confront Kōsuke at his office.

They walked in and found that there were only three or

four people in the office. They told one of the clerks who they were and that they wanted to talk to Ōkita and were led to a reception area at the back of the room. The man who came to see them a few minutes later was in his late thirties, almost six feet tall, and very well built. He was wearing a khaki shirt and looked as if he had just come in from a job.

"How do you do, my name is Ōkita," he said.

"How do you do. To get straight to the point, I presume that you know about the murder of the president of the Tanzawa Country Club?"

"Yes."

"Well, we would like to ask you one or two questions connected with the case." Momozaki glanced around the office and saw that everybody was looking their way. "Perhaps you would not mind accompanying us to the station." They had intended to take him to the police station all along and just made the pretense of worrying about what other people might think in order to put him off his guard.

Ōkita looked at them for a moment and then nodded in agreement. He was a good-looking man with well-defined features and a sloping forehead. He asked them to wait for a few minutes, then, after giving his employees several instructions, he went through to the back of the building and returned a few minutes later wearing a dark gray suit.

Back at the Himonya police station, Detective Inspector Momozaki and Assistant Inspector Hida from HQ were in charge of the interrogation. Ōkita made no effort to hide the fact that Nasuno had owed him one hundred and twenty million yen or that this had been the source of a lot of ill will between them.

"I did the job according to the plans from the very beginning and they kept finding fault with it for the sole reason of delaying payment of what they owe me."

Even though they were talking about the same thing, Ōkita's view of it was the exact opposite of Kawai's. He had answered their questions in a quiet, reasonable manner until they got to the subject of the outstanding money, when he became quite excited. Momozaki got the impression that although he was a quiet, soft-spoken man, he could be very obstinate when he thought he was in the right and had a quick temper.

"By the way, where did you go on the evening of the sixth?"

"Oh, that night I had a rather strange experience." He calmed down again, but there was a strange expression in his eyes as he spoke. "It was about ten-thirty, I think, I had a phone call from a woman; it was a wrong number, but the woman said that she couldn't see very well and her breathing sounded very ragged, as if she were in pain." He looked out of the window at Meguro Avenue as his thoughts went back to that night. "She said that she did not have any more ten-yen coins and asked me if I could pass on a message for her. I agreed, but although I was sure I dialed the number she gave me, I couldn't get through. The message had been to say that she was standing in a phone booth outside a large church in Himonya and to ask the other party to come and pick her up. She sounded to me as if she had had some kind of accident and I decided to go and see if she was all right. It was very cold that night and it was raining hard.

"I left home at about eleven-fifteen, but when I got to the phone booth all I found was a handkerchief and a note saying that she was waiting at a nearby coffee bar. More than an hour had passed since I first received her phone call, so I couldn't blame her for not waiting. Anyway, I managed to find the coffee bar that she had mentioned, but when I got there I was told that a woman answering her description had left shortly before I arrived, so the whole episode was a complete waste of time."

Momozaki and Hida exchanged a glance, and when they turned back to Kōsuke, there was no trace of friendliness in their faces.

"Did you go straight home from the coffee bar?" Hida asked in an offhand tone. The detective who had been sent from Central Headquarters was a small, well-built man with a slight stoop. He was still only thirty-four, which made him ten years younger than Momozaki, but was very shrewd.

"Yes, I did."

"What time did you get back?"

"About half past twelve, I think."

"Am I right in saying that the woman who phoned your house at ten-thirty was completely unknown to you?"

"Yes, it was a wrong number."

"Did she tell you her name?"

"When she asked me to pass on her message, she did mention it. It was Take something, Takeda or Takeshita, I think."

"Do you remember what number it was she asked you to call?"

"No, I should have written it down when she told me, but there wasn't any paper handy, so I tried to memorize it. That's why I couldn't pass her message on." He frowned as he tried to remember what it was, but it was no good.

"What was the name of the people she was trying to contact?"

"I can't remember that either."

Hida gave an irritable sigh.

"Are you sure you don't have a clue as to who it was that phoned you?"

"None whatsoever."

"How about the voice or her manner of speaking?"

"She had a very deep voice—oh, yes, she also had a bit of an accent. I don't know what accent it was, but I remember thinking that she had probably just arrived in Tokyo from the country and didn't know her way around yet."

"How old would you say she was?"

"Somewhere between thirty and fifty."

"Are you sure that she was calling from a pay phone?"

"Yes, there is no mistake about that—she was cut off after three minutes, and anyway, I found the note and her handkerchief in the phone booth opposite the church."

"Do you still have those objects in your possession?"

"No, I seem to remember throwing them away."

Hida and Momozaki both looked very grave. Hida then leaned forward and looked at Kōsuke calculatingly.

"We all get people dialing our number by mistake and I can quite understand that a woman who was in trouble and did not have any more change might ask you to pass on her message, but I think that it is a little hard to believe that you would go out on a wet night to help a complete stranger. I think that it is taking human kindness a bit too far.''

''Personally, I wouldn't call it kindness so much as responsibility,'' Kōsuke answered, meeting Hida's gaze. ''I had agreed to pass on the woman's message, but due to my own carelessness I was unable to do so. However, I was unable to contact the woman to tell her that and so she would be waiting in a cold phone booth for goodness knows how long for someone to come and pick her up. I think it would have been much more unnatural for me to have just left her there.''

''I see . . .''

''If it had been a man, I might not have bothered, but as it was, it was a woman with bad eyesight who sounded sick or injured. I know the area slightly—it is very bleak at night—and on top of that it was very wet and cold that night. It was only fifteen or twenty minutes away by car, and rather than sit and worry about it all night, I thought it would be much easier just to go and have a look,'' he said, bristling with indignation. He looked the quiet type, but once he had decided that he was in the right, he would become quite vehement.

''Very well, I think we understand how you feel about it,'' said Momozaki, taking over the interrogation. ''So you say that you left home at about eleven-fifteen, and roughly what time did you arrive at the church in Himonya?''

The church was only a short distance from the police station and under its jurisdiction, so Momozaki had known immediately where Kōsuke was talking about.

''It's only twenty minutes from my house, but it took me a little time to find it, so let's say around eleven-forty or perhaps a little later.''

''You say that you went into the phone booth and found a handkerchief and a note saying that she was waiting in a nearby coffee bar, is that correct?''

''Yes, the coffee bar was called Eri, I think. It was about two blocks down to the east. I'd soon be able to find it if I went there again.''

"And what time did you enter this coffee bar?"

"At around eleven-fifty or twelve o'clock, I think."

"Did you know that Mr. Nasuno lived nearby in Oh-okayama?"

"Yes."

"Have you ever been there?"

"Yes, quite a while ago, I went as far as the front door."

He explained that when he had first taken on the job of constructing the Tanzawa course, he, Kinumura, and Nasuno had gone drinking together in Ginza, and as they lived in the same direction, he and Nasuno had shared a car home. The car had driven right up to the front door, which meant that Kōsuke knew that there was a thirty-yard driveway leading up to the house from the road.

"Did you know that Mr. Nasuno was having the driveway resurfaced recently and that he had to walk to the house from the road?"

"No, I had no idea."

He shook his head and denied it as Momozaki had thought he would, but as he did so, the detective noticed a shadow of something cross his features.

"It is only about five minutes to the Nasunos' house from the church; it's about the same distance from the coffee bar Eri, too," Momozaki said as if he were thinking out loud. "Is there any way that you can prove that you were at the telephone booth at approximately eleven-forty and at the coffee bar from eleven-fifty to twelve o'clock?" he asked quietly, and fixed Kōsuke with a steady look. It was not necessary for him to point out that this was a key point.

A look of concern crossed Kōsuke's features.

"The people in the coffee bar should remember me, but as I said, there wasn't anyone at the phone booth."

"You did not ask anyone in the area for directions or anything?"

"No, I did not see a soul on foot and there were hardly even any other cars."

"Yes, it is a lonely area at night," Momozaki said with a nod. "But you have no idea of the woman's identity; you can't remember the number she asked you to call. Is there nothing else you can remember?

"Seiji Nasuno was murdered at some time between eleven-forty and twelve o'clock, so if you can prove that you were where you said you were at those times, it will put a completely different light on the situation. We will go and check out the coffee bar, but are you sure that there is no one else who can vouch for the fact that you had a phone call from a strange woman who asked you to pass on a message for her?"

Kōsuke sat with his chin on his hands, deep in thought. The sun shining in through the window struck him in the face and highlighted the worry in his eyes.

"Actually, although it is a little embarrassing to say, our maid sometimes listens in to our phone conversations," he said, without lifting his head from his hands. "That night I answered the phone in the bedroom and I am pretty sure that Tome was listening in on the extension in the kitchen, so she might be able to tell you the woman's name."

"Do you mean to say that you let your maid listen in to your calls without doing anything about it?" Hida asked in his blunt fashion.

"No, I did broach the subject with her once and she stopped for a while. If my wife or I are at home we usually answer the phone ourselves, but sometimes Tome picks up the receiver at the same time and doesn't replace it. She only does it out of curiosity and doesn't mean any harm; anyway, I get most of my calls at the office, so it doesn't really affect me that much."

"Has she been with you long?"

"Eight or nine years; she was recommended to us by my wife's family." A look of pain passed across his features again.

Once the questioning was finished, Hida and Kōsuke went out to check up on as much of his story as they could. They went in a squad car, Hida and Kōsuke sitting in the back while a uniformed officer drove. A weak westerly sun shone through the clouds, but it was already low in the sky and sunset was not far away.

They turned off Meguro Avenue, and after going for about seven hundred yards they came to a large white church with a large cross on the roof. It was only about three minutes from the police station by car.

"That's the phone booth," Kōsuke said, pointing to the right of the church.

At Hida's prompting they got out of the car and walked over to the booth. Kōsuke opened the door and pointed to the ledge next to the phone where he had found the handkerchief and note.

"It said that she was waiting in a coffee bar called Eri and the name on the top and the signature were the same as the ones she mentioned on the phone, so it had to be her."

"But if she was lost, how did she know where the coffee bar was?"

"I don't know. Maybe she had some idea of the immediate vicinity or she had walked around looking for somewhere to wait out of the cold."

They went back to the car, drove east for two blocks, then turned right at a crossroads and were able to see a sign advertising the coffee bar Eri. Even in the afternoon the streets were virtually deserted and it only took them about one minute to get there, although it would have taken a woman on foot at least ten times as long.

Hida looked pointedly at his watch.

"That night I drove in the opposite direction to begin with, so it took me a little while to find," Kōsuke said hurriedly.

Inside there were three student-looking types sitting by the jukebox and one man sitting at the bar. Behind the bar there was a waitress of about twenty-five or -six and a middle-aged man who was obviously the manager.

"Oh, you are the ones who were here the other night when I came in, aren't you?" Kōsuke said to the couple as soon as he walked in. Everyone in the room looked over at them.

Hida showed them his identification and said, "I wonder if you could answer a few questions to help us with our inquiries."

"Is it to do with the murder of the golf-club owner?" the manager asked.

"Yeah, you could say that. This man says that he came

in here that night a short while before twelve o'clock; do
you remember him?"

The couple regarded Kōsuke in silence for a few moments, then they both nodded. They did not seem very
positive, but they seemed to remember him vaguely.

"I came in and asked you if a woman had been here
and you told me that she had come in about twenty minutes earlier and had left a few moments before I arrived.
Surely you must remember," Kōsuke said to the manager.

"Now you come to mention it, I do seem to remember
having a conversation like that."

"I think you said that she was wearing a black raincoat
and that she had telephoned somewhere but did not seem
to get an answer, so she had given up and gone out. When
I heard that I also left," Kōsuke said to the waitress, and
although she nodded, Hida got the impression that they
felt intimidated by Kōsuke and were just agreeing to hu-
mor him. Hida had him go out and wait in the car while
he questioned the couple. As a result, he was able to learn
that they both remembered that a man resembling Kōsuke
had come in late, three nights before, looking for a woman,
but neither of them could remember their conversation with
him in any detail.

"Had the woman he was looking for really been in?"

"I don't know if it was the woman that he was looking
for or not, but a woman had come in on her own and
seemed to have been waiting for someone."

"She was wearing a black raincoat and sat over there,"
the waitress said. "I remember taking her a cup of hot
lemon."

She pointed to the table in the corner, but she could not
give a better description of the woman and could not even
be sure that it was Kōsuke who had come in later. The
shop was very dark and he had only been there for a few
minutes.

"Do you remember what time he came?"

"I think it was before midnight," the manager said, and
glanced over toward the waitress. "Kaz was still here, so
I think it must have been between eleven-fifty and twelve
o'clock."

"How long was he in here?"

"Only two or three minutes, I think. He went out without ordering anything."

In that case, even if they were willing to swear that it was Kōsuke who had come in, it would not provide him with an alibi, Hida thought with satisfaction. Even if he had killed Nasuno, he could easily have driven over afterward and made an appearance in the coffee bar in order to create an alibi; it was only a five-minute drive by car.

"When the man came in, did he appear to be upset or nervous? Did you notice any blood on his clothing?"

The couple exchanged a glance again.

"Now, that you mention it, he did seem a bit flustered."

While Hida was checking out Kōsuke's alibi at the coffee bar, two other detectives visited his house. It was the same couple who had been there during the day, and when Shimako came to the door, they said that they wanted to check on some things with the maid, Tome. They took her into the living room and the two of them sat down opposite her.

"This afternoon when we spoke to you, you said that when the phone rang at about ten-thirty on the evening of the sixth, you answered it in the kitchen, but when you heard Mr. Ōkita speaking on the other extension you hung up. However, are you sure that you hung up right away and didn't listen to his conversation for a while?"

"Of course I didn't," Tome said, shaking her head positively.

"That is strange, because Mr. Ōkita definitely says that he heard the sound of the other extension being replaced after he finished speaking. It is very important that we know the contents of that telephone call and we would be very grateful if you could help us."

"As I said before, I picked up the extension in the kitchen, but as soon as I heard the boss speaking I hung up. When the boss or the missus are at home, they generally answer the phone and I always hang up as soon as I hear them speak."

"You said it was a woman's voice, didn't you?"

"Yes."

"What was the conversation about?"

"From what I heard, I got the impression it was a wrong number."

"Why did you think that?"

"Because she asked for a different name; however, I did not hear any more."

No matter what the detectives asked, Tome refused to admit that she had listened to the whole conversation. The detectives asked Shimako if they could check the two phones, then they went back to the police station.

A meeting was held at the station so Hida and the two detectives who checked the house could make their reports. During this period Kōsuke was not allowed to go home and another detective took over the interrogation.

"If Tome Yazawa's story is to be believed, a woman phoned the Ōkita house by mistake, but we do not know if the contents are as Ōkita reported them or not."

"We must bear in mind that she has been working for the Ōkitas for nine years now and is distantly related to Mrs. Ōkita, so she is virtually a member of the family. There is always a chance that she might lie to protect Ōkita if he or his wife asked her to, so I think that even if she could change her story later to bring it further into line with Ōkita's, we should treat it with a certain amount of suspicion."

Commissioner Yamane from headquarters, the officer in charge of the investigation, listened to their reports in silence before speaking. "I think that there is one more possibility that we must not overlook. I think that we are all agreed that Ōkita had sufficient motive to kill Nasuno and that he was in the area at the critical time without an alibi, so he also had the opportunity. Finally the maid, Tome, is virtually a member of the family and as such her testimony does not hold very much weight, although it is stronger than his wife's would have been."

"Do you mean that he may have asked her to make a false statement about his having received a phone call in order to supply him with an alibi?" one of the younger detectives asked.

"That is quite possible, but first we must try to discover just how close a relationship there is between the Ōkitas and the maid. However, when I said that there was one more possibility, what I meant was that Ōkita could have asked an accomplice to phone that night and give that story. He probably guessed that if the phone rang late at night while his wife was away, Tome would listen in to call and, by so doing, provide him with an alibi later. There are two other people living at the Ōkitas, the maid and the young lodger, and so it would be difficult for him to go out without anyone realizing and he could not trust them to keep silent. It would be much easier altogether if he were just to get a friend to make a call and pretend it was a wrong number. He would not even have to tell the friend what it was for; he could just pretend it was a practical joke.''

He glanced around the room, looking for approval of his idea. His eyes fell on Momozaki.

"Even the suspect admits that he was in the neighborhood at the time of the murder, so there is no question about that, but I find it a little hard to believe that he just happened to have received a phone call that caused him to go there at that precise time.''

"I don't know about that,'' Hida said, thrusting his head forward excitedly. "Perhaps it all happened as he said, but that was what triggered it off. He had had a violent argument with Nasuno over the payment for his work five days before the murder, but he did not get any satisfaction. At the same time his bills are becoming due for payment every day and he is at his wit's end. That night he has a phone call from a stranger, but due to a mix-up of phone numbers he is not able to pass on her message. Rather than sit there and worry, he decides to go and look for her, but when he get there he finds the telephone booth empty. Looking around, he realizes that he is near Nasuno's house and decides to try once more to get him to pay. He waits at the gate and when Nasuno arrives they get into an argument, and losing his temper, Ōkita hits Nasuno with a golf club. Ōkita plays golf, so it would not be strange for him to keep a club in his car for when he goes to practice.''

# 5

# Evidence

AFTER HE HAD BEEN CROSS-EXAMINED FOR SEV-
eral hours, Kōsuke realized with a chill that the detectives'
attitude toward him was changing subtly and that the majority of them obviously thought him guilty. He had first
been asked down to the station at two in the afternoon,
but it was past seven before they finally let him go. The
fact that he had been within five minutes' drive of the
scene of the murder, coupled with the fact that he had
sufficient motive, was enough for most of them. He realized with a fateful clarity that the only reason they eventually let him go was because they lacked sufficient
evidence to keep him.

He caught a taxi in front of the police station and went
directly back to the office. He had telephoned the staff
earlier and told them to leave when it was time, so when
he got there at about 7:30, it was quite dark except for a
dim light at the entrance. He let himself in and went to
his cold office.

There were no messages for him on his desk, just a list
of three names of people who had phoned him. He glanced
over them and felt a thrill when he noticed the name Nasuno among them. Now that Nasuno had been murdered,

the only person of that name who could possibly have called him was Chiharu.

Nasuno's funeral had been held that day. No doubt when the people from the Uchibō club and Tanzawa club gathered together, the main topic of conversation had been who the murderer was, and it was likely that Kōsuke's name had come up. He could visualize the atmosphere there and could not help but wonder why Chiharu had chosen this particular day to phone him. Was it to hear his story in person or was she phoning to demonstrate that she trusted him? Kōsuke chose to believe the latter. When they had last met, she seemed very worried about the trouble between him and her father and she had asked if it would be okay for her to call.

He stretched out and picked up the phone. For a moment he was about to telephone her, but then he forced himself to replace the receiver. He realized that it would be best if he were to stay away from her until the police realized his innocence. But what if things only became worse? Thoughts of what might happen filled him with a vague fear, and in order to take his mind off it he tried to submerge himself in his work. He would have to plead with Kawai to pay the money that was still outstanding or at least enough of it for him to pay for the trees and turf he had bought for the job.

He was worrying about this when he heard the sound of the front door opening and several men entering the building. He thought that it must be the detectives come back to continue their inquiries and felt his body tense with anticipation. His office was not far from the front door and the men walked over, talking as they came. It seemed to Kōsuke that they spoke in a very rough way for detectives and he stood up in alarm. He opened the door and stepped out of the office and as he did so he found himself surrounded on three sides. There were four of them, all young with crew cuts. One of them was wearing a dark suit while the other three had brightly colored jackets and checked shirts. Kōsuke could tell right away that they were Japanese gangsters or *yakuzas*.

"Are you Ōkita?" one of them asked in a curiously high-pitched voice.

Kōsuke nodded in silence.

"We're here on behalf of Mr. Kuretani and have come to pick you up."

"Kuretani?"

"Yes, that's right, Noboru Kuretani, president of the Seicho Company and editor in chief of *Economic Growth*. Surely you must have heard of him."

Kōsuke could feel that the young man was making fun of him, but there was nothing he could say. Although he had never met Kuretani personally, he remembered hearing Kinumura mention him.

"Shall we go? Mr. Kuretani is waiting for you in his office."

"What does he want with me?"

"I am afraid you will have to ask him that yourself. We were just told to come and pick you up."

"But I still have a lot of work to do."

"Yes, we realize that you must be very busy, and you must be feeling exhausted after being kept by the police for so long." Although the man's words were polite enough, his tone held a hidden menace. Not only that, but he also knew that Kōsuke had been at the police station all afternoon. "We won't keep you long, but we would appreciate it if you would come with us."

One of the men slipped around behind Kōsuke and he found himself surrounded. He tried to ignore them and walk away, but when he did, they all stuck to him. Although none of them was particularly tall, they were all powerfully built and looked as if they could take care of themselves.

They all walked out into the dark plot in front of the office. Kōsuke's car was inside the garage there, but there was a strange sedan parked across the entrance, blocking it. The man in the dark suit nodded toward it and slipped his hand inside his jacket to indicate that he was armed. Kōsuke realized that he had no alternative but to go along with them for the time being. He got in the back of the car and one man sat on either side of him. The man in the suit got into the driver's seat and the fourth man got in next to him. The car started with a squeal of tires and headed off past the farmers' fields that still dotted the residential area and made its way toward the road.

Strangely enough, squashed into the backseat of the car, Kōsuke found himself relaxing a bit, and started to try to guess why Kuretani would have sent his men to pick him up. He couldn't think of any reason, but he guessed that he'd find out soon enough. The men didn't talk to him anymore and just chatted among themselves, the topic of their conversation seeming to revolve around women and mah-jongg.

He thought back over the conversation he had had with Kinumura about Kuretani and remembered that Kinumura had told him that Kuretani did not employ any *yakuza* himself but borrowed them from the Takafuji gang whenever he needed them. Usually he pretended that he had nothing to do with the underworld and was nothing more than a magazine editor.

Every now and again he felt the fear build up in his stomach, but he forced himself to remain calm until the car pulled up in front of a condominium.

"This is it," the man next to him said in a low voice. "After you."

Kōsuke got out and the four men surrounded him again. The building was six stories high, and although it was getting a little old now, there were several other companies in it. They got into the elevator and went up to the fourth floor.

They walked along the corridor until they came to a door with a blue plate with white lettering that said SEI-CHO. The doors on either side also had company names on them, but it was late now and there was no sign of anyone else on the whole floor. The man who was in the lead walked in without knocking and the man behind Kōsuke pushed him in.

The room inside was filled with desks and looked like an ordinary office. There was no one in the room, but one of the men walked over to another door and this time he stopped and knocked. After hearing a reply, he opened the door and they led Kōsuke inside.

There was a leather-covered three-piece suite inside the room, and standing in front of an ebony desk, a swarthy man looked out of the window. His hair was neatly combed, and he was wearing gold-rimmed, tinted glasses. He was about fifty years old, had a slight paunch, and looked every inch a company executive.

Kōsuke was led up to the sofa and pushed roughly into it. The driver went out again and the remaining three men sat in the other chairs or stood casually by. They did not look particularly interested in the proceedings, but they kept Kōsuke surrounded.

The swarthy-looking man turned in his direction. "My name is Kuretani," he said in a deep voice, and lowered himself into the chair opposite. Unlike the younger men, he was wearing a very conservative dark brown suit and tie. "The reason I asked you over here today was so that we might discuss the death of Mr. Nasuno the other day."

Kōsuke noticed that there was a large mole on his cheek, just under his glasses.

"As you probably know, his funeral was held today and of course I attended. I thought that it was terrible that so great a man should suffer such a terrible death. We go back a long way, he and I, it must be twenty years now. . . ."

Kōsuke had been watching Kuretani's mouth as he spoke, wondering when he would get to the point, then suddenly something about it sickened him and he looked around the room instead. His eyes landed on some calligraphy in a frame above the desk. Written in black ink with a strong hand were the words "Love your brother man."

"We were both still in our early thirties when we met. Nasuno had already started his own company and I had left the stockbrokers where I had worked and started a trade paper; that's how we met. He taught me all kinds of things, and when either of us was in trouble, we would always help each other out. We became inseparable friends, and as the years passed, a real platonic love grew up between us."

He seemed to like talking about love and friendship, but his cruel lips and cold way of talking belied his words.

"For that reason I hate whoever it was who did that to him and I have sworn that he will be made to pay for what he has done."

He leaned forward and put his hand to his hip, and as he did so Kōsuke was surprised to see that the dark suit was lined with a bright garish material. He noticed that Kuretani's breathing had become labored, and looking up at his face, he saw that the eyes behind the tinted glasses were fixed on him with a burning hatred.

"Why did you kill Nasuno?" he demanded threateningly.

"You've got to be kidding!" Kōsuke almost shouted in surprise.

"What do you mean? You were at the police station all afternoon, weren't you?"

"I was just there to clear up a few points."

"Don't give me that; they're not going to keep you there that long unless they're pretty sure that you're the man they're after."

"Not at all; there are any number of other people who had just as much motive to kill him as I did." Kōsuke was shocked to hear that even Kuretani suspected him and found himself struggling to prove his innocence.

"Shut up!" Kuretani said, raising his voice. "It's no use lying, I've got proof!"

"Proof? What kind of proof could you possible have?"

"One of the people on my editorial staff saw you that night."

"Where?"

"In front of Mr. Nasuno's house. He saw you come out of the gate of Mr. Nasuno's house at approximately eleven-fifty on the night of the sixth."

"That's a lie!"

"He lives in an apartment in Midorigaoka and that night he walked past Mr. Nasuno's house on his way home after playing mah-jongg. He knows you by sight from the Tanzawa Country Club, where you were working, and he says that he saw you run out of the gate, panting and looking very pale."

"Don't be ridiculous. That's a complete fabrication and you know it!"

"He is prepared to go to the police with his story, so why don't you just stop playing the innocent and come clean?'' Kuretani was obviously an old hand at threatening people.

"You're lying. You can't expect the police to believe a story like that.''

"Oh, yeah? In that case I'll have him go to the police tomorrow, shall I? He has also got witnesses to prove what time he left the mah-jongg parlor; they can go, too, and back up his story if that's the way you want it.''

"It's all lies, all of it. . . .''

Even as he tried to refute it, he knew that it was no good. Kuretani's connections with the underworld were well known, but if enough of his men were to swear that they had seen Kōsuke, the police would have no choice but to believe them. In fact, the police might welcome it, as all they wanted was a bit of concrete evidence in order to arrest him.

Kuretani was watching him closely, and as soon as he noticed the dismay in his face, he continued.

"I only heard the story myself last night; the man in question went away on a business trip the day after the murder and only came back yesterday. Naturally, as soon as I heard about it, my first thought was to go straight to the police, but after thinking it over for a day, I have changed my mind.'' He sat up straight and continued in a solemn voice as if he were a judge passing sentence. "As I mentioned just now, Nasuno and I were very close and I can never forgive the man who did that to him, so I decided that rather than hand you over to the police, I would punish you myself.''

He placed his hands on his hips and Kōsuke could again see the strange bright lining of his suit. He felt the young men stand up and move in behind him and the room was filled with a suffocating tension.

He wanted to cry out that it was not him, but the fear and tension were so much that he could not find his voice. He felt that if he were to say anything, it would move the men to action, and aside from Kuretani, there were the other three strong-looking men to reckon with. The three men seemed to be waiting for some kind of sign from Kuretani and the room was completely silent. Several minutes passed, or maybe it was only seconds. Suddenly a cat cried—it sounded as if it was in the office somewhere—a small, lonely sound.

Kuretani stood up, and removing his hands from his hips, he scratched his nose. "If your wife heard about it, I am sure she would be very upset," he said with regret. "Your mother and sister, too. They live in Ōhashi, I hear; it's quite close to here. I go past their house every day, you know."

Although Kuretani's words sounded suddenly soft and concerned, it was only another way of pressuring him, and Kōsuke felt genuinely threatened. His sister lived in a condominium with her husband and their sixty-year-old mother.

"When I say that I want to punish you myself for what you did, I do not mean that I want to punish you physically. Nasuno was a gentle man and I do not think he would be very pleased if I did that. No, I want to make you pay for what you did in a way that he would approve of." He looked over at one of the young men and a message seemed to pass between them.

"Normally I would make you pay more than adequate compensation for what you did, but unfortunately your company is on its last legs. . . ."

At that moment the door opened and the man in the suit who had driven the car walked in carrying a thin briefcase. Kuretani took the case, and removing a document from it with a beringed hand, he offered it to Kōsuke. It was a printed receipt for a loan and "Seicho Company" had been filled in as the lender. It read:

*Article one: The lender hereby gives the borrower twenty million yen and said borrower hereby certifies that he has received said sum. . . .*

The amount was written in ballpoint pen and the name of the borrower left blank. There was also a letter of attorney.

"I know that your company is likely to go bust any day and that your house and land will all be mortgaged, so I am not going to ask you for any money. But someone of your age, with a wife and house, must have a life insurance policy for twenty or thirty million yen. If you were to die suddenly, your wife could expect to get at least that much." He paused and licked his lips. "Don't get me wrong. I'm not suggesting that anything is going to happen to you. I'm not even relying on your life insurance. Your wife's family is apparently quite well off; her father was an executive in a bank, wasn't he? When he retired he bought a big tract of land in Chigasaki, which I am sure must be worth at least twenty or thirty million."

Kuretani had not stopped at checking out his mother and sister; he had even found out all about his wife's family.

"Therefore, I want you to get your wife to fill in her name and address in her own handwriting and to put her seal on the bottom. I will also need a power of attorney, which will have to be notarized, and as Monday is a holiday, I will send one of my men around to pick it up on Tuesday evening. Just make sure that you have everything ready for him when he arrives."

When Kōsuke heard that Kuretani wanted him to have it notarized, he realized that he was dealing with a professional. "Why do you have to drag my wife into this?"

"Because you haven't got any money of your own. You'll have to use your life insurance money to pay back Mr. Nasuno for what you did."

"You've got to be joking!" After all his fine words, it boiled down to simple blackmail.

"Get your wife to fill in all the forms by Tuesday evening. If you agree, we'll let you go home tonight."

"I've got no reason to do that."

"What about the witness who saw you?"

"But I did not do anything."

The exchange continued for a short while, then Kuretani took a deep breath and stood up. "You shouldn't underestimate me, you know. You don't know how I work. Show him."

This last was to the young thugs, who had been poised behind him, waiting for the opportunity. They grabbed him roughly by the arms and pulled him to his feet. They dragged him in to the next room and opened a door. Suddenly he could hear the cat quite clearly. The door led to the condominium's bathroom and on the tiled floor there was a basket that contained a kitten.

"Shall I do it?" asked one of the young men.

"Yes, go ahead," replied Kuretani from behind them. "This is what I meant when I said that I would punish you for what you did. This will show you what kind of people you are dealing with."

The young man in the checked shirt walked into the bathroom with a can of gasoline, and after looking down at the kitten for a moment, he poured the contents of the can over the basket. He walked back out and everyone looked on in horror while the kitten wailed piteously. After a few more minutes the man lit a match and threw it into the basket. The basket caught fire with a bang and the room was filled with the terrible scream of an animal in pain.

The tenth of October was Sports Day, which meant that this year the national holiday fell on a Sunday. The skies over Tokyo were heavy and gray and it promised to be a miserable, cold day.

Shimako got up at nine o'clock, and after having breakfast in the kitchen, she went back to the lounge next to her bedroom and sat on the sofa in silence. She suffered from low blood pressure and was never very lively in the morning, but this day in particular she just sat staring into space and did not seem to have any energy at all.

She always felt a bit under the weather at the change of the seasons or when the bad weather continued at the beginning of autumn, which was why she had gone back to stay at her parents' house the previous week. Her sister still lived there; she had never married and ran a small calligraphy school. Shimako could really relax when she was there and enjoyed a visit more than anything.

Shimako was thirty-four and had been married to Kōsuke for nine years now. After she graduated from a women's college she had entered a large landscape gardener's, and it was there that she met Kōsuke. He was the son of a nursery gardener and planned to open a landscape-gardening firm of his own. He managed this in 1972 when he founded Wakashiba Landscaping, Inc., But as a result,

Shimako had to wait until 1973, when she was twenty-five, before she could marry him. Unfortunately, soon after their marriage Japan suffered from the oil shock, and although Kōsuke managed to bring the company through countless crises, this time it looked like the end.

Although Kōsuke never spoke to her about business, she could tell from his manner that something had gone seriously wrong recently. The previous night he had come in at a little before eleven looking particularly haggard and had just collapsed into bed without saying a word. She wondered if he was feeling okay, but this morning he got up before eight o'clock and went to the office. Today was a holiday, but when she asked him where he was going, he just said that he had a few things to tie up.

Even though Kōsuke did not like to talk about business at home, he had occasionally mentioned the trouble he was having over the Tanzawa Country Club and Shimako could still hear the anger that had been in his voice when he cursed Nasuno. Now, on top of everything else, he was also under suspicion for murdering Nasuno. Although he had not said anything himself yet, the police had come to interview her and Tome twice the day before, once in the morning and once in the afternoon, and they made no attempt to hide their belief that Kōsuke was guilty.

She knew he claimed to have received a telephone call from a strange woman, but despite this alibi, she felt that his case was hopeless.

She looked out into the garden, which was filled with pine trees, boxwood, and other nonflowering evergreens. Most people probably think that a landscape gardener would have a beautifully kept garden filled with all kinds of plants and trees, but the truth couldn't have been further from that. This was especially true of Kōsuke and illustrated the way that he saved everything for work and was almost indifferent about what happened in the home.

Even though it was a holiday, the whole neighborhood was unusually quiet. Tome was working in the kitchen and Shimako had bumped into Hideo, the lodger, after she had finished her meal. Although they had given him a job at the request of his father, he did not seem to enjoy being a gardener and he occasionally demonstrated this in his behavior toward Kōsuke and Shimako. At first glance he seemed to be a very quiet boy, but at times he could be very obstinate if he wanted to be, and Shimako guessed that he must be going through a difficult period.

Apart from the sound of Hideo's and Tome's voices in the distance, the house was very quiet, and sitting back on the sofa looking out at the bleak garden, she found herself thinking about the Nasuno murder and Kōsuke's position. Her pulse started to pound and she became very tense as fear and loneliness moved in on her.

If only we had children at a time like this, she thought longingly, although she probably did so more in an effort to take her mind off her predicament than anything else.

Shimako and Kōsuke had never had any children; it was physically difficult for her to conceive, and although she did manage to become pregnant once, the child had never seen the light of day. Kōsuke had a gentle side and a violent side to his character; he was basically a very kind man, but he had a vicious streak. He would lose his temper at the slightest thing and sometimes he even hit Shimako.

Not that it could be called a slight thing, she thought. All the same, if he had not pushed me away like that . . .

She had almost forgotten the reason for their argument that night. All she could remember was being knocked over and hitting the corner of the table. She had collapsed and the next morning she had had a miscarriage.

If the child had been born, he would have been two now.

As always when she thought about it, she started to cry quietly to herself, although she was no doubt unconsciously whipping up her resentment toward her husband in order to take her mind off the worry and tension she felt.

At that moment she heard Tome shout something from the kitchen and Hideo also seemed very excited; or did the sound come from the garden?

She looked up. Her nerves were at such a pitch that she could almost feel that there was something wrong. Presently she heard the sound of footsteps running down the hall. Tome opened the door before Shimako had the chance to get to her feet.

"Excuse me, ma'am . . ." Tome's gray hair was drawn back into a bun and her face was as white as a sheet.

"What is it?"

"There is something I think you should see."

So saying, she hurried back down the hall toward the kitchen and Shimako had no choice but to follow her. The glass doors were open and Hideo was standing in the garden in a sweater and jeans. He still looked like a schoolboy with a thin face and glasses, but when he saw Shimako, he frowned and a strange look came over his face.

The garden outside the kitchen was filled with low shrubs and on the left-hand side there was a prefab shed. When she looked in that direction, she noticed that the ground under the floor of the shed had been dug out and scattered around the garden. She immediately guessed that it was the work of one of the local dogs, Ess, who often escaped at night and came to play in their garden. He had a habit of digging holes there, and although Shimako kept telling herself that she should go and complain to the owners, she still had not done anything; every time it happened, she left it to Tome or Hideo to fill in the holes.

"I only noticed it just now and asked Hideo to fill it in, but when he had a closer look, he found these."

Tome pointed to one side where there was a yellow mud-stained towel and a cotton work glove. Hideo picked up the towel and Shimako could see that it was a sports towel, a little smaller than a bathtowel, and that it had dark stains on it. The glove also had similar stains on it. Hideo stood looking at her as if waiting for her to say something, but when she remained silent, he could not stand it anymore.

"I think that the black stains may be blood," he said.

Shimako remained silent.

"The glove has similar stains."

"We could only find one glove. I think that Ess might have run off with the other one," Tome added.

"There is something else, too," Hideo said, looking toward the shed with distaste.

"What do you mean, something else?" Shimako asked in a weak voice.

"There is something else under the shed, at the back," Tome said, "but I said that we should call you before we did anything else."

Shimako walked out into the garden in her slippers and crouched down behind Hideo to look under the shed. He produced a shovel and proceeded to prod about under the floor. Finally she saw something glint in the dark and he pulled out a shiny golf club and a white towel.

"I think that is all," he said, and stood up, brushing the earth off his trousers.

The white towel was also covered with mud and had the same black stains on it. The golf club was a number-five iron and did not look particularly dirty.

"I think it's blood," Hideo said again. "He must have used the white towel to wipe the golf club clean."

"What is that supposed to mean?"

"Well, what I mean is that someone wiped the blood off this golf club with the towel and hid them under the shed together with the glove."

"Who do you mean, someone?" Shimako looked at him in bewilderment, but he could not meet her eye and looked over toward Tome. They exchanged a knowing look and an unnatural silence continued.

"If Ess took the other glove, perhaps we should try to find it," Tome said suddenly.

"All the same, I think we should hand these over to the police first." Halfway through the sentence he turned to look at Shimako.

"The police?"

"Yes, the police are still investigating the murder of the president of the Tanzawa Country Club and they say that they still have not found the murder weapon."

"What has that got to do with this?"

Hideo looked embarrassed for a moment. He had been interrogated by the police at work and knew that they suspected Kōsuke, but now he found that he suspected him, too, and a defiant look came over his face. Shimako stared at him fixedly for a few minutes.

"Wait a little while. I want to talk it over with Kōsuke

first,'' she said in a strained voice. ''He should still be in the office; we can always go to the police later.''

She ran back into the kitchen and grabbed the telephone.

# 6

# A Parting in the Fields

It was a little after three o'clock on Sunday the tenth when Chiharu Nasuno had the telephone call. Usually she would either be at work or out practicing her golf somewhere at that time of day, but her father's funeral had only taken place the day before and she had decided to stay away from work until after the public funeral on the fourteenth. In orthodox Buddhism, the family members hold a private funeral service first and then hold a formal service five days later, this latter being a kind of memorial service for the dead. Chiharu's sister, who was married to a doctor in Yokohama, had also been staying at the house since the murder and it was she who answered the phone. When she heard that it was for Chiharu, she went through to the room with the family shrine and whispered, "Telephone for you."

"Who is it?"

"I'm not sure; he said something about the Uchibō club."

Chiharu made her way to the telephone, thinking that it was probably the caddie master. "Hello, Nasuno speaking."

"Is that Chiharu?" The moment she heard the man's

68

powerful voice on the phone she felt something like a shock of electricity thrill through her body, although it was probably a few moments before she guessed who it was.

"Yes, it's me."

There was a moment's pause, then: "It's Kōsuke speaking."

"Yes . . ." She found that she could not say any more. It was the first she had heard from him since the murder and he had not even come to the funeral the day before. She had thought this a little strange as he and Nasuno had been in business together, but she had heard from Kinumura that Kōsuke and her father had had a very violent argument a mere five days before the murder. Kinumura had been the one who had first introduced them to each other and he was very upset that things had not turned out well between them.

She had also heard rumors that Kōsuke had become one of the main suspects in the murder case and she guessed that he had only refrained from calling her out of consideration for her position.

"Did you phone me yesterday?" he asked.

"Yes."

She had telephoned his office at about six o'clock but was told that he was out. She had not left a message but had mentioned her name and she guessed that his secretary must have left a message.

"I would like to offer you my most sincere condolences and I must apologize for not coming to see you in person," he said in a very formal tone. "The funeral service will be on the fourteenth, will it?"

"Yes."

"I had hoped that I could at least come to that—" He seemed to be at a sudden loss for words and broke off in midsentence.

"It will be the seven-day memorial service in four days' time. It seems so fast. . . ."

"You must be feeling exhausted."

Hearing his deep voice on the phone, she felt the grief that had been building up inside her slowly start to dissipate. The day before she had come back from the funeral and wanted nothing so much as to talk to him, so she had gone to the empty reception room and called his office. She had acted wholly on impulse and had no clear idea of what she wanted to say to him if he had been there. They had been seeing each other about twice a month for a meal or a game of golf for two years, and although neither of them was a great talker, when he stopped calling her, she felt as if something important had gone out of her life. She knew that he was married and that their relationship could never come to much, but all the same, she felt that his existence was vital for her well-being.

After a few moments of silence, Kōsuke seemed to make up his mind about something and took a deep breath. "I don't suppose you are free to go out today, are you?"

"Yes, we aren't having many visitors today."

"I would like to meet you if that's possible. I may not be able to see you again for some time."

Chiharu could hear the pain in his deep voice as he said this, but he soon managed to get his feelings back under control.

"I know that I should really come around to your house to pay my respects, but what with one thing and another, I don't think that would be very wise at the moment."

Chiharu realized he was referring to the fact that he was the main suspect for her father's murder and that everyone knew it.

"If you do agree to meet me, I think it would be best if we did it someplace where we won't be seen. I don't want to cause any trouble for you later." His voice sounded very calm, but she could feel the underlying tension. "If you could possibly come out to meet me . . ."

"Yes, it's okay," she said without a moment's hesitation. Admittedly it was only a few days since her father's sudden death, but there were no religious services today, so there was no reason why she shouldn't go out. She realized that he was being so circumspect because he wasn't sure how she would react to him now that he was a suspect. Although she believed in his innocence, she knew that her mother and sister would be very upset if she told them who she was going to meet. "There is nothing to stop me from going out for two or three hours."

"In that case, you couldn't come to Kokubunji, could you?"

"Kokubunji . . . ?"

"Do you remember that coffee bar we visited there once on our way back from the golf club at Chichibu?"

"Yes, it was called the Coral Tree, wasn't it?" It was about a year since they had been there, but she found that she could remember it very well.

"Yes, that's the one. I'm in Ekoda at the moment and if I leave right away I should be there by about four o'clock."

"Okay, I'll get ready right away."

"Thank you," Kōsuke said quietly, and hung up.

She ran upstairs to her room and changed out of her black suit into a one-piece. She picked up a beige coat and handbag and ran downstairs again. At the front door she met one of the secretaries from the Tanzawa Country Club who had come to help at the house.

"Please tell my mother that I have to pop out for a short while but that I should be back by evening," she said in an offhand way, and put her shoes on.

After the murder, boards had been placed over the driveway so cars could drive all the way up from the road and Chiharu was able to keep her yellow BMW 320 in the garage next to the front door again.

"I may not be able to see you again for some time."

Kōsuke's deep voice seemed to echo through her mind as she gazed through the windshield of her car. She wondered what he could have meant by that; she knew about the rumors that he was the murderer, but she wondered if something else had come up. Thinking of his tense manner on the phone, she realized that this must be what had happened; her knuckles turned white as she gripped the steering wheel.

Luckily, since it was Sunday afternoon, the roads were not so crowded, and when she got onto the Chuo expressway she was able to gun it.

I must be mad to go off like this without saying anything to my mother or sister, she thought.

Of course she was grieving for her father. That day she had been praticing her golf at the Tanzawa club when the police telephoned to give her the news. At first she could not believe it and thought that there must have been some kind of a mistake, but she would never forget the shock she had felt when she saw her father laid out in front of the family shrine with that terrible wound on his forehead. She spent the next two days crying, and found it difficult to believe that the human body could hold so many tears.

It was later that she started to feel the anger and rage build up inside her. She would have been able to accept her father's death if it had been due to accident or illness, but the thought that someone had purposely put an end to his life in such a horrible way and was even now behaving as if nothing had happened, was enough to make her shake with rage.

She heard all the rumors about Kōsuke and was very surprised when Kinumura told her about the trouble between him and her father over the one hundred and twenty million yen. It was the first she had heard of it. He also told her that Kōsuke's alibi was weak and that all the evidence seemed to point to him, but strangely enough, she found that none of the hatred she felt for the murderer was directed at him. While she wanted the murderer to be arrested as much as anybody else, she was also worried about Kōsuke's fate and she guessed that her feeling was due to her certainty of his innocence. When she realized this, she felt her eyes fill with tears.

As she left the expressway at Kunitachi, the clock in the dashboard said 4:07; thanks to the roads being empty she had made even better time than she had hoped for. The leaves on the trees that lined the streets still only hinted at the colors she remembered from the last time she came this way. That had been in November when she and Kōsuke had stopped here on their way back from playing golf in Chichibu.

She soon found herself driving past small woods and nursery gardens and remembered Kōsuke telling her that he bought most of his trees in this area. Although there are several parts of Japan that are famous for their nursery gardens, not many people know that the Kokubunji area of Tokyo also produces a lot of trees. Kōsuke had told her that even when he was not busy he liked to come here and stroll through the fields of trees, and that day he had brought her here especially to share it with her.

She drove down a familiar quiet street, bordered by red-leaved hedges and with several signs advertising nursery gardens. She saw a red-lacquered shrine on her left and then the road became steep. It was just as she remembered it and she drove up it without any hesitation. Halfway up the hill on the right, there was a small brick building slightly set back from the road with a parking lot out front and a sign saying THE CORAL TREE COFFEE BAR on the roof.

She swung into the lot and looked around for Kōsuke's gray sedan, but there was no sign of it, so she walked inside and looked around. There were a number of benches divided by flower pots, but most of them were taken. Because it was a cloudy Sunday, a lot of young couples had obviously decided to come here to spend the afternoon together. Since she could see no sign of Kōsuke, she sat down at an empty table to wait. After the waitress brought her a glass of water and took her order, she changed seats so she could sit and watch the door. She looked at her watch; it was now eleven minutes past four. When he had called, he had said that he was on his way over from Ekoda and she had expected him to be there waiting for her when she arrived. As she waited, she found her disappointment changing to worry.

When she saw Kōsuke push through the swinging door, she felt both relief and a new kind of worry. He was wearing a dark blue coat and sunglasses; she had never seen him wear sunglasses before except in the middle of summer. Apart from that he did not look any different than usual, but the minute he walked into the room, she could almost feel the tension in him. He nodded slightly to her and then looked around the room before he made his way over to her table.

He took off his coat and sat down opposite her. She smelled the mixture of after-shave and cigarette smoke that she always connected with him. The waitress came over with the coffee for her and a glass of water for him.

He also ordered coffee, but he waited until the waitress left their table before he took off his sunglasses.

Their eyes met and held for some minutes. Chiharu gazed at him as if she were seeing him for the first time in many years. He had thick eyebrows, a high-bridged nose, slightly sunken eyes, and strong, relaxed good looks. His forehead sloped back slightly. His lips were slightly full and he had a good tan. She had to admit that it was her favorite kind of face.

"I'm sorry I'm late," he said in a deep voice, and his eyes smiled. "Did I keep you waiting long?"

"No, only about ten minutes."

"I stopped by to visit a gardener near here and could not get away again. I hope you didn't mind me calling you like that, without any warning."

"Not at all."

"Was it difficult for you to get away?"

She shook her head. "Not really. There are no special services today and we don't expect many visitors."

"I was very sorry to hear about your father. It must have been very hard for you," he said, repeating what he said on the phone and bowing to her. "I suppose you were questioned by the police, too. It must be a very difficult time for you all."

Chiharu bowed her head and could feel the tears building up in her eyes. She sat in silence for a short while, then looked up again. There was nothing she couldn't discuss with him, there couldn't be, that was what their whole relationship was based on.

"I hear that things haven't been very easy for you either."

Kōsuke met her question calmly. "Yes, actually I was with the police when you phoned yesterday."

The waitress brought him his coffee and he lit a cigarette while he waited for her to go away. At the table on the other side of the aisle were three university students who seemed to have run out of things to say and were sitting in silence.

"They questioned me for a long time and I didn't get back to the office until about seven o'clock. They had found out about the trouble between my company and the

Tanzawa Country Club and wanted to know the details of that and of my alibi." He kept his eyes fixed on a point on the table and spoke in a low voice. As he continued a look of pain came over his face. "I could only tell them things as they happened. With regard to the trouble over the payment for the Tanzawa course, they had information of their own."

He gazed at the steam rising from his coffee cup and sat deep in thought, but then he appeared to make up his mind not to go into any details of the trouble. "Unfortunately, they only have my word to go on about my alibi."

"Oh . . ." She had heard that he did not have an alibi but didn't know any details. She sat gazing at him and waited for him to continue.

"Actually, that night I was in Himonya from about eleven-forty to twelve o'clock, which is when they say your father was killed."

She looked at him questioningly.

"I had a telephone call, from a woman. It was a wrong number . . ." He made a wry face. "She rang me by mistake, but she didn't have any more loose change. She said that her sight was poor, and judging from her breathing, I'd say that she was in pain. . . ."

He went on to explain that she had asked him to pass on her message and how, when he had been unable to do so, he had gone to look for her himself.

"That night was very cold and the rain was terrible, so I thought that if I drove her to where she wanted to go, she would be all right."

"Are you sure you don't know who she was?"

"Yes, I can't remember very well now, but she seemed to have an accent and I didn't recognize her voice at all."

"Did you go to the phone booth?"

"Yes, but by the time I got there more than an hour had passed since I first received her phone call and she was nowhere to be seen. There was only a note saying that she had gone to a coffee bar called Eri to wait. I went to look for her, but I arrived just after she had left." He gave a sigh and took a sip of his cold coffee.

"Did you tell the police that?"

"Yes, there was nothing else I could say."

"And what did they say?"

"After I had finished they went with me to the phone booth and the coffee bar to check my story. The people in the coffee bar confirmed that I had been there a short while before twelve o'clock, but the police seem to think I could just as easily have gone there after the murder. Of course there was nothing to prove that I had been to the phone booth."

"If only you could prove that you had received the phone call."

"No, I realize now that even that would be pointless."

He shook his head and looked around the café again. His eyes came to rest on the students at the next table, and Chiharu could not help but think that he already looked like a fugitive. His eyes came back to her and he continued in a low voice.

"The police seem to think that I made up the story about the phone call, but even if I could prove I didn't, they'd just assume I had an accomplice make the call at my request."

"But what if it really was a wrong number?"

"In that case they'd think that it was what triggered the murder."

This was the first time he had used the word *murder* in front of Chiharu.

"If it really was a wrong number and I had gone to meet the woman as I said, they'd simply assume that when I found myself near your house, I stopped off and murdered your father."

Chiharu sighed. For the first time she realized just what a difficult position he was in. The police had three scenarios and were just trying to decide which one to use to arrest him.

There must be some other answer, she thought, but at that moment Kōsuke stood up and picked up the bill.

"Let's go."

He was obviously worried about being seen by the people in the café and already had the look of a hunted man about him.

Outside it was still overcast and the early autumn dusk was already starting to fall. There was a smell of rain on the wind and the moisture served to make it feel a little warm. Chiharu could see her yellow BMW in the parking lot, but there was no sign of Kōsuke's gray sedan.

Kōsuke came through the swinging door and she noticed him take in the surroundings with a quick look.

"Let's go for a walk."

"Okay."

They walked up the hill from the café until they came to an area of nursery fields. They were filled with trees about ten to twelve feet tall, which were ready to be sold to gardeners and landscapers. The fields were separated by narrow dirt roads and Kōsuke turned into one of these. Chiharu looked at the trees; there were willows, camellias, pine, laurel, and many, many others that she could not begin to name. The further they walked, the quieter it became. They could not hear the cars and there was no sign of any other people, only a clear breeze blowing through the trees and rustling the leaves.

"A little longer and this path will be deep in leaves, the maples will turn bright red, and it will look really beautiful." His voice sounded a lot more relaxed.

They walked through the trees, the sleeves of their raincoats lightly brushing against each other. She noticed that he was unwinding with each step, but she did not say anything; she just waited for him to start talking.

"How are you doing these days?"

"Do you mean my golf?"

"Yes."

"Well, my approach could be better."

"But you try very hard. I'm sure you will be all right next year." He was referring to the pro exam she intended to take the following year in order to become a professional.

"But now that father's been . . . since that I don't know what's going to happen."

Kōsuke stopped and they automatically turned to face each other. He frowned and his face was twisted with emotion, but then the moment passed and he was able to speak again. "I probably won't be able to see you again for some time. That was why I asked you to come all the way out here today to meet me."

They were standing in a field of fairly high trees and the wind made a low moaning sound as it blew through the branches.

"As I said earlier on, the police don't accept my alibi and they feel that I had adequate motive to murder your father. They only let me go because they lacked enough evidence to arrest me, but after this morning, it is hopeless."

"Why? What happened?"

Kōsuke took a deep breath and held it for a few moments, but in the end he did not answer her directly. "As things are, the police may come to arrest me at any time, and I am also being threatened by someone else. If I am arrested, there is no way my company can avoid going bankrupt. . . . Everything seems to be conspiring against me." He gave a brief laugh.

"But what are you going to do?"

"I don't know. There doesn't seem to be much I can do, but while I'm still free to move around, I want to do all I can to ensure that my company stays solvent for as long as possible."

He stood gazing at her face again for a few minutes before he continued in a low voice. "Either way I probably won't be able to see you again for some time; that's why I forced myself to phone you today. I know it was unreasonable of me, the murder suspect, to expect you, the victim's daughter, to come and meet me, but I knew that if I missed this chance, I might never get another one."

"Do you plan to go somewhere?"

"No—well, I might go and try to borrow some capital. . . ." he said more to himself than to her. The truth of the matter was that he did not have any clear idea of what he was going to do himself. "I suppose that if worse comes to worst, I will just put the whole matter in Mr. Sako's hands."

"Who is that?"

"Oh, he's a lawyer in Kyōbashi whom I employ to look after the company's business. I've known him for a long time and he's someone that I can trust."

"Are things really that bad?"

He made another pained expression. "Of course, if I could only get the police to believe me, everything would be fine, but I have no way of proving my alibi."

Chiharu was silent.

"I am not going to ask you to believe me. It would be unfair to put you in that position. I just wanted to see you—thank you for coming." He put his arms on her shoulders and stood looking down at her. He stopped frowning and his face became really peaceful, although she could see that there were tears in his eyes.

"No, I believe you." The words gushed out of her and tears ran down her cheeks.

"Thank you," he said in relief, and sighed. His hands held her strongly, then pulling her toward him, he slipped them around her back and cradled her in his arms as if she were something very precious. His lips brushed her forehead gently, then moved down to her nose before finding her lips. It was their first kiss. How long they stood motionless in each other's arms neither of them knew. Chiharu's mind was a complete blank, then suddenly a thought floated through the void.

I have loved him since the first time we met, I have always known that. . . . I just never realized it before.

When he released her, she buried her head in his chest, crying.

"What can we do? How can we save you?"

"I don't know. I suppose that if I managed to find the woman who telephoned and had her testify that everything was just as I said and that she had left a note in the phone booth, then my alibi would become much stronger, but I don't think there's much chance of that happening."

"Why not? Why do you give up so easily?"

"I think . . ." After a few seconds' hesitation, he started to answer, then he suddenly glanced over to one side. There was a man in a gardener's jacket coming toward them and he was watching them curiously.

"You must go home," Kōsuke said firmly. "Quickly, before anyone sees you with me. They must be worrying about you at home."

"But what about you?"

"You must never tell anyone that you met me here to-day."

"But . . ."

"Whatever happens, just pretend that you have nothing to do with me."

"But what . . ."

"I'm very glad that you came to meet me here today."

The gardener disappeared behind some trees, and putting his hands on her shoulders again, Kōsuke turned her back in the direction they had come. She found that she could not oppose him.

"I will never forget you. I love you."

She could feel his breath on her neck, then he kissed her from behind. Suddenly she could no longer feel his hands or lips, and by the time she looked around his tall figure was rapidly disappearing between the trees.

# 7

# The Disappearance

THE POLICE FIRST LEARNED ABOUT THE DISCOVERY of the two bloodstained towels, the glove, and the golf club under the shed at Kōsuke's house at nine o'clock in the evening of the tenth when Hideo Naitō telephoned, saying that he did so on Shimako's behalf.

Inspector Momozaki was still at the station, and as soon as he heard the news, he hurried around to the house with a young detective. When they got there they found Shimako, Hideo, and Tome waiting for them with the items in question laid out on newspaper on the dining-room floor. He examined them closely and was very interested in the dark stains on the towels and glove that Hideo had said looked like blood. At first glance there did not seem to be anything unusual about the golf club, but when it was examined closely under the light, traces of something like dry blood could be made out on the head, and it looked as if they were all that remained after it had been hurriedly wiped clean with the towel.

"Where did you find these?" Momozaki asked Shimako, who looked exhausted and was as white as a sheet.

"I found them first . . ." Hideo said after a few minutes when she did not answer. He looked very excited.

81

"The soil under the shed over there had been dug up, and when I went to fill in the hole I noticed the yellow towel. When I looked around at the back, I came up with all these other things."

"You say that the soil had been dug up?"

"Yes, it was probably one of the dogs in the neighborhood."

He went on to explain how one of the local dogs often dug holes in the garden at night and how he or Tome would have to go out in the morning and tidy up after it.

"Morning? Do you mean to say that you found all these this morning?"

"Yes, at about nine-fifteen," Hideo said, exchanging a look with Tome.

Momozaki looked from Hideo and Tome to Shimako. He thought of asking why it had taken twelve hours for them to contact the police about their discovery but decided it could wait for now. Instead he opened the door Hideo had indicated, and borrowing a pair of sandals, he went out to look at the shed. He could see quite well in the light that spilled out of the kitchen door, and with the aid of the younger detective's flashlight, he examined the hole in the ground. It was about a foot and a half in diameter and there was earth scattered all over the place.

"When I found the towel, I tried to leave everything as it was," Hideo said.

"Does the dog often dig holes like this?"

"Yes, but it belongs to one of the neighbors and we didn't want to make a fuss," Tome said.

It appeared that the dog had just happened to dig up the evidence buried under the shed. Momozaki knew it was still too early to call the items evidence, but he thought it very unlikely that they were unconnected with the murder. Nasuno had been struck on the forehead with a blunt instrument and several of the men thought it had been a golf club, just like the one that had been found. The murder weapon had not been found at the scene of the crime. He could not help but feel this was it.

"Did you only find the one glove?" he asked Hideo.

"Yes, I guess the dog must have carried the other one off."

The dog had either dug up the towels by accident or had been attracted by the smell of blood; either way the area around the shed would have to be examined more closely and the dog's owners interviewed. He telephoned the station for more men.

He returned to the kitchen where Shimako had remained sitting in a chair. Although she had been questioned the previous day by the police, it was the first time that Momozaki had seen her and he was struck by her cold beauty. He had heard that she was rather weak physically and he had to agree that her complexion was extremely pale.

"Do these towels and glove belong to your household?"

"I don't know. I don't recall having seen them before."

Neither of the towels had any patterns or labels on them.

"How about the golf club?"

She looked at him questioningly for a moment. "I don't play golf."

"But your husband does, doesn't he?"

"Yes."

"Is it your husband's club?"

"I don't believe so."

"Is your husband home?"

"No."

"Could you tell me where he is?"

"He has been at the office all day."

"So that means he still doesn't know about your find, right?"

A strange expression came over the face of Tome and Hideo, who were standing to one side, listening. Shimako took a quick breath and looked as if she were about to be sick.

"I telephoned him and told him about it," she finally managed to answer.

"What time was this?"

"Soon after we found it, a little before ten, I think."

"And what did he say when you told him?" Momozaki shot a quick glance at Tome and Hideo. If Shimako lied, he might be able to tell from their expressions.

"He didn't seem to understand what I was talking about at first but said he'd come and have a look."

"Did he come home?"

"Yes, a little after ten."

"I see, and then?"

"He asked Hideo to tell him exactly how he came to find them, but he seemed to be very puzzled by it all."

"Is this your husband's club?"

"No, he said that he had never seen it before."

"Did your husband have any idea how these things got there?"

"I don't know," Shimako replied with a sigh.

"What did Ōkita say when he saw these things?" Momozaki asked, turning to Hideo and Tome.

"He seemed to be very surprised; he just looked at them for some time," stammered Hideo.

"He didn't say anything in particular," mumbled Tome.

It seemed obvious to Momozaki that Kōsuke had been careful not to say anything that could be held against him later, not in front of Tome or Hideo anyway. He turned back to Shimako again.

"What did your husband do after that?"

"Yes, well . . . He said he wasn't sure what he should do and that we'd discuss it again when he came home tonight, then he went back out again."

"What time was this?"

"I think he went out about eleven-thirty."

"Where did he go?"

"He said he was going back to the office. He has been very busy recently and even has to work on Sundays."

"And you have not seen him since then?"

"No."

"Any telephone calls?"

"No."

"Then he must still be there."

Even as he said this he had a nasty suspicion that Kōsuke wouldn't be. Just to make sure, though, he had the other detective telephone, but as he had guessed, there was no answer.

The other detectives arrived from the Himonya police station and he set them to search the area around the shed, talk to the neighbors, and go and look for Kōsuke at his office. When he had organized all this, he went back to the kitchen where Shimako, Tome, and Hideo had been kept waiting. Their cross-examination was not yet over.

"You say that Ōkita came home at a little after ten and then went out again at eleven-thirty. During the time he was here did he say anything about reporting the find to the police?" He looked over at Tome and Hideo first, but they just shook their heads in silence. He turned to Shimako.

"No, as I said earlier, he said that he would think about it after he returned home and then hurried out again."

"And you have not heard from him since then? You mean that you waited until after nine o'clock and then contacted us anyway without discussing it with him first?"

"Yes, Hideo said I should. He said that if I left it too long without doing anything, you might suspect us, too."

"That's right; in fact, I told her that we should phone you as soon as I found them," Hideo said, slightly over-eagerly. "But Mrs. Ōkita said that we should contact Mr. Ōkita first and we have been waiting for his decision ever since."

"I didn't know what we should do, but Hideo's find seemed to be important and it had nothing to do with any of us, so I thought we should call the police right away, too." Shimako seemed to be battling with some strong emotion and her eyes were brimming with tears. Her usually pale face had become even whiter and the shadows under her eyes became very pronounced.

"What exactly did your husband do during the hour and a half he was in the house?"

"After looking at the hole by the shed and the golf club, he went through to his study and got some papers ready to take out with him."

"I see."

Although Shimako didn't seem to realize what she had said, Momozaki was more than satisfied with her answer. She had let it slip that she'd had a chance to talk with Kōsuke alone. They could have used that opportunity to discuss what Kōsuke should do next and decide when she should telephone the police to tell them about Hideo's discovery. It was unfortunate for Kōsuke that the evidence was found by the maid and the lodger, as it meant that if he tried to hide it, his position would only become more dangerous.

"I don't feel very well; would you mind if I went into the other room to lie down?" Shimako asked desperately. She had always suffered from anemia and Momozaki realized that she had had a big shock that morning and been under a lot of stress ever since. She looked pale in the extreme and the tears in her eyes stopped her from focusing properly. However, Momozaki suspected that that was not all; he guessed that being forced to sit in the kitchen and be questioned in front of her maid and the lodger while the detectives were running around in the background had been a blow to her pride.

"Of course. I am sorry, please feel free to go through to the living room, but I am afraid that I still have a few questions I'd like to ask you. It won't take much longer, I assure you."

Shimako frowned in annoyance and walked out of the room without saying a word. She led Momozaki along the hall and through the first of two doors. The room contained a dressing table and a wardrobe; in the middle there was a low table and a sofa. The curtains had not been drawn and Momozaki saw that the room looked out onto a garden surrounded by a hedge.

"Does this lead to the bedroom?" Momozaki asked, indicating the other door in the room.

"Yes."

"You have a telephone in the bedroom, don't you?"

"Yes, next to the bed."

That must mean that this was the room that Kōsuke claimed to have been in on the night of the murder when he got the phone call that was to send him to Himonya to look for the woman. The detectives who had come to the house after Kōsuke had been questioned had checked on the phone, so Momozaki didn't ask if he could open the door.

Although the newly discovered evidence would seem to confirm Kōsuke's guilt, Momozaki felt that he could not ignore the man's strange alibi altogether. "I understand that you were not here on the night of the Nasuno murder."

"No, I was at my mother's house in Chigasaki."

"I take it that your husband has told you what happened that night in detail."

"No, he didn't, but I think I know more or less what happened from what Tome and the detectives who came yesterday told me."

"Well, he says that he felt so sorry for a woman who had dialed his number by mistake that he drove all the way over to Himonya to help her, and I must admit that there are a lot of people at the investigation HQ who find it a little difficult to believe. They seem to feel that it's taking ordinary human kindness a little too far."

"But the woman said that her eyesight was bad, didn't she?"

"Yes, she said that was why she made a mistake when she dialed the number."

"In that case I think it quite likely that my husband would go to her aid." She had been sitting back exhaustedly on the couch, but now she sat up straight and her eyes glittered earnestly. "My husband always goes out of his way to help blind people."

"Is there any particular reason for this?"

"Yes, you see, he used to have a cousin who was two years older than him; she was said to have been extremely beautiful, but she was blind. When my husband was in the first year of senior high, she was attending a special school for the blind. She used to go there on her own by train, but one day got off at the wrong station for some reason and became lost. She soon realized her mistake and started to make her way back to the station, asking people the way as she went. However, whether it was because she was upset or in a hurry, I don't know, but she fell into the storm drain next to the road and broke her spine. She was rushed to the hospital, but it was no good; about a month later she died of her injuries.

"My husband went to visit her in the hospital every day, and when he heard how it had happened, he was enraged. He said that if only the people she had asked had taken a bit more time to help her, had led her by the hand, then the accident need never have happened. According to his sister, he had had a crush on his cousin and so felt the shock all the more.''

''I see.''

''As soon as I heard about the phone call, I knew my husband wouldn't be able to ignore it, especially as it was his fault that he couldn't pass on her message. He wouldn't be able to stand the thought of her waiting in that phone booth for someone who would never come.''

''I see . . .''

If Shimako's story was to be believed, it certainly explained Kōsuke's behavior that night, but there was still another way to look at it. The episode with his cousin could have given him the original idea for his alibi and he might even have counted on his wife telling the police about it to make his actions seem more believable.

Momozaki moved in his seat. ''When your husband went out for the second time today, did he tell you where he was going?''

''To the office.''

''Is there anywhere else he might have gone?''

''I suppose he could have gone to see some of his suppliers; perhaps you should ask Mr. Shōnouchi, the managing director.''

Momozaki got the addresses of the directors at the company, his lawyer, his clients, his sister, and anyone else he might have gone to visit. ''Just one more thing: when he went out at eleven-thirty, he didn't take anything with him, did he?''

''Well, of course he had his attaché case. . . .''

''Are you sure that's all? He didn't take a large sum of cash or a change of clothes?''

Shimako collapsed back into her chair and shook her head in despair.

The golf club, the towels, and the work glove that were found under the shed were all sent to the forensic department at police headquarters. It was found that the stains on the towels and glove were in fact blood and the head of the golf club reacted positively to a Luminol test. The blood in each instance was type B, which was the same as that of the victim. Most damning of all was the fact that the shape of the head of the golf club matched that of the wound on Nasuno's skull.

All this, coupled with the fact that Kōsuke was already one of the main suspects, left little doubt that he was the murderer. The police guessed that he wore the gloves when he committed the murder and that he used the towels to clean off the bloodstains and to wipe the club clean of blood and fingerprints afterward. They assumed that the club and towels belonged to him, but when they searched his house on the night of the tenth, they couldn't find a trace of any other golf equipment.

"He usually keeps his clubs in the trunk of his car, but recently he has been very busy and he hasn't had the time to play for a long while," Shimako said.

They still had no idea where he had gone, but by checking on his business acquaintances, they were able to find out his movements up until the evening of the tenth.

After he left his home at 11:30 he went back to his office where he telephoned Shōnouchi, the managing director, and called him into the office. They talked together for some time and Kōsuke gave him detailed instructions about the running of the company for some time to come. He then telephoned the company's lawyer, Takashi Sako, who was at home in Nakano for the holiday. He went to visit him and they discussed the company's bonds and debts in detail until he left at a little after 3:00. At 3:45, he appeared at the Miyoshi nursery gardens, where he talked to the owner, Atsumaru Miyoshi, who was one of his main suppliers. He told him that as he could not pay his bill he would return all the plants he presently held in stock and asked him to come pick them up.

He then drove away in the direction of the nursery fields and nobody knew what happened to him after that. He didn't even contact his home. Around midnight, the police began to suspect that he had gone into hiding, and a description of him and his car was circulated to all the police stations in Tokyo.

A little after one o'clock on the morning of the eleventh they received a report that Kōsuke's car had been spotted outside Ueno station. Ueno station is the main terminal in Tokyo that handles trains leaving for the north of the country, but even though the lot where his car was found was open twenty-four hours, it was virtually empty at that time of night.

The police had suspected that he might try to escape and had ordered a special check at all the main stations and airports, and that is why it was found so promptly. By checking the parking ticket, they found that the car had been left since seven o'clock the previous evening.

They opened the trunk with a key that Shimako had provided and inside they found a set of golf clubs of the same make as the five iron that was found under the shed in Kōsuke's garden. Worse still, the five iron was missing and the police took this to be definitive proof of Kōsuke's guilt.

The way they saw it, on the night of the sixth Kōsuke had lain in wait for Nasuno to return from Ginza, and after another argument about the money that remained due for work on the Tanzawa Country Club he had produced the club, which he had hidden while they talked, and hit Nasuno on the temple with it. Returning home, he had hidden the club, towels, and gloves that he had used in the crime under the shed in his garden, thinking that he could move them to a safer hiding place later on. However, the police got on to his trail quicker than he had expected, and with detectives going in and out of his house at all hours he didn't have the opportunity to move them. The worst came when a local dog had dug up the evidence and left it to be found by the lodger and the maid. When Shimako telephoned and told him this, he knew he wouldn't be able to make Tome or Hideo keep quiet for long. He went home, and after making preparations for his flight, he got Shimako to agree to keep the matter from the police until nine o'clock at night so he would at least have that much of a lead on them.

By two o'clock that morning, they had taken out a warrant for Kōsuke's arrest and a nationwide search was instigated. That morning the newspapers and television news all carried photographs of him and the story made the headlines.

* * *

Chiharu first heard about it when she saw the story on the eight o'clock news, and looking at the newspaper, she found a large photograph of him on the front page. As she read the article she felt that there had been some terrible mistake somewhere. The story only traced his movements up to four o'clock, so at least her meeting with him was still a secret.

She kept remembering how he had looked as he disappeared into the dusk the night before, then after sitting in a daze for some time, she took the paper and went up to her room. She wanted to keep the news from her mother for as long as possible. Once she got to her own room, she let herself relax and broke down in tears over the paper.

She remembered the times they had been together, especially the previous day. She remembered the strange tension she had noticed in him when he walked into the coffee bar, his strong arms holding her in the quiet of the nursery garden, his lips on hers when they shared their first kiss, and the smell of his after-shave.

I have always known that I loved him, ever since the very first time we met . . .

As she sat blankly, thinking back over what he had said, she found herself seized by a terrible melancholy.

"I may not be able to see you again for some time. . . ."

"After this morning, it is hopeless. . . ."

"The police may come and arrest me at any time. . . ."

"I just wanted to see you. . . ."

His words came back to her, one by one, each engraved on her heart.

When he had met her, he already knew about the club and towels that had been found in his garden and that it was only a matter of time before the police started on his trail. He had taken the time to see her and say good-bye before he decided to try to escape on his own.

Had he really gone into hiding? She wanted to deny it, but she guessed that the thought of arrest and the humiliation that would follow had been too much for him. But where would he go? What would he do? Suicide? No! She couldn't believe that he would commit suicide. Doing so would be the same as admitting his guilt.

That was it. He must have decided that if he was arrested, it would be the end, he would not be able to do anything to prove his innocence.

She sat gazing into space. She wanted more than anything to believe in his innocence. If she couldn't, she wouldn't know what to say to her father, because now that Kōsuke had been accused of the murder, she realized as never before just how much she loved him.

# 8

# The Bait in the Trap

IT WAS THE MORNING OF TUESDAY THE TWELFTH when Chiharu telephoned the lawyer, Takashi Sako, at his office in Kyōbashi.

She remembered Kōsuke saying that if worse came to worst, he would put the whole matter in the hands of his attorney, and when she read in the newspaper that he had been to see him before he disappeared, she wondered if he had mentioned where he was going to run to. The day before being a holiday, she had phoned him at his home, but a woman that she took to be his wife told her he had gone out for the day and would not return until late.

The weather had been very overcast since the tenth and it finally started to drizzle that morning. It seemed that every rain shower brought winter that much closer and it was very chilly. Chiharu was alone in the house except for her mother and the maid, and going into the reception room, she used the phone on the sideboard there. It rang twice and was answered by a young man's voice.

"Hello, Sako, attorney-at-law, may I help you?"

"Yes, my name is Nasuno. I wondered if Mr. Sako was there."

"Yes, he is."

"Well, may I speak to him, please?"

"Excuse me, but could you tell me what your business is?" the man asked in a polite tone.

"Yes, er . . ."

She could hear another phone ring in the background and a woman's voice answer it. She had been about to say she was calling about Kōsuke, but she hesitated, thinking it might be unwise to mention his name on the telephone to a secretary.

"As I said just now, my name is Nasuno; my father was the president of the Tanzawa Club, and I would like to talk to him about the case."

"Oh, I see." He was silent for a moment, then, "Could you hold the line for a moment, please?"

His voice was replaced by a recording of organ music and Chiharu felt her pulse quicken. When he heard who she was, Sako was likely to be on his guard, but as far as she was concerned, she was not phoning as the victim's daughter so much as Kōsuke's lover. The organ music came to a sudden end and jerked her out of her reverie.

"Hello, I'm sorry to have kept you waiting."

It was a strong, deep male voice and Chiharu felt a shock of excitement run through her.

"Sako speaking."

She felt sure that it was Kōsuke, so similar were their voices, and it was all she could do to stop herself from crying out in excitement.

"Hello, Sako speaking."

She shook her head in an attempt to bring herself back down to earth. "Oh, hello, I am sorry to call you suddenly like this. I am Seiji Nasuno's daughter, Chiharu."

For a minute there she had almost believed that it had been Kōsuke, but when she thought about it, she realized it was impossible. "I would like to talk to you about my father's case . . . although not because he was my father, but . . ." The harder she tried to explain, the more confused she became.

"What exactly do you mean?"

"Well, you see, I have known Mr. Ōkita for some time and . . ." She paused for a moment, then made up her mind. "Well, to tell the truth, I met him for a short while at around four o'clock on the afternoon of the tenth and I got your name from him.''

''I see, and what do you want me to do?'' he asked. Chiharu did not know exactly what kind of reaction she expected, but she had definitely hoped for a little more than that.

''Well, if it is possible, I would like to come in and see you.'' Chiharu chose her words carefully in an effort to communicate how she felt. When she told him that she was the last person to have seen Kōsuke before he disappeared, she had expected him at least to show a bit of excitement, but as it was, she did not know how to proceed. ''I don't suppose I could possibly see you today, could I?''

''Let me see . . .'' Sako was silent for a few moments while he thought over his schedule for the day. ''In that case, how about three-thirty?''

''At your office?''

''Yes.''

Chiharu was at a loss for words. She had expected him to treat her request a little more seriously when he heard what she wanted to talk to him about and she wondered if she would be able to talk at a busy office.

''Okay, I will see you at three-thirty then.''

''Do you know where it is?''

''Er, Kyōbashi, isn't it?''

''Yes, two blocks from Tokyo station, on the third floor.'' He told her the name of the building and hung up.

When Chiharu put the phone down she found that she was drenched in perspiration. Kōsuke had told her that whatever happened she was not to say that she had met him in the fields and that she was to pretend that she had absolutely nothing to do with him, but already she had told someone. However, she thought, she had no choice; Sako was the only one who may know where Kōsuke had gone and she did not think he would have seen her if she had not told him.

She followed Sako's instructions and found that his office was in a six-story brick building that contained the offices of several companies. She got out of the elevator on the third floor and found a glass door with his name etched on it. She knocked and a young woman in a dark blue suit appeared.

"Hello, my name is Nasuno."

"Yes, please come in." The woman seemed to be expecting her and led her through the office to a reception room. Chiharu noticed that there was another young woman and a young man in the office. The reception room did not have any windows and the walls were lined with bookcases filled with law books. There was a leather-covered three-piece suite, and although the building was a little old, Chiharu realized that Sako must be quite a high-powered attorney to be able to keep an office of this size in the center of Tokyo.

A big man in a dark brown suit walked into the room. "How do you do, my name is Sako."

His voice was very reminiscent of Kōsuke's, but that was where the resemblance ended. His slightly red face with thin lips, a strong chin, and tortoise-shell glasses bore no similarity to Kōsuke's, although he was similar in build.

"Please take a seat."

They sat down opposite each other and Chiharu saw that he was in his late forties. He looked very astute and so severe that Chiharu found herself unable to speak.

"You said that you wanted to speak to me about Kōsuke Ōkita."

"Yes, as I mentioned on the telephone, I saw him at Kokubunji on the afternoon of the tenth, and although he seemed very tense, I don't believe that he disappeared just to avoid being arrested. I know that I am the victim's daughter, but I have known Mr. Ōkita for some time and I don't believe that it is in his character to ever hurt anyone. I was hoping you would be able to tell me something, whether he has really gone into hiding, and if he has, where he has gone."

Sako sat listening to her in silence, and when he finally spoke, it was to shatter her hopes. "I haven't heard from him since the tenth either and I have absolutely no idea where he might have disappeared to."

"Didn't he talk about the case when he came to see you that day?"

Sako looked steadily at her for a few moments as if

sizing her up before he spoke. "When he came to see me, we spoke mainly about business. As you probably know, when he finished work on the Tanzawa Country Club in July, your father made several claims against his work and had him redo several areas. He has long since completed them, but he still has to be paid, and there is almost one hundred and twenty million yen outstanding. For a company the size of his, that is a lot of money, and if he doesn't get paid soon he will have to declare himself bankrupt." He said in an expressionless voice, "That afternoon we spoke about the bills that were about to become due and how he was to get the money to pay them."

"Do you mean that you didn't talk about the murder case at all?" Chiharu asked again.

"He did give me a quick rundown of the case so far," Sako said, his eyes fixed on the opposite wall. Chiharu wondered what he meant by a rundown and whether Kōsuke had told him where he was going to hide, but she didn't have the nerve to ask. Anyway, she didn't think that this careful lawyer was likely to tell her the first time they met.

"What do you think about his disappearance and his being put on the wanted list?"

"I don't have an opinion. As I said, I have absolutely no idea where he might've disappeared to," he said again, obviously in an effort to avoid the subject, but he had not counted on Chiharu's determination.

"So, do you think that he really is the murderer?"

"Well, I must admit that whatever way you look at it, he's in a very difficult situation," he said without moving. "There's no denying that he had adequate motive; he is known to have been quite upset about your father's failure to pay and the police seem to take the view that he killed him thinking that the vice-president of the company would be easier to deal with.

"Then there is his alibi. Even if we could get a statement from his maid saying that he did indeed receive a phone call as he said, the police would merely say that he had made use of his maid's habit of eavesdropping to provide himself with an alibi. In fact, there are already people who are saying that. Of course that is not to say that he was the only suspect that they had; there were several other people they were watching, but they'll all be forgotten now.''

''Why is that?''

''Because he has gone into hiding. I've seen a lot of cases in the past, and no matter how bad their position, innocent people just don't try to escape. If a suspect tries to escape when he is cornered, nine out of ten times, he's the real murderer. If you try to escape, that's the end.''

Sako pursed his lips and frowned; it was obvious that he was cross with Kōsuke. Chiharu sat with her head bowed; halfway through his speech she had found herself unable to stop crying; it seemed that when his own lawyer pronounced him guilty, there was no more hope.

Sako realized that he may have been a little too blunt with her and continued in a calmer tone. ''There is one other way of looking at it. Ōkita was very concerned about the payment that was shortly to be due to the gardeners who supply him with his trees and grass. Although all the banks in Tokyo have already lent him as much as they are prepared to, he did mention going to talk to his old college friends who live in the country and asking them for a loan. He could have left Tokyo on a quite innocent errand of that sort and the police panicked when they found him missing.''

''Now you come to mention it,'' Chiharu said, raising her tearstained face, ''when I met him at Kokubunji, he said that he wanted to do all he could to secure the future of the company while he was still free to move around. I asked him what he intended to do and he started to say he was going to try to raise some money but then broke off in midsentence. I don't think he was quite sure himself what he wanted to do.''

''Yes, I can understand how difficult it must be to go and see someone for the first time in years and ask them for a large loan. Also Ōkita's the kind of man who doesn't like to talk about something until he's made up his mind about it.''

There was a knock on the door and the young girl from the office entered with a tray of tea. She put the tea down on the table in front of them and said something to Sako in a low voice; it seemed to be about an appointment. The lawyer seemed to be a very busy man, but there were still one or two things that Chiharu wanted to ask.

"You said just now that the police suspected several other people may have been connected with my father's murder, but what kind of people do you mean?"

"Well, with your father being the president of two golf clubs, there are a large number of people who could stand to gain by his death."

"Yes . . . ?" Chiharu sat watching him expectantly and he switched his gaze back to the opposite wall again.

"As you know, a golf club is very different from other types of companies; the club starts to collect money from its prospective members when it's still in the planning stages and then proceeds to keep this money as an interest-free loan for anything from five to ten years. Naturally this money is used for the construction and running of the club, but there is no rule governing the number of members or the amount of money collected, and some places collect more than is really necessary and use it for other ends. This is more common than many people think, and as a result there is a lot of dispute over the way golf clubs are run."

Sako was careful only to talk in generalizations, but no matter how single-mindedly Chiharu devoted herself to her golf, even she had noticed all the strife among the members at the Uchibō club.

"Not only do they use the money for other ends, but it is not unusual to hear of new clubs where the owner takes the money for his own. Of course they use several techniques to hide what they have done; for instance they get the merchants they work with to charge extra and then give them a kickback, or else the agents who look for new members may charge a huge commission and then pay it back to the owner. There are all sorts of techniques, but I think you can see that when the president of a golf club is murdered, there are likely to be a large number of suspects for the police to check on."

"But if Kōsuke is innocent and there is someone else out there who is guilty, why did he disappear?"

"As I said before, I have absolutely no idea."

Her persistence seemed to have had its effect on him and he gave her a wry smile. "If we are to assume that he is innocent, it must mean that he felt trapped and decided to go into hiding, or as I mentioned just now, he did not mean to disappear and the police misread his motives and put him on the wanted list."

"So that must mean he is hiding somewhere."

"Not necessarily; there are one or two other possibilities. He could have been caught in a trap and kidnapped or he could even have been . . . But there is no point in worrying about that now; the police have started a nationwide search for him and we are sure to learn something soon."

He stopped smiling and she remembered her first impression of him as a cold, calculating, middle-aged lawyer.

"Anyway, for the time being we can do nothing but wait and see." He put his hands together in a pose that Chiharu took to mean that their meeting was over. She thanked him very much for his time and he showed some compassion for the first time.

"Be careful on your way home."

It was four o'clock when Chiharu left Sako's office, which meant that she had been with him for just thirty minutes. It was still drizzling and Chiharu felt very depressed. She had not really expected Sako to be able to tell her where Kōsuke was, but she had hoped he would be a little more helpful. Even if he didn't know where Kōsuke was, she felt he could have discussed the case with her in more detail and advised her about the future. She had really wanted him to be more friendly, but she realized that as Kōsuke's lawyer he could hardly be expected to fall all over himself to help Nasuno's daughter, and she cursed herself for having been so foolish. She walked back to the parking lot where she had left her car without even noticing the rain.

She sat in the car without starting the engine and thought about the case again. Any way she looked at it, Kōsuke was in a bad position. He had had a violent argument with Nasuno in his office a mere five days before the murder, he had ample motive, and his alibi was not very strong. Added to this, a bloodstained golf club and towels found in his garden made him the main suspect in the case to date. A mere four days after the murder and he was in the situation where he had to either run or face arrest, and he seemed to have chosen the former. As Sako had said, if you run, that is the end, and now it was widely accepted that Kōsuke was the murderer. But what if the whole thing had been planned that way from the beginning? What if Kōsuke had fallen into a cleverly planned trap?

The idea seemed to come to Chiharu suddenly, but she realized that it had been lurking at the back of her mind all the time. Everybody knew about the trouble between Kōsuke and her father, and if someone wanted to kill the latter they could have thought that this was the perfect chance to do so and lay the blame at Kōsuke's door.

No matter how much the evidence pointed to Kōsuke's guilt, he only needed a firm alibi to be okay. When she thought of this, she realized that it was in fact very unusual for him not to have an alibi. She did not meet him that often, but she knew from his conversation that he very rarely went out for a drink, and as his office was only about fifty yards from his house, there was hardly a moment when he would not be able to account for his movements. If she found herself in the same situation, she would find it much harder to prove her alibi. Every day she drove to the golf course in Uchibō, and on a crowded evening it sometimes took as long as three hours to get home—three hours that she would not be able to account for—and even when she did get home, there was only her mother and father to vouch for her, while Kōsuke had a maid and a lodger as well as his wife.

The only time for which Kōsuke could not account would be at two or three in the morning, and at that time it would be almost impossible to kill Nasuno without attracting attention, so the first thing the murderer would have to do would be to destroy Kōsuke's alibi. Yes, when she thought about it, the only piece of evidence against Kōsuke that was not very clear was his alibi. She stared across the gloomy parking lot while she tried to remember his exact words two days before at Kokubunji.

He had said that he'd had a telephone call from an un-known woman and as a result he had gone to Himonya to look for her at approximately the same time as the murder took place. When he was interviewed by the police, he had told them the whole story and had taken them to see the phone booth and the coffee bar in question, but they didn't believe him. They pointed out that both of the places were within five minutes' drive of the house and that he could have gone there after he killed her father. One group said that he'd had an accomplice make the call to provide him with an alibi, while another group thought that he may indeed have received the call, but when he had arrived at Himonya, he remembered that he was near Nasuno's house and went and murdered him. Either way, Kōsuke was con-sidered guilty, but even when he told her about it, she had wondered if there was not another answer that would ex-plain it all, and she realized now that he had also begun to think the same way.

He had told her that the only way to prove his truthful-ness would be to find the woman who had telephoned him, but that he didn't think this was likely. He was about to tell her why when he had noticed a man approaching them and told her to go. She realized now, however, that he was not just being defeatist, that he had realized that the woman had only existed in order to destroy his alibi. Still, Chi-haru felt he was too quick to give up: the woman must exist somewhere. She had made the phone call, written the note, and visited the coffee bar, so there must be some way of finding her and making her give a statement to the police.

Chiharu had a rough idea where the Eri coffee bar was and decided to go there. She started the car and drove out of the lot. It was still raining as she headed toward the expressway ramp and she thought over everything again. She was so engrossed in her thoughts that she did not even notice the jam on the expressway, and it was not until she had left it and was driving along Meguro Avenue beside Meguro station that she became aware of the big black sedan that seemed to have been following her for some time.

She didn't know how long it had been there, but when

she got to Gonnosuke hill she swung into a side road and drove down it as fast as the yellow BMW would go until she got to Yamanote Avenue. She turned left and drove to the Ōtori shrine before turning back into Meguro Avenue.

She glanced down at the car clock and saw that it was still only seven minutes past five. The rain showed no sign of letting up and a lot of cars had turned on their lights already. Due to the rain the homeward rush had started earlier than usual and the streets were already crowded. She drove up the hill hoping to get through the green light before it changed, but the cars in front of her came to a stop and she was forced to brake. She looked in her rear-view mirror, and although it was difficult to tell in the dark, she thought that the sedan two cars back was the same one that had been following her; she thought that she could recognize the driver's profile. She felt a shock of fear tingle through her body at her failure to lose them on her detour through the back streets, but if someone did want to follow her the fact that she was driving a bright yellow import would make the job quite simple.

"Be careful on your way home."

Sako's final words came back to her, but she still couldn't bring herself to believe that someone would really be following her. She drove on, but the street was becoming crowded and she could not drive as fast as she would have liked. No matter how often she tried to tell herself that everything was okay, she could feel the fear building in the pit of her stomach.

She thought of her father and of the pride he had obviously felt when she had started to play golf. He had only two daughters, and as a result he tended to spoil them. Chiharu had often complained about him, but now that he was gone she realized just how much she loved him. Yet here she was not caring about anything but Kōsuke.

"Father, please forgive me . . ."

She felt tears roll down her cheeks and once they started they wouldn't stop. Ever since her father's death her grief had kept itself at a certain distance from her, and then every so often it would suddenly assault her again.

"But I want to find the person who did that to you."

She knew that it was not Kōsuke; she believed in him and she felt that her father forgave her for doing so.

She came to the stoplight at the Himonya junction and turned left; she decided that she might as well visit the phone booth opposite the church before she went to the coffee bar.

No sooner had she turned than the area became almost deserted. The dusk deepened rapidly and there was nobody in sight. Another car turned into the road and started to speed away. It passed Chiharu, the rain thrown up from its tires like smoke. Before long she noticed the white walls of the church with a cross on top of its steeple; she had never taken much notice of it before, but it was near her house so she had been able to find her way with no trouble. To the right of the church was a telephone booth surrounded by Himalayan pine trees.

She parked her car and went into the phone booth. Six days before, Kōsuke had come here in the middle of the night, parked his car, and opened this very same door. For a moment she thought she could smell his after-shave lotion. She put her hand out to the yellow telephone and was about to leave when she changed her mind and decided that as long as she was there she might as well phone her home. When she had left to see Sako at a little after two, she had not said where she was going and her mother would probably be getting worried by now.

She dialed the number and was a little surprised when it was answered before the second ring.

"Hello, Nasuno speaking." She was even more surprised to hear a man's voice; it was rather deep and cultured.

"Hello, this is Chiharu . . ."

"Oh, hello, Chiharu, this is Kinumura."

"Oh, this is a surprise."

"Yes, I am sorry, I was here to discuss the arrangements for Thursday and I had just finished a phone call to my office."

Thursday was the day for the public funeral.

"Oh, I see, I was just ringing to say that I was on my way home."

"Yes, your mother was getting worried about you."

"I'm sorry, I am nearby, but there is one more place that I want to visit first."

"Okay, I'll pass it on."

She hung up. Kinumura seemed to be taking Nasuno's death very hard because it was he who had first introduced him to Kōsuke, but Chiharu felt a lot better after hearing his voice. She got back into her car and drove on through the rain. Two blocks to the east she saw a large red sign with the name ERI on it and as she drew closer she noticed several cars parked in front of its striped awning.

She drove on a bit until she could find a place to park, then getting out, she locked the car door and started to walk back to the coffee bar. The next moment she stopped as she saw a sedan pull up on the other side of the street and two young men with crew cuts get out, one wearing a yellow shirt, the other a sky-blue one. Her feet felt glued to the sidewalk as she realized with a sinking feeling that she recognized both the car and the driver's profile.

The two young men hurried over to where Chiharu stood and were soon standing on either side of her. They were both well built and the muscles stood out in their shoulders.

"You're Mr. Nasuno's daughter, aren't you?" the man in the yellow shirt asked. Both were eyeing her figure with obvious interest.

"We would like to offer you our deepest condolences over your loss."

"I'd heard that you played golf and I see that all the exercise has given you a good body."

They spoke with coarse accents and their tone seemed to carry a hidden threat. Chiharu felt her pulse quicken.

"Mr. Nasuno was very good to us when he was alive and he often spoke to us of you."

"There is someone who would like to speak to you and I wondered if you would be good enough to come with us. We can go in our car, so, if you'd care to come this way . . ."

The man in the blue shirt put his arm around her shoulders. He was wearing dark glasses and two-tone shoes. Chiharu tried to pull back, but her legs would not obey her. The black sedan was still parked on the opposite side of the street and the driver was sitting there watching them. He was wearing a dark suit and had his hair cropped short. His head was rather pointed, which gave him the strange profile that Chiharu had noticed in her rearview mirror. A million thoughts rushed through her head, but she was speechless.

"Come on this way. There is nothing to be afraid of, we only want to talk."

"Where to?" Chiharu asked, finally finding her voice.

"It's not far, just to our office. Our boss wants to speak to you."

"Why? I . . ."

"He wants to ask you something."

Chiharu looked at him questioningly.

"Surely you must realize by now, he wants to talk to you about Ōkita."

Chiharu felt another shock of fear run through her body.

"You want to know where Ōkita has gone and so does our boss. He just wants to exchange information with you so you will be able to find him all the quicker."

The two men moved in closer and she could smell the sweat on their bodies.

"Who are you?"

"We work for a magazine; it's called *Economic Growth*. We really are deeply indebted to your late father, you know."

Chiharu had never heard of the magazine, but it was easy to guess that it was not an ordinary magazine. Her whole body rebelled against the idea of going with them, but she was helpless to resist them. She wished that there were some passersby who could help her, but everyone who passed just hid their heads behind their umbrellas and pretended that they didn't see anything. The two men grabbed her arms and led her toward the car; they were not holding her tightly enough to hurt, but she realized that it would be useless to try to escape.

Her heart beat wildly as she tried to think what she should do. Should she cry out? But it was already dark and there was nobody around, only a steady stream of cars that rushed by, their headlights gleaming off the wet road, their tires sending up clouds of spray, but none of them showed the least inclination to stop. Then suddenly, like a prayer answered, one of them came to a sudden halt in front of them, its horn blaring. The driver got out and walked around the front of the car, blocking their way. He was wearing a dark blue suit and gold-rimmed glasses.

"Kinumura!" Chiharu found her voice at last, and wrenching her arms free, she hurried over to him.

"Chiharu, what's going on here?" he asked, his eyes never leaving the two men.

"These two men suddenly grabbed me."

"What's the idea then?"

"Who are you?" the one in the yellow shirt asked back.

"I am a friend of Chiharu's; now, suppose you tell me what you want with her."

"It's nothing to do with you."

"But she obviously didn't want to go with you."

"She's got it all wrong, you know," muttered the one in the yellow shirt and sunglasses, looking uneasily at the cars that were building up around them. Kinumura had stopped his car in the middle of the road and it was causing something of a jam. "Our boss wanted to speak to her and we came to pick her up, that's all."

"Who is this boss?"

"Mr. Kuretani of *Economic Growth*."

"Chiharu, did you say that you would go with them?"

"Never!" She shook her head violently and clung to Kinumura.

"Look at her, she's terrified. You can't just go around scaring people, you know; you could be arrested for threatening behavior."

One of the drivers behind them blew his car's horn and opened his window. "What do you think you're doing!" he shouted angrily.

"Next time you try to abduct people against their will I'll call the police."

"You'll what . . . ?"

At that moment another car blew its horn briefly and the two men looked over in that direction. The driver got out of the black sedan and nodded to his two accomplices. Several other people could also be seen getting out of their cars.

"Shit!" said the one in the yellow shirt, looking menacingly at Kinumura.

"We'll come again then, when it's more convenient for you," the other one said politely to Chiharu, then hurried away, kicking the hood of Kinumura's car as he went.

After watching the other car move away, Kinumura hurriedly moved his own car out of the middle of the road, then putting an arm around Chiharu, he led her into the coffee bar.

They sat in a booth and Kinumura took off his jacket and wiped the perspiration from his face. The waitress came over and they both ordered coffee.

"People like that don't like to have any witnesses," Kinumura explained. "If it was just you and you went to the police afterward, they could just deny everything and there would be nothing you could do about it. But as soon as there's a witness who can state that you were scared, they can be accused of intimidation, and if they have a record, there's a good chance of their going to prison."

"I wonder who they were."

"Just some of Kuretani's thugs, or maybe it would be truer to say some thugs he borrowed from the gang he is affiliated with."

"Kuretani?"

"Yes, a small-time gangster who runs a publishing swindle. It's true that he was an acquaintance of your father's; in fact, he's one of the shareholders at the Tanzawa Country Club."

"But why did he want me to . . ."

"I've no idea." Having wiped the perspiration off his face, he cleared his throat and took a drink of water.

"I wonder what would have happened if you hadn't come along just now. Was it a coincidence? Your coming, I mean."

"Yes, I was going home from your house and I just decided to come around this way. Maybe I had a premonition. When you telephoned, you said you were calling from near home and that you had one more place to visit before you came back. I guessed that you were phoning from a phone booth and it occurred to me that it might be the one opposite that church and that the other place you said you were going to visit was this coffee bar.''

''You should become a detective; you certainly seem to be cut out for it.''

''No, it's just that I'd been thinking of coming here to see what kind of place it was, too, so it was the first thing that sprang to mind.''

The waitress brought their coffees and went away again. There were four other customers in the shop, and they saw the manager working busily behind the bar. They both felt exhausted after their encounter and the hot coffee tasted heavenly. Chiharu finally managed to relax and suddenly felt like crying. First there had been her meeting with the lawyer Sako; he had been very polite but rather aloof. Then she had been followed by the black sedan and gone through the most frightening experience of her life. But now, at last, she was with a friend she could relax with.

''Okita told me that the two of you sometimes played golf together, and to tell the truth, you are the first person I thought of when I heard he had been put on the wanted list. I thought you might not be able to believe it either.''

''Do you mean that you think he's innocent, too?''

Kinumura did not answer immediately, but his anguished look was enough to tell Chiharu that he did.

''All the same, I wonder where he could have gone to.''

# 9

# Lake Tazawa

THE WARRANT FOR KŌSUKE'S ARREST WAS IS-
sued at two o'clock on the morning of October 11 and
right away a wanted poster bearing his photograph, his
address, his description, and a list of places he was likely
to visit was sent electronically to all the prefectural police
headquarters around the country. The list of places he was
likely to visit included the addresses of any relatives or
friends and areas that he knew well. In Kōsuke's case this
was very short, as all his relatives lived in Tokyo and his
wife's home was close by in Chigasaki, so the men from
HQ could cover that themselves. Of course there was always his college friends, but when Shimako was questioned about them, she said that she had absolutely no idea
who they were, and it was not until his colleagues from
Wakashiba and the landscape gardeners he had worked
for were questioned that they learned he had a strong af-
finity with the north country. He had been in the ski club
in college and had often gone there for skiing; also on his
honeymoon he had chosen to go to Lake Towada and the
Tsugaru coastline in the north. This, added to the fact that
his car was found in a lot near the main train terminal for
the north, meant that he had probably gone that way, so

the investigation HQ got in touch with the six prefectural headquarters in the north and told them to keep a special lookout for him.

Once the prefectural headquarters receive a wanted poster, they make copies and send them around to all the local police stations by motorcycle, where they are split up and displayed at all the various police boxes. All this takes a little time, but the television reported the fact that Kōsuke was wanted in connection with Nasuno's murder on the morning of the eleventh and most of the newspapers also carried the story, although those in the outlying areas did not get it until the next day.

The police did not know for sure that he had gone to the north country; he could have left his car by that station purposely to mislead the investigators, and anyway "north" was too vague an area for the police to do anything positive. They had no choice but to rely on the news reports and wait for the public to tip them off. Luckily they did not have long to wait. On the morning of the thirteenth the Akita prefectural headquarters had a report from the police station at Kakunodate saying that he had been spotted. They sent the report on to police headquarters in Tokyo and it arrived at the Himonya station just as the morning conference was coming to a close. Commissioner Yamane, who received the message, addressed them all.

"The police station at Kakunodate has had a report from the owner of a hotel on the shores of Lake Tazawa saying that he suspected one of his guests of having committed suicide in the lake. They went to investigate and found that while this may well have been the case, the guest answered the description of Kōsuke Ōkita, and so they got in touch with us right away."

Being a supervisor from the investigation branch at Central Headquarters, Commissioner Yamane was in charge of the Nasuno case. He came originally from Iwate Prefecture and still had a slight northern accent.

"Where exactly is this Lake Tazawa, sir?" one of the younger detectives asked. Most of the men on the case were from Tokyo and had never heard of it.

"It is in Akita Prefecture, about halfway up, near the border with Iwate."

There was a map of Tokyo and one of the local area on the wall but none of the whole country, so the detectives had to try and picture the area he meant as well as they were able.

"The lake has a depth of four hundred and fifty feet, making it the deepest in the country, and the water seems to draw you in when you look at it." Yamane gazed into space for a moment as he visualized the scenery that only he knew. "As a result it is a favorite place for people wishing to commit suicide, and the owners of the hotels in the area make a point of keeping their eyes on single guests. If the guest is a single woman, they will watch her actions closely, but in this case the guest had been a man, and as he seemed to be very relaxed they did not really pay him much attention. Of course, they had seen Ōkita's picture on the television and in the papers, but they never thought he would come to their hotel."

The guest, calling himself Kawamura, had checked into the Ryūjin Hotel at a little after five on the evening of the twelfth. He had phoned about an hour before to inquire about a room and was told that although it was the season for the maple leaves, there were still a few vacancies. He had walked to the hotel from the direction of the bus stop carrying a Boston bag and with a newspaper tucked under his arm. He looked a little over forty, he had well-defined features and was wearing sunglasses with a blue raincoat draped over his shoulders. He looked like a typical office worker or salesman.

He signed the register as Akira Kawamura and gave an address in Sendai city. The Ryūjin Hotel has over twenty rooms; half of them are Japanese style, and it was to one of these on the second floor that he was led. He had his meal in his room with a bottle of sake and told the maid he wouldn't be needing her. He sat reading the paper, and when the maid came back at nine o'clock to clear away the meal and make his bed, he was sitting in a chair looking out of his window over the dark lake.

"Breakfast next morning was at eight o'clock, so the maid went to wake him at seven-forty. She called him from the corridor, but there was no answer. His door was not locked, so she went in and found the bed made but no sign of Kawamura." Yamane related the story to the other detectives. "His pajamas had also been folded neatly, but the Boston bag was still there, so she assumed that he had just gone out for a walk before breakfast."

"Could he go out without passing the reception area?" asked Hida, who had been sent from headquarters with Yamane.

"Yes, there is an emergency staircase at the end of the corridor and the guests left their shoes outside their own rooms, not at reception as in most Japanese-style hotels. The maid noticed that his shoes were missing when she arrived."

The maid put the bed away in its cupboard, moved the table back into the middle of the room, and laid breakfast. She rang his room at 8:30, but there was no answer. At 8:45 she went up again but found the meal untouched and that was when she started to worry. There was a mist over the lake that morning and a cold wind was blowing; it was not the kind of day for a long walk at the water's edge.

At nine o'clock the staff searched the area, but when they could find no sign of their missing guest the manager and the receptionist took it upon themselves to search his room. His bag contained a change of underwear and some toiletries, but nothing else. His suit and coat were missing from the wardrobe and his newspaper was lying in the clothes basket with one of the hotel's envelopes lying on top of it. They opened the envelope to find a fifty-thousand-yen note and a single sheet of hotel writing paper inside with the following message:

*I am sorry for all the trouble I caused.*

It was written with a ballpoint pen in a strong hand but was not signed. The newspaper was the previous day's national and it had been opened to the page that held the story about Kōsuke. It was a northern edition and the story was not as long as it had been in Tokyo, but when the manager held it in his hand, he realized for the first time that the man in the picture was the image of his missing guest.

* * *

Assistant Inspector Hida and Detective Fujio took the 4:10 flight to Akita that afternoon. They arrived at 5:15; it had been good weather in Tokyo, but it was drizzling there and the damp evening air was so cold that it felt like the end of autumn.

It took them about fifteen minutes by express from Akita to Ōmagari where they changed to a local train, which took them to Kakunodate. They arrived at Kakunodate at a little after eight; it was an old castle town built next to the River Hinokinai and many of the old samurai houses had been preserved. They paused for a few moments to look at the station building, which had been built to represent the gatehouse of a samurai house. While Fujio, who was still only twenty-five or -six, seemed to be impressed, Hida did not say a word; he just lit a cigarette. Hida was thirty-four, round-shouldered, and tended to be overweight, but his step was light and he had the build of a good rugby player.

They took a taxi in front of the station and told the driver to take them to the police station, then settled back to watch as the town unfolded itself outside the windows. They were here because it seemed likely that the man who had called himself Kawamura had in fact been Kōsuke. When the police first came up from the town, they had shown the hotel staff Kōsuke's photograph, and they had all agreed that this was the same man. Even the blue coat and sunglasses he was wearing when he arrived matched the description they had received from the gardener he had visited in Kokubunji. They checked the address he had given in Sendai but found that there was no one of that name living there.

The hotel staff immediately guessed that he had committed suicide in the lake. They assumed that the money he had left was to make up for all the trouble he had caused them and that the note was a kind of suicide note. The police and fire brigade searched the shoreline, and sure enough, about five hundred yards from the hotel, near a statue of Princess Tatsuko, they found a pair of men's shoes on top of a rock. The place where they were found was an especially popular place for potential suicides, and when this information reached the Himonya station, it was decided to send Hida and Fujio up to help in the investigation.

The police station in Kakunodate was a modern white building, and they found the station chief and his subordinates all waiting to greet them. After the introductions were completed the assistant chief, Inspector Tōgo, brought them up-to-date with the situation. He was a man in his midforties, slim, and with only a slight trace of an accent.

"The Ryūjin Hotel is on the southern side of the lake and the place where we found the shoes is farther to the west, near the Katajiri bus stop." He pointed out both areas with a ballpoint pen on a colored map of the area that was fixed on the wall.

"There is a gold-colored statue of Princess Tatsuko here and along with two other areas it is a favorite spot for people who want to commit suicide. The shore is made of basalt and it drops off sharply close to the shore. The shoes were found there, placed neatly on a rock, the toes pointing toward the lake."

He indicated a pair of shoes that were standing on newspaper on the floor. They were casual loafers, well worn and very big.

"The name inside is that of a popular shoe store in Tokyo." This had already been checked by phone.

"What have you done about searching the lake?" Hida prompted.

"We sent a boat out at around noon and dragged the area with hooks, but it was no good. That method is only really good for shallow water up to sixty feet or so, but as I mentioned earlier, the shore drops away suddenly at this point and is very deep, so after we had tried dragging it, we sent in the divers, a couple of local lads who often do this kind of thing for us."

"I see."

"However, a hundred and fifty feet is as deep as even the divers can go. This case being a bit different from the average suicide, I kept them at it for a long time, but I am afraid that they were not able to come up with anything."

"You mean that they couldn't find the body?" Hida

asked, feeling an emotion that was not exactly disappointment; rather, he felt that he had been half expecting this.

"Yes, but that is not unusual. If we get a report immediately and start the search right away, there is a fair chance of us finding the body, but once it has sunk into a deep part, it never comes up again," said the station chief, who was sitting down in front of Hida.

"Last May a whole family committed suicide here and their relatives asked us to use divers to find the bodies. We searched for several days, and although we found the body of another suicide that had not been reported, we never did find the bodies of the family. A lot of suicides go unreported, so goodness knows how many bodies there must be in the lake altogether."

"It sounds a bit like Aokigahara," murmured Fujio, referring to the dense forest around Mt. Fuji where it was reported that countless numbers of people had entered, never to be seen again.

This was the first Hida had heard of bodies disappearing once they entered the lake; his superior, Yamane, had known a fair deal about the area, but that was one detail he hadn't mentioned.

"What causes them to disappear like that?"

"It's due to its depth," the chief replied. "At its deepest part it is over one thousand three hundred feet deep, making it the deepest lake in the country. At the same time the water is cold; at most it never goes over forty degrees, so it is like a gigantic refrigerator, and the bodies don't decompose, they just sink to the bottom and stay there."

"I see."

"We searched quite a large area around the statue today," said the assistant chief. "Tomorrow I thought we would continue the search a little to the north." He pointed to an area called the Sitting Stone on the map. "The lake around here is only about sixty feet deep, so if he is there we should be able to find him." However, he did not look very hopeful. The shoes that they had found on the rock were the same size as Kōsuke wore and it was generally accepted among the local police that after he had taken them off he had proceeded to swim out into the lake until he could swim no more.

"Is the lake warm enough to swim in at the moment?"

"No. Swimming is permitted from the end of July to the end of September, but it would be out of the question now."

He would, however, have been able to swim for a while, until his hands and feet became numb and he sank to the depths of the lake.

"Do you have any idea what time he disappeared?"

"The maid says she made his bed up at nine o'clock and nobody has seen him since; the bath in his room shows no sign of having been used either. I'd say that if he wanted to get out without anyone seeing him, the best time would be somewhere between eleven o'clock last night and five o'clock this morning."

They went to look at the belongings that the man had left behind. Apart from his shoes, there was a change of underwear, his toiletries, the fifty thousand yen, and the note. Hida stood looking at the note for a short while. He would have to get a copy off to Tokyo to have the handwriting checked and also to have it checked for fingerprints. If either of them matched Kōsuke's, it would then be definite that it was he who had disappeared from the Ryūjin Hotel.

He was pretty sure that it was Kōsuke. He felt the newspaper had obviously been left open on that page as a hint to his real identity, but then why didn't he sign the note with his real name? That was the only thing he could not understand; why leave the newspaper as a clue to his identity when he could just as easily have signed his real name?

Going on the assumption that the man who checked into the hotel was in fact Kōsuke, Hida decided to try to trace his footsteps up to his arrival there, and in order to do this he had to enlist the help of the Akita and Iwate police.

The people in the hotel said that they thought that the man had come by bus and walked from the bus stop at Katajiri. There was a bus that made the one-hour journey around the lake from Lake Tazawa station; it was a white bus with a maroon stripe down the side and was quite crowded during mornings and evenings with schoolchildren. Hida got the local police on the job immediately and had them make door-to-door inquiries around all of the bus stops. This was completed by the following morning and they managed to find three people who remembered having seen someone who answered Kōsuke's description: the ticket collector at the station, an old lady who ran the station kiosk, and a waitress in the coffee bar outside the station.

The ticket collector said he was fairly sure that a tall man in a dark blue overcoat had given him a ticket and walked out of the station sometime after three o'clock. Lake Tazawa is on the line from Morioka, in Iwate Prefecture, to Ōmagari, in Akita, and the 3:23 from Morioka to Ōmagari is the only train to stop there between three and four. Thus it was assumed that the man had arrived on this train.

The woman who ran the station kiosk said that a man of Kōsuke's description had bought a magazine and cigarettes. The waitress said that he had used the telephone next to the register, and although she had not listened to his conversation, she seemed to remember him looking at a timetable or hotel guide as he spoke.

Another witness was the driver of the bus. The bus made nine trips around the lake every day from the station, driving in a counterclockwise direction in the morning and clockwise in the afternoon to make it more convenient for the passengers. One of the buses arrived at the Katajiri stop at about five past five in the evening, and when the driver was questioned he said he had a vague recollection of somebody matching Kōsuke's description getting off the bus there. About ten people got off the bus there, seven of them locals and the rest tourists. Among them he thought he remembered seeing a man in a navy-blue raincoat who had walked off toward the lake in the direction of the hotels.

The police had managed to trace his movements from the station, but they still didn't know where he had been from the time he left Kokubunji at around four o'clock on the tenth until he surfaced here at three-thirty on the twelfth.

In the meantime the search of the lake continued and Hida and Fujio went along to watch. The water of the lake was a dark blue-gray and looked very cold. On the southwest side stood the beautiful golden statue of a woman supposed to represent Princess Tatsuko, who, according to legend, had turned into a dragon and ruled the lake. Hida had read the story in a guidebook on his way up; it told of a dragon from Hachiro Lagoon, farther north, that had fallen in love with the princess and how they spent each winter together at Tazawa before he went back north in the spring. As a result of their passion, Tazawa never freezes in the winter and grows annually deeper while Hachiro Lagoon becomes shallower.

The ground around the statue was made of basalt and small waves were lapping against it, making a lonely sound. Under the gray sky the water looked very cold and gray, but when Hida went up to the shore and looked closer, he saw that it was really a pale emerald green. All of a sudden he remembered Yamane saying how the lake seemed to draw you into it and he understood what Yamane had meant. There was a light mist over the lake and every now and again the opposite shore would come into view only to disappear again. The green of the surrounding mountains was flecked here and there with the reds and golds of approaching autumn.

"This is where we found the shoes," Inspector Tōgo said, indicating a rock about six feet from the water's edge. "This area is especially popular with people who want to commit suicide because the bottom of the lake drops away very close to shore."

The spot where they were standing was only two or three minutes from the Ryūjin Hotel. A cold wind was blowing, causing Hida to draw his bull neck into the collar of his jacket in an effort to keep warm. He looked from the hotel to the statue and on down to the shore as he tried to imagine Kōsuke sneaking down the fire exit and coming to this spot in the dead of night. He would have stood here and looked around for a moment, then, slowly removing his shoes, have walked down to the water's edge. After a brief pause, he would have taken a deep breath and started to swim out into the lake for as long as he could. Hida relived the scene in his mind for some time, then plunged a hand into a pocket to look for a cigarette. He was a short, well-built man, with little excess fat. He stood frowning out over the lake, the cigarette hanging from his mouth.

"I don't like it."

No matter how much he tried, he could not bring himself to believe the scenario he had composed. One reason was that he didn't believe that Kōsuke was the kind of man to commit suicide, and the other—he hadn't realized it until now—was because bodies were seldom recovered from Lake Tazawa.

Tōgo led them around to the Sitting Stone area on the northern shore of the lake. There was a large red-lacquered *torii*, or archway, on a rock by the lake and a flight of stone steps leading up from the road to a small shrine on the top of a hill there.

"This is another area that is very popular for suicides, and if his body is in the lake here, we stand a reasonable chance of finding it," he explained.

But if Kōsuke had committed suicide at this spot, he had had to walk about three miles barefoot. Even though there was a good road running the whole way, this seemed unlikely, and so they did not hold much hope of finding the body.

"He could have wandered along the lakeside while he tried to summon up the courage to take the leap, so to speak," Tōgo suggested, none too hopefully. "It may seem a bit unnatural, but you can never tell what a person will do when they have decided to commit suicide. They're not behaving rationally to begin with. Anyway, a day and half have passed since he disappeared, and if we're going to find him anywhere, it will have to be where the water is no deeper than sixty feet."

It was obvious from his tone that Tōgo was not very hopeful either. They had searched the area around the statue very carefully, and if this had been a normal suicide, this is as far as they would have gone. But Kōsuke was wanted for murder, and even if there was only a slight hope of finding the body, Tōgo thought it worth the effort.

They were using four boats to drag the bottom of the lake with hooks.

While this was going on, the inquiry into Kōsuke's movements before he arrived at Kakunodate was continuing. He had left his car at the parking lot at Ueno station at seven o'clock on the evening of the tenth and there were ten trains that night after seven o'clock heading in the Morioka—Aomori direction. These all arrived between three and nine the following morning, and if he had changed at Ōmiya and taken the bullet train, he would have arrived the same night. But where had he been staying before he appeared at Tazawa? It had been decided to concentrate the search on Morioka as the man who had been spotted had arrived on a train from that direction.

The search at the lake continued until lunchtime, but it failed to turn up anything new, so they decided to call it off. However, the search in Morioka did come up with something at last. On the night of the eleventh, a man matching Kōsuke's description had checked into a hotel near Iwate Park.

In this way, the movements of the man gradually came together, and on the evening of the fifteenth they were finally able to say definitely that it was Kōsuke Ōkita that they were following. The fingerprints from the note left in the hotel and a copy of the note itself had been sent to Central Headquarters in Tokyo; the fingerprints matched the large number of Kōsuke's that had been found in his home and office, while the handwriting was also judged to be his. As soon as this was confirmed, the police got in contact with Kakunodate.

EIGHT O'CLOCK, OCTOBER 15.

A large blackboard was set up on one side of the conference room with the following written on it:

*Kōsuke Ōkita's Movements*

| | |
|---|---|
| 1) October 10, 7:00 P.M.: | Catches express from Ueno or bullet train from Ōmiya bound for the northeast. |
| 2) October 11, 4:00 P.M.: | Checks into the V.I.P. Inn in Morioka. |

| 3) October 12, 3:23 P.M.: | Arrives at Lake Tazawa station. |
| 4) October 12, 5:05 P.M.: | Gets off bus and checks into Ryūjin Hotel. |
| 5) October 12, 11:00 P.M.– October 13, 5:00 A.M.: | May have committed suicide in lake. |

"As you can see, number one is only a guess, but I think that there would be no harm taking it at face value. We have witnesses for numbers two to four, so we have a rough idea of what the suspect did since he disappeared from Tokyo. . . ."

Hida looked around at the detectives who were gathered in front of him. Apart from the local detectives, there were also representatives of the Iwate and Akita headquarters, who were there to help coordinate the inquiries. There were about thirty of them altogether; most were older than the thirty-four-year-old Hida, but he did not let this bother him.

"As I see it, the problem is number five. Personally I think there's a strong possibility that his suicide was all a hoax to throw us off the scent and that he is still on the run."

A murmur ran around the room at this remark. While none of the men present were convinced that Kōsuke was dead, Hida's certainty that it had been a trick surprised them.

"The first reason I have for saying this is that from what I know of his character I think suicide extremely unlikely. I personally interrogated him and checked up on his alibi, and I can tell you that the impression I got was not of a weak man who would be easily driven to suicide, but of a man with a fiery temperament, who, no matter how far he was driven into a corner, would never give up.

"Second, there is the fact that bodies that disappear in Lake Tazawa are seldom seen again. If it had been any other lake, we might find the body, but since this isn't true of Lake Tazawa, it is the ideal place to stage a fake suicide. I find the third point the hardest to swallow," he said, hitting the table with three fingers. "I think that there was something strange about his behavior just before he disappeared. If he had decided that he couldn't go on running and that he was going to make an end of it, I feel sure that he would have left a note to this effect. Given his character, it would have been the natural thing to do.''

"But he did leave a note."

"What, you mean the 'I am sorry for all the trouble I caused'? One line without a signature? It was sure to take us some time to confirm that Ōkita had written it; it's almost as if he wanted to disappear without anyone knowing.''

"I see, but he had left a newspaper under the note, opened to the article about him. Surely he meant that as a hint.''

"Yes, a hint!" Hida said forcefully. "If he left a note, he must have known that we would check the writing and the fingerprints. He wanted us to know that he had committed suicide, but it would seem that he didn't want us to know for two or three days.''

"You mean he wanted to give himself time?" one of the detectives from the Akita HQ asked.

"Exactly. If we had known that it was Ōkita from the beginning, we would have instigated a general search of the area at the same time as searching the lake, and that would have meant that he'd be trapped.''

"I see what you mean; when you think of it in that light there is definitely something fishy about his behavior,'' said the chief of the Kakunodate police. "He left a note and money in his room and we found his shoes beside the lake, but in my experience, people who make their preparations as carefully as that usually leave some positive piece of identification—their calling card, season ticket, driving license, or something—but in this case there was nothing.''

"He would need all those things while he was on the run, especially money. No, I think he bought another bag and change of clothing in Morioka and took that with him when he left the hotel. He wanted us to think him dead when, in fact, he was really on the run again.''

A vision of Kōsuke running along the side of the lake

flashed in front of Hida's eyes and this time it rang true, not like the vision he had had of him swimming out into the dark waters of the lake.

# 10

# The Fake Suicide

REPORTS THAT A MAN MATCHING KŌSUKE'S DEscription appeared to have committed suicide in Lake Tazawa were in all the morning papers on the fourteenth, which, as chance would have it, was also the day of Seiji Nasuno's funeral. The service was held in a hall in Meguro and the guests all agreed that it was only fitting that the suicide should have happened on the same day. However, two days later, it was announced that the body could not be found and that there was a strong possibility of the suicide having been a fake. The papers all took up the story enthusiastically, with gaudy headlines splashed across the front pages. Even ten days after the murder, it still made good copy.

Tōru Kinumura sat in his office, engrossed in the story. He had read it at his apartment in Takaido before he left for work at 10:30, but as he had a different paper delivered to the office, he read the story again to see if he could glean any new information. The bad weather had finally cleared up and the sun flooded through the office windows. One of the girls who had been working for him for a long time came in with a cup of tea, but when she saw the look on his face, she stopped for a moment. He had the newspaper spread over the desk and was crouched over it intently. He was frowning and looked as if he were enduring some terrible pain. She put the tea down on the corner of the desk, and for the first time he became aware of her presence. He looked up and pushed his glasses back, but before he could open his mouth to speak, the phone by his elbow rang. He answered it.

"Hello, Camellia."

"Kinumura? It's me, Chiharu." She sounded strangely tense and nothing like her usual lively self. "Did you see the news on TV this morning?"

"No, I haven't watched TV yet; why, what's wrong?"

"They're saying now that Kōsuke's suicide may have been a fake."

"Oh, I know. I was just reading about it in the paper. Are you phoning from home?"

"No, the golf course. I just happened to look at the TV in the clubhouse when the news came on. It was a real shock." Chiharu had not been to work or to practice her golf from the time of the murder until the funeral service was finished, but today she had left early and driven out to the Uchibō club. "Why do you think that they suspect his suicide to be a fake?"

"It says here that when they couldn't find his body, the police became suspicious and started trying to discover what he did after he left the hotel. As a result, they were able to learn that a stranger matching Kōsuke's description was seen on the first bus the next morning."

Kinumura realized that only having seen the TV report, she would not know much detail, so he looked down at the paper again before continuing.

"The first bus leaves Tazawa station every morning at six-thirty and makes a trip around the lake to pick up the locals who are on their way to work. It was too early for the tourists, but the day after Kōsuke is supposed to have committed suicide, several people say they saw a tall stranger with a brown jacket over his shoulders board the bus. A man answering that description was also spotted in front of the station, and the police suspect that this may have been Kōsuke," he said, reading the newspaper as he spoke.

"You mean they think he got up in the middle of the night and, after leaving his shoes by the lake, disappeared again on the bus?"

"Well, they don't know for sure whether the man on the bus was indeed Kōsuke, but the police and the press certainly seem to think there's a good chance it was."

Kinumura also thought the man on the bus was Kōsuke and guessed that he had tried to fake a suicide to give himself some breathing space in which to make good his getaway. However, now that the police realized that they had been hoodwinked, it was going to be much worse than before. The police would consider catching him a matter of honor; Kinumura could visualize pictures of Kōsuke being plastered all over the country until he was finally brought to justice.

"But that means that Kōsuke is still alive, doesn't it?" Chiharu asked in a strangely excited voice. Kinumura realized suddenly just how much this meant to her and could not just brush her off with an easy answer.

"Let's talk about it later. Can you meet me tonight?" he asked. She had obviously been thinking the same thing because she agreed without a moment's hesitation.

They arranged to meet at eight o'clock at a hotel in Akasaka. Ever since they had talked at the coffee bar in Himonya four nights before, a kind of camaraderie had grown up between them.

He put the phone down and sat looking at the activity in the office for a while, then stood up and walked over to filing cabinets in the main office. He squatted down and pretended to be looking for something, but really he was listening to one of the girls, Yaeko, make her sales pitch.

"How's your game recently? . . . I say, that's incredible, you've certainly improved a lot. . . . Yes, we're getting really good reports about it, you must let me take you over there one day and show you around. . . ."

She had a very clear voice and he could hear her easily despite the fact that there were two or three girls in between. Her everyday voice was deep and uncultured, but when she got on the phone, she sounded like someone else altogether. Even though he realized it was her job,

Kinumura could not help but be amazed by the change that came over her when she was talking business.

However, this was not why he was keeping an eye on her; he had noticed that she sometimes slipped into his room when she thought he was out in order to go through the firm's books and generally seemed to be keeping her eye on him. She was twenty-seven or -eight, had a good figure and full lips. She dyed her hair brown and had it permed in a tight curl. She had joined the company when the Tanzawa club was almost finished and the second sales campaign was just starting, and as far as he could remember, it had been Vice-President Kawai who had recommended her.

He could picture Kawai's fat face and shifty eyes, and as he did, he found his thoughts going back over the Uchibō club stockholders meeting three days before. Approximately seventy percent of the stock was held by Nasuno and Kawai, the rest being held by a number of small shareholders. Eleven of the small shareholders were relatives or friends of Nasuno, such as Kuretani or Kinumura himself, who held two percent of the stock, and did not count. The remainder had been sold when the club was still little more than an idea and not even all the land had been bought. One hundred five-hundred-yen shares had been added to each membership to make them seem more appealing in order to raise the capital to continue. There were about one hundred and thirty of these shareholders altogether, and although most of these did not even bother to attend the meetings, twenty of them were quite militant and demanded to know what had happened to the three billion yen that was said to have disappeared. They seemed to know that there were really eight thousand members instead of the four thousand eight hundred that was the official number, and this would mean that three billion yen were floating around somewhere, unaccounted for. When they pressed Kawai for an answer, he just answered blandly that he had no idea and put the blame on his late partner, Nasuno.

That evening at 8:30, Kinumura met Chiharu in the lobby of the hotel in Akasaka. As they had agreed on the phone that morning, Chiharu had called him from the lobby when she arrived and he had come up from his office, which was very close by. She was wearing a dark brown one-piece dress with a brown blazer over her shoulders and a light brown scarf, and she looked striking among the other people in the lobby, most of whom were wearing much brighter clothes. Tall, slim, and beautifully tanned, she looked every inch a sportswoman and tended to stand out wherever she went.

"Thank you very much for the other day," she said with a bow as he walked toward her. She could have been referring to his help at the funeral, but he knew she meant the time two evenings before when he had saved her from Kuretani's gang.

"Forget it, it was nothing. Have you eaten yet?"

"No."

"Well, shall we go upstairs then?"

By upstairs, he meant the restaurant on the fortieth floor where the diners are entertained with harp and piano music while they look out over the lights of Tokyo.

"Okay," Chiharu said with a nod, and started toward the elevators, then stopped. "On second thought, you wouldn't mind if we went down to the basement, would you?" she said, dropping her eyes.

"Not at all, either way is fine."

There were several restaurants in the basement and they chose a dark Spanish one. They sat down opposite each other at a table by the wall under a poster advertising a bullfight. There was a small porcelain lamp on their table and Kinumura studied her in its light. Her slim, brown arm still looked the same and she still had the same fresh beauty, but when he looked in her eyes, he realized that she had changed. That was probably why she had not wanted to go up to the restaurant on the fortieth floor; she didn't feel like the bright lights anymore, or maybe it would remind her of Kōsuke. Kinumura had known that they were in love for some time, perhaps even longer than they themselves had realized.

Kinumura ordered for them both, parma ham, Catalonian salad, and a mussel and scallop paella; for drinks he ordered sangria.

"Have you had any more trouble with strange men hanging around since then?" he asked with a smile once the waiter had gone away.

"No, I haven't," she said, raising her eyes. "What do you think they were trying to achieve, forcing me into their car like that? They did say that they were going to take me to see Kuretani, but what do you think?"

"They said that they were looking for Kōsuke also, didn't they?"

"Yes. They said they wanted to exchange news with me about him."

"I thought so; it occurred to me later that maybe it was all just a demonstration."

"A demonstration?"

"Yes, to show that they were not involved in his disappearance themselves."

After Kinumura had rescued her, they had gone into the coffee bar to calm down, and while they were there, Chiharu had told him what she had heard from the lawyer, Sako.

"When you told me about your conversation with Sako, you said that he told you that you shouldn't take Kōsuke's disappearance on face value and that he may even have been kidnapped. Well, the police must be thinking in the same way because they're the experts when it comes to disappearances and Kuretani may have told his men to pick you up like that to discuss Kōsuke's disappearance in order to demonstrate that he didn't know anything about it."

"I thought of something later on," Chiharu said, seemingly making her mind up about something. "The truth is that I met Kōsuke on the tenth, shortly before he disappeared. He told me that apart from being suspected by the police, he was being threatened by someone else. He could well have been referring to Kuretani."

Kinumura wasn't ready for this; she had told him before about her meeting with Sako, but he had never for one minute suspected that she had seen Kōsuke on the day he disappeared. "I hadn't known that, but I don't think it's directly connected to his disappearance. Kōsuke is not the kind of man to let mere threats worry him."

"Yes, I agree." She showed a smile for the first time; at last she had found an ally.

Their sangria arrived with a thin slice of orange floating on the top; their eyes met as they toasted each other in silence.

"All the same, I wonder what the truth is about that telephone call. There's no way of proving Kōsuke's alibi unless we can find the woman who made it."

She sighed, unable to forget Kōsuke's predicament for a moment, and Kinumura could hear the sadness in her voice. The only reason she went to the Eri coffee bar had been to try to find out something to back up Kōsuke's story. She and Kinumura had talked to the manager and the waitress but hadn't been able to come up with any more than the police had.

"I can't help but feel that the woman phoned Kōsuke to get him out of the house." The sangria had brought a flush to her cheeks. "She could have faked an accent and pretended to be in trouble, then given him a number and asked him to pass on a message. Of course she chose the number at random, so when he tried to pass on her message, nobody would know what he was talking about and he would start to worry about her. She guessed that he would come looking for her and had left the note in the phone booth directing him to the coffee bar in order to keep him in the area as long as possible and destroy his alibi."

"I see; that would mean that she was in league with the murderer. He must have known about the trouble between Kōsuke and your father and decided to set Kōsuke up to take the blame for the murder. If that was the case, everything has gone just as he planned."

They sat in silence and exchanged a tense look. The restaurant was becoming crowded as the evening wore on, but the tables were set a fair distance apart and Latin-American music was playing in the background, so they were not disturbed. After a short silence Kinumura had an idea.

"You said just now that the woman might have faked an accent and it reminded me of something. One of the girls in my office who is working on telephone sales can change her voice any way she likes in order to appeal to her customers, and it occurred to me that she would have no trouble faking an accent. I had my suspicions about her for something else, so I checked up on her background, and what do you know? She is Kawai's mistress.''

Chiharu looked at him excitedly.

''Kawai recommended her originally and she does very well at her work. She has a good figure and is the kind of girl that men find it hard to refuse, but she behaves strangely in the office sometimes, so I asked one of the clerks who has been with me for a long time and who works as my secretary to check up on her and she told me that she is Kawai's mistress.

''One of the other girls had gone out with her to meet some clients at a coffee bar, and when they finished the other girl left, but she soon returned to pick up something she had forgotten. She got back just as a big foreign car pulled up and the first girl got in. She looked to see who was driving, and to her surprise she saw it was Kawai. Did you know that he drove his own car?''

''Yes.''

''Normally I wouldn't think anything of it, but if you look at it in the context of the murder, it takes on a new light altogether.'' He leaned forward and lowered his voice. ''Did you know that there was a stockholders meeting at Uchibō last Wednesday? I realize I shouldn't really be telling you this, but a few of the stockholders demanded to know what had happened to the three billion yen that they claim has disappeared. You see, they claim that although there are only supposed to be four thousand eight hundred members, there were as many as eight thousand memberships sold, and that your father and Kawai split the extra money between them. There have always been rumors about it, but when it was announced that the guaranty money would not be returned for another five years, things came to a head.

''When he was pressed for an explanation, what do you think Kawai said? He said he had nothing to do with the sales side of the operation, that it had all been done by your father, and as a result he had absolutely no idea what could have happened to the money they claim has disappeared.''

''And what is the truth?''

''I am afraid it's true that there are at least three thousand more members than there are supposed to be. Camellia was set up originally as the sole agent for the club, but there are any number of ways to sell memberships without going through the company. However, one thing is for sure: it wasn't all your father's fault. Kawai had just as much input; he just thinks that now your father is dead, he can get away with it by blaming him.''

He knocked back the rest of his sangria, and calling the waiter over, he ordered a scotch and water. The alcohol and excitement had combined to make his face quite red.

''A golf club is rather different from most businesses. A membership is nothing more than a piece of paper and nobody is to know many are sold or how much money is collected. For this reason a lot of fraud is connected with golf clubs, and if two people run it and one of them dies, nothing can stop the remaining partner from denying all knowledge of any wrongdoing.''

''Mr. Sako, the lawyer, said the same thing. He also said that a lot of people stood to gain by my father's death and so the police wouldn't be concentrating solely on Kōsuke.''

''A directors' meeting was held immediately after your father's death. It was decided to leave the post of president open for the time being, but Kawai is now the president in all but name. If you wanted to know who benefited the most from the murder, you wouldn't have to look far.'' He seemed to realize he'd said too much and held his napkin to his mouth for a few moments. ''There's the problem of his girlfriend's behavior as well, so just leave it to me. I'll try to investigate it as well as I can.''

They sat in silence again until their paella arrived. Kinumura urged Chiharu to eat more and she complied without protest, but then suddenly put her fork down.

''Do you think it was really a fake suicide?''

''Yes, I do,'' he answered with a nod.

''Will it make things worse for him?''

''Yes, the police will think he's made a fool of them,

and with everyone watching the case like this, it will be a matter of pride for them to arrest him as soon as possible.''

"The extra news coverage will also make it more likely that he is recognized and someone could easily tip off the police."

"Yes."

"But I want him to be alive," she whispered. "I feel sure that the truth will come out in the end, I really do. I just hope he doesn't do anything stupid before then. I want him to be alive more than anything."

It was almost as if she were talking to Kōsuke instead of Kinumura and then tears started to pour down her cheeks.

# 11

# The Postman Comes

EVERY DAY WAS A CONTINUING NIGHTMARE FOR Shimako. Not a day had passed since she phoned the police to tell them of Hideo's discovery that the police hadn't been marching in and out of the house.

First, Inspector Momozaki and the identification team had arrived at about ten o'clock that night, and while the others were checking the articles in the garden, she had to put up with Momozaki's persistent questioning. Next, there had been the search of the house. Of course Momozaki asked her permission before starting and made it clear that it was strictly voluntary, but he didn't seem to be in the mood to take no for an answer.

The search had lasted until twelve o'clock that night and at six o'clock next morning she was awoken to be told that a nationwide search had been instigated for Kōsuke.

Finally four men had come and covered the bedroom, the lounge, Kōsuke's desk, and even the crockery with white powder as they searched the house for fingerprints. They also took Shimako's, Tome's, and Hideo's fingerprints, causing Hideo to complain.

"What do you need my fingerprints for? I haven't done anything."

135

"So we can tell which ones belong to Ōkita," one of them answered simply. Shimako realized they meant to collect all the fingerprints in the house, then subtract those that could be identified until they were left with a complete set of Kōsuke's. After they had finished, two of them went off, but the other two remained and questioned her repeatedly about where Kōsuke could have gone. Momozaki had asked her the same thing the night before and she answered exactly the same thing. She told them the address of Kōsuke's sister and her own parents' house, but apart from that, she merely shook her head and said that she had absolutely no idea.

She had thought they would go away when they realized that they could learn no more, but she was wrong. They hung around talking in the kitchen for a while, then one of them went out into the garden, and when he returned the other went out in his place. She realized then that the house was being kept under a continual watch both inside and out.

The seven o'clock news that morning dealt with the search for Kōsuke and his picture appeared on the screen. A few minutes later the phone rang, and when Shimako went to answer it, the detective who had been smoking a cigarette by the window suddenly appeared at her shoulder and studied her expression while she spoke.

"Excuse me for asking," he said when she hung up, "but who was that on the phone?"

"My mother in Chigasaki."

"And what did she want?"

"She saw the news about Kōsuke and phoned to see what it was all about."

"She didn't say she'd been in touch with your husband or anything like that?"

"No."

"If you hear anything about your husband's whereabouts, please let us know instantly. If you cooperate with us, we'll do our best to keep out of your way."

From the way he spoke, she realized that they meant to keep up their watch, and she wasn't wrong. From that day on they arrived at eight o'clock every morning and stayed till about ten at night. They spent most of their time out of doors, but they were always there somewhere. Sometimes there would only be one, sometimes two, and it was always someone different, but one thing didn't change: Shimako was kept under a close watch. Whenever the phone rang, one would appear to ask who it was, and when the mail arrived they would look at the name of the sender to make sure it was not Kōsuke trying to get in touch with her. She thought they left her alone at night, but even here she was wrong.

"I just heard that there's a policeman staying in the upstairs room of the house opposite," Tome said when she came in from shopping one day. "I could hardly believe my ears." She had overheard two of their neighbors talking about it and hurried home to tell Shimako. "He would have a clear view of the front of the house and the garage from there."

Shimako went to stay at her parents' house in Chigasaki once after Kōsuke was put on the wanted list, but she was followed by a detective and the house was put under surveillance. Her mother and sister became exhausted, and in the end she couldn't stand it any longer and returned to Tokyo.

She learned of Kōsuke's stay at the hotel by Lake Tazawa on the twelfth when the police came to see her on the afternoon of the thirteenth. As before, it was Inspector Momozaki who questioned her.

"Have you heard any more from your husband since he disappeared?"

"No, nothing whatsoever."

"Did he mention that he would be going to the north of the country when he left the house on the tenth?"

"No, he didn't."

"Does he have any friends living in the area around Lake Tazawa?"

"I don't know. I suppose some of his old friends from college could live in that area, but I wouldn't know. He didn't speak of them as a rule."

Even Momozaki, who was a very quiet, understanding man, was obviously becoming annoyed with her refusal to be more helpful.

"Has my husband really committed suicide?"

"What do you think?"

Shimako did not answer.

"We have sent two of our men up by plane to investigate and we should know more soon."

Every day was torture for Shimako, and as her loneliness grew, she felt she was going mad.

On the fourteenth she couldn't stand the idea of remaining cooped up in the house a moment longer, and putting on a black suit, she left the house. She didn't care if she was followed; she didn't care about anything. She stopped a taxi and told it to go to a funeral parlor in Meguro. She remembered one of the detectives mentioning that Nasuno's funeral was to be held that day at two o'clock and had made up her mind to attend.

When she arrived, she found the garden filled with wreaths and the entrance to the parlor crowded with mourners. If Kōsuke had appeared, there would probably have been a riot, but as it was, nobody was likely to know Shimako. She signed the guest book in her maiden name.

She walked into the room where the service was to be held, and taking in a chair at the back, she sat facing the picture of Nasuno and closed her eyes. After a few minutes she opened them and looked around the dark room. The service was about to start and she noticed Kinumura hurrying busily up the aisle. When he saw her, he stopped in his tracks and stared at her as if he couldn't believe his eyes. Of all the people present, he was probably the only one who could recognize her, and when his attention was diverted for a moment, she quietly slipped out. She guessed that the detectives who had followed her there would assume she had gone in Kōsuke's place to try to make amends with the deceased.

When she returned home, she felt so bad that she lay on the bed for a long while.

On the sixteenth the papers announced that Kōsuke's suicide was probably a fake and Shimako could almost feel the interest that was focused on their house. From that time even Tome was followed when she went to the shops, and that evening Hideo said he couldn't stand it any longer and went back to his parents' house in Saitama.

While she knew that the police must be doing everything in their power to find Kōsuke, Shimako found herself living in a kind of vacuum. Nobody wanted to see her and she couldn't even go out without a policeman tailing her. Her fears of going mad grew.

Things continued like this for ten days after Kōsuke's disappearance, and the twentieth dawned a lovely, fine day. Tokyo had not had a day like this in weeks, although there was a strong wind and lots of clouds, which made the day suddenly dark as they crossed the sun.

Shimako did not get up as early these days as she had and it was usually eleven o'clock before she appeared in the kitchen for breakfast. After eating she went back to her lounge and stayed there alone. She had lost her appetite these days; as a result her anemia had grown worse and she would often suffer from dizziness and nausea.

This morning's detective had already announced himself at the front door and Shimako was sitting looking vacantly out at the garden. She had not put a foot outside the house since she went to Nasuno's funeral and she felt as if she had no place left to run.

She wondered what Kōsuke was doing now and where he was hiding. When Momozaki had asked her whether she thought he had really committed suicide she had honestly not known what to answer. Her thoughts kept chasing each other around and around in her head. She wondered if this was how it felt to go mad.

At that moment the front doorbell rang. It was 12:20, and although she didn't know why, she decided to go and answer it. This was the time of day when Tome liked to do the housework, and many was the time that she had been using the vacuum cleaner and not heard the bell, leaving the guests waiting on the porch until she had finished. Not that there had been many guests since Kōsuke went on the run—only the laundry and the delivery boys from the local shops.

When she opened the door, she found a mailman in his blue uniform and hat standing with a white envelope in his outstretched hand.

"Express delivery."

"Thank you."

It was addressed to Shimako and on the back it said

Ichizō Tanaka and had an address in Naka-ku, Nagoya city. It was written with a blue ballpoint pen in a strange, square hand.

The mailman closed the door and Shimako heard him drive away on his motorbike just before the door opened again and a detective walked in. She knew him by sight and guessed that he had been hiding in the bushes by the gate when the mailman arrived.

"I see you've had a special delivery," he said, peering at the envelope in her hand. "Would you mind if I take a look?" he asked politely, and took it from her.

"Naka-ku, Nagoya. Is this person a friend of yours?"

"Yes," she said with a nod, but the detective didn't seem to believe her, so she added: "He used to work for us before he moved to Nagoya."

She took the envelope back and turned away from him angrily. His attitude had only exacerbated her anger, and the longer she was kept a virtual prisoner in her own home, the shorter her temper became.

She walked past Tome, who was bent over the vacuum cleaner in the living room, and returned to her lounge in the back of the house. When she got there, she stood looking at the envelope in her hand. The truth of the matter was that she had never heard of the man whose name was written on the back, but she had been so angered by the detective's senseless prying that she had lied before she realized what she was saying.

She didn't know about Kōsuke, but she certainly didn't know anyone in Nagoya, and apart from having changed trains there once several years before, she had no knowledge about the city at all. However, there was no getting away from the fact that the letter was addressed to her, and looking at the envelope, she saw that it had been posted in Nagoya the day before.

"What funny square writing," she said to herself as she went to fetch some scissors. "Anyone would think it was written with a ruler."

She opened the envelope to reveal a single sheet of writing paper that had been folded into four. She unfolded it and found that it was written in the same strange, square letters with the same blue ballpoint pen.

*Shimako Ōkita,*
*We have got your husband and if you want to see*
*him again you must pay us ¥20 million. When we*
*get the money, we will let you meet him, then we will*
*smuggle him out of the country safely. If you contact*
*the police, we will kill him immediately.*
*We have mailed you proof that we have him in our*
*possession by special delivery, so you better get the*
*money together right away.*

*Ichizō Tanaka*

Halfway through the letter, her heart started to beat as
if it were about to burst and her eyes kept wandering in-
voluntarily from the paper, but when she finally managed
to finish it, she had a fair grasp of its contents.

Someone had kidnapped Kōsuke as he was hiding from
the police and they wanted Shimako to pay a ransom. But
twenty million! They had told her to get the money together and obviously meant to contact her again later;
however, they said they were going to send her definite
proof that they were in fact holding Kōsuke first.

Of course it could be a hoax. She had read in a magazine somewhere that the families of wanted men often had
to put up with a lot of harassment, and in her own case
she'd had a few nasty phone calls soon after the news was
first announced, but this was the first letter. However, she
didn't believe it was a hoax; she had a nasty feeling that
Kōsuke was being held somewhere and didn't know what
to do. The letter said that if she contacted the police, they
would kill him, but this was something she could not handle on her own. She sat down on the sofa and her hands,
lying in her lap, trembled slightly.

Outside the sun went in behind a cloud, and it seemed
to her that there was a man crouching behind the trees that
were still blowing restlessly in the wind. It was probably
that detective again. He had not believed her story about
the letter and had slipped around the garden in an effort
to see her reaction.

If she showed it to the detective, he would know what
to do, but she couldn't bring herself to do that. If she
found out later that Kōsuke had been killed, it would be

almost as if she had done it herself. She wondered if she should try to get the money ready, but she doubted that there was that much money in the house or in the company, which only left her mother. Even if she asked her, she didn't think her mother could gather together that much money without arousing the suspicions of the police.

It had to be a hoax, but it said that they had sent proof by express mail. Probably nothing would come, but if a parcel had been sent at the same time as the letter, how much longer would it take to arrive? She tried to calm herself down and convince herself that she would hear nothing more of it, but she couldn't stop herself from trying to guess what they would send her. Would it be his watch? His diary? His driver's license or perhaps a tape recording of his voice? She remembered once reading a detective story where the parents of a kidnapped child had received a tape of the child's voice.

Had he really been kidnapped? If this letter was not a hoax, it could only mean that he had been and that if she told the police, he could easily be killed. She decided that just to be on the safe side, she'd try to keep the police out of the matter, but this wasn't going to be all that easy. The detective on duty today seemed to suspect something when the letter arrived, and if she was to get a parcel from the same place, he might easily ask her to show him the contents. She would have to try to get the parcel without the police knowing about it.

She looked down at the envelope she was still holding in her hand and noticed the postmark. "NAGOYA CENTRAL 82. 10.19.12-18." She guessed that this meant that it must have been posted at Nagoya central post office between twelve and six on the afternoon of October 19, 1982. It had arrived at noon on the twentieth, which meant that it took exactly one day to be delivered. She wondered when the next delivery would be and seemed to remember once having received an express letter from her sister at about two in the afternoon. She wondered if that was the time of the next delivery.

She tried to stand up but was taken by a dizzy spell and collapsed back into her chair, crying.

"Why isn't there anyone who can help me when I really need them—like now?"

Tome looked over inquiringly when a pale-faced Shimako walked into the dining room. Recently she would go back to her private lounge after a late breakfast, and if Tome wanted anything, she would have to go through and ask.

Tome had finished vacuuming the dining room and had just started on the corridor when Shimako appeared. She moved out of the way to let her pass. A strong wind was still blowing and a cloud blew across the sun just as Shimako appeared, making the room grow dark and accenting her paleness. Her eyes were rimmed with red from crying, but a pale complexion suited her and she looked stunningly beautiful. She gazed out vaguely into the garden.

"There wasn't a small parcel delivered for me yesterday or today, was there?"

"No."

"That's okay then. Where's the detective?"

"He was in here chatting until just now; that's why I'm so behind with my work. But he's disappeared somewhere again."

She looked at Shimako again for a minute before going out to continue cleaning the hall. Shimako pulled up a chair and sat down. She looked at the clock and saw that it was five past one. She guessed that the detective was still watching her from the garden. The watch had been kept up for ten days now and they had just begun to relax their vigilance when the letter arrived to put them back on their guard. She knew the detective suspected her of trying to hide something and she was determined to get the parcel, if it arrived, before he could see it.

Tome came in and asked her what she wanted for lunch, and when she learned that she did not want anything, she decided to leave the cleaning until later and go to the shops. Left alone in the house, it occurred to Shimako that this would be a good opportunity to telephone the local post office and find out what time the special deliveries were made.

"Yes, express letters are delivered four times a day,"

she was told, "at nine, twelve, one-thirty, and four." The one-thirty delivery should reach you at Kinuta by two at the latest."

So the next delivery is at two, she thought, and sat listening for the sound of the postman's bike on the drive, but all she could hear was the wind. The minute hand of the clock crawled toward two o'clock and still nothing.

"So it was a hoax after all."

No sooner had she murmured this to herself than the front doorbell rang. She jumped to her feet and had another dizzy spell. The doorbell rang again and she managed to force herself to stagger through to answer it.

"Express delivery," said a young man in a postman's uniform.

She heard footsteps behind her and swung around to find that it was Tome, who had just come back from the shops and come through the kitchen to answer the door. When she saw Shimako there before her, she stopped in surprise.

The postman handed her a small package with a label attached. It was long and thin and was lightweight. She saw that it was addressed to her, but when she noticed the name Ichizō Tanaka on the back of the label, she felt quite faint again. The postman soon went on his business and left Tome and Shimako alone in the hall. Tome looked suspiciously from the parcel to Shimako's face and back.

"I wonder what it is? Who is it from?" Tome stretched out her hand, but before she could touch the label, Shimako turned around and walked back to her room. She felt as if she were walking on air, and when she got into her room, she closed the door and collapsed back into the sofa. She put the package down on the table and could hear her heart pounding in her ears.

The package was about six inches long, two inches wide, and one inch high. It was wrapped in brown paper and tied neatly with string. Her name was written on the label as well as on the paper on both sides of the package, and on the reverse side of the label was the same name and address in the same writing as the letter. There was a red "express" stamp in one corner, and instead of a stamp, there was a white label with a post office stamp on it.

After looking at it for some time, she stood up and walked to the window but could see no sign of the detective. She thought of closing the curtains, but that would only make him more suspicious if he was watching.

She went back to the sofa and picked up a pair of scissors; her hand was shaking visibly. She cut the string and opened the paper; inside there was an oblong case with a clear top like the ones used to pack fountain pens. Inside the case she could see something that had been wrapped in gauze and then put in a plastic bag. She opened the box and removed the object. She took it out of the plastic bag and noticed that the gauze had a dark stain at one end. Taking a deep breath, she peeled away the layers of gauze to reveal a small, dark purple object. She sat and looked at it for a moment before she suddenly gave a short scream and averted her gaze.

The box had contained a man's finger.

She clutched the sofa with both hands and bowed her head. The sight of the finger remained in her mind and she could not free herself of it. She had no idea how long she sat like this, but it was some time before she could open her eyes. When she had read the letter that morning, she thought the evidence they would send would be Kōsuke's diary, driver's license, or some other innocent thing. That they would send her his finger had never even occurred to her. But could she be sure that it was in fact Kōsuke's finger?

She forced herself to look at the object again and saw that it was indeed a finger. There were spots of blood on it here and there and the whole thing was a dark purple, but there could be no doubt about its nature. It had been removed at the first joint and seemed to curve to the right slightly in a way that made her think it might be a little finger. It looked thick, but she guessed that a man's finger would probably be about that size.

Suppressing an urge to be sick, she forced herself to study it more closely. It was then that she noticed the diagonal scar running down from the fingernail to the joint. She knew that she had seen it before and remembered Kōsuke telling her he had gotten it during his college years when he injured himself skiing.

She buried her face in her hands, overcome with fear and despair. Suddenly she couldn't stand it; if she stayed any longer on her own, she would go mad. She knew she couldn't cope alone but that if she told the police she would be condemning Kōsuke to death.

If only there was someone who could help me, she thought.

She picked up the telephone and dialed a number. It was soon answered by a woman's voice.

"Hello, Camellia."

"Hello, is Mr. Kinumura there, please?"

"Yes, just a moment, please."

The background noise was replaced by music as she was put on hold. Shimako listened for the sound of the receiver being picked up in the kitchen. Ever since she had been questioned by the police, Tome seemed to have lost her appetite for eavesdropping, but this wasn't Shimako's worry. Tome had told her that when she had received a call from a friend the week before, one of the detectives had picked up the extension and listened in to her conversation. They obviously didn't trust her and were suspicious of any contact she had.

"Hello, Kinumura speaking."

"Hello, it is me, Shimako Okita."

Kinumura gave a short gasp of surprise. "Oh, hello . . ."

"I'm sorry to bother you like this."

"Not at all, although didn't I see you at the funeral?"

"Yes, but I only dropped in for a moment." She chose her words carefully, just on the off chance that one of the detectives might be listening in. "I would like to ask you a favor. You couldn't come over to the house, could you?" There was no reply. "There are some things I would like to discuss with you about the house and the company. I'm very sorry to disturb you at work like this."

"You mean right away?"

"Yes, as soon as possible . . . I'll go mad if I am left like this." Even though she was trying to keep herself under control, she couldn't keep the tears out of her voice.

"I see. I'll be straight over then," he answered in a calm voice.

Shimako replaced the receiver and collapsed over the

phone with a groan, then, pulling herself together, returned to the lounge and redid her makeup to hide the signs of her crying. She couldn't do anything about her red eyes though, so she put on a pair of sunglasses and walked out of the room.

Two detectives were in the kitchen when she got there. She guessed that the detective had been suspicious of the letter and her subsequent behavior, so he had called in reinforcements.

"Mr. Kinumura from Camellia will be coming over to see me. He is the only man I know connected with my husband's business and there are several things I'd like to discuss with him."

She said this hoping to put them off their guard, but she realized that it was hopeless. She went into the dining room and sat down in front of the television. The two detectives moved away to leave her on her own, but she knew they wouldn't go far.

I seem to be doing my best to make sure they suspect me, she thought, turning on the television. But I can't help it. If I stayed on my own, I'd go mad.

A little before three o'clock there was a knock at the door, but Shimako forced herself to remain where she was while Tome went to the door.

"Good afternoon."

"Good afternoon, Mr. Kinumura. This is a surprise."

Tome came back to the dining room and Shimako turned off the television before going to the door.

"Good afternoon," he said when he saw her.

"Good afternoon. I'm sorry for having dragged you all the way over here like this."

"Oh, don't worry about it. Has something happened?"

"No, there is just something I'd like to discuss with you."

Kinumura realized she didn't want to talk in front of Tome and did not ask any more.

"Please come through," Shimako said, and led him into her lounge after telling Tome that they would not be needing any tea.

As soon as she closed the door, she gave a groan and collapsed onto the sofa.

"What's wrong, what happened?" Kinumura asked in a gentle voice, then looked out through the window. Shimako tried to get her emotions back under control.

"At the moment two detectives are watching the house and they seem to suspect me of something, so we must be careful that they don't overhear us."

Kinumura said nothing.

"Something terrible has happened." She pointed to the envelope and the package on the desk. She had rewrapped the finger and returned it to the plastic case. "This letter arrived this morning and the parcel arrived just before I phoned you."

Kinumura sat down opposite her and opened the letter thoughtfully. He read it through once, turned pale, then read it again. "Do you know this Ichizō Tanaka?"

"No, not at all."

"How about this address?"

"No."

"And this parcel arrived later?"

"Yes."

"What is in it?"

Shimako tried to answer but couldn't find her voice. Kinumura picked up the plastic case and inspected it. It would seem to have originally held a fountain pen and it had a company name written on the lid. When he opened the gauze and saw what it contained, he gave a short cry and turned away. Shimako kept her head bowed.

"Do . . . do you think that this is really . . . Kōsuke's finger?" he stuttered, and hurriedly replaced it in the box. A cold sweat had broken out on his forehead.

"I think so; there is a scar below the nail."

"But why . . ."

"I didn't know what to do. It said in the letter that if I told the police they would kill him, so I tried to keep it from them. But when the parcel arrived I just couldn't stand it anymore, and that was when I phoned you. I told the police you were coming to help me with business. . . . I didn't know what else to do."

Kinumura looked back out of the window. The sun had hidden itself behind the clouds again and the trees were blowing violently in the wind. He turned back to her and put a hand on her trembling shoulder. "You've got to try to calm down. We must be calm and try to work out our next step."

"I suppose I must try to get the money together."

"But if you do that, the police are sure to get wind of it. Anyway, how are you supposed to get it to them?"

Shimako sat sobbing while Kinumura held a muttered debate with himself.

"If they told you to go somewhere to hand the money over, the police are sure to follow you and the house is under constant surveillance. Surely they can't have left that out of their plans." He dropped into silence, shaking his head every now and again. "No. Whatever you do, the police would be sure to get wind of it. It would be better if you were to tell them from the beginning and leave it in their hands. I don't think we have any choice."

Shimako didn't say anything; she had given up trying to formulate plans the minute Kinumura arrived and was happy to let him decide. At approximately 3:30, Kinumura went out of the kitchen into the garden and called the detectives over.

"There's something I'd like to discuss with you," he said to the elder one, and led him into the lounge. The letter and the plastic case were lying on the table. "I am afraid that Mrs. Okita isn't feeling very well and is lying down in the bedroom, so I will explain everything for her."

He told the detective everything just as Shimako had told him. Even the veteran detective looked a bit shocked when he saw the contents of the box.

The detective rang the Himonya station and Momozaki hurried over with three other detectives. First he looked at the letter and the finger, then he took over one of the rooms on the second floor and set up a portable radio. Next he wired a tape recorder to the telephone in the bedroom and had the station arrange with the telephone exchange to have any incoming calls traced. From then on all contact with the station was to be made by radio to leave the phone free for the kidnapper's call.

When Momozaki arrived, Shimako had been feeling faint and was lying down on the bed, but the situation did not allow her to remain there and she had to get up and wait by the phone with a detective. Kinumura remained in the house, too.

Momozaki didn't expect the kidnappers to phone, but he had to make all the necessary preparations just in case. When he had finished, he studied the letter and the package in detail before cross-examining Shimako.

"No, I don't know this Tanaka and I don't have any acquaintances in Nagoya." Shimako looked as if she was going to pass out at any moment. Her face was deathly pale and it seemed to be all she could do to remain upright. She shook her head weakly in answer to Momozaki's questions.

"So you cannot remember your husband ever saying that he was going to visit anyone in Nagoya?"

"No."

"Have you had any contact from your husband since he disappeared?"

"No! How many times must I tell you before you believe me?" She was obviously on the verge of hysteria and looked over to Kinumura for help.

"Do you think it is really your husband's finger?"

"Yes, I recognize the scar." She gave a deep sigh. "But at least I now know that he is still alive."

# 12

# The Finger

A DETECTIVE TOOK THE LETTER, THE PLASTIC box, and its contents to the Himonya station to be analyzed, and at five o'clock a special meeting was called to discuss this new twist to the case. Although Kōsuke's house fell under the jurisdiction of the Seijo station, it was agreed that the kidnapping should be dealt with by the men who were looking for Kōsuke.

Normally in a kidnapping case, the police keep the press informed but have them refrain from publishing the story until the case is solved. This is done to protect the victim, particularly when the victim is a woman or a child. But in this case where the victim was a man in his prime who was also wanted by the police in connection with a murder investigation, it was decided to keep the press out of it altogether.

"According to the postmark on the letter, which was delivered to Ōkita's house at twelve-twenty this afternoon, it was posted at the Nagoya Central Post Office between twelve and six on the nineteenth," Commissioner Yamane said, addressing the investigation team. "We checked with the post office and it would appear that it was actually posted between four and four-fifty. It came to Tokyo on the seven o'clock truck and arrived at Seijo this morning via the Tokyo Central Post Office. The parcel was also posted at the same time and arrived at the Seijo post office together with the letter, but due to their delivery schedules, it was a little delayed. This means that the kidnapper appeared at the central post office in Nagoya between four and four-fifty yesterday and posted the letter and the package together.''

''Does the man in the post office remember what he looks like?'' one of the detectives called out.

''No, as you know the postal laws in this country do not allow the post office to divulge who sent what where. On top of that, the post office closes at five o'clock, so the period before that is the most crowded of the day. In order for the people working there to remember anyone, they would have to have some very special characteristics indeed.''

Between four and five, the Nagoya Central Post Office handles over thirty express packages and each window deals with over eighty customers, so it would be hard for them to be expected to remember a particular person. It was assumed that whoever had sent the letter had sent it express instead of registered and chosen the busiest time of the day specifically in order to remain anonymous.

''Is there any hope of tracing the plastic case or the paper it was wrapped in?''

This question was answered by the officer who had been assigned to investigate this angle. ''As you know, there was a manufacturer's name on the case and we got in touch with them right away. Unfortunately, they told us that it belonged to a ballpoint pen that could be purchased for two thousand yen at stationery or department stores throughout the country. The same goes for the brown paper, label, and string—they all come from a wrapping set that can be purchased at any supermarket.''

''How about the finger; has it been definitely identified as belonging to Ōkita?''

''It's still being checked by the identification section at the moment, but we expect to get confirmation any minute now,'' Yamane replied. ''As far as we can tell, it is the little finger from a man's left hand, and Mrs. Ōkita is fairly positive it's her husband's as she recognizes a scar below the fingernail. Decomposition has not progressed very far, so it should be easy to check the fingerprint.''

They had checked the paper, the plastic case, and the finger itself, but the writer had obviously used a ruler, so the writing was devoid of individuality. Momozaki and five other detectives were staking out the Ōkitas' home and there was nothing else that any of them could do now until word came through from the identification section.

"If we are to assume the finger really does belong to Ōkita, it would mean that the suicide at Lake Tazawa was, in fact, a hoax, and—''

This was Hida who had been the first to suspect that Kōsuke had faked his suicide, but before he could finish his thought the phone ran and the room became suddenly silent as everyone waited expectantly. The identification section at headquarters and the detectives at Kōsuke's home were both to contact the investigation HQ as soon as they had any news. The station chief picked up the phone and listened for a few moments before handing it to Yamane.

"It's from headquarters.''

Yamane spoke on the phone for a few minutes and everyone kept their eyes on him until he finally put it down and turned to them. "They say that there's no doubt that the finger is the little finger from Ōkita's left hand.''

Everyone started to talk at once and Yamane waited until the room quieted down before continuing.

"The finger was removed between three and five days ago, but the method of preservation until it was posted is unknown. It is thought that it was removed with a carving knife, and it was not a clean cut; there was a certain amount of damage to the tissue surrounding the wound.''

The room became quiet again apart from one or two people clearing their throats as they tried to imagine what it must be like to have a finger removed.

"Further tests are to be made on the finger at the university hospital. The finger has already been delivered, and they are just waiting for a warrant.''

The police did not have their own autopsy section; they used one of the large university hospitals in the city. Even though the object for examination was only a finger, it was still treated as a body in the eyes of the law, and this made it necessary to obtain a warrant from a judge.

"But what else is there to know?" one of the younger detectives asked.

"There is still one very important point to clear up," Yamane replied. "We have to ascertain whether the finger was removed from Ōkita's body before or after death. This will give us some indication as to whether he is still alive. Unfortunately, the identification section could not say for sure, but there is a professor at the hospital who specializes in wound tissue, and he should be able to give us a definite answer."

They still didn't know if Kōsuke was dead or alive, but as with any other kidnapping, they would work on the assumption that he was alive until they had proof to the contrary.

"They say that the finger was removed three to five days ago, which would mean that it was cut off between the fifteenth and the seventeenth," Hida said. "Ōkita disappeared from the hotel by Lake Tazawa on the thirteenth, and as we think he left of his own volition, then *if* he was kidnapped, it was probably on the fifteenth or later." He stressed the *if* because he still doubted Kōsuke's actions. "However, are we to assume that he made his own way down to Nagoya and was kidnapped there?"

"His wife says she has no idea. She doesn't think he knew the city or anyone in it."

"Maybe he thought it would be easier to disappear in a town where nobody knew him and we would not expect him to go."

"Ōkita's wife has been very unhelpful throughout the investigation, which is only to be expected considering she is the suspect's wife, but I don't think we should take everything she says at face value," Yamane said. "However, Momozaki learned from Kinumura that Ōkita would appear to have been threatened by Noboru Kuretani immediately before his disappearance. Kuretani has links with the Takafuji gang, who in turn has links with the other gangs all over the country, so he could easily be involved."

They had come across Kuretani in their initial inquiries

about the Nasuno murder, and although they knew that he was involved with gangsters and often forced Nasuno to give him money, they couldn't find evidence of any recent disagreements between the two, so they didn't seriously consider him a suspect. However, cutting off people's little fingers was something of a specialty among Japanese gangsters, and even if Kuretani was not directly involved in Nasuno's murder, he was an obvious suspect for the kidnapping.

"Kinumura says that his men also tried to kidnap Nasuno's daughter, Chiharu. I think that there's definitely a case for investigating him."

"Even if there's no sign of his having left Tokyo himself, he could easily have sent one of his men."

"Maybe one of the other gangs he is connected to just happened to come across Ōkita and he suggested holding him for ransom."

"Anyway, Kuretani seems to be involved in this somehow. Even if his object is money, he might enjoy hurting Ōkita as a way of getting revenge for Nasuno's murder."

"Surely it could also be the work of a gang without connections to either Nasuno or Ōkita," one of the younger detectives said. "Ōkita's wanted poster is on display all over the country. Maybe someone recognized him, but instead of coming to tell us, they kidnapped him and demanded a ransom. Cutting off his finger could have been done not only to prove that they were holding him but also to make him weaker and easier to control."

Several of the other detectives murmured in agreement.

"Of course there'd have to be more than one of them, but that doesn't necessarily make them gangsters. Any number of gangs of young people around today wouldn't hesitate at something like that."

Whatever was the case, it was generally agreed that Kōsuke had made his own way to Nagoya and been kidnapped there. It was too dangerous for anyone to try to transport him across the country after he was kidnapped.

"I don't agree." Hida stood up and stuck his chin out aggressively. "I think we agree that Ōkita faked a suicide at Lake Tazawa and that he was very clever about it. He left sufficient clues for us to guess his true identity, but he did so in such a way as to win himself time to make his escape. We tend to think he faked his suicide on impulse, but I suggest that it was a very cleverly planned attempt.'' He looked around him, as if daring anyone to find fault with his logic. He had lost Kōsuke at Lake Tazawa, but this made him all the more determined not to lose him the next time. "After he left Lake Tazawa, he made his way down to Nagoya, but he was running short of money. The only person he could contact for help would be his wife, but he knew she would be kept under surveillance, so he hit on the idea of pretending to be kidnapped and asked his wife to send him a ransom. I think it's just the kind of thing we could expect from a man like him.''

"So you mean to say that he cut his own finger off?''

"Why not? Gangsters do it all the time. I spoke to a doctor about it once, and he told me that if you wrap elastic around the base of the finger for about fifteen minutes, it becomes quite numb. Then all that remains to do is to place a knife against it and hit the knife hard. He said that if the wound is seen to by a doctor, it will heal in about a week, and will heal on its own as long as it doesn't get infected. Therefore I think it is quite possible he left Nagoya immediately after he sent the letter and came back to Tokyo to collect the money from his wife.''

There was a brief silence as they thought over his idea.

"But the report said that it was not a clean cut. Surely if he cut off his own finger, he would make sure he did it with the least possible pain.''

"Also, how did he expect to be able to get the money from his wife without being spotted by us? Anyway, the sight of his finger was sure to give his wife a shock and make it all the more likely that she would come to us. No, I don't think there was enough likelihood of success to justify losing a finger.''

This time nobody seemed very eager to accept Hida's "fake'' theory.

"We'll be able to settle that when we find out whether Ōkita is alive or—''

Yamane was interrupted by the phone ringing again.

\* \* \*

Meanwhile, at the Ōkita home, Shimako, Momozaki, and another detective were sitting by the telephone in the bedroom waiting for a call from the kidnappers. In the lounge next door Kinumura was watching them while a detective was stationed upstairs by the transceiver and another by the kitchen telephone. The usual detectives were still on duty, one out in the garden guarding the back of the house and the other under the trees out front. It was 8:30. The wind had dropped at last and everything was quiet outside.

Five hours had passed since Kinumura contacted the police. The finger and the letter had been taken to the police station and Momozaki had spent most of the time questioning Shimako, Tome, and Kinumura. They had started making arrangements for the money, but nothing more had been heard from the kidnappers. After Momozaki finished his questioning, Kinumura prepared to go back to his office, but at that moment confirmation came in over the radio that the finger really did belong to Kōsuke and Shimako became really frightened.

"Please don't go now," she begged him. "I couldn't bear to be left on my own. I don't know what I'd do."

Despite the several detectives and Tome in the house with her, she was unable to calm down and already looked on the verge of a breakdown, so he agreed to stay. He went out to a phone booth and telephoned his company, telling them that something urgent had come up and that he would not be back that day.

The telephone rang once at seven o'clock, but it was only Kōsuke's sister who lived at Ōhashi. Shimako didn't tell her anything and hung up as soon as possible.

"It's quite possible that they won't telephone," Momozaki said, seeing how exhausted Shimako looked. He was forty-four years old, had been a detective for twenty years and the chief detective at the Himonya station for the last two, yet he still managed to have a pleasant voice and give the impression that he was a man to trust.

"His being a wanted man, they must know that his house will be under surveillance and that there is even a chance that his phone will be tapped. That might be why they contacted you by mail to begin with; they'll probably use the same technique next time, too.''

"What do you think they'll say?''

"They'll probably tell you to take the money to some prearranged spot.''

"But I haven't been able to raise the money.''

"Just take what you can and it'll be all right. We'll be following you and I guarantee that we will catch the men responsible.''

"But what happens if you don't?''

The letter had told her to prepare twenty million yen, but the police had said that this would not be necessary. In a normal kidnapping the victim is released on payment of the ransom, but in this case the kidnappers had merely promised to let Kōsuke go free in a foreign country, which was the last thing the police wanted. They were determined to catch not only the kidnappers but Kōsuke as well. Shimako, however, was not satisfied; she managed to borrow three million yen from the bank, and after having the police talk to the bank manager and explain the situation, she arranged for Tome to pick it up after hours. That was the most she could manage; Kōsuke had used all the rest of their savings to save his company—even their house and land had been mortgaged. Shimako had wanted to ask her parents for a loan, but Momozaki said this wasn't yet necessary and persuaded her to wait.

"When they get in touch with you, just do exactly what they tell you. I assure you that we won't let them know we're following you and I guarantee that we will arrest them.''

He tried to sound as confident as possible in order to raise her spirits, but then he realized that he was also, in effect, promising to arrest her husband, and he dropped into an awkward silence.

"What do you think their next move will be?'' Kinumura asked, folding his arms.

"I don't know. To tell the truth there's something about this case I don't quite understand.''

He sounded like he was trying to imply something and Shimako lost her temper.

"What is there that you don't understand? I had a finger

sent to me that turned out to belong to my husband, so I think it's pretty obvious that he's been kidnapped. Oh, when I think what it must have been like for him when they cut it off . . . I just don't know what I should do!''

She buried her face in the bedspread and burst into tears. The tension was proving to be too much for her; it was now ten days since Kōsuke had disappeared and she couldn't take it anymore, her nerves were in shreds.

Kinumura rubbed her back self-consciously and tried to comfort her. ''Calm down, you shouldn't let yourself become so upset. After all, as you said, the mere fact that they were able to send you one of his fingers proves that he's alive.''

While he was busying himself with her, a young detective who had been left in charge of the radio on the second floor came in. ''HQ just called to say they've received the medical report on the finger, sir.''

Momozaki left the telephone and walked toward him; he could see from his expression that something was wrong. The young detective took a deep breath.

''The finger was removed after death.''

He spoke in a low voice, but everyone in the room could hear him. Momozaki made no reply, so he repeated himself.

''HQ had a report from the university hospital to say that the finger had definitely been removed after death.''

''After death . . .'' Momozaki repeated in a low voice. ''After death . . . You mean that it was cut off a dead body?'' He knew that the whole room was listening to him, but that couldn't be helped. They'd have to be told anyway.

''Yes, sir. The identification branch thought that might be the case, so they sent it to the hospital, and after a careful examination of the cut no trace was found of red or white corpuscles in the tissue, which could only mean that the finger was removed after death.''

''There can be no mistake?''

''Apparently it's sometimes hard to be sure, but in this case, it wasn't a clean cut, which made it quite easy to check. That doctors seemed quite sure and he has never been known to be wrong before. HQ is going to tell the press tonight and tomorrow they'll start a full investigation.''

Momozaki looked at his watch; it was 8:10. ''I doubt that we shall be hearing any more from them tonight.''

The room fell into silence; the only sound was the sobs that came from Shimako, lying on the bed, her face buried in the eiderdown. Kinumura walked over to the window and looked out; the wind had dropped and it had become quite foggy.

Momozaki thought of Kōsuke's strong features and realized that he would never see them again. It was ironic, but when the finger arrived both Kinumura and Shimako had thought that it was proof that Kōsuke was still alive. The truth had been quite the opposite.

# 13

# A Shadow in the Fog

WEDNESDAY THE TWENTIETH HAD STARTED OFF very windy, and although everyone had expected a fine day, the wind brought in clouds and the weather was very unsettled. By evening the sky was overcast with rain clouds and a thick fog filled the city streets.

The view of downtown Shinjuku from the seven-story condominium in Higashi-Ōkubo was usually very impressive at night, but today the neon lights seemed to melt into each other in the fog like an oil painting.

"Strange weather today," Risaburō Kawai said, looking out the window from the bed where he was lying. He turned away, lit a cigarette, and stared up at the ceiling. He blew out a stream of smoke, then reached out to stroke the back of the naked girl next to him.

Keiko Tani was lying with her back turned partially toward him and her full breasts rose gently as she breathed. She let out a small groan of ecstasy as his roving fingers stirred the embers of fulfilled passion.

"How is the Tanzawa club doing; is it selling?" asked Kawai.

"No, it doesn't seem to be doing very well."

"Roughly how much has been sold?"

"Well, if you add all the agents, I'd say maybe twelve hundred memberships have been sold altogether, but no more."

"Hmm . . ." Kawai had already known that things were not going as well as they had hoped. "But Nasuno said that there were about three hundred companies that had said they were going to join."

"I think he must have been exaggerating," she answered in a bored voice. "Things started to pick up in the summer, but it didn't last. It looks as if we're still in the depression."

"Nasuno sounded quite certain about it."

"Kinumura is the same. He keeps saying it just needs one more big effort, but really I think he's heading for a nervous breakdown."

"Yes, he looks as if he's good at his job, but really he's a very weak man." Kawai's hooded eyes sparkled with a cold light as he spoke.

It had been Kawai who had first gotten her the job at Camellia. He had come across her working for another golf agent and offered her a job—not because he thought she was especially qualified, but because she was his type of woman. He had rented this condominium for her and they'd been together for almost a year now.

"There might be a depression, but the Uchibō club's reputation does nothing to help either; all the agents say so."

"What do you mean?"

"They say that the guaranty money won't be returned for another five years and rumor has it that there's three billion yen unaccounted for."

Kawai just smiled and said nothing. Keiko was never one to mince her words and as a result he was able to learn all sorts of rumors that would otherwise never reach his ears. She was almost worth the money he spent on her regardless of the sex they shared.

"There's no need to worry. Rumors like that never last long and we'll be able to sell eventually. Not only is the golfing population growing annually, but they play more than they used to. Businessmen have to play golf or they can't do their jobs, and it's even becoming popular with housewives and high school students. It's getting so every-one plays golf, but there's only a limited number of courses, and what with all these new regulations and the price of making a new course, that number will only grow by four or five a year. The law of supply and demand guarantees that we'll be able to sell eventually—we just have to sit back and wait.''

This appraisal was correct; in fact, although he was sell-ing memberships for three and a half million at the mo-ment, he intended to raise the price after the club was opened. The problem was what to do about money in the meantime; so many clubs went bankrupt or changed hands in the first few months because they lacked the capital to tide them over until they had a full roster of members. In some cases the management disappeared with all the membership money without even constructing a course—and this was one of the reasons for the many new regula-tions governing the opening of a club.

Kawai realized now that they had been a bit too opti-mistic in 1978 when they got permission to open the Tan-zawa club. Fresh from the killing they had made with the Uchibō club, they were hungry to repeat their success. Unfortunately, they hadn't reckoned with the difference in the market between the pre-oil-shock boom years of the sixties and the present day.

''You're right. People soon forget about rumors, so you have nothing to worry about,'' Keiko said, and crawling over to him, she took his cigarette. Something in her tone made him look up. ''Just what do you mean?''

''Well, they say that now that Mr. Nasuno is out of the way, you're the one who stands to benefit the most.''

''Who says?''

''It's only a rumor, but you must admit there's a certain amount of truth in it. You can lay the blame for the miss-ing money on him and now you're the sole boss of both the Uchibō and Tanzawa clubs.'' She drew on his cigarette and stubbed it out in the ashtray.

''Don't be ridiculous!'' he shouted angrily. ''I suppose it was that Kinumura who started it, was it?''

''I wouldn't be surprised; he always was a devoted fol-lower of the late Mr. Nasuno. He keeps on about how Mr.

Nasuno found him working for a small construction company and gave him his chance to be a success.''

"That's not all he gave him," Kawai said, turning over and stroking Keiko's thighs. Keiko looked over at him questioningly. "Yes, about eight hundred million of the Uchibō's money was rerouted to Camellia."

"Rerouted?"

"Yes." He didn't say any more but sat and gazed into space as he thought back over the conversation he had had with Nasuno shortly before he died.

When the Uchibō Country Club was opened in 1972 there were officially four thousand eight hundred members and the final entry fee was fifteen hundred thousand yen guaranty and three hundred thousand membership. Of this Camellia, as sole agent, took three hundred thousand commission, as did the agent who actually made the sale. This left one hundred and twenty thousand per member. Although the earlier sales had been cheaper and the real average was closer to one million, it still came to a total of four billion eight hundred million yen. A large portion of the land for the course was rented, and since at that time it only cost about one hundred million per hole to construct a course, they easily covered their costs. Of course they had borrowed heavily to cover their initial costs, but the sales went smoothly and they were able to pay off their loans on schedule.

This is the authorized version, but at the same time they also sold many memberships without going through Camellia and by selling them at discounted prices they managed to sell another three thousand—which grossed them approximately three billion yen. This they divided between them—the missing three billion that some of the shareholders were complaining about. Nor was this the only fraud they were guilty of. Although it was very easy for them to sell memberships "under the table," there was always the chance that word would get out and they might be asked to repay the guaranty money. They wanted at least to create the impression that they were aboveboard. That was where Camellia came in.

As sole agent for the club, Camellia deserved to be rewarded for signing the members, but really it was the sales agents who found them. Camellia did nothing and there was no reason why it should be paid a margin. Usually the job was done by the sales section of the club itself, but Nasuno saw that this was a good way to increase his profits and set it up as a separate company, leaving Kinumura in charge. Altogether, Camellia showed an income of one thousand four hundred million yen; the running costs for the three years it was in operation came to one hundred million. They had to pay five hundred million in taxes, but this still left eight hundred million, which Nasuno appropriated for his own use. All the major stockholders at the time were connected with Nasuno or Kawai, so nobody complained.

After sales for the Uchibō club ended in 1973, Camellia functioned as an ordinary membership dealer, buying any cheap Uchibō memberships that appeared on the market and dealing in the memberships of other clubs. From 1979 it became the sole representative for the Tanzawa club, and employing several salesgirls, it started to deal in sales aggressively. However, for about ten years Camellia had been functioning with the eight hundred million it had gotten from the Uchibō club, and had no doubt increased this amount, although Kawai had had no idea what was done with the money.

"Kinumura only had to get Nasuno's okay to go and do whatever he wanted with the money," he said suddenly. "So whatever their relationship, it had to be connected with the money somehow."

He had not inquired into what Nasuno did with the eight hundred million he had managed to acquire because Kawai had also acquired approximately the same amount for himself by other means. The land they purchased for the golf course could easily have been bought directly from the owners, but Kawai started a real estate company to deal with it and skimmed a margin off the top of all the sales. The same thing went for the furniture and equipment for the clubhouse, the lawn mowers, the sprinklers, etc. They had all been bought from local dealers he knew for inflated prices and he had received a rebate afterward. In this way both Nasuno and Kawai acquired approximately one billion yen each while still balancing the books.

For ten years they were happy to let things stand as they were, without inquiring too closely into the other's affairs.

"Do you mean to say that now that Nasuno is dead, all that money is Kinumura's to do with as he likes?" Keiko asked, looking up at Kawai, her interest aroused.

"Well, I imagine that after controlling it for the last ten years he probably thinks that it's his money, but I'm afraid that things aren't quite as simple as that. The money might be in Camellia's name, but it really belongs to the Uchibō club." He seemed to have conveniently forgotten about the money he had acquired at the same time. "I also hold stock in Camellia; of course we gave Kinumura a certain amount, but I have more, and if it comes down to it, I can always call a stockholders meeting and force him out. Of course I wouldn't need to do anything so drastic as long as the Tanzawa club sold well, but as things are . . ."

When Nasuno had first brought up the idea of the Tanzawa course, Kawai had been eager to join him. Of course they both knew that things had changed since the oil shock in 1973, but there were still a number of new clubs opening every year and they were eager to repeat the success of the Uchibō club, so they went into it very optimistically. Things, though, had changed much more than they had anticipated.

First there was the land. The new laws on conservation required them to leave a large amount of land wooded, and this meant that they would need almost three hundred acres. Of this almost half would have to be bought, and although they started off buying it at about twenty-four-and-a-half million an acre, some of the landowners held out for a higher price. In the end they spent four billion on the land and another five hundred million to secure the one hundred and forty acres they were able to rent. All in all the land alone set them back four and a half billion yen.

Recently, constructing a course in the Tokyo area costs about four hundred million per hole, but this is only an average figure. In the case of a club like the Tanzawa where most of the land is very steep, leveling is expensive, and as the club was near a residential area, they had to ensure that there was no fire hazard. They finally came to an

agreement with the general contractor at a figure of four
billion, excluding the landscaping, and this meant that with
the price of the land they would have to pay eight and a
half billion before they even started work on the course
itself. After that there was the clubhouse, the services, and
the landscaping to pay for. All in all they would have to
invest about ten billion yen before they could even start.

At the beginning they agreed that each should invest one
billion and they also managed to borrow a further two
billion from the banks, although in order to do so they had
to use the Uchibō club as collateral—a fact they withheld
from the members. This gave them a total of four billion;
they were relying on the money they would collect from
the new members to make up the rest. They started advertising for members even before they received permission from the local council to open the club, and they
anticipated having about three thousand members by the
time that the club opened.

This was where they had made their biggest mistake. It
was already three months since the provisional opening
and they had only managed to get twelve hundred members. The members had had to pay three million five hundred thousand yen guaranty and three hundred thousand
for membership; of this seven hundred thousand went to
the sales agent, and Camellia, which this time was working at cost, took another hundred thousand or so, which
left three million. Not all of the members had paid the full
price, however, and they only managed to collect about
three billion—which left them three billion short. They
owed the general contractor approximately one and a half
billion, but they planned to postpone payment for as long
as possible and then palm the workers off with memberships instead of money. They had intended to swindle
Wakashiba Landscaping, Inc., and the people who outfit-
ted the clubhouse from the beginning, but that still left the
money they owed for the land. This came to about one
and a half billion yen, and payment was due when work
on the course was finished. Usually work does not start
on a golf course until all the land has been bought and
paid for, but in this case they had agreed to defer payment
until after work was completed. This was now due and it

could not be delayed any longer; if the owners applied for a court order, they could seize the land and the club would be unable to open.

Nasuno and Kawai had managed to delay the payment for a while, saying that the landscaping had not been completed satisfactorily, but already some of the landowners were threatening to go to court, so they had met and agreed to invest another seven hundred and fifty million each. This way they could pay off the debt during October.

Kawai could still remember that late-September day. Nasuno had come to his room, and although they had never discussed their private finances before, Nasuno told him all about Camellia and his other investments. Sixteen days later he was dead, and Kawai wondered if he had had some kind of premonition.

He looked out of the window at the fog, which was swallowing up the city and mixing the neon lights. His bare skin seemed cold against the blanket.

"I wonder where Ōkita is hiding," he said.

"Do you think that his suicide at Lake Tazawa was really a fake?"

"I don't know."

"Maybe he went abroad."

"No, I think that would have been impossible, but he didn't strike me as the suicidal type."

He thought back to the day after Nasuno's death when Ōkita had come to his office. At first glance he seemed quiet and intellectual, but he had been a tough man to deal with.

When Nasuno had seen the general contractor's estimate, he suggested that a small company do the landscaping to keep costs down. Then, when the work was finished, they could postpone payment until the landscapers agreed to settle for about half of the original fee. Kinumura mentioned one of his college friends who ran such a company, and so it was decided that the work should go to Ōkita. Kawai worked a similar scam on the furniture and fittings for the clubhouse but had had nothing to do with the landscaping.

"If he hasn't committed suicide, they'll catch him in the end," Keiko said, turning toward him and moving her hand up his chest. "But when you think of it, it was lucky for you that he decided to disappear like that, wasn't it?"

"What's that supposed to mean?"

"Well, if he hadn't disappeared like that, you'd probably have had the police hanging around you as well, which could have been a little inconvenient."

"The same could be said for a lot of people. Kuretani, for one, must have been very relieved." He put his arms around her, then paused and looked out the window again. "Oh, yes, Ōkita's wife came to the funeral, you know."

"Really? You mean that the wife of the man who killed Mr. Nasuno actually came to his funeral? I wonder why."

"She was only there for a short time. I did not know who she was, but when I asked afterward, I was told that it was Ōkita's wife."

"What do you think she wanted?"

"I don't know."

He moved over on top of her and kissed her neck, then moved down to her breast. As he did so his hands started to move over her body, but this failed to excite him as it usually did; he had too much on his mind. He glanced over at the clock by the bed and noticed that it was 9:25. He decided to leave by ten o'clock. He was a great believer in going to bed early and rarely stayed at Keiko's condominium past eleven o'clock.

Risaburō's Kawai's house was in Kamiogi in the Suginami ward of Tokyo, a little to the south of Ōme Avenue. Although the area has become quite built up recently, several small woods and marshes remain, and it still retains something of its old character.

To get to his house you turn off Ōme Avenue into a fairly wide tree-lined street, and about halfway there, you come to a small bar named Pico, which is open until eleven o'clock every night. The walls are painted white, and inside there is only room for a counter and two tables. At night it is lit with orange lights and has a homey feel about it.

On the night of the twentieth the western part of Tokyo was covered with a thick fog, and the Kamiogi area was empty, just the occasional car driving slowly by, its headlights slicing into the heavy mists.

Around 10:25 a man pushed open the door of the Pico bar and walked in. He was wearing a black windbreaker with the hood up and dark sunglasses; in one hand he carried a long thin bag that looked as if it contained a golf club. He kept the other hand in his pocket.

There were four other customers at the counter, drinking and chatting with the young couple who ran the place. Three were students and one was an artist; they all lived nearby and were regulars there. They all looked up when the man entered and were rather surprised that he didn't remove his hood. He went straight over to one of the tables and sat down in the shadows, then he took out a cigarette and sat smoking it, his head bowed. The landlord's wife went over with a hand towel and a glass of water.

"Hello, it's ice cold out today, isn't it?" she said in a friendly way, but he didn't even look up at her.

"Scotch and water."

She went back to the counter, then returned with the drink and a small dish of peanuts.

When she finally moved away, he gave a deep sigh, removed his hood, and took a deep drag on his cigarette. He sat with his back half turned to the counter, looking out of the window for the time it took him to smoke two cigarettes, his only movement an occasional raising of his glass to his mouth. The windows were all steamed up, but there was nothing to be seen outside except the heavy mist floating across the street. This did not deter the man, who seemed to be waiting for something and kept his eyes fixed on the window. The other customers continued chatting to the landlord and his wife, but his brooding figure seemed to cast a pall over the evening.

They all assumed that he was waiting for someone, but at 10:35 he suddenly stood up, leaving his drink unfinished. He put his hood up and walked over to the cash register at one end of the counter; the landlord's wife went over to him.

"That will be six hundred yen, please," she said in a pleasant voice.

He put a five-thousand-yen note down on the counter

and she noticed that he was wearing leather gloves. While he was waiting for his change, he used the pay phone. He covered the receiver with his hand and started to talk in a low voice.

"Hello? Oh, hello, it's me." He raised his voice a little. "It's me, can't you tell, Kōsuke . . . that's right."

He looked over his shoulder at the landlord's wife, obviously uneasy about being overheard, so she hurried back to the other customers. He turned his back to them and continued to talk, then put the phone down and picked up his change.

"Good night."

"Come again."

The man ignored their farewells and pushed his way out into the night.

The man was next seen at a twenty-four-hour Laundromat about two hundred yards down the street from the Pico. A young office worker who lived in an apartment nearby was sitting on a seat in front of the washing machines reading a comic while he waited for his wash. He glanced up and saw a man in a black windbreaker with the hood up and dark glasses. The man acted rather furtive, and when he noticed the young office worker, he stopped dead in his tracks for a moment, then walked over to the pay phone that was by the door.

It was a quarter past eleven when Kawai approached Kamiogi in his Mercedes. He would be fifty-three this year and he had two mistresses. He had bought the condominium in Ōkubo for Keiko Tani a year before and his other mistress ran a bar in the Ginza area. He usually visited them both once or twice a week, although he very rarely stayed the night with either of them. He wasn't scared of his wife; he simply slept better in his own bed. Recently he had the added pleasure of playing with his grandson in the morning before he went to work. Kawai's twenty-seven-year-old son lived with them and ran the hotel, parking lots, and rental buildings that Kawai owned in Chiba city. Kawai was originally from Chiba, so it was only natural that his business interests were mostly centered around that area. A year ago his first grandson had been born, and Kawai thought it the best thing that had ever happened to him. His eldest daughter, who had married an office worker and lived in Hodogaya, had had a daughter soon afterward, and she often brought her to visit on the weekends. His youngest daughter had only gotten married in June, to a man who worked for an airline company, and they now lived in Sapporo, but she had telephoned this week to say that she was already three months pregnant.

He was delighted by his grandchildren; they made him feel really pleased to be alive. He regretted Nasuno's death, but at the same time he couldn't help feeling it had been the man's own fault. He should have been more careful. As he drove along that night, he found that his grief over Nasuno's death and his feelings of guilt toward Kōsuke were diminishing. He had come out the winner but still couldn't afford to let his guard down. There were still Kuretani and his men to deal with and he knew that he'd have to force them out of the Tanzawa club soon.

He turned off Ōme Avenue and headed toward his home. He was late tonight and his grandson would already be in bed. When he thought of his grandchildren, he felt that no matter how much money he left them when he died, it would never be too much.

The farther he drove from the city center, the thicker the fog became. The cedar trees on either side of the road seemed to be floating on a sea of mist. He slowed down and continued carefully down the street, noticing that the Pico bar, which was usually open when he passed, was already closed for the night. Looking down at the car clock, he saw that it was 11:17. It was unusual for him to be this late. For some reason Keiko had not wanted him to leave, and with all the fog he had had to drive slower than usual.

He turned left after the Pico. The houses on both sides of the street were set back from the road behind fences or hedges and there was only the occasional light shining weakly through the fog. Visibility was only a few yards as he turned left again; his gate was at the end of the street. The gravel road up which Kawai drove his silver Mercedes was less than four yards wide. He braked suddenly. There, only about two yards in front of the car, was a tricycle that some child had left in the middle of the road.

He looked on either side of the road. On the right side there was the fence of the corner house and on the left a dark grove of trees. He opened the door and got out. There was nobody in sight. He walked over to the tricycle and saw that it was very rusty and broken. As he bent down to grasp the handlebars he heard a noise—whether it was a footfall or what he was not sure—and then something moved in front of the headlights. He looked up and saw what looked like a man in a black windbreaker with the hood up and dark glasses, but he couldn't make out his features. The figure stepped forward and Kawai saw to his horror that he held what looked like a golf club. He approached the motionless Kawai in silence.

"Wh-who are you?"

The man halted in front of him and stood in silence for a few moments. "Kōsuke Ōkita," he finally whispered.

"Ō-Ōkita . . ."

Kawai wanted to cry out for help, he wanted to run, but his body wouldn't obey him. The next moment the dark shadow raised the golf club and brought it down savagely. Kawai fell to the ground and the next blow hit him in the head. His face seemed to be glued to the road. As his consciousness started to dim, his lips finally moved.

"No . . . no . . . that was all Nasuno's idea. . . ."

# 14

# A Sudden Turn

IT WAS ESTIMATED THAT THE FINGER THAT WAS delivered to Kōsuke's house had been amputated three to five days before it was examined by the police surgeon. They had no way of telling how it had been preserved before it was put into the parcel, which was why they allowed two days leeway, but either way, it meant that Kōsuke had been killed between October 15 and 17. He had last been spotted on a bus at Lake Tazawa on the morning of the thirteenth and it was assumed that he had continued to elude the police until he was kidnapped. The kidnappers then murdered him and probably disposed of the body immediately.

When Momozaki got the report over the radio at Kō-suke's house he decided that it was very unlikely that they would hear from the kidnappers that night. He had not really expected them to contact Shimako by phone at all, but he had set things up so any call could be traced just in case.

He told her that it would not be necessary for her to wait by the phone any longer and he realized that it would be hopeless to expect her to anyway as she seemed to be at the end of her tether. Ever since she had heard that

Kōsuke was dead, she had lain on the bed with her head buried in the bedclothes, and every so often her body was racked by heavy sobs.

"You just go and lie down in another room, I'll have one of my men stand by the phone."

"But what if they should phone?" Kinumura asked in a low voice.

"In that case the detective will pretend to be the lodger and ask them what they want. I admit that there's a chance that they'll become suspicious, but that can't be helped. It will be in the press tomorrow anyway."

Shimako was completely exhausted and Tome had to help her out of the room. Momozaki left three detectives, one by the radio and two by the telephone. He, too, decided to call it a day and left the house with Kinumura.

"Thank you for staying to help," Momozaki said as they were about to part.

"Not at all, but what's going to happen now?"

"We'll have to stop our present search for Ōkita and try to find his body instead," Momozaki answered disappointedly.

It was nine o'clock when Momozaki left the Ōkitas' house and headed back to the Himonya station. The wind had dropped and to his surprise a heavy fog was blanketing the capital. By the time he got back to the station, his superior from Central HQ had also arrived and was waiting for him so they could hold a meeting and decide how to proceed with the case.

It was decided that there was no point in keeping it a secret from the press any longer as they were sure to get wind of it anyway, so they called a press conference for 10:30.

The reporters still had no idea what had been happening, and when they heard about the press conference, they all guessed that it was because Kōsuke had been arrested somewhere.

"This afternoon at twelve-twenty, an express letter arrived at Kōsuke Ōkita's house in Kinuta, Setagaya ward, from an Ichizō Tanaka at two-seventeen Sakai, Naka-ku, Nagoya. . . ."

Momozaki went on to explain the contents of the letter,

and when he held it up for them to see, there was a loud clicking of camera shutters.

"At two o'clock an express package arrived from the same sender. It contained a man's little finger wrapped in gauze. Approximately one and a half hours later, at three-thirty P.M., our men, who were keeping the house under observation, were informed."

There was a brief outburst from the reporters, then everyone became silent as they waited for him to continue.

"A team of our men went to the house and arranged to have any incoming calls traced and at the same time the finger was sent to headquarters to be examined. We compared it with the examples we have of Ōkita's fingerprints and are now able to state, beyond a shadow of doubt, that it did indeed belong to him."

There was another excited outburst and one of the reporters at the back, unable to wait, called out, "What condition was the finger in?"

"It had been amputated between the first and second joints. The instrument used is thought to have been a carving knife, but it wasn't very sharp and there was a certain amount of damage to the tissue surrounding the cut.

"We had the finger sent to a university hospital for a more detailed examination." He paused for a minute before giving the result. "The doctor in charge of the examination is an expert in his field, and after a careful study he stated that it had been amputated after death."

"After death? Do you mean to say that Kōsuke Ōkita is dead?"

"Yes, we can only assume that Ōkita's been murdered and our investigations will now concentrate on finding his body and whoever it was who was responsible."

He could not help showing the disappointment he felt. Even if they managed to find the men who had killed Kōsuke, they'd never be able to learn the details of Nasuno's murder or whether in fact Kōsuke was really the murderer.

"Maybe that was why he was murdered," said a small voice, insinuating itself into his brain.

"Can you give us some idea as to how you intend to proceed with this case?"

He paused for a moment, then answered in a calm voice.

"Ōkita disappeared from the hotel at Lake Tazawa on the night of the twelfth and we have several witnesses who report having seen him on a bus the following morning. We intend to follow the trail he left after he disappeared and feel confident that it will lead us to whoever it was who kidnapped him. At the same time we will continue with our investigations of the letter and the package. Ōkita's wife says that she has never heard of the sender before and so do the people at his office. We checked the address, and it turns out to be that of a park in the city, so we are assuming that whoever it was used a false name and address. However, we feel it is likely that he has some connection with Nagoya, at the very least he or one of his confederates had to appear at the Nagoya Central Post Office on the afternoon of the nineteenth, so we intend to ask the Aichi prefectural police to help us investigate that end."

"Do you have any leads at the moment?"

"No, I'm afraid not."

"Do you think that the murder was done for the ransom?"

"I'm afraid that we are not in a situation to say at the moment."

He answered very noncommittally, but his personal opinion was that a kidnapper who sent a ransom demand to the house of a wanted man, and then sent the little finger of a dead man as proof, was not only very violent but very stupid, too.

"Do you think they'll try to contact Ōkita's wife again?"

"I don't know, but we have men standing by just in case."

However, there was no contact that night, and the following morning the course of the investigation took a sudden turn.

That morning Kawai's wife, Machiko, woke up at five o'clock and looked over at the bed next to her. It was just as she had made it the night before.

So he didn't come home after all, she thought irritably.

She knew all about the two women her husband kept in town. When he was younger he was always one for the women and they used to have endless arguments about it, but when they reached their midforties she just gave up complaining about it. She realized that she should be thankful that he didn't move in with a younger woman or that he hadn't had any other children, so she just kept quiet and counted her blessings.

At about the same time that she stopped complaining, Kawai stopped staying out all night. They had enlarged the house when their son was married so he could live with them, and after their first grandchild was born Kawai couldn't wait to come home just to see it. This was not to say that he never stayed away all night—sometimes he would telephone to say that he would be away for the night on business, but she had no way of telling if it was really business that kept him busy.

Last night she had been unable to sleep. She finally managed to doze off, however, and when she looked at the clock she saw that it was five past five.

He could at least have phoned, she thought angrily. She had put the phone through to the bedroom before she went to bed, so she knew there was no way she hadn't heard it if it rang. She wondered where he had spent the night and guessed that it was with that woman who ran a bar in Ginza. He had been seeing her for a long time and he still seemed to be having a relationship with her.

It was still dark outside and she tried to go back to sleep, but it was hopeless. At six o'clock it started to get light, and getting up, she put on a skirt, cardigan, and some thick socks before venturing out onto the landing. The house was in the suburbs and it was two or three degrees colder than in Tokyo, so it was quite chilly still. She tiptoed past her son's room, but there was not a sound to be heard. Their son, who had taken over the businesses her husband had started before he became involved in the golf club, didn't have to get up as early as the average office worker. As a result his wife and child also slept late every day.

She put on a pair of sandals and opened the front door. She wanted to make sure that the car was not in the garage. She was still scared after what had happened to her husband's partner, Nasuno.

It was colder outside than she had expected and she clutched her cardigan to her as she walked through the front garden. The fog of the night before had cleared away, but there was still a light morning mist. The door of the concrete garage on one side of the house was open; she could see her son's white Skyline, but there was no sign of her husband's silver Mercedes.

She walked over to the garage and stood gazing at the empty space for a few minutes. She turned back to the house, then changed her mind and walked over to the front gate. Her son had purposely left the wrought-iron gate unlocked, but as Kawai had not returned, it still remained open.

Machiko walked out of the gate and down the gravel hill—why, she didn't know. Just to be sure, she thought, and anyway she found the cool air strangely bracing. The road was only about twelve feet wide and the houses on both sides were surrounded with high fences or hedges. At this time of the day the area was still quiet and looked deserted.

She walked down to the main road. There was the wooden fence of a house on the right and a small grove of trees with some wasteland behind it on the left. The day became brighter as she walked and she noticed a child's small tricycle lying in the weeds in front of the trees. She wondered who it could belong to as there were no young children living nearby. As she drew closer she saw that it was broken and rusty, and frowning, she realized that someone must have dumped it there.

The wasteland was still filled with mist, but when she looked into it, she saw to her surprise that there was a car hidden among the high weeds, shining brightly in the sun. She made her way toward it, hardly believing her eyes, and felt her pulse thunder in her ears as she realized that it was her husband's car. She couldn't see the license, but she felt sure she recognized the golf magazine lying on the back shelf.

She went up to the driver's side and looked in. All the windows were shut and nobody was inside, but the door was not closed properly and the keys were still in the ignition. A brown leather briefcase was laying on the passenger seat; it was the case that Kawai always carried with him.

She walked around the front of the car and stopped dead in her tracks. A man in a gray suit was lying facedown in the grass next to the passenger door, his arms stretched out in front of him. His head was buried in the weeds, but she could tell who it was even from behind.

"Oh . . ." she said. "Oh . . ." Her voice failed her and she ran to the man's side. She shook him and called out his name, but there was no answer. When she pulled him up into a sitting position, she noticed for the first time that the top of his head and the area behind his ear were covered with blood. His face was an unnatural gray and there were bloodstains under his blank eyes. His shoulders that she was clutching also felt strangely stiff.

A scream finally escaped her lips and she ran back to the house, stumbling as she went. She woke her son and his wife and he ran back to the wasteland to check. When he realized that his mother had not been wrong, he hurried back and telephoned the police station, which was just on the other side of Ōme Avenue. Kawai had always said that the area was so quiet at night that it was dangerous and he had pasted the number of the police station on the wall above the phone.

It was a little after 6:30 when detectives and members of the identification section arrived from Ogikubo police station. The assistant inspector who had been in charge of the night shift, a man in his midthirties, accompanied the identification team when they went to study the body.

Kawai had been hit three times, on the forehead, the crown, and behind the left ear. The wounds were all open and there had been heavy bleeding. The assailant had used a length of pipe or a similar blunt object, but there was no sign of the weapon in the vicinity of the body. Rigor mortis had already started in the arms, legs, and neck, and the face showed death spots that did not disappear when the body was moved, so it was reckoned that between six and eight hours had passed since the time of death.

"It would appear that the body was moved here from

the road, sir," said one of the men, who had been ordered to search the surrounding area for clues. "There are bloodstains on the road and spots of blood on the earth and grass between here and there."

The body also showed signs of having been dragged there; the front of Kawai's gray suit had muddy streaks running down it and bits of grass and gravel had stuck to the fabric. They went to look at the spot that the constable had found and saw that there was a large amount of blood there. It was farther down the hill, just in from the asphalt road, and they wondered if he had been attacked there. On one side there was the fence of an old house and on the other there was a copse of trees with a nine-foot-wide track leading through it to the wasteland where the body had been found.

On one side of the road, among a tangle of weeds, they found a broken old tricycle and beside it a fresh footprint. Next to the road, on a muddy, sunless strip of ground about a foot in width, which did not have any gravel on it and was not covered by weeds, they found the clear imprint of a large sneaker. One of the officers produced a tape measure.

"Eleven and a half inches—quite a big shoe. The imprint of the sole is still very clear, so I don't think it has been worn much. The footprint looks very fresh, too."

They couldn't say for sure that this footprint belonged to the murderer, but it seemed likely that it did.

They heard from his family that the Mercedes was Kawai's personal car and that he commuted to work in it daily. This meant that he had returned in the car the night before, but although bloodstains were on the road, none were in the car. This could only mean that for some reason Kawai had gotten out of the car at the bottom of the hill and was attacked on the road.

"I suppose the murderer was lying in wait for him to return."

"But why would the victim get out of his car?" another of the officers countered.

"Do you think it was an acquaintance?"

The young officer who had found the tricycle in the weeds had an idea. "If that tricycle had been left in the middle of the road, Kawai would have had to get out and move it before he could continue.''

''That's a point. He drove a big car, so it would be difficult for him to try to drive past without moving it.''

Looking at the narrow road with muddy ditches on either side, two or three other detectives also nodded in agreement. If one accepted the theory that the murderer used the tricycle as a trap, then the footprint they had found beside it seemed even more likely to belong to the murderer. The shoe had been eleven and a half inches long and four inches wide at the widest point, so it must have been a big man who had been wearing it.

The men from the first division at Central Headquarters arrived and the investigation began in earnest. They interviewed the family, and what they heard only strengthened the tricycle theory.

''After what happened to Mr. Nasuno my husband had been very careful. It's very unlikely that he would get out of the car under normal circumstances.''

Kawai's wife Machiko was plump and fifty-one, two years younger than her husband. She seemed to be very much in control of her emotions and answered the detectives questions quite calmly.

''He was always a very wary man, and after what happened to Mr. Nasuno he was even more careful. He said that he now had two golf clubs to run and he could never tell where there might be enemies waiting for him. He always told me that he couldn't trust anyone.''

''So if he had seen an acquaintance waiting for him on the road when he came home last night, you think it unlikely that he would have got out to talk to him?''

''Yes, very. He very rarely invited any of his business associates back here, and if it was something urgent, they would telephone first and arrange to see him.'' She stared into space, imagining the things the detective suggested. ''If my husband had come home and found someone hanging around outside waiting for him, I think he'd have been very suspicious indeed.''

The detective nodded understandingly; he knew a lot of rich men were paranoid about safety, but this meant that the perpetrator was not necessarily someone who knew Kawai.

"Did you notice an old tricycle lying by the entrance to the wasteland?"

The inspector and another detective were sitting in a large reception room next to the front door. The inspector was looking out into the front garden as he questioned her.

"Yes," Machiko replied without hesitation.

"Has it been there long?"

"No. I saw it for the first time this morning. There aren't many children small enough to ride a tricycle in this area."

"One of the wheels is coming off; no one could ride it now," said the other detective. "I think someone must have found it dumped somewhere and brought it here."

"Now that you mention it, there's a place near here where all sorts of things like that are dumped." Machiko described a large ditch on the other side of the wasteland that could be seen from the main road.

The murderer could easily have found the tricycle there, brought it over, put it in the middle of the road, and then lain in wait for Kawai to return. Afterward he drove the car into the wasteland and dragged the body in there to try to delay discovery as long as possible. If the murderer had been working alone, this scenario seemed very likely, but if there had been a gang of them, one of them only had to stand in the middle of the road to stop the car and then the others could have dragged Kawai out of the car and killed him.

"Did your husband keep the driver's door locked when he drove?"

"I don't know."

When the car was found in the wasteland, the passenger door and the rear doors had been locked and only the driver's door had been left unlocked.

"You didn't hear a car horn blowing last night, did you?"

"No, not at all."

"What time did he intend to come home?"

"I don't know for sure, but it would be after nine o'clock. In the morning he told me he wouldn't be in for supper." Kawai always liked to eat his evening meal by nine o'clock; he said that it was bad for his digestion to eat later than that, and if he thought he was going to be late, he would have something out. "He usually came home by eleven o'clock, though."

"Did he talk about business much at home?"

"No, never."

Apparently he didn't talk about it to his son either.

"Were there any people at work or socially who he talked about business with?"

"I don't think so, although he used to get on very well with Mr. Nasuno."

"Excuse me for asking," the inspector said, looking embarrassed, "but did he have any, er . . . female friends?"

Machiko dropped her eyes and bit her lip. She was silent for a few moments, then she took a short breath. "There would appear to have been two people like that."

She told them that one ran a bar in Ginza and that the other was a young woman who sold memberships for the golf club. Machiko's cousin's daughter worked for the Tanzawa golf club and she passed on all the rumors she heard.

"His grandson will have his first birthday soon," she said abruptly. "Recently Risaburō seemed to prefer him to all his women friends; in fact maybe his grandson was the only person he really trusted."

The inspector then interviewed Kawai's son, Kōichiro, and his wife. Kōichiro was twenty-seven and skinny, but he had inherited his father's shifty eyes.

"I went to the office in Chiba yesterday, and when I came home at about nine-thirty I saw that Father was still out, so I left the front gate open."

He had gone to bed at about eleven o'clock but had not heard a car horn or any voices. It was unlikely that he would have heard the sound of the car's engine from the house.

"There was an unusually heavy fog last night and the whole area seemed strangely quiet." He gazed into space as he spoke, as if he were imagining the mysterious murderer looming up out of the fog.

From the family's statements, the police guessed that the murder took place sometime after 9:30.

While the family of the victim was being questioned, the other detectives were checking the neighbors to see if they had heard anything suspicious. The Pico bar opened at ten in the morning, and when two of the local detectives arrived there, the morning mists had completely disappeared and the sun was shining brightly on the white building. The blinds had only been opened a few minutes before the police arrived, so there were still no customers, just the landlord and his wife. They were both about twenty-seven or -eight and were very surprised when they saw the policemen's identity cards and heard why they were there.

"We think it happened sometime after nine o'clock last night and we wondered if you could help us. Did you hear any screams or see anyone suspicious?"

Instead of answering, the landlord asked them a question of his own. "This Kawai, he was the vice-president of a golf club, wasn't he?"

"Yes."

"The Tanzawa Country Club, wasn't it? We read about the case in the papers this morning."

He and his wife looked at each other in astonishment and so did the police. That morning the newspapers had carried the story of Kōsuke's kidnapping and the report that he was dead on their front pages.

"At the moment we don't know if there's any connection between this and the Nasuno case," the younger of the two detectives said, but the landlord and his wife continued to look at each other in silence.

"You were open until eleven o'clock last night, weren't you?"

"Yes, we closed at a little after eleven."

"Did you have many customers?"

"About the same as usual, a few students and office workers who live nearby. They were all regulars—" He broke off suddenly and looked toward his wife again. They seemed to be holding a silent conversation. It was she who spoke first.

"Now that you mention it, there was a rather strange man in here last night."

"Strange? In what way?" the elder officer asked. This time it was the landlord who took up the story.

"Well, as a rule we only get regulars in here after ten o'clock at night, but last night a customer came in here at about ten-thirty and neither of us had seen him before."

"Was it a man?"

"Yes, he was wearing a black windbreaker with the hood up like this. . . ." The wife used both hands to show what the hood had looked like.

"He was wearing large dark glasses and was alone. He seemed a bit strange."

Last night had been foggy, but it had not been raining or especially cold, so it seemed odd to the detectives that the man should have walked into the bar with his hood up. They started asking for particulars and it soon became apparent that the wife had had the most contact with the man.

"He sat at that table over there and ordered a scotch and water. He sat facing the window, as if he didn't want his face to be seen and it wasn't until I had given him his drink that he removed his hood."

"Was he carrying anything with him?"

"Yeah, right, now that you mention it, he was carrying a long thin case that looked as if it contained a golf club or something."

"A golf club?"

This was too much of a coincidence and immediately brought to mind the Nasuno case. The injuries were similar, and if what she said was true, so were the murder weapons.

"What time did this man leave here?"

"He only stayed long enough to drink one scotch and then soon left. I think it must have been about ten-forty."

"Which direction did he go in after he left?"

"No, just a minute, he made a phone call before he left."

"Are you sure?" the detective asked tensely.

"Yes, over there." She nodded toward the pay phone by the door. "I was doing his bill. . . ." It all seemed to come back to her as she spoke. "He had one scotch and water, and when I asked for six hundred yen he paid with a five-thousand note. Oh, yes, he was wearing black leather gloves.''

"Hmm, gloves . . .''

"He made the call while he was waiting for his change.''

"What did he say, could you hear anything?''

"No, he had his hand around the receiver and was mumbling. He made it obvious that he didn't want to be overheard, so I just left his change and went back to the other customers.''

"So you were unable to hear anything at all?''

She didn't answer right away but stood staring at the phone in silence as she struggled to remember. "He seemed to be phoning someone he knew well. I'm almost positive that he said 'Hello, it's me. . . .' ''

"Yes, then what?''

"I remember he said 'It's me . . . Kōsuke.' I'm certain that's what he said.''

"But Kōsuke was the name . . .''

The landlord looked from his wife to the younger detective, who was obviously making an effort to remain calm.

"That's right, Ōkita's name was Kōsuke, but are you sure that the man said that that was his name?''

"Yes, he said his name and then indicated that he wanted me to go away.''

The two detectives exchanged a glance.

"And how about you, sir, did you hear what he said?''

"No, I was over here behind the counter talking to the other customers.''

They checked the time that the man had been in the bar, and after talking it over, the couple came to the conclusion that it was between 10:25 and 10:40. They then asked the names and addresses of the customers who had been there at the same time and left the bar.

"But it can't be!'' one of the detectives said angrily when they got outside

"Do you think she made a mistake or was it just a coincidence?''

"I don't know, but I do know one thing. It could not have been Kōsuke Ōkita. . . . He was already dead!''

# 15

# A Dead Man's Crime

THE NEWS THAT KŌSUKE ŌKITA HAD BEEN KID-
napped while he was on the run and later murdered was
announced at the Himonya police station at 9:30 on the
evening of the twentieth and it appeared on the eleven
o'clock news on TV and radio that night.

Next morning the news appeared again in more detail
and the morning papers also carried the story along with
photographs of the ransom note. That same morning Risaburō Kawai's body was found near his home. Obviously
there was some connection between this murder and those
of Nasuno and Kōsuke, but the police couldn't tell what
it was, and so it was decided to open a new murder headquarters at the Ogikubo police station to investigate this
case.

At eleven o'clock, about forty minutes after the two
detectives had finished their inquiries at the Pico, a young
man phoned the police station and asked for the chief detective. Cases like these always provoked a flurry of telephone calls from the public with various tips and
information. Most of them were quite coincidental and
some of them were just hoaxes, but the police couldn't

188

afford to ignore any of them, so the detective in charge of the investigation took the call.

"Oh hello, my name is Sawada, I live at two Kita-cho, Nishiogi. . . ."

The detective leaned forward in anticipation. People who give their name and address first tend to give the most reliable tips.

"I just heard about the murder at Kamiogi on the car radio and . . . well, something happened last night and I wondered at the time whether I should tell you about it."

"I see. Could you be a little more precise?"

"Yes. You see, I work for a firm that makes kitchen appliances and as my home is in Kyūshū, I'm living in the company's dormitory."

That explained his accent, which the detective had not been able to place.

"Last night I went to a nearby Laundromat at around ten-thirty to wash my baseball uniform as the washing machine in the dormitory can't handle much at one time."

"I see."

"I was sitting there alone reading a magazine for about ten minutes when a man suddenly came in. He gave me quite a shock. He wasn't carrying any laundry and he was rather strangely dressed."

"What exactly was he wearing?"

"It was a kind of black windbreaker and he had the hood up; also he was wearing sunglasses even though it was dark outside."

"You say he had the hood up?"

"Yes, it was really foggy last night, and when he appeared out of the fog dressed like that he really scared me, although he seemed equally surprised to see me. The Laundromat is open twenty-four hours a day, but it's usually empty at night and he obviously didn't expect to find anyone there."

"Are you sure he didn't just come to do some laundry?"

"Yes, when he saw me, he sort of turned away and hurried over to the telephone."

Sawada explained how the man had crouched over the phone and dialed a number. He soon started talking, and although he kept his voice low, it was very quiet in the Laundromat and he had been able to hear fragments of the conversation.

"First of all he said 'This is Ōkita.' I'm quite sure that was what he said. He repeated it twice."

"So the man said 'This is Ōkita'; anything else?" When the detective repeated the man's words, the other people around him looked up in surprise.

"Yes, he seemed to be talking about work. He sounded like he was talking to a nursery gardener or something. I heard him mention the price of turf and seedlings, but I could only hear fragments of what he was saying. I got the impression that he knew the other party very well, though. He spoke for two or three minutes, then he suddenly hung up and hurried out into the fog."

"I see; and how old would you say he was?"

"It's hard to say as his face was hidden by the hood and the sunglasses, but judging by his build, I'd say he was in his thirties or forties."

"How tall would you say he was?"

"Well, it might be due to his hood, but I got the impression that he was very tall."

"Can you remember anything else? The color of his trousers? What kind of shoes he was wearing? Anything at all would be a great help."

The man was silent for a few minutes while he thought about it. "Yes, I think he was wearing sneakers."

"Are you sure?"

"Yes. When he said his name, I knew there was something, but I couldn't remember what. Then, when I got back to my room, I remembered about the murder of the golf club owner and wondered if I should contact you. I decided to leave it, but when I heard about the murder in Kamiogi on the radio, I realized that it was near where I had seen the man and thought that you should know."

The detective thanked him and checked his address once more. He put the phone down and turned to the other detectives, who were all sitting watching him.

"He says that Ōkita appeared out of the fog. . . ."

* * *

The investigation of the Tanzawa and Uchibō golf clubs started in earnest, and one of the things that soon came to light was Kawai's weakness for women. Although he didn't look it, he was very popular with women and made no secret of his various relationships. The longest running of these affairs was with the owner of a bar in Ginza, and there was also a young woman who worked at Camellia, who he kept in a condominium in Shinjuku. They checked with Camellia and soon learned that her name was Keiko Tani and that she was twenty-eight years old.

It was a little before noon on the twenty-first when the detectives turned up at the office looking for her, but they were informed that she had not appeared that day. There were about twenty girls working there and they started at 9:30 in the morning. They sometimes had appointments with their customers first thing in the morning, but if that was the case, they were supposed to phone in and explain where they were. But nobody had heard anything from Keiko.

The police went to her residence, which turned out to be a middle-class rental condominium. Her rooms were on the seventh floor, with a good view of the Shinjuku skyscrapers. Unlike the night before, it was a lovely, clear day and the sun was glinting off the buildings.

She did not have her name on the door, but they had asked the caretaker which was her apartment. They rang the bell three times, but there was no answer and the door was locked.

Had she taken the day off to go somewhere or had something happened to her due to her connection with Kawai?

"Ms. Tani, are you there?"

The detective knocked on the door, then put his ear to it. He heard a slight movement inside and heaved a sigh of relief.

"Ms. Tani. May we speak to you for a few minutes?"

"Who is it?" came a hoarse voice.

"We are from the Ogikubo police station."

There was another short silence, then the door opened the length of the security chain. Her short hair had a tight curl and her well-proportioned body was wrapped in a colorful gown. The detectives showed her their IDs.

"Excuse us for turning up like this, Ms. Tani, but do you know about the murder?"

She just stood without answering and looked at them with her mouth half open, but the detectives realized that she had heard about it.

"We wondered if you could answer one or two questions for us. . . ."

She closed the door for a minute and removed the chain, then she reluctantly beckoned them in. The drapes were only open a little, but the light that flooded into the room was adequate to show the mess that it was in. They sat down facing her over a table littered with magazines, glasses, an ashtray, and a half-eaten bunch of grapes. The detectives noticed that there were two glasses and two different types of cigarette butts in the ashtray. When they asked her about her relationship with Kawai, she answered quite frankly.

"I moved into this apartment about a year ago and he came to see me—oh, once or twice a week." Her deep voice sounded bored.

"Have you heard that Mr. Kawai was found murdered near his house this morning?" the detective asked again.

"Yes, on the TV." She nodded slightly and bit her lip. The detective suddenly realized that she wasn't bored: she was petrified.

"Mr. Kawai left work a little early last night, at about five o'clock, and his secretary tells us that he didn't have any other business appointments. Did he come to see you?"

He stared at her, and after a moment she nodded. There was no point in her trying to hide it; they could easily find out if they wanted to.

"From what time?"

"We met in the basement of a hotel in Shinjuku at half past five."

They had had a Chinese meal together and then come back to this apartment in his Mercedes at around 7:30. He had left his car in the parking lot in the basement as usual.

"How long did he stay here?"

"He left this room at a little after ten."

"Does he usually leave at that time?"

"Yes. He likes to get back to his house by eleven every night."

"Did he have any telephone calls while he was here?"

"No."

"Did he mention that he would be seeing anyone on his way home?"

"No, not a word."

"What did you talk about while he was here?"

"Nothing in particular."

"You say that he was here for two and a half hours. You must have talked about something."

"We talked about the sales of the Tanzawa club and Mr. Nasuno and things."

"What did he say about Mr. Nasuno?"

"Just that it was a shame what happened to him."

"Is that all?"

"Yes! That's why I said we didn't talk about anything in particular!" she screamed in a shrill voice, sounding like a completely different woman all of a sudden.

"Nothing unusual happened. He went out of that door as he always does. To think that he was killed on his way home—who could have done it? What are you police doing? Why don't you hurry up and catch whoever it was!"

Through their inquiries, the police had managed to build up a fairly complete picture of Kawai's movements up until the time of his death.

According to Keiko Tani, he had left her apartment at a little after ten, so by the time he got to his car in the basement and drove it out, it would have been about ten minutes past. It's only about twelve miles from her condominium to his house, but Ōme Avenue is always crowded after ten at night and it would take between forty and fifty minutes on a normal night. As the night of his death had been unusually foggy, they estimated about an hour. The autopsy put the time of death between eleven and twelve, which tied in exactly with what they knew. The autopsy also showed that he had died of multiple fractures of the skull caused by blows from a blunt object with square sides such as a golf club or a similar weapon. That similarity between the injuries and the fact that the murder occurred outside his home made it impossible not to connect it with the Nasuno murder.

The murderer had waited for him on the road leading to his house, and after Kawai stopped the car, by some subterfuge the murderer go him out and killed him—although how this was done depended on how many assailants there were. After the murder, his body and the car were hidden in the wasteland to delay discovery of the crime for as long as possible. There was no sign of robbery, so it was thought that the murder was committed out of enmity or jealousy.

Nasuno and Kawai had held seventy percent of the stock for the Tanzawa and Uchibō golf clubs between them and most of the remaining stockholders were under their influence. Of course Nasuno's stock would all go to his dependents and the position of president had been left open, but until his death Kawai had been in sole command of the company, and at one point it was suspected that Kawai had killed Nasuno in order to obtain sole control over the three billion yen that was said to be missing from the accounts. Now that Kawai had also become a victim, however, it was thought that they had both been murdered in order that some third party could gain control of the money. They needed to make further inquiries to see just who was in a position to benefit.

With regard to his two lovers, the one in Ginza had been working in her bar at the time of the murder, so she had an alibi, and Keiko Tani said she had gone to bed after Kawai had left and did not know about the murder until she saw a report on the television. The detectives felt inclined to believe her but thought that it would be worth checking out both women's backgrounds just in case.

On the other hand there was the man that the couple who ran the Pico had seen. At first the police had not taken the report very seriously, but after talking with Sawada, the man who had seen a similar figure in the Laundromat, they decided they couldn't ignore it.

"We have interviewed the owners of the bar, the other customers who had been there at the time, and the man Sawada who saw the same figure in the Laundromat a short while afterward,'' Momozaki said, opening his notebook. It was eight o'clock on the evening of the twenty-first and he was holding a conference to bring all the detectives up-to-date on the latest developments in the case. It had been a lovely clear day, but the temperature outside the conference room was now dropping.

The Himonya station was about to start an open investigation of Kōsuke's death that morning when news of Kawai's murder came in. It seemed obvious that there was a connection between all the murders, so that afternoon Momozaki had gone to the Ogikubo station to catch up on events there. Now he was bringing his colleagues up-to-date.

"The man in question arrived at the bar at approximately ten-twenty and remained until ten-forty. During that time he smoked two cigarettes, drank half a glass of scotch and water, and made one telephone call. He turned up next at a Laundromat about two hundred yards away at ten-forty-five and made another phone call from there. He was wearing a black windbreaker with the hood turned up, brown or gray trousers, white sneakers, and was carrying what looked like a golf club in a case."

Several of the detectives gazed into space as they tried to visualize the man.

"He was between five nine and six feet tall, but he was wearing large sunglasses and kept his face averted, so we do not know what he looked like or how old he was. However, all the witnesses think he was somewhere in his thirties or forties. Finally, when he spoke on the telephone, he used the names Kōsuke and Okita."

A number of the detectives in the room were hearing this for the first time and looked perplexed. The description that Momozaki had just given them would have fitted Kōsuke exactly, but . . .

"The man left the Laundromat at ten-fifty, and as it is only a leisurely seven- or eight-minute walk from there to the victim's house, he could have arrived in plenty of time to waylay Mr. Kawai as he returned home. Add to this the fact that the footprint of a sneaker was found in the vicinity and that Mr. Kawai would appear to have been killed with a golf club and I think there is a strong possibility

that this is our murderer. Our colleagues at Ogikubo think
so, too.'' Momozaki paused for a moment and looked
around the room.

''However, the only problem is that the suspect, Kōsuke
Ōkita, died sometime between the fifteenth and the seventeenth of this month.''

Having covered developments in the Kawai murder, the
subject turned to Kōsuke's kidnap and murder. Since the
finger had been delivered to Kōsuke's wife, the investigation had changed course. Until then the object had been
to find Kōsuke and get him to confess to Nasuno's murder,
but now they were concentrating on finding Kōsuke's kidnappers and his body. A detailed explanation of the events
leading up to Nasuno's death could wait.

The investigation had been divided into two parts, one
to trace Kōsuke's route from the time he left the Lake
Tazawa hotel until he was murdered in Nagoya and the
other to find some trace of Kōsuke or his kidnappers in
Nagoya itself. The local police were dealing with this second part, and they had already started to make door-to-
door inquiries among the hotels in the area.

It was still not known whether the kidnapping was the
work of a group of people or just one man, but if it was
one man, he was probably an acquaintance of the victim's
who had offered to hide him and then murdered him when
he got the chance. The police were concentrating on this
at the moment and were questioning everyone who had
contact with the victim; in particular, they were checking
on their alibis for the evening of the nineteenth, as it was
at this time that the letter and package were mailed to
Shimako. If the kidnapper was working alone, he'd had to
go to Nagoya to post them.

''We've checked all his contacts at work and at the Tanzawa golf club, but we still haven't come up with anything,'' the inspector in charge of this side of the
investigation said glumly.

Of course, Kinumura and Kawai had come under special scrutiny, but both of them had airtight alibis. Kawai
had gone out to the Tanzawa course in the afternoon but
had been back at the office at six o'clock and had then

gone out for a meal with his head accountant and the people from the contractors who had done the work on the course. Kinumura had been at Camellia until 6:30 and had more than ten girls willing to back him up. After that he had taken two managers of a travel agency to dinner in Akasaka to try to persuade them to join the Tanzawa club. He had stayed with them until eleven o'clock, as both they and the hostesses of a Roppongi bar could confirm. Neither Kinumura nor Kawai appeared to have been out of Tokyo between the fifteenth and twentieth, and neither of them seemed to have any particular accomplices either.

The only person connected with the Tanzawa club who did not have a firm alibi was Kuretani. Commissioner Yamane nodded to Hida, who had been in charge of questioning him.

"Today I questioned the four so-called editors of his magazine, *Economic Growth*, individually, then I questioned Kuretani himself." Hida had obviously been looking forward to making his report. "Kuretani and the others all say they had nothing to do with Ōkita's kidnapping and were in Tokyo all day on the nineteenth, but none of them are to be trusted. They call themselves editors, but that's a lot of rubbish; one of them's a driver that Kuretani has on loan from the local gang boss—he has a crew cut, carries a knife hidden in his jacket, and is obviously a *yakuza*. Another is the girl who answers the phone, or maybe I should say grandma—she is well over fifty and her son was a gangster who was killed; Kuretani is looking after her as a favor to the gang boss. The other two look respectable enough, but they're swindlers and would think nothing of lying to a policeman.

"Anyway to make a long story short, they all say the same thing: Kuretani was in his office in Daikanyama all day, but when I asked for specific times, who telephoned or who came to visit, their stories all varied slightly, which proves that they're lying. Obviously they're making it all up in order to supply Kuretani with a fake alibi."

"I heard they tried to kidnap Nasuno's daughter earlier on," the commissioner said, and Momozaki took over the story.

"Yes, I went to visit Chiharu, his second daughter, this

afternoon in order to get the details firsthand. Apparently it was on the evening of the twelfth, the day after we took out the warrant on Ōkita. She was walking along a street in Himonya when a group of men who said they were from Kuretani tried to force her into their car. Also, when we were making inquiries around Ōkita's company, we heard that the day before he disappeared, the ninth, he was led away from his office at about eight o'clock in the evening by a group of *yakuzas* and driven off in a car. That would mean that soon after he returned to his office after being interrogated by us, he was forced to go somewhere else, and I think that we can be sure that this was also the work of Kuretani's men."

"I agree," Hida said in his usual confident way, "and I think it likely that Kuretani got in touch with one of the gangs in the Nagoya area that he is connected with and arranged for them to kidnap Ōkita."

Sending Kōsuke's finger to his wife was so typical of the way that *yakuzas* work that even Hida, who had originally suspected Kōsuke of faking his own kidnapping, was convinced that it was the work of Kuretani. They decided to check whether Kuretani or any of his men had been anywhere near Nagoya recently.

"But if it was the work of Kuretani," one of the veteran detectives said doubtfully, "surely he'd have known that we would be able to tell whether the finger had been removed before or after death."

"They were probably banking on Ōkita's wife not coming to us. They'd know that if she did, there wouldn't be much hope of them getting the money anyway."

"It seems a bit unlikely, but I suppose they might think it was worth giving it a try."

"Yes, I agree." Hida leaned forward with excitement. "After all, they're nothing but a group of petty crooks and swindlers. They probably came across Ōkita hiding out somewhere and kidnapped him. However, it would be difficult to keep big man like him prisoner for long, so they killed him and sent his finger to her as proof that they were holding him. When they realized we were still watching the house and had caught wind of what was going on, they changed their plan and one of them dressed up as Ōkita and killed Kawai.''

Everyone looked at him in surprise.

"Do you mean to say you think that Kuretani was responsible for Kawai's murder, too?"

"Why not? People like him are not all that clever and it may not have occurred to him that we would be able to tell that the finger was cut off after death. When he realized that his plan wasn't going to work, he dressed up a man of similar age and build as Ōkita to look like him, then had him kill Kawai, hoping that we would think that Ōkita had escaped and killed Kawai in revenge.''

"So you think that the man who turned up in the bar and the Laundromat was one of Kuretani's men and that he was trying to imitate Ōkita on purpose?"

"When Nasuno was still alive, he often used to give Kuretani money, but when the golf club fell into Kawai's hands, he probably refused to give him any more. However, Kuretani is a stockholder in the club, and he might be planning to try to take it over.''

"I agree that the man who appeared at Kamiogi last night and killed Kawai was trying to make it look as if it was the work of Ōkita,'' the commissioner said. "I don't know whether it was the work of the gang who kidnapped Ōkita or not, but I think it was definitely an attempt to pin the blame on Ōkita because the timing would have seemed to be perfect. At the time of the murder, we still had not announced Ōkita's kidnapping or murder, and I think this is a very important point.'' He stared into space for a moment, then added, "One thing's for sure: Ōkita's finger was removed after he died and dead men do not commit murder.''

The room was silent as they all listened to Yamane's soft, northern accent.

"The news of Ōkita's death did not appear on TV until eleven o'clock, but the man masquerading as Ōkita had shown up in the bar and the Laundromat between ten-twenty-five and ten-fifty. What is more, he tried to draw as much attention to himself as possible by wearing strange clothes, carrying a golf club, and behaving in a suspicious fashion. He then purposely paid his bill with a five-thousand-yen note in order to ensure that the barkeeper would be close by when he said his name was Kōsuke on the phone; then he went to the Laundromat in order to let the office worker Sawada overhear him say that his last name was Ōkita. After he had prepared all his witnesses he proceeded to the Kawai house, where he killed Kawai the same way he killed Nasuno, even going to the trouble to leave a footprint the same size as Okita's, just in case we managed to miss all the other clues.''

A number of the detectives nodded deeply. When it was put like this, it seemed obvious that it had all been planned to throw them off the scent.

"Therefore," Yamane continued, "I think it's safe to say that whoever was responsible didn't know that Ōkita was dead, or if it was one of the kidnappers, they thought they were the only ones who knew. Either way they thought that if they pretended that it was the work of Ōkita, both we and the general public would fall for it.''

"However, as luck would have it, we found out about Ōkita's death a mere two hours before the crime, so all their efforts were wasted," Momozaki said, folding his arms. He thought back to the previous night when the news of Ōkita's death had been radioed through to him at the Ōkitas' house; it had been 8:50.

At that time only a limited number of policemen at HQ and the Himonya station and the people present at the Ōkitas' house had known about Ōkita's death. The general public first heard of it on the eleven o'clock news, although a majority didn't know anything until they woke up the next morning.

Momozaki agreed with the commissioner that the murder had been committed by someone who didn't know that the police already knew that Kōsuke was dead. He cleared his mind of all the ideas he had had about the case and forced himself to think it over again from the beginning. He looked out of the window at the night sky and saw an image of Kōsuke as he had been when they had last met.

# 16

# The Face

Floodlights lit the green net and grass, making the practice range stand out in the dark; the surrounding woods and the fairway stretching away to the south had already been swallowed up in the night. It was raining heavily and the raindrops streaked across the area in front of the bright lights like small comets in the misty night.

Small white balls shot across the open space at regular intervals to hit the opposite net and fall to the earth again. Chiharu kept hitting the balls with machinelike regularity in the deserted range and the sound of her shots filled the air with weak reverberations.

It was November 5 and the place was deserted. The evenings closed in early, and with all the rain they had had that day, no one had even wanted to play until sunset. The lights in the restaurant were already out and only the lobby and the office showed any sign of life. After she had finished her work in the caddie master's office, she had come through to the practice range to hit some balls. She often stayed after work to practice her putting under the watchful eye of the head coach or to come in here and work on her drive, but tonight was different. Tonight she was not interested in her style, she just wanted to immerse herself in something and forget everything else, even if only for a short time. It was the first time she had held a club in two weeks, and though it felt nice to get back to golf again, she wasn't really concentrating, wasn't even interested in where the the balls went.

She had missed work for two weeks with a cold. She managed to rouse herself to attend the Buddhist ceremony for her father on the twenty-first day after his death, but it only made her cold worse and she had spent nearly all the time since then lying in bed unable to move. Nothing like this had ever happened to her before; it only went to show how exhausted she had become, both mentally and physically.

She had first heard about Kōsuke's death on the morning of the twenty-first. She had gotten up early as usual and was listening to the six o'clock news on the radio when they mentioned the kidnapping. She couldn't believe her ears and ran down to see the morning newspaper, but there it was, just as the radio had said. They even had a photograph of Kōsuke and a picture of the pen case that had been sent to Shimako. The newspaper said the pen case had contained one of Kōsuke's fingers, which had been removed after he was dead. She had read the story two or three times. That was all she could remember; the rest was all a blank.

The next thing she could remember was Kinumura telephoning her to see how she was. He told her about Kawai's murder, which had already been reported on the radio, but it was the first that Chiharu had heard about it as she had spent the whole morning locked in her room.

That afternoon, at about three o'clock, Momozaki had come to see her, and her mother had insisted that she come down and see what he wanted. She didn't feel like meeting anyone, but if she had to talk to the police at all, she was glad that it was Momozaki. He had been very kind and understanding after her father's death and she had thought later how lucky they had been. If it had been a different policeman, the whole ordeal could have been a lot worse. When she came down, she found that he was interested in hearing details of her near kidnapping by Kuretani's men after Kōsuke had first disappeared.

"Yes, it was about five-thirty on the evening of, er . . . the twelfth, I think." She frowned and tried to tell him everything in as much detail as possible. "They said that they worked for a magazine called *Economic Growth*, and that their boss wanted to speak to me."

"Did they say what about?"

"They said they also wanted to know where Kōsuke Ōkita had gone and suggested that we pool our information." She told how they had grabbed her by the arms and would have forced her into their car had Kinumura not come along in the nick of time and saved her.

"Was it a complete coincidence, his coming along like that?"

"No, I had telephoned home a short while before and he had answered the phone."

"I see." Momozaki nodded. "To be quite honest with you, I've already talked to Mr. Kinumura about it. He thinks the whole thing may have been done to demonstrate their ignorance of Ōkita's whereabouts, but the way things have turned out, I'm not so sure anymore." The last part of his speech seemed to be addressed to himself.

"Do you think that Kuretani's group was responsible for Ōkita's kidnapping then?" Chiharu had to pronounce each word distinctly in order to keep the tremble out of her voice.

"There is always that possibility. Even if their object was money, Kuretani always said that he was a close friend of your father, and he may have killed Ōkita for revenge. Incidentally, what were you doing in that part of Himonya at that time of the day?"

He had obviously realized she was accosted quite near her house. She thought back to that day; she had just come up with the theory that the phone call Kōsuke had received on the night of the murder might have been made especially to lure him out of the house and so destroy his alibi, and she had decided to go to the coffee bar where the woman was said to have waited in order to try to find out if she really had existed.

"There is a coffee bar called Eri in that street and I just thought that I'd like to visit it."

"Oh, you mean the one that Ōkita visited on the night your father was killed?"

"Yes."

"And did you have any particular reason to want to go there?"

"Well, the newspaper said that the woman who had telephoned Ōkita that night had been in that coffee bar until a few moments before he arrived."

"And you wanted to ask the people there about her?"

Chiharu didn't answer.

"The people in the coffee bar say there was definitely a thin woman in a black raincoat who had left a short while before Ōkita, but I think it was probably just a coincidence. The whole story was probably just an attempt on Ōkita's part to make an alibi."

"But there is another way of looking at it. Perhaps the real murderer had an accomplice who made the phone call for the sole reason of getting Ōkita to leave the house. . . ."

"The real murderer?"

He looked hard at her and she felt that he could read her most secret thoughts. She thought he would admit that her theory had some validity, but he just sat and looked at her in silence. He might seem to be a nice man, but after all he was a policeman and one of the men responsible for the warrant having been taken out on Kōsuke.

She kept thinking about it as she hit the balls into the night. Normally she would watch each ball and correct her swing, but today she just wanted to forget. She kept hitting the balls until her body was drenched with perspiration and eventually all the other thoughts disappeared from her mind. All that remained was a vision of Kōsuke's face, floating before her eyes.

On the twenty-first her temperature rose and she spent the following two weeks in bed. Her temperature rose and fell, but she completely lost her appetite and spent nearly the whole time in bed. The only thing she did every day was check the newspapers for news about Kōsuke. She kept praying for an item saying that they had made a mistake and that his finger had really been amputated while he was still alive or a report that he had been arrested somewhere. Even if he was arrested, she wouldn't care; at least he'd still be alive. However, the investigations of both Kōsuke's kidnapping and Kawai's murder seemed to be going badly.

Two or three days after the story of the kidnapping came out, the owner of a small hotel in the Taito area of Nagoya reported that Kōsuke had stayed there on the fifteenth and sixteenth of October. He had not thought anything of it at the time, but when he read the reports that Kōsuke had been in Nagoya, it occurred to him that he had been a guest in the hotel. After that, however, there was no news at all.

There had been a lot of fuss about the missing three billion at the Uchibō club after Kawai died and it was announced that the public prosecutor's office would investigate the claims, but there were no reports of what happened after that. Several people from the office came to see her mother, but she didn't feel well enough to get up, so she didn't know what they talked about.

She couldn't help but feel amazed at the speed with which the general public lost interest in the case. Every day the newspapers seemed to have some new scandal to interest their readers, and she assumed that they all thought that the case was closed when Kōsuke's finger was delivered and it was assumed that he was dead.

She finally felt well enough to get out of bed on the fourth of November. It was thirty days since her father died and twenty-five days since Kōsuke disappeared. She had lost six and a half pounds and felt very weak, but she decided it was no use sitting around at home moping and went to the Uchibō club the next day.

Even though she knew that Kōsuke was dead, she still refused to believe it until she actually saw his body. The thought that he might have died without being able to clear his name was too much for her to bear, and tears streamed down her cold cheeks to mingle with the rain. She was convinced now that the woman who had called him on the night that her father had died had done so to destroy his alibi, and that he had been killed as a direct result of this.

The wind blew the rain on her until she was soaked from head to foot, but she didn't pause for a minute. She just continued to hit the balls wildly out into the night. She still believed in Kōsuke's innocence, but she had no way to prove it, and her impotence brought fresh tears to her eyes.

The next morning, at ten o'clock, Chiharu boarded the bullet train for Nagoya. The day before, as she drove back from the Uchibō club, she had made up her mind that if she could never see Kōsuke again, the least she could do would be to visit the places that he had before he died.

The rain of the day before had vanished and there was a lot of blue sky visible between the clouds. The train left the tangle of Tokyo streets behind and struck out across the plains toward the west. The mountains to the right of the tracks were the Tanzawa range; already the foliage of the trees that covered them was tinged with the colors of autumn. The rice in the paddy fields on either side of the train had already been harvested and the countryside was preparing for the bitter winter that would soon be upon it.

The Tanzawa golf course was at the eastern foot of the mountains and Chiharu thought with emotion of how her father, who had liked gardening, had said that he wanted to plant lots of beautiful blossoming trees between the fairways and make the course famous for its beauty. She knew that there had been a lot of trouble due to his refusal to pay the contractors, but that was a side of him she had never seen. She only knew him as a kind, handsome man who was always smiling and who would generally let her have her own way.

Although she was not involved directly in the running of the clubs, now that her father and Kawai were no longer in charge, the staff reported to her mother, and she had overheard enough to get a good idea of how things stood. Without Kawai or Nasuno to hold them off, the people who claimed that there was three billion yen missing from the books had become even more vocal in their complaints, and it looked as if the public prosecutor's office or the inland revenue were going to investigate the allegations. Of course Kawai and Nasuno had held seventy percent of the stock between them and this would go to their heirs, but until the question of the missing money was solved they were helpless to do anything. There was also the money owed to the contractors and the owners of the land and allegations from members of the Uchibō club that their guaranty money had been used to construct the Tanzawa club. On top of everything else it looked as if Kuretani was trying to take over the Tanzawa club for his own ends.

The bullet train pulled into Nagoya station at one minute past twelve, and when Chiharu stood on the platform, she found the weather cold but fine. She handed in her ticket and walked along by the mosaic wall toward the main entrance. She passed many other platforms for local trains and expresses; the whole station seemed to be overflowing with people, all hurrying somewhere.

She walked outside and found a large fountain and lines of taxis, all waiting to zoom up to the boarding point before diving out into the fray once more. The whole area was covered with tall buildings, and looking up the street opposite the station, she could see the sun shining brightly behind the haze. The wind was a lot stronger than she had expected and she hugged herself to keep warm. She stood absorbing the view and felt her heart quicken as she thought that Kōsuke had probably stood in exactly the same place and seen the same things.

He had stayed at a cheap hotel in the eastern part of the city on the fifteenth and sixteenth of October, but what he had done on the two previous nights after he disappeared from Lake Tazawa wasn't known. He could have come by plane to Tokyo or Osaka and then taken a train, or he could have come the whole way by train, but either way he would have had to come through the doorway she had just passed and probably stood in this very spot. She wondered if he had chosen to come through during the rush hour when there would be more people about to hide him. When she thought of him, exhausted and red-eyed behind his sunglasses, she felt tears come to her eyes.

She went back into the station to buy a local map, and while she did so, she asked where the central post office was.

"Just turn left down there and it's about a hundred yards away."

She had only asked for reference and was surprised to hear that it was so close. She walked out past the subway entrance into the square, and there, behind the bus terminal, she saw a large, white, six-story building with the words NAGOYA CENTRAL POST OFFICE written vertically on it.

She felt herself drawn to it, and as she walked in through the front door she read a sign saying, THE TWENTY-THIRD OF EVERY MONTH IS LETTER DAY.

She walked in, but unlike the station, the place was almost deserted. Windows 9 and 10 dealt with parcels and at each there was a large set of scales with a postman in a blue uniform sitting behind it. Although the place was almost deserted now, she tried to imagine what it had been like on the evening of the nineteenth when someone had come here just before it closed and posted the package containing Kōsuke's finger to his wife.

The postmen were chatting to each other to pass the time, but when they saw Chiharu staring at them, they eyed her suspiciously. When she felt their eyes on her, she shook her head and walked out again. Proof of Kōsuke's death had definitely been sent from there, but she had not come all the way to Nagoya just to see that.

She walked back to the station. According to the newspaper reports on the twenty-third, Kōsuke was seen on the fifteenth and sixteenth in a small hotel called the Excel, in Yashiro-dai, Meitō ward. The proprietor of the hotel did not pay much attention to the guest at the time, but when he read that Kōsuke had come to Nagoya and had probably been killed there, it occurred to him that his guest may well have been him. The police showed him a picture of Kōsuke, and he said that although the man had been wearing sunglasses when he checked in, he was pretty sure that it was the same man. The clothes that he had been wearing matched those that Kōsuke was reported to have been wearing when he boarded the bus at Tazawa, and apparently the man kept very much to himself, only going out occasionally.

Chiharu opened her map and saw that the Meitō ward

was in the very east of the city near the Nagoya inter-change on the expressway, so she went over to the taxi stand and stood in line.

When she got in she asked for Yashiro-dai and the driver turned on the meter and drove off in silence. There was less traffic on the streets than she had expected and it was not long before they came to a large square with a fountain in it. Chiharu had been to Nagoya once before with her father when she was a student and she seemed to remember that this was the center of the downtown area. They drove through the square without any delays.

"The streets are empty during lunch hour," the driver said suddenly in a loud voice. "Come one o'clock and it will take ages to get through there." When she had first gotten in, he had ignored her, but he sounded very friendly now. "This area has changed a lot recently, you know?"

"Is it far to Yashiro-dai?"

"If we keep up at this pace, we should get there in about thirty minutes."

She looked out of the window, thinking that maybe Kō-suke had also come along this very route, but then she noticed that they were passing subway stations at regular intervals and she guessed that he had probably come by train as that way he was less likely to draw attention to himself. The road was wide and straight and in the dis-tance she could see a large green hill. When they drew near, they passed a junction with the name East Hill Park and she remembered that she had passed it when she came here with her father. He had been invited to watch a golf tournament at a club in this area and for some reason she had decided to go with him, even though she didn't play golf at that time. The club had been in the suburbs of the city and she realized that they must have passed this way when they went there.

She thought back to that trip and to all the other good times she had had with her father and became very mel-ancholy again.

After a while they pulled up at a traffic light and the driver turned to her. "Which part of Yashiro-dai do you want?" he asked.

"There's a hotel there called the Excel, do you know it?"

"I'm not sure. There aren't any big hotels in this area, you know," he answered, and drove off as the light changed.

They turned left into another wide street, this one bordered on both sides with car showrooms. They continued halfway up a gentle hill and then the driver came to a halt.

"There are several hotels up that road to the right, if my memory serves me right."

Chiharu looked in the direction that he indicated and saw that the road had a no-entry sign on it. "It's all right, I'll walk from here. How much is it, please?"

She got out of the cab and set off up the road. This was also a hill, and after a short while she came to a group of hotels, just as the driver had said.

As soon as she saw them, she was glad she had walked. On one side of the road was a small park and the buildings on the other were all built to represent European castles or fairy-tale houses and had curtains over the entrance to their parking lots so anyone who visited them could remain anonymous. Even Chiharu, who had very little knowledge of such things, could see at a glance that they were obviously all drive-ins for sex.

Chiharu was shocked as she crossed the hill and walked down the other side. The area, apart from where she was standing, was a quiet, residential one and she could not understand why there should be so many hotels gathered in this one spot, but from what she could see the parking areas all seemed to be full, so they must be making a good living. They all had gaudy signs protruding into the street, advertising empty rooms or such dubious attractions as a "miracle chair."

She finally came to the Excel, standing slightly apart from the others, with its name written on a rusty sign. It was a square four-story building covered with brown tiles, and it was quite a contrast to the other garish buildings, although judging by the gloomy entrance hall and the dark garage in the basement, she guessed that there was not much difference in the type of clientele. Next to the front gate was a sign saying ONE NIGHT . . . ¥4,000 ONE HOUR . . . ¥2,800 INCLUDING SAUNA.

At first she was shocked that Kōsuke would have chosen such an establishment, but when she thought about it, she could see the logic behind his decision. People who visited such places did not want to be seen by anyone, so the staff kept their contact with the customers to a minimum and tried to avoid looking them in the face. This would be ideal for someone in Kōsuke's circumstances: not only could he keep out of sight, but establishments like this were cheaper than normal hotels.

When she came to Nagoya, she had intended to stay in the same hotel that Kōsuke had, preferably in the same room, but now she realized this was out of the question. Instead she just impressed the image of the hotel on her mind and set off back down the hill. When she came to the park she walked in. There were several cherry trees whose leaves were turning red and a small group of nursery-school children playing on a seesaw. She walked over to the railings on the other side and found herself on the edge of a small cliff. She could see green mountains in the distance beyond the roofs of the buildings and the telephone poles of Nagoya, and directly below her, a yellow train roared by.

A strong wind tugged at her hair and she wondered if Kōsuke had also stood here in the wind, gazing at the view while he tried to decide what he should do next. The police still hadn't determined Kōsuke's movements after he had left the hotel, so there was no way that she could follow in his footsteps any further. She felt despair and loneliness build up inside her again.

"Anyone would think that I came all the way here simply to cry," she said to herself scornfully.

Chiharu walked down the hill beside the park until she came to a golf practice range. She noticed that it had a coffee bar, and as she was still feeling weak after her illness, she decided to go in and rest. Since it was midafternoon most of the people practicing were housewives in their thirties and forties, but the coffee bar was fairly empty. She managed to get a seat overlooking the lawn.

After drinking the hot coffee and listening to the familiar sound of people hitting golf balls for a while, she began to feel stronger and wondered what she should do next. She had come to Nagoya on the spur of the moment with the thought of following in Kōsuke's footsteps, but his trail ended at the hotel she had just seen and she didn't have a clear idea where to go from there.

She suddenly had a thought and, opening her handbag, took out a magazine clipping. It was an interview between a famous actress and a professor who had made a special study of speech characteristics; she cut it out of the magazine two weeks ago. The professor had suddenly become famous a short while before when he identified a man who had kidnapped a small child by his voice print. As was to be expected, the interview was about voice prints.

*"Although identical twins may even sound identical, if you were to check their voice prints, you would find that they were in fact quite different."*

*"How about impersonators? They can copy people's voices exactly."*

*"They have similar voices to begin with and then by copying the other person's accent and mannerisms, they manage to fool their audience, but if you were to look at their voice print, you would see that they are in fact completely different."*

*"So it's quite easy to fool the ear?"*

*"Yes, the ear may be a marvelous instrument, but it's not very discriminating."*

*"In the case of kidnappings, usually the only time you hear the voice is on the phone. Does that make any difference?"*

*"Yes, for economic reasons the telephone only transmits a certain group of frequencies, which tends to make all voices sound similar."*

*"But you can still tell them apart?"*

*"Yes, even though they may sound similar, their voice print remains different."*

*"So you can't be fooled that easily. . . ."*

The part about fooling people on the telephone had caught Chiharu's eye. The professor's name was Kazuto Akiyoshi and he worked in the technology department of a private university here in Nagoya.

She went to the pay phone by the entrance of the coffee bar and looked up the number of the university. She copied the number into her diary and then dialed it. It was 1:45 on a Saturday afternoon and she realized that the professor might well have left for the day, but it was worth a try. The phone was answered after two rings.

"Tōmei University."

"Hello, my name is Nasuno and I would like to speak to Professor Akiyoshi in the technology department."

"One moment, please."

She hadn't expected to be put through so easily. She waited for the phone to be answered.

"Hello?"

It was a soft-spoken man's voice.

"Oh, hello; is that Professor Akiyoshi?"

"Yes, speaking."

"I'm sorry to telephone suddenly like this, but I read your interview in a magazine a short while ago and there is something that I'd like to discuss with you if you have the time."

"What kind of thing?"

"About people's voices . . . voices on the telephone in particular. I must say, though, that I work at a golf club in Tokyo and am not involved in this field at all. It's just that there's something I would very much appreciate your opinion about."

There was a few moments' pause.

"Did you come here from Tokyo?"

"Yes."

"Well, in that case the least I can do is listen to what you have to say. If you would like to come to the university, I'll be free from three o'clock."

"Thank you very much. I'll see you at the university at three o'clock then." She hung up and realized that she had been perspiring heavily. She had forgotten to ask directions to the university, so she opened the phone directory again and copied down the address.

She walked over to the girl at the cash register. "Excuse me, but how long does it take to get to Takamine in the Showa ward from here?"

"Takamine?"

"Yes, Tōmei University."

"Oh, you should get there in about thirty minutes."

Chiharu thanked her and went back to her table. She was very glad she'd been able to get an appointment with the professor, not because she necessarily expected him to be able to help her, but because she knew that if she returned to Tokyo without seeing him, she'd regret it later.

At 2:15 she left the coffee bar and walked down to the main road, where she managed to catch a taxi. She noticed a man in a suit walking along the road under the yellow leaves of the ginkgo trees and for some reason he reminded her of Momozaki.

She had met the detective three times and he struck her as a very nice man, but when it came to the question of Kōsuke's guilt, their opinions were completely opposite—although that was only to be expected given his position as chief detective in the police station that took out the warrant for Kōsuke's arrest. Their views about the telephone call that Kōsuke claimed to have received on the night of the murder were also opposed. He thought it was just part of a false alibi, but she could not think so. That last time she had seen Kōsuke at Kokubunji, he had given her his version of the story and she'd believed him. She realized that he had already been on the run at the time, yet he had taken the trouble to see her to say good-bye. He had spoken to her in a gentle voice and there had been tears in his eyes. He was not the kind of man who could kill someone and she just couldn't believe he'd been lying.

Did that mean that the phone call that night had been a coincidence? She couldn't bring herself to believe so; no matter how she thought about it, she always came back to the same answer. The woman had telephoned him in order to destroy his alibi. But who could it have been? There must be some way that she could catch her and so prove Kōsuke's innocence.

The taxi blew its horn and swung around a corner. Chiharu looked around and saw that they had already arrived. There was a long driveway bordered with oleander and several groups of students walking around in various directions. The taxi pulled up in front of a black stone gateway and Chiharu got out. Many motorcycles and scooters were lined up outside on the street and Chiharu felt a wave of nostalgia for her own college days.

She waited for ten minutes, then went up to the office next to the gate.

"Hello," she said. "I'd like to see Professor Akiyoshi of the technology department, please."

"Do you have an appointment?"

"Yes, my name is Nasuno."

The man at the gate rang through and checked. "You will find him on the left-hand side of the first floor of that building over there, in the Audiovisual Education Laboratory."

She walked across a brown lawn to the building that the man had pointed out. It seemed to be set aside for the members of the faculty, but now it was quiet and seemed almost deserted. She found the room without any trouble and knocked on the heavy-looking stainless-steel door. The door soon opened and she found herself facing a young woman.

"Hello, my name is Nasuno."

"Hello, please come in."

She led her into a square room whose concrete walls were covered with all kinds of apparatus, from an old phonograph to a machine that appeared to have several recording tapes inside its transparent case. The secretary directed her to a sofa and then went through to the next room. A short while later the door opened again and a well-built man in his fifties came out to greet her.

"How do you do, my name is Akiyoshi."

"Oh, hello. I'm sorry to come and see you at such short notice. . . ."

"That's okay, please take a seat," he said good-humoredly, and sat down opposite her. He regarded her closely for a few moments, then said, "You said on the telephone just now that you worked for a golf club."

"Yes."

"Do you play?"

"Yes."

"I thought so; you sounded like someone who does sports."

"Can you tell that from my voice?"

"Yes, you can tell even more from a voice print, however—whether the person drinks much, his physical condition."

His easy way of talking set Chiharu at ease. "As I said on the telephone, there's something I'd like to ask you concerning a person's voice."

"What does a voice have to do with golf?"

"No, this is nothing to do with golf. . . ." On her way over in the taxi she had tried to think of a good way to broach the subject, but she couldn't think of anything suitable. "What I want to know is, to what extent is it possible to disguise one's voice?"

"For instance?"

"Well, let's say I wanted to telephone a friend without them realizing that it was me. Would that be possible?"

"Of course. Haven't you ever been fooled?"

"I don't think so."

"You've probably been fooled without even realizing it. It's especially easy on the telephone because the range of the voice is severely limited."

"What do you mean?"

"Well, for economic reasons, the range transmitted by the phone is limited to between three hundred and four thousand eight hundred hertz, so all voices become somewhat standardized."

"You mean that they all resemble each other?"

"To a certain degree, but of course if they're talking normally it's easy to recognize them."

"I see."

"So you want to telephone a friend without them realizing it is you, do you?" Akiyoshi asked, his eyes laughing mischievously.

"Not at all. A friend of mine was put in a very embarrassing situation due to a phone call he had." Chiharu chose her words with care. "I don't know if the call was actually made by a stranger or whether it was made out of malice by someone who knew him, but if it was the latter, I'd like to try to find out who it was.''

"And therefore you'd like to know how much a person can disguise their voice, is that it?''

"In a nutshell, yes.''

The professor leaned back in his chair and pursed his lips thoughtfully. "Well, first of all, a lot depends on the person who receives the call. Let me give you an example: if you were staying in a hotel abroad and you had a call from someone, no matter how easily you might recognize their voice, if you thought that it was impossible for them to telephone you there, your mind would automatically think it is somebody else. On the other hand, if you're waiting for a call from somebody and the phone rings, if the person sounds even slightly like the person you were expecting, the chances are that you'll automatically assume it's them and start to talk. I'm sure that you must have experienced something like this.''

"Yes, so what you're saying is that if we're not expecting a call, it's very easy to be deceived?''

"Yes, especially if the voice is disguised in some way.''

"Could you give me an example?''

"Yes, there are several mechanical ways of disguising the voice, but easiest of all is to change the pitch. If you usually speak in a very high voice, speak in a low one, or alternatively, if you usually speak in low voice, speak in a higher one. This is especially true of women; if they speak in a deep voice, they give a very different impression on the telephone, and if they alter their intonation, the speed with which they speak, and their accent, then I would say that it would be most unusual if they didn't fool the person on the other end of the line.''

"Actually, I get a lot of people coming to see me because they want to improve the image they project on the phone. For instance, for people in sales, the way they speak can mean the difference between a successful sale and a failure.''

The secretary brought in some tea and Akiyoshi took a sip before continuing. He seemed to be warming to his theme as he spoke.

"I tell them to try to change the pitch, speed, and intonation of speaking as this will enable them to change their voice a lot. Haven't you ever heard someone's voice and wished you could speak like that?"

"Yes."

"Well, if you made an effort to copy their intonation and mannerisms you would actually sound like them. If you recorded a favorite actor and then consciously tried to mimic him, you'd soon find yourself talking like him. Accents are the same, you know. We copy them without knowing it, and before we realize it, we're talking in the same accent."

Chiharu thought back to what Kōsuke had told her about the phone call. When he had picked it up, he heard the tone that meant that it was from a phone booth and then a woman's voice had asked for someone else. He asked what number she wanted and the one she gave him had been correct, except for the last two digits. If the woman had really been a stranger, then Chiharu's visit to the professor would have been meaningless, but if in fact it was really someone Kōsuke knew, then the woman had already fulfilled one of the conditions that the professor had stated. By making Kōsuke believe it was a wrong number, she had already put him off his guard. Even if he thought her voice sounded familiar, he'd automatically assume it was a coincidence.

Next, when it came to her voice, what was it that he had said? "It was a deep voice with a slight country brogue and she was gasping slightly as if she was in pain." All these characteristics were just what the professor had said would be necessary to disguise one's voice, so it seemed quite feasible that she could well have been someone known to Kōsuke.

"You said just now that there were several mechanical ways of disguising the voice. I wonder if you could be a little more specific?"

"Of course. Actually, I made a special research of this subject in order to try to catch kidnappers. Obviously after they have kidnapped someone they have to contact the relatives to demand ransom, and they need to disguise their voices as much as possible, so I thought it would be worth my while to make a study of it myself.''

"I see.''

"Well, there are several ways, but probably the easiest is to use a hearing aid.''

"A hearing aid?''

"Yes, you know, the type that deaf people carry in their pockets, about this size.'' He produced a packet of cigarettes. "A hearing aid is a lot more complex than most people think; it doesn't simply amplify sounds but also adjusts them to the frequencies that the wearer finds easiest to hear. It has a tone knob and an automatic range control, or ARC, that cuts out all the frequencies the wearer has trouble hearing. For instance, a person who has trouble hearing deep sounds will find that they actually distort what he's hearing, so he just adjusts his ARC to cut them out altogether and listens to the higher frequencies.''

"You mean it will change the pitch of the speaker's voice?''

"Yes, to a certain extent, and it's particularly effective if the wires leading to the earphone are disconnected and fixed directly to the microphone in a telephone. If someone with a high voice were to speak in a low one and then turn the ARC to its lowest setting, then the ARC will distort the voice and make it completely unrecognizable to the person on the other end of the phone.''

Especially if they add an accent, gasp painfully, and pretend it's a wrong number, Chiharu thought to herself with a strange satisfaction.

"The human ear can be a very delicate instrument indeed, but it can also be fooled very easily, and I always try to stress this to the police when I'm called in to help with an investigation. Nothing of what I have told you today is new, I'm afraid. It's all in a book I wrote on the subject a few years ago, but I hope I've been able to be of some help.''

As she walked back over the brown grass toward the main gate, dusk was already drawing in and there were not nearly so many students sitting around the base of the fountain as there had been when she had arrived. She walked back down the driveway she had driven up in the taxi, and when she got to the gate she saw a phone booth and entered it.

She was feeling exhausted after the day's events and realized that she was still weak after her long illness. She didn't feel up to the long trip back to Tokyo that night and so she looked up the number of the hotel overlooking Nagoya castle, where she had stayed when she came to Nagoya with her father.

She got through to the hotel and managed to book a single room, but as she was replacing the receiver, she remembered what the professor had said, and twisting the cover, she found that it opened quite easily to reveal the microphone. She turned it upside down, saw just two wires connecting it, and realized it would be very easy to attach the wires of a hearing aid to it.

If the woman who had phoned Kōsuke that night had in fact used a hearing aid, she could easily have connected it without being seen. The phone booth she had called from had been on a very deserted street and the booth itself was surrounded by trees. Then again, she could just as easily have used a private phone. All she had to do was play a short tone before she started to speak and then cut herself off after three minutes and Kōsuke would never suspect anything. After that she only had to go to the phone booth in question and leave the note and handkerchief on the shelf beside the phone before Kōsuke arrived and the trap would be complete.

Chiharu caught a taxi and got in. She gave the driver the name of the hotel and lay back in the seat. She was more tired than she had thought and sat watching the passing scenery blankly.

For all her efforts she had only been able to establish the possibility that Kōsuke had been phoned by someone he knew. She realized now that she could achieve very little on her own and wondered whether Momozaki would follow up her theory if she were to tell him everything she had learned.

She closed her eyes.

They arrived at her hotel in thirty minutes and she was shown up to a room on the ninth floor overlooking the castle keep. She remembered from her visit here with her father that the castle was floodlit in the evening and seemed to float in the night sky. She thought over that long-ago trip and realized that she had no shared memories of Kōsuke, only the kiss in the fields at Kokubunji.

She bathed and telephoned her mother to give her the name and phone number of the hotel, then she drew the curtains and lay down on the bed. She still wasn't hungry and she thought she would just have a short rest, but no sooner did her head hit the pillow than she fell fast asleep.

She was awoken by the sound of the phone ringing by her bed. The room was quite dark except for a small night-light by the door and she realized that she had slept longer than she had intended. She reached out and picked up the phone.

"Hello?"

"Hello, is that Chiharu Nasuno?"

"Yes."

"Hello, Chiharu, how are you?"

It was a strong masculine voice and she felt hope and confusion well up inside her, but she forced herself to try to remain calm.

Is this a dream? she thought. Am I imagining it? No, I remember, I have had this experience before, but when was it, who was I talking to?

No matter how she thought, she could not remember.

"Who is this speaking?" she asked hurriedly.

# 17

# The Phone Again

KŌSUKE'S AMPUTATED FINGER TURNED OUT TO be proof of his death, and so the police watch on his house came to an end. The first night after the finger was delivered, Inspector Momozaki had left three men in the house in case the kidnappers tried to contact Shimako again, but the next day, after the announcement of his death in the papers, they, too, returned to the police station and Shimako and Tome had the house to themselves again for the first time in nine days. The police had only been there in case Kōsuke tried to return or to contact his wife, but now that he was officially declared dead, there was no need for them to remain.

The house regained a certain illusion of normality, but Shimako still could not relax. When the police were there, she had felt cut off from the world, and this feeling had grown to be an obsession with her. She had stayed at home alone worrying about it until her nerves became quite frayed, and even now she could not unwind. When she thought of her husband being kidnapped, killed, and mutilated, she felt faint, and knew she would never be free of her fear until his murderers had been caught and brought to justice.

At the same time Kōsuke was still the suspect for the Nasuno murder and everyone thought of her as the wife of a murderer. She couldn't bear to meet anyone and ended up staying in the house all the time. Her sister telephoned and told her to come and stay in Chigasaki, but she refused, saying that she didn't want to go anywhere until Kōsuke's murderers were apprehended. However, after she put the phone down she felt even lonelier and wondered if she would be able to continue like this without going mad.

Three days after Kōsuke's murder had been announced, the managing director of the Wakashiba company, Shōnouchi, telephoned and then came to see her. He was in his fifties and had worked for Kōsuke's father. He had been running the company since Kōsuke disappeared and he had come to bring her up-to-date on matters, but his news was not very good.

"We have bills due for payment on the fifteenth and the twentieth, and as things stand we won't be able to pay them. One of them is for the Miyoshi nurseries in Kokubunji, but I was talking to Mr. Miyoshi on the phone the other day and he says that he realizes that things must be hard for us at the moment and that he will not press us for payment until things quiet down. He says that Kōsuke went to visit him the day before he disappeared and told him to come to the company and collect all the plants we had there in order to keep his losses at a minimum. He felt that Kōsuke was doing his best under difficult circumstances and he couldn't believe that he was the type of man who would ever kill anyone, so he'll wait until things sort themselves out. We're lucky to be dealing with people like that. The other company says that if they force us into bankruptcy, they'll only lose in the long run, so they'll give us a little longer before they press for payment."

He put his hands together and sighed. "However, now that Kōsuke has been pronounced dead, things can't go on like this. A lot of people gave us time because they liked and trusted him, but now they have no reason to put off their demands any longer. Of course, if the Tanzawa Country Club paid its bills, there'd be no problem, but as things have turned out I don't think there's much chance of that.''

"When is the next bill due?"

"Next month, but I think that it'll be impossible for us to pay everything that's due this year.''

"You mean we'll go bankrupt?''

"Yes, I'm afraid so.''

"What will happen to the house and land?''

Even Shimako was surprised at how calmly she was taking all this. "I spoke to Mr. Sako, the lawyer, about it and he says that if we declare ourselves bankrupt, representatives for the company, the banks, and yourself will have to meet, and if, after discussions, the banks think we won't be able to pay, your property will be seized in order to cover the debts.''

"Does that mean I'll have to move out of the house this year?''

"No, even if the worse comes to the worst, you won't have to move out that soon.'' He frowned painfully. "You won't have to leave here until about March or April at the earliest, and depending on how things go, Mr. Sako says you could very well remain here for much longer.''

She realized that he had been to see the lawyer before he came here, so he would be able to give her a complete picture of the future. "Next year—everything should have sorted itself out by then,'' she said more to herself than to him. By "everything'' she meant that Kōsuke's body would have been found, his killers arrested, and Nasuno's and Kawai's murderers caught. Ever since she heard that Kōsuke was dead she had dreaded seeing his body, even though she realized that once she had, everything could be settled and forgotten.

Without a body she couldn't even hold a funeral. His sister was already burning incense for him on their family altar, but Shimako couldn't bring herself to do that.

November came and the police still hadn't found the body or arrested the kidnappers. They had no new clues to the identity of Kawai's murderer either, and although both inquiries were continuing day and night, they didn't appear to be making any progress. The public seemed to have forgotten the case, but for Shimako there was no respite.

November 13 dawned, overcast and cold, and there was a bitter wind blowing from the north. By evening the wind had dropped slightly, but it started to rain and the night quickly became colder.

By 10:30 Shimako had changed into her nightgown and was ready for bed. Although she couldn't sleep very well, she had started to retire earlier since Kōsuke had disappeared. Tome had already gone to her own room and the house had dropped into silence. Shimako could hear the rain beating on the roof outside the window.

The bedroom had two single beds with a night table between them. A long bedspread covered one of the beds and the other was turned down, ready for her to get in. The phone was on the night table.

Shimako thought it must have been like this when Kōsuke received that fateful call on the night of Nasuno's murder. He was alone in the bedroom and a cold rain was falling outside. At that moment the phone rang, its bell piercing the silence and causing Shimako's heart to miss a beat. She looked over at the digital clock and saw that it was 10:30—the same time as the mystery call that had started the whole nightmare. She realized this was only a coincidence, a result of her thinking of that night, but all the same . . .

She picked up the phone with anticipation.

There was a tone on the line that meant that the call was from a pay phone.

"Hello?"

A man's voice answered. "Hello, is that the Ōkita house?"

"Yes?"

Her heart started to pound uneasily again. She recognized that voice; it was a deep, powerful, masculine voice, but no, it could not be. She shook her head in denial.

"It's been a long time. How are you doing?" That voice really was familiar, but it *couldn't* be. "It must have been very hard for you this last month, how are you feeling?"

"Excuse me, but . . ." Shimako asked in a hoarse voice. "Who is this calling, please?"

"Are the police still watching the house?" He continued speaking as if Shimako hadn't said a word. "I suppose this phone might be tapped, too."

The voice was identical to her husband's; it could only be him, but that was impossible!

"Who is this speaking, please?" she asked a little crossly.

The man on the other end of the line still ignored her and continued to question her. "Is there anyone there with you now?"

The accent and intonation were identical to Kōsuke's, but he spoke more slowly and carefully, as if he were scared that someone was listening in and was trying to find out what the situation was.

However, that could not be.

"*Stop it!*" she screamed, and slammed the phone down. She collapsed onto the bed and clenched her fists.

It has to be a hoax, she told herself. It's someone playing a trick on me.

She kept repeating this to herself, but for some reason she couldn't get herself to believe it.

The next day the telephone remained quiet most of the time; it rang once in the afternoon and once in the evening. Shimako ignored it both times and Tome answered it in the kitchen. Tome didn't call her and didn't mention anything during the meal, so it couldn't have been anything important.

The fifteenth was another uneventful day, the weather was still bad, and in the evening it started to rain again. Shimako's sister called from Chigasaki at about 9:30. Shimako told her everything about Shōnouchi's visit.

"So if the company goes bankrupt, you'll have to leave that house, will you?" her sister asked a bit resentfully.

"Yes, but it'll be next year at the earliest and by then everything should have sorted itself out."

"That's true, you'll be able to get off to a fresh start."

Shimako felt much better after talking to her sister, and took a nice hot bath. She had a good long soak and by the time she got back into the bedroom it was 10:30.

The phone rang again and she figured it was just her sister again, with something she had forgotten to mention.

She slipped a gown over her shoulders and sat down on the bed.

She picked up the phone, but the moment she heard the buzz of a pay phone she felt a flash of fear pierce her heart.

"Hello, is that the Ōkita residence?"

It was that voice again!

"Is that Shimako?"

She didn't reply.

"Are you alone?"

"Who is speaking? If this is your idea of a joke, I don't think it's very funny."

"It's not a joke," admonished the voice that sounded just like Kōsuke's. "I want to speak to you. However, I want to make sure that nobody else is listening."

He was still testing.

"If you don't tell me who you are, I'm going to hang up."

"You mean you can't recognize my voice?"

It had to be his voice.

"Who are you? You can't be my husband, he's dead—so please stop this, I've had enough!"

She realized she had put the phone down and was pressing down the receiver with both hands. She looked at the clock and saw that it was 10:37—the same time as the mystery call again.

"Perhaps . . . But no, it couldn't be. . . . "

She found herself trembling violently.

The next day it had stopped raining and there were blue skies for a change. The house was quiet again; Shimako had made a brief appearance in the dining room that morning and said that she didn't feel well. Then she had gone back to her bedroom. Tome left to do the shopping and returned at about two o'clock. She walked into the kitchen and opened the door. As she did so, a man of medium height with a slight stoop and wearing a dark raincoat suddenly appeared from behind one of the trees and hurried toward her. His appearance was so sudden that she almost screamed, but then she realized that she recognized him. He was about forty years old, had a dark complexion, and a scar on his face. He was one of the detectives from the Himonya station who had been assigned to watch the house. She thought his name was Wakura or something like that.

"Hello, how have you been?" he asked with a grin. "I'm sorry if I gave you a start."

"No, that's all right," she replied with an answering smile.

It is not a very nice feeling to be kept under twenty-four-hour surveillance, but meeting the same people every day, she had gotten to know them and now they seemed almost like old friends.

"What can we do for you today?"

"Oh, don't worry, it's nothing like that. I just wanted to make sure that everything was okay. You never know, until we find the body the kidnappers may try to get in touch with you again."

"What's happening? Are you still working on the case then?"

"Of course, every day we've got men making door-to-door inquiries and searching for the body."

He sat down on the doorstep and lit a cigarette. Tome fetched an ashtray and came back to him. He might be a detective, but what with Shimako locked away in her room day after day, she was desperate for someone to talk to. That wasn't all—there was something strange going on in this house, she could feel it, so she was not altogether sorry that he had come.

"Is Mrs. Ōkita at home today?" He nodded toward the back of the house, exhaling a stream of smoke.

"Yes, she hasn't felt well all day and is lying down in her room."

"Yes, I see her curtains are drawn." He couldn't see her room from where he was sitting, so it was obvious he had checked around the house before he let himself be seen. "She isn't very strong; it must have been a terrible strain on her."

"Yes, that's true." Her tone made it obvious that there was more to it than that.

"Is there something else?"

"Well, it's just that lately we've been getting these strange telephone calls. . . . "

"What do you mean, strange?"

Tome brought one of the kitchen chairs over to where he was sitting. She sat down and looked at him in silence for a while as she tried to think of a way to phrase it.

"Do you mean that they're connected to Mr. Ōkita's disappearance?"

"I don't know, I haven't heard them myself."

"What do you mean?"

"When I answer, whoever it is hangs up without saying anything."

"Does Mrs. Ōkita usually answer the phone herself?"

"No, not necessarily. I let it ring three or four times, and if the missus doesn't take it in her room, I answer it in the kitchen." She spoke very stiffly and Wakura remembered the talk of her eavesdropping, which she had been questioned about at length. Apparently since then she was very careful about what she said about the telephone.

"I see, and you say that they hang up when you answer?"

"Yes, yesterday and the day before, it must have happened about four times. The day before yesterday the missus didn't answer the phone at all, and when I answered, I would say, 'Hello, the Ōkita residence,' and the line went dead right away."

"Didn't you hear the voice at all?"

"Not for the first three times, but the fourth time I picked up the phone and didn't say anything. A man's voice said hello, but when I said yes, he hung up. He obviously realized it wasn't the missus."

"So you mean that they'd have spoken if it was Mrs. Ōkita?"

"Yes, maybe, and I'm sure that there was something strange about it."

Wakura watched her with interest.

"It was three days ago, on the thirteenth, the phone rang at about ten-thirty. I was already in bed and the missus took it, but I was worried that I hadn't fastened the shutters properly, so I got up to check."

"Yes."

"Well, I heard her saying 'Who is it?' and 'Stop it!'

Then she banged the phone down. Since then she's stopped answering the phone.''

"I see. I think you're right. It was probably the same person that hangs up when you answer.''

"That's not all; it happened again.''

"When?''

"Last night. Her sister rang from Chigasaki at about nine-thirty. I answered it and put it through and they spoke for a long time. After that the missus took a bath.''

She explained that Shimako stayed in the bath until about 10:30, and after that she had taken her turn in the bath. No sooner did she get in than the phone rang. She started to get out, but she heard Shimako answer it, so she left it.

"It was at the same time as the call on the thirteenth and I wondered if it was from the same person, so I got out and went through to the hall.''

It would appear that instead of listening to the calls on the extension in the kitchen, she now listened through the door, but she didn't seem to realize that she was doing anything wrong.

" 'Who is this . . . stop it . . . I've had enough!' ''

She heard the same cries from Shimako and then the sound of the phone being slammed down.

"She's stayed in bed all day today and I feel sure that it was a result of that call.''

"Hmm . . .'' said Wakura, thinking, and took out another cigarette. "I don't know, it was probably just someone doing it for kicks.''

"But how could they tell the difference between my voice and the missus's? It seems kind of unlikely to me.''

"What did this man's voice sound like?''

"It's hard to say, I only heard him say hello, but it was a strong male voice.''

"How old would you say?''

"About the same as the boss.''

By "the boss'' Tome meant Kōsuke. Wakura lit his cigarette, then changed the subject.

"Did Mr. and Mrs. Ōkita get on well?''

Tome blinked two or three times and dropped her eyes to her lap. She seemed to be embarrassed, but after a moment she sighed and spoke. "The boss was a very busy man and he never was much of a talker at home."

"But you must've known if they got on well or not; you've been living with them for many years now."

"That's true, I've been with them since they were newlyweds. I've been friends with the missus's family for ages now, and when they got married they suggested that I come and help look after the house. The missus isn't very strong and my husband died a long time ago."

"So when you first came they were still very in love, were they?"

"Yes, but he kept her waiting until the company was off the ground."

"You mean he kept her waiting too long?"

"Yes, by the time they married they were already quite settled in their ways, but it's only in the last three years that things were like this. If only they'd had a child."

Wakura turned to her and leaned forward. He felt he was on to something at last. "Do you mean that they didn't get on as well as they might have?"

"Yes, the missus often goes to stay with her mother at Chigasaki and the boss always worked late. On the few occasions when they did have their dinner together, they hardly had a word for each other. If they'd had a child that time, they would at least have had something to talk about."

"What do you mean 'that time.' Do you mean that she was pregnant once?"

Tome looked very worried but seemed to realize that it would come out eventually, so she sighed again and made up her mind to talk. "The missus suffers from anemia and it was very difficult for her to get pregnant, but she managed three years ago, only to have a miscarriage three months later."

"So she wasn't physically capable of it then."

"Well, I suppose that also played a part, but there was another reason. . . . They had a fight and he hit her."

"Did he often hit her?"

"No, he wasn't basically a violent man, but sometimes he lost his temper and hit her without realizing what he was doing."

"But all the same, to hit her when she was pregnant . . . What was the argument about?"

"I wasn't there at the time."

She was obviously trying to avoid answering.

"But you must have heard their voices or asked her afterward."

The fact that Tome was refusing to speak could only mean that it was something important.

"Had she discovered that he had been having an affair? But no, if that was the case, she'd have hit him. How about the opposite?"

Tome looked at him angrily.

"Was she having an affair with someone?"

"She did nothing of the kind. She's not that kind of woman. But I don't know what the argument was about in any detail."

Wakura realized there was nothing to be gained by pursuing it any further.

"Anyway, Shimako had a miscarriage after Ōkita hit her and there's been very little love lost between them since."

The detective who had come to see Tome popped in every other day just to check on Shimako's condition. He would wait until he knew that Shimako was not around, then make his way over to the kitchen, where Tome was waiting for him.

"No, we have not had any more strange calls since then; in fact the missus seems to have gotten over it now and even answered a call from her sister herself today."

"Anyway, don't forget what I told you," Wakura said, and hurried away.

The weather started to deteriorate on the twentieth and on the twenty-first it started to rain. Winter was approaching and it seemed that it drew closer each time it rained.

Listening to the rain pounding on the roof, Tome had a bad feeling about the day. It was probably because the weather reminded her of the day that Nasuno was killed. At 10:15 P.M. Shimako got out of the bath and went straight to bed so as not to catch a chill.

After she had retired to her room, Tome went to the

bathroom and opened and closed the sliding door. It was surprising how the sound carried through the silent house and Shimako would now think Tome was in the bath. Tome then crept back to her room, where she started to fold the laundry to pass the time. She had left the door separating her room from the kitchen open and could see the telephone from where she sat.

She kept looking over at the clock on the table. She had finished folding the clothes and was about to put them away by the time the hands crawled around to 10:30. She was just starting to stand up when the phone rang. Although she had been waiting for it, it came as a shock all the same. She hurried through to the kitchen extension and stood waiting for Shimako to answer. This was the first time it had rung at this hour since the sixteenth and she could feel her heart racing. Was it the same man? Would Shimako answer it? These two thoughts chased each other through her mind as she stood counting the rings.

Finally, halfway through the sixth ring, the phone suddenly became silent. Had Shimako answered it or had the other party given up and hung up? She reached out and gently removed the receiver, but she was so excited that her hand slipped slightly, which made a slight noise on the line. She put the phone to her ear and heard that a conversation had already started.

"Hello, Ōkita speaking," Shimako said tensely. There was a pause.

"Hello." It was a man's voice. "Is that Mrs. Watanabe?"

"What?"

"Isn't that the Watanabe residence?"

"No."

"Isn't it 416-329X?"

Tome held her breath and listened.

"Sorry, you have the wrong number."

There was another pause and Tome thought the man was going to hang up.

"Just a minute," the man said hurriedly, and Tome thought that her heart would stop: the voice was identical to Kōsuke's. "I'm sorry, I seem to have dialed the wrong number; you see my eyes aren't very good."

Shimako remained silent.

"I don't quite know how to say this, but I don't suppose you could be kind enough to phone Mr. Watanabe for me, could you? I haven't got any more coins and there aren't any shops open near here where I could get some change."

Shimako still refused to speak.

"Please, I'd be very grateful. You see, my eyes are very bad. . . ."

Tome could hear someone breathing heavily on the phone, although this seemed to be Shimako, not the man. The man's tone was very cool; in fact it was identical to Kōsuke's voice when he was angry about something and was complaining to Shimako about it.

"Who . . . who are you?" Shimako asked in a hoarse voice.

"My name is Takeshita."

Shimako gave a faint scream.

"I'm in a phone booth next to the church in Himonya and I would be very grateful if you could phone the number I'm going to give you and ask them to come and pick me up. . . ."

There was a loud noise as Shimako hung up, but Tome still had her receiver off the hook so the line was still connected. The man on the other end of the line was silent, then he quietly hung up, too.

Tome staggered back to her room and sat down on the floor. Her heart was pounding as if it was going to burst and she clutched her chest with both hands.

Who could it have been?

Tome had listened in to the call that Kōsuke had received on October 16 at approximately the same time. It had been virtually identical to this one except that the caller had been a woman, and soon afterward he had hurried out, almost as if she had lured him.

She sat trembling and felt as if someone were taking their revenge on her. She had sworn never to listen in to people's calls again, but this time had been different—she had only done it because Detective Wakura had asked her to.

She heard the sound of footsteps and saw Shimako hurrying along the hall toward her, wearing a black raincoat and with a blue scarf over her hair. It was probably due to the scarf, but she looked deathly pale.

"Are you going out?" Tome asked, but Shimako didn't even look in her direction; she just went straight to the front door, her face showing the terrible strain she was feeling. Tome felt another shock as she realized that Shimako had also been lured out by the telephone.

The minute that she stepped out the door, Shimako felt the warmth being sucked out of her. She had been quite hot after her bath, but it was a cold, wet night, and she could almost feel the heat leaving her. She walked along, one hand holding an umbrella while the other clenched a handkerchief in her pocket. Her whole body was tense and most of her willpower was needed just to keep the cold at bay.

The area in which she lived was well known for its narrow, twisting streets, and although none of the surrounding houses were particularly large, they were all set back from the road and very little light reached Shimako as she hurried through the night toward the main road. Her breath was white in the night air and her footsteps echoed in the silence.

There used to be a large number of nursery gardeners in the area, and even now there were still plenty of small fields and trees. She walked past a cabbage field and could see a nursery full of young camellias on the other side. She could see them blooming in the night and wished she had some blooming trees in her garden instead of the pine, boxwood, and other evergreens that Kōsuke had planted. It was typical of him to devote himself entirely to his job and to ignore his own wife and family.

She finally came to the end of the deserted street and arrived at the main road. It was full of vehicles, many of them trucks with illuminated displays on their sides, and they thundered through the night in a cloud of spray. She stood at the curb keeping her eyes peeled for a taxi. Her feet were soaked and she felt so cold that her mind was numb. However, she had known exactly what she was going to do from the moment she hung up the phone and got dressed, and it would take more than a little rain to stop her now.

She finally caught an empty cab and told it to go to Eifukuchō. She collapsed into the backseat and suddenly felt faint. The heater thawed out her cold body and her pulse quickened as she realized what she had done. It was the same as the time when she had decided to go to Nasuno's funeral, police or no police, but now she came back to her senses and looked out the rear window. She could see nothing but the lights of the cars following and she gave up worrying about it. She was more concerned about her destination; she had never been there at night before and wasn't sure she could recognize the place. She was relieved to see an overpass she recognized and told the driver to turn left and then at the second right, and when they came to a seven-story condominium, she told him to stop.

It was a new building with a brick and plaster façade and a fairly large garden around it. She walked in and hurried across the deserted lobby to the elevators, her heels tapping on the floor as she went.

She got into the elevator, and as it started to ascend she took out a compact and inspected her face in the mirror. As she had taken a bath just prior to leaving, she was not wearing any makeup and her face looked unnaturally pale. The elevator soon arrived at the sixth floor and she stepped out. A corridor stretched out in front of her, a row of doors on the left and the right open to the rear garden. A cold rain was blowing in from the outside and her back got wet as she walked along. She came to the door she wanted, and fighting back the panic that was rising up inside her, she pressed the bell.

In the few minutes before anyone answered she felt her body growing stiff and her knees start to tremble. Finally a man's voice answered, but Shimako just stood there in silence. Eventually she heard the peephole opening and then the door was hurriedly unlocked.

Suddenly Kinumura was standing in front of her. He looked at her for a moment, and when he realized that she really was Shimako, an expression of surprise came over his features. At the same moment she staggered toward him.

"I'm scared. . . . I'm so scared that I don't know what to do. . . . " she said, sobbing. "I'll go mad if I have to stay on my own any longer. I didn't know what to do, please don't send me away."

He stood, holding her in his arms, and looked into her eyes with a mixture of sadness and sympathy. "Of course I won't send you away."

"I can't bear to be on my own any longer."

"Come on, quickly, come inside."

He hugged her to him and at the same time looked quickly up and down the corridor. He led her into the room and then stepped into the corridor again and checked the garden. He saw no sign of anyone, so he hurried back into the apartment and locked the door.

He supported Shimako from behind and helped her off with her wet coat and shoes. She was wearing a sweater and a knit dress that she had changed into before she fled from the house. The apartment consisted of four rooms and he led her through to a large living room at the end of a short hall. The heating was turned up high, soft music was playing on the stereo, and there was a glass of brandy and some magazines on the table. It was obvious that he had been reading until she arrived. The neatness of the apartment said a lot about his character, although he did have a lady in once a week to help keep the place clean.

He sat her down in the comfortable armchair where he had been sitting and then waited for her to calm down a little before trying to find out what had scared her so.

"You should have something to drink; it'll help warm you up." He poured her a brandy and held it up to her mouth. "Come on now, you must try to drink just a little."

She finally managed to take a sip, then taking the glass from his hands, she set it down on the table.

"It must have been very cold. Did you come by taxi?"

Shimako nodded.

"Did you call for one?"

"No."

"You mean you walked until you found one? No wonder you were soaked."

"I had an umbrella—oh, I seem to have forgotten it in the taxi." Her mouth twitched into what might have been a smile.

"Does Tome know you've come out? If not, it might be best if you phoned her. She's probably worried about you."

"No, she knows." Her voice became a bit stronger. "She ought to know; she was listening."

"Listening? What do you mean?"

"To the telephone. Who can it be? That was the third time he's called." Her voice took on a wild edge and she hid her face in her hands. "It was the same time as that night and he said the same thing."

Kinumura spoke to her soothingly and managed to get the whole story out of her. He kept drinking the whole time she spoke.

"So, you had a phone call on the thirteenth, the fifteenth, and again tonight at a little after ten-thirty?"

"Yes, the first two times it sounded just as if it was Kōsuke, on the run still and phoning to see what the situation was at home."

"It couldn't have been Kōsuke and you know it," Kinumura said, showing his irritation for the first time. "It's only because you wanted it to be him that he sounded similar."

"But what he said, it was the same as that call."

"Anyone could have said it. Kōsuke gave a statement about the call and it appeared in several papers, so it's no secret. Then again, maybe whoever it was realized that Tome was listening in and just pretended it was a wrong number." He bit his upper lip and gazed into his glass as he thought. "I don't know for sure," he said with a sigh. "But I feel sure that Kuretani is behind this somehow."

"How about Kōsuke's kidnap and murder?"

"Yes, that, too." Kinumura couldn't think of anything else. "When they sent you Kōsuke's finger, they never thought we'd be able to tell that it had been removed after death, but your house was under surveillance and things didn't go as they hoped. When they realized this, they got one of their men to dress up like Kōsuke and had him murder Kawai to make it look as if Kōsuke was still alive.'' He held Shimako's eye and nodded comfortingly. ''What other answer could there be? Unless, of course, it was Kōsuke's ghost out for revenge.''

He saw the fear come back into her face and quickly continued. ''There's no way it was Kōsuke, so it has to be one of Kuretani's gang. They probably knew that by frightening you, you'd come to see me eventually and then they could start threatening me. They probably hope to frighten me so much that I'll give up my stock in Camellia and the Tanzawa club, and then in the confusion they'll try to take over the club for themselves. That's the only reason why they're trying to threaten you, I'm sure of it. You mustn't allow yourself to give in to their threats.''

He went out into the kitchen and made some hot lemon for Shimako, who still looked cold. He was thirty-six years old, and nine years ago, when the Uchibō club had just opened, he had married the daughter of one of the members, whom he had met while he was playing golf there. They got married very quickly, but it only lasted two years. The official reason was that they didn't get along and had come to a mutual agreement, but the real reason was that he had been so involved in his work that he didn't have any time for her and she started to go out drinking on her own every night. Eventually she found another man; after the divorce she married him and now they had two children. Ever since then Kinumura had tried to devote himself to his work, and as could be seen from his neat apartment, he made a good bachelor.

He took the drink to her and she sat with the glass in her hands, feeling the warmth spread through her body. Eventually he was pleased to see her start to relax and think things over calmly.

''All the same, his voice and way of speaking were identical to Kōsuke's. If you had heard him, you'd have been surprised, too.''

''There probably just happened to be someone at Kuretani's who sounded like that.''

''But then there's the part about Tome listening in. I took the call in the bedroom and heard a slight sound as she picked up the phone in the kitchen. Someone who didn't know Tome's quirks would never have noticed, so why should he pretend he had gotten a wrong number?''

''I see what you mean. They'd have to be very conversant with the goings-on in your house or they'd never realize.''

Their gazes met.

''Is there anyone you can think of who has known you for some time whose voice sounds similar to Kōsuke's?''

''Yes, now you mention it, there is someone.''

The idea had been floating around in her mind for some time, but it was not until now that she realized it.

''Who is that?''

''Sako, the lawyer for the company.'' Something about the lawyer had always reminded her of Kōsuke, despite the big difference in their ages and their looks, but it was not until now that she realized that it was their voices. ''It was a long time ago now, but once when I was waiting for a call from Kōsuke, Sako rang and it was a few moments before I realized who it was.''

''The fact that you were waiting for a call only helped you to jump to conclusions. It was probably the same with that call tonight. There's nothing to be scared of. That's a good thought about the lawyer, though; he would definitely know a fair amount about the house.''

''Do you think it was him then?''

''I can't say at the moment, but it's a distinct possibility. One of Kuretani's gang may be using him.''

''What should I do?''

''The best thing is for you to just ignore it. If the phone rings, don't answer it. They're sure to give up in the end. The most important thing is for you to keep your spirits up.'' He stood up from his chair and knelt down in front of her, then putting his hands on her shoulders, he said, ''You have to be brave. It won't be for much longer.''

''How much longer must I wait?''

''Not long, until the spring.''

''Next spring,'' she repeated in a sad voice, full of yearning for something she could not attain. ''Okay, I suppose everything will have been cleared up by then.''

"Of course it will, and everyone will have forgotten all about the past."

"It won't be for much longer," she repeated in a small voice, and the fear came back into her eyes.

Kinumura held her with both hands and helped her to her feet. "Come on, you'd better be going now."

Her whole body tensed and she seemed to rebel against his words like a child.

"Come on, Tome will be waiting for you. We don't want her to get worried and start a fuss, now, do we?"

Shimako seemed about to say something but held it back and started weakly toward the door. She stopped and looked as if she were about to cry as she stared at Kinumura's face, then she slipped her arms around him. She continued to look into his face and her eyes held all the loneliness and fear that she felt. He seemed to be fighting an internal battle and tried not to meet her gaze, but it was no good.

"If I wait, everything will be all right?"

"Of course it will."

"I can really believe that?"

Suddenly he seemed to lose control of his emotions and he held her to him. Their lips met and tears started to flow from his eyes, leaving two trails down his cheeks.

It was twenty past twelve before Shimako left Kinumura's apartment. As they walked along the corridor toward the elevator, Shimako kept her face buried deep inside the upturned collar of her raincoat, but Kinumura kept looking around as if he were worried that they were being watched. They took the elevator down to the garage in the basement, and a few minutes later Kinumura's brown, two-tone sedan was driven out onto the street. A light drizzle was still falling and Shimako's face shone whitely in the streetlights as they made their way toward the main road.

No sooner had they turned the corner than a black sedan moved off after them. It had been parked in the shadow of a building about twenty yards down from Kinumura's condominium with its lights off.

Kinumura's car wound its way through the quiet residential streets until it came to a halt at the junction near Shimako's house. Only ten minutes had passed since they left his apartment.

The light at the end of Shimako's driveway illuminated the nearby bushes, and the two of them could be seen silhouetted against it as they leaned toward each other for a moment, then drew away.

Shimako got out, wearing her scarf again and holding a hand over her mouth. She kept her head bowed as she hurried over to her gate, but once she got there, she paused for a moment to look back at Kinumura's car before disappearing into the darkness.

Kinumura waited until he was sure she wasn't going to return, then he pulled off quietly and headed back home. As he did so, the same black sedan followed him at exactly the same distance. He parked his car in the basement garage again. As he made his way up to his apartment he looked around once more to see if anyone was watching him, but he never realized he had been followed for the whole trip.

The lights came on in his room, and after about ten minutes the black sedan started up and set off toward Kō-shū Avenue again. Driving the car was a young detective from the Himonya police station, and sitting next to him in the passenger seat was Detective Wakura. He had intimated to Tome that he was checking on the house now and again, but in fact Momozaki had ordered that they resume their twenty-four-hour surveillance.

When he arrived back at the station, he found Momozaki still there and made his report.

"Now I see why Shimako went to Nasuno's funeral on the fourteenth of October. I thought it strange at the time, but it wasn't until tonight that I understood the real reason."

He didn't go into details as he guessed that Momozaki would be able to work it out for himself as soon as he heard the rest of the report.

"Shimako left her house at ten-forty-two and I heard from Tome later that she had received a phone call shortly before she departed."

He went on to tell how Shimako's destination had been

Kinumura's apartment and that she had stayed there from approximately eleven to 12:20 when Kinumura had driven her back in his car.

"While she was in Kinumura's apartment, I went back to Kinuta to talk to Tome. I had asked her to listen in if there were any more strange phone calls."

"Yes, and . . . ?"

"She was terrified; she said that the voice on the phone was identical to Ōkita's and that the contents of the call were the same as the one of the night of Nasuno's murder."

"The same . . . ?"

"Yes, the voice was a man's, but it was identical in all other respects."

"That means . . . that means that she really did listen in to the call that night after all."

"Yes, I checked on that point, too, and this time she didn't attempt to hide it. She said that she picked up the phone in the kitchen immediately after Ōkita did and listened to the whole call. She had been very embarrassed when we questioned her about it and pretended she only heard the first few lines before hanging up, and she stuck to her story until tonight."

"So the story of the wrong number was not a lie after all."

Although this did not necessarily mean that Kōsuke was innocent, Momozaki had been of the opinion that Kōsuke had made up the whole story. To hear that it was really the truth came as a bit of a shock.

He suddenly thought of Chiharu, who had come to see him eleven days before on November 10. She had phoned soon after he arrived at the station at eight o'clock and asked if she could see him. He realized that she must have taken the morning off work especially to see him, so he agreed to meet her.

The last time he had seen her had been immediately after the Kawai murder and she had been sick in bed. As he talked to her, he had suddenly realized that she was in love with Kōsuke.

He met her in the lobby and showed her through to a reception room, where they could talk in private. She still looked a little underweight, but on the whole she looked much better than when they had last met.

"The reason I have come to see you today is that last weekend I went to Nagoya and met with Professor Akiyoshi at Tōmei University." She told him about the work the professor had done on speech analysis. "He told me of several simple ways of disguising one's speech and has convinced me that it would have been quite feasible for the woman who called Kōsuke on the night of my father's murder to be someone that he knew well."

"But surely it was just as likely to have been a complete stranger."

"Yes, that's true, but the reason I suspect that it might be someone who knew him is that the contents of her call could almost have been designed specifically to lure him out of the house. That would only be known by someone conversant with his past. It was a cold, wet night and most people would just forget about it when they couldn't pass on the message the first time, but I believe that whoever it was knew that Kōsuke had a soft spot for blind people and that was why she claimed that her eyes were bad."

"What do you mean?" Momozaki remembered some such talk at the time, but he wanted to hear it from her.

"He used to have a blind cousin who was two years older than him, and when he was still in high school she got lost and fell into a ditch. She died as a result of her injuries and Kōsuke always said that if only the people around her had been more helpful it need never have happened. For this reason he always went out of his way to help blind people, and I think that whoever it was who rang him that night knew this. He wouldn't have been able to rest if he thought a blind woman, especially one who sounded as if she were ill or in pain, was waiting in a cold phone booth for someone who would never come because he had failed to pass on her message."

Momozaki listened to her in silence. He had always assumed that Kōsuke had killed Nasuno and that the story about the phone call was bogus, but now he realized the call could indeed have been a very cleverly laid trap to lure him out of the house.

"Kōsuke didn't like to talk about himself very much

and there can't be many people who knew about his cousin, which is why I thought it might be someone who knew him very well."

"I see," Momozaki said, nodding slowly. "If the call was indeed a trick, you could very well be right."

But what about all the other evidence they had against him? The evidence found in his garden was the most damning thing for Kōsuke. He had been put on the list of suspects from the very beginning, since he had both a motive and the opportunity to kill Nasuno, but it was not until the golf club, towels, and glove were found under his shed that the police took out a warrant for his arrest. The blood on the towels was of the same type as Nasuno's, and the golf club belonged to Kōsuke, so there seemed to be little room for doubt that he was the murderer.

On the other hand, if one were to assume that the telephone call was a trap, the evidence could just as easily have been faked, too. A person close to Kōsuke would have known that Kōsuke kept his golf clubs in the trunk of his car and could easily have slipped one out without Kōsuke knowing. After that, it would be a simple thing to put it under the shed with the towels to make it look as if a dog had dug them up and then wait for Tome or the lodger to find them.

He realized that Chiharu was not asking him to do anything, just to try to look at the case from a different point of view, and he found to his surprise that when he did, all kinds of possibilities presented themselves.

His colleagues at the Ogikubo station were not making very much progress on their investigations of Kawai's murder either. Their main suspect was Kuretani; he had probably found Kōsuke on the run and murdered him, then sent Shimako a ransom note in the hope that he could make some money. When this failed, he dressed up one of his men to look like Kōsuke and had him murder Kawai, the idea being that he would be able to take over the Tanzawa golf club in the confusion that followed. The inquiries, though, were not going very well. They were also investigating everyone connected with the Uchibō golf club, since they suspected that the missing three billion yen could be at the bottom of the murders, but these inquiries had also drawn a blank.

Momozaki gave Wakura a look of gratitude.

"Well, things finally seem to be moving."

"Yes, but who do you think is making the phone calls to Ōkita's wife?"

# 18

# The Phantom Fugitive

WITHOUT NASUNO AND KAWAI AROUND TO keep things under control, the Uchibō and Tanzawa clubs soon fell into chaos. Anger at the extension of the deposit period of the guaranty money boiled over and finally the inland revenue and the public prosecutor's office were called in to see what had happened to the mysterious three billion yen.

Kinumura heard about this on the twenty-fourth of November, but since he had had nothing to do with the three billion, he decided to wait and see how things progressed. He guessed that the money would be deducted from the estates of Nasuno and Kawai and that their heirs would probably lose their stock in the clubs, too. The inland revenue would probably demand their share of anything that was left, so it seemed that very little of the huge fortunes the two men managed to amass for themselves would revert to their heirs.

Anyway, until the whole problem was solved, the members union and the board of directors would continue to run the Uchibō club. As for the Tanzawa club, the contractor and the landowners each had about fifteen hundred million outstanding, and it looked as if the contractor

247

would take over the club in lieu of payment. They proposed to pay the money owed to the landowners, and it was the executives from the contractors who were handling all the negotiations.

If the management changed, the name of the club would probably also change, but in the meantime, Kinumura continued as before. He went into the office every day and tried to drum up interest in the club, but with all the scandal in the newspapers he got little response. Sales had gone badly from the beginning, and only twelve hundred memberships had been sold—only half the anticipated number. Still, as Kawai had liked to say, people soon forget, and Kinumura knew it was only a matter of time before sales started to pick up again. Time solves most problems as long as people remain patient.

On November 25 Kinumura arrived at his apartment in Eifukuchō at twenty past ten. It was a very large, luxurious apartment by Japanese standards and he had been living there since it was built four years ago. He turned the heat up and changed into a sport shirt, then pouring himself a brandy, he picked up the newspaper and took it to his favorite armchair.

His apartment was on the sixth floor and he could see the lights of the Setagaya ward spread out below him. When he first moved in, he had wished that the lights were brighter, but now he'd grown to like them as they were and found the sight very relaxing. They shone coldly in the night air and spoke of the approaching winter. He found himself drawn to one red light in particular and sat looking at it blankly.

He had made sure he was home by eleven o'clock every night for the last four nights because at eleven o'clock Shimako phoned. When she had shown up at his apartment in the middle of the night, soaking wet and terrified, he had recommended that she stop answering the phone, but she said that she would go mad if she was cut off from the world even more. He had then suggested that she call him every night at eleven o'clock.

"That's a good idea. Tome will be in the bath at that time and there won't be any chance of her listening in."

The next night she had phoned him at exactly eleven

o'clock and told him that neither she nor Tome was answering any calls. He could tell from her tone just how important her calls to him were and the responsibility was quite frightening.

He suspected Sako, the lawyer, was making the calls, although he had no idea what Sako hoped to gain from it. Kōsuke had introduced them once, but Kinumura didn't know him well and couldn't tell whether he was calling for his own ends or whether he was working for Kuretani. He guessed, however, that he would be getting a phone call from him himself in the near future, so he was not particularly surprised when the phone suddenly started to ring at 10:30. He knew it was either Shimako phoning early or it was his turn to talk to the mystery man.

He stood up and went to the phone in the corner of the room. He found, somewhat to his surprise, that his pulse had quickened. He let it ring four times, then picked it up.

"Hello?"

"Is that Mr. Kinumura?" It was a deep male voice.

"Yes."

"Mr. Tōru Kinumura?"

He listened as hard as he could. It certainly sounded like Kōsuke, but that was impossible. "That's correct, who's speaking, please?"

"I'm sorry to phone you so late." The caller seemed to sense Kinumura's confusion and paused, then continued in an amused voice. "My name is Sako. I represent the Wakashiba company. I believe we met once."

"I was right."

"What?"

"Oh, I'm sorry, I remember you."

He really did sound exactly like Kōsuke and it didn't sound like it was an act.

"I'm sorry to phone you so late like this, but something unexpected has come up. The woman who made the anonymous call has come to my house and admitted it."

"Anonymous call?"

"Yes, surely you must remember—Kōsuke claimed that on the night Mr. Nasuno was murdered he had a telephone call from a woman who pretended she had dialed a wrong number, and he went to Himonya to look for her. However, as he was not able to say who she was, the police didn't accept this as an alibi.''

"Yes.''

"Well, that woman has turned up at my house and told me everything. I told her to go to the police as what she has to say proves that Kōsuke was telling the truth and it throws a completely new light on the case.'' He seemed to be listening for Kinumura's reaction as he spoke. "However, she says that before she goes to the police, she wants to see you. Apparently she knows you very well.''

Kinumura still remained silent.

"She says she's willing to go to the police, if you will go with her.''

"She couldn't—'' Kinumura burst out, stopped himself, then realized that his reply was not inappropriate and quickly forced himself to relax. "It seems a little strange to me that a woman who got through to Kōsuke after she accidentally dialed a wrong number should know me.''

"It wasn't necessarily an accident, but it's a very complicated situation and I wondered if it wouldn't be asking too much to have you come to my house.''

"What, now?''

"Yes, I live in Ekoda, so it should only take you about fifteen minutes at this time of night. I would come to see you, but she is exhausted and doesn't seem to be very well.''

Kinumura remained silent.

"Well, if you can't come, I suppose I'll just have to call the police and have them come over and interrogate her. I know that Kōsuke is dead now, but he's still the prime suspect for a crime he didn't commit, and I think it's only fair that the case should be cleared up.''

"No, of course I will come,'' Kinumura said quickly.

"Well, I'll tell you how to get here. Have you got something to write with? Go along Ōme Avenue toward Shinjuku, turn left at the fourth set of lights, and proceed until you get to a primary school, then turn left. Turn right in front of a big temple then left by a large bamboo grove. You'll find my house at the end of the street.''

Kinumura wrote down the directions absentmindedly,

his mind working furiously. So it was Sako who had been phoning Shimako after all, but what had he hoped to gain by frightening her? Would it really be the best thing to go to his house now?

"Okay, I see, I'll be right over." He put the phone down, returned to the armchair he had been sitting in, and knocked back his brandy in one gulp.

So he had been right about Sako making the calls. He had to admit that his voice did resemble Kōsuke's, but Kōsuke could hardly have come back from the dead. When he thought about it calmly, this was self-evident, but Shimako had been so terrified by the calls that he found some of her fear rubbing off on him.

He was relieved to know who the calls were from, but what was their purpose? Was Sako in league with Kuretani or working alone? If he was just trying to test Kinumura's reactions, it would be best if he went; otherwise it would look as if he had something to hide.

If Sako was working for Kuretani, Kinumura could expect to be threatened in some way, but he couldn't bring himself to believe that a practicing lawyer would lend himself to something like that. No, Sako had probably found some woman who was willing to make a statement to the police and so provide Kōsuke with an alibi. If he, Kinumura, were to go, he could probably make some kind of an arrangement with the lawyer.

There was one other possibility, however, and that was what he dreaded the most. He recalled Sako's words: *She says that she's willing to go to the police if you'll go with her.*

He hurried over to the telephone and dialed a number from memory. The phone rang seven times, but there was no answer; then making up his mind, he put the phone down and headed for the bedroom. Going to the closet, he took out a pullover and put it on over his sport shirt, then put a blazer on top of that. Thinking it might be cold outside, he took out a scarf and wrapped it around his neck.

All the time he was doing this he was still debating with himself the wisdom of going. He thought he had made up his mind, it was the logical thing to do, but a tiny voice in the back of his mind told him to stay. For some reason his thoughts went back to Kōsuke, and he wondered if he felt the same way the night that Nasuno was killed.

If he were living in America, he'd have taken a gun with him, but this was Japan and he couldn't do that. But only a fool would go completely defenseless—who knew what might happen?—so after a few minutes' deliberation he went to the cloakroom and took a golf club out of his golf bag.

Kinumura took the elevator down to the basement garage and got into his car; he placed the golf club against the passenger seat with its head on the floor. It was 10:40 when he drove out and there was a light mist floating above the road. Most of the buildings around his condominium were taken up by offices, so the area was very quiet at this time of night.

There were still a lot of cars on the streets, but the traffic was moving smoothly. As he drove he found himself getting over the shock of the call and thinking clearly. It was obvious that Sako wanted to discuss something, and if he had not agreed to come, he would put himself at a severe disadvantage.

He turned into Ome Avenue and took out the directions. When he came to the fourth set of traffic lights, he pulled over to the side and looked around. Sure enough, there was a building that looked like a school on the left-hand side, so he pulled over again and turned left. The road suddenly became very deserted and the only cars to be seen were those parked at the edge of the sidewalk. He eventually came to a temple on the left, as Sako had said he would. It was a very large temple and the wall seemed to go on forever. He kept his eyes on the opposite side of the road and looked for the next turn; Sako had said there was a sign advertising a pawnshop, and sure enough, there it was. The road became really dark and he drove past several old buildings interspersed with fields and woods.

He couldn't see any lights in his rearview mirror, and after driving for several hundred yards he came to the bamboo grove on the left. He slowed down and turned into the narrow road next to it. There was a large two-story building on one side of the road that looked like an expensive Japanese restaurant, but there were no lights showing anywhere. It looked to Kinumura as if the road had been made solely to serve the restaurant and he wondered if Sako really did live at the end.

He was peering into the night, looking for the house, when he suddenly braked the car. There, standing in the middle of the road, all by itself, was a child's tricycle.

He felt a wave of fear wash over him and sat staring at the tricycle, his breath coming in ragged gasps. Kinumura found himself thinking that the tricycle sparkling in the light of the car's headlights looked brand-new. It was not an old broken one that someone had found dumped somewhere and placed in the middle of the road for his own purposes.

He finally managed to tear his eyes off the tricycle and look around. The road was empty; there was the bamboo grove on the left and the restaurant on the right with an estate van parked in front of it. The road was about twelve feet wide, and as his car was not all that large, he would normally have been able to squeeze by the tricycle, but the position of the van made this impossible. He looked around carefully. No lights were on in the restaurant and the bamboo grove was pitch black. He couldn't see to the end of the road, but it looked as if it might end very soon and there was no sign of any movement in that direction.

If it was a dead end, no other cars would be using it. Kinumura continued to think it over. Was it merely a coincidence, or was Sako testing him? Was Sako sitting up in his house at this very moment watching him?

He felt very irritated with himself. He was not a child to be frightened off by a mere tricycle, but at the same time he couldn't ignore the fact that there was a certain amount of danger involved in his getting out of the car to move it. Maybe that was what Sako was after; some of the newspapers had mentioned an old tricycle found near Kawai's body, but it would be unnatural for him to show excessive fear.

He looked around carefully again and edged the car forward until it was almost touching the bike, then gripping the handle of the golf club with his left hand, he opened

the door with his right. As he did so the interior light came
on.

He couldn't discern any suspicious movement, so making up his mind, he finally stepped out of the car. He left
the car door half open and hurried over to the tricycle. He
picked it up in his right hand and threw it toward the van,
then transferring the club to his right hand, he started back
toward the car. At that moment he saw something move
and strained his eyes in that direction. There was no moon
and the road was wrapped in a mantle of darkness, but he
could have sworn that he had seen a movement out of the
corner of his eye. The only light was that of his car's
headlights, but they revealed nothing.

He waited for an endless moment, then let his breath
out with a chuckle. It suddenly seemed ridiculous that he,
a full-grown man, should be frightened by shadows in the
night. He started back to the car only to stop again, fear
seizing his heart with its icy talons. There, no more than
two or three yards off, was the shadow of a man. He was
standing just outside the light of the headlights and it was
probably when he moved out of the shelter of the bamboo
that Kinumura spotted him. He forced himself to remain
still while all his instincts screamed for flight and his heart
thundered in his ears as if it were about to burst. The other
man didn't move a muscle. Only the white mist of his
breath set him apart from the trees and bamboo around
him.

Kinumura forced himself to look at him. He looked extremely tall, but no, it was the hood he was wearing; a
pair of dark glasses glittered slightly in the light from the
road. He seemed to be wearing a windbreaker, a black
windbreaker with a hood, and dark glasses. As the details
gradually became clear, Kinumura began to panic. They
stood like this in silence for several seconds, Kinumura's
breath coming raggedly until he finally found his voice.

"Who . . . who are you?"

"Who do you think I am?"

"Ōkita . . ." he replied before he realized what he was
saying, so similar were their voices. The other gave a deep
laugh.

"What are you talking about? Kōsuke Ōkita is supposed to be dead, isn't he?"

Kinumura did not answer.

"Anyway, even if I was Ōkita, why would that scare you so much?"

"I'm not scared, but . . . but it's a bit of a shock to meet someone who's supposed to be dead."

"But that's not all, is it? It would spoil all your plans if Kōsuke was still alive, wouldn't it? Surely, if you were really Kōsuke's friend, you'd be delighted to find that he was still alive after all."

"What?"

"Don't worry. Kōsuke is dead, after all; the police received a finger that was undoubtedly his and that had definitely been removed after death, so there's no question of his still being alive. However, until his body is found, people with guilty consciences will go on fearing the phantom fugitive. You, for instance, and Shimako."

"Who are you?"

The hooded man gave a deep chuckle. "I'm Sako; I phoned you just now."

"Then what are you doing here?"

"I came to meet you. I didn't want you to get lost, and anyway I wanted to talk, just you and me."

He spoke in a relaxed tone, but his voice still sounded identical to Kōsuke's. He had to be doing it on purpose!

"You're the one who phoned Shimako, aren't you?" Kinumura said, changing to the offensive. "You used the fact that your voice resembles Kōsuke's to try to threaten her, didn't you?"

"That is correct, I did phone her."

"Why?"

"I wanted to check her reaction."

"I thought as much. So what you said on the phone to me just now, about the woman who made the telephone call on the night of the Nasuno murder, that was all a lie, too, was it?"

"No, that was the truth," the man answered quietly. "She came to see me this evening and told me all about the telephone call she made. She said she was willing to go to the police if you went with her." He spoke calmly and his voice held a ring of truth that made Kinumura start to tremble.

"Where is she now, this woman?"

"She was very excited and was quite exhausted, so she's resting at my house."

"You haven't called the police yet then?"

"No, you said you'd come and I wanted to speak to you first. That's why I waited for you here."

"I've got nothing to say to you."

"Really?"

"Why would I want to speak to you? In fact, I think I'm going to sue you for making threatening phone calls."

"Oh, really? In that case, I'd like to know how it happens that you know the contents of my calls to Shimako."

"Because she told me. I was a close friend to both of the Ōkitas, and now that Kōsuke is dead, she had nobody else to turn to."

"Friends? I'm sure there's more to it than that. The third time I telephoned Shimako, she lost all self-control and ran to your apartment. She stayed with you for nearly two hours, and when you drove her home, you kissed in the car before she got out. You see, I always phoned her from the phone booth near her house, and so I was able to watch her from the moment she left the house until she finally returned. I must say it was very illuminating.

"I admit that I impersonated Kōsuke on the phone and intimidated her, but I didn't do it without reason, you know."

The tall, dark shadow in the windbreaker continued to stand just outside the lights of the car and speak in a deep, strong voice. Kinumura found himself frozen to the spot, like a rabbit mesmerized by a snake.

"I had a telephone call from Kōsuke on the twelfth of October, a day and a half after he went on the run. No, that's not quite correct—he never meant to go on the run, he had only gone to Morioka to visit a college friend to try to borrow some money to keep his company solvent. However, when the police found him missing, they jumped to the wrong conclusion and took out a warrant for his arrest."

Kinumura tried to swallow his fear, but he couldn't stop listening.

"He said he had a call at the office from Shimako at about ten o'clock on October tenth to tell him about the golf club and towels that were found under the shed in his garden. She told him that Tome and Naitō were making a fuss, and it was at that moment that he realized he had been set up. The day before he had been cross-examined by the police and he knew they suspected him. He'd had both the motive and the opportunity to commit the murder, and with the evidence that had been planted in his garden, he knew there'd be no avoiding arrest.

"He'd been threatened by the Kuretani gang the night before and his first thought was that it was their work, and as the 'evidence' had already been seen by the maid and the lodger, he couldn't avoid it coming to the notice of the police. Also, he knew that as soon as the police saw it, they wouldn't hesitate any longer to arrest him." He gave a deep sigh and his breath shone whitely in the car lights.

"However, he still wasn't all that worried. He knew he was innocent and he believed that this would become evident eventually. However, he realized that he'd probably be arrested and it would be some time before he could move around freely. Before that happened there was something that he had to do.

"As soon as he had the call from Shimako, he hurried home and took her to the back of the house where they could talk in private. He told her that if he was arrested right away, the company would go bankrupt, since there were two bills that were due for payment and he didn't have the necessary money to pay them. He wanted to do as much as possible to protect the company while he still had the chance because even if he was found innocent, it would be too late if the company had already collapsed."

Kinumura could see the logic in this. Kōsuke had started the company himself and it now employed thirty people, so it would have special meaning to him.

"He told her that he might have to go away in order to try to raise the necessary funds and that he wanted her to keep the evidence secret until he telephoned her to tell her that he had the money. After that she should call the police, and although it might mean that he had to go to prison for a while, he was innocent, so there was no need for her to worry.

"He then returned to the office at eleven-thirty, called the managing director, and gave him detailed instructions on how to run the company in his absence. After that he came and visited me at my home and gave me a detailed report on the state of the company. I could see he was very strained, and although he didn't tell me about the 'evidence,' I guessed that things weren't going very well for him in the Nasuno case, so I gave him a piece of advice. I told him that no matter what happened, he shouldn't try to escape. If he was innocent, he shouldn't go on the run; if he did, that would be the end.

"When he phoned me on the twelfth, he spoke as if he was calling from Morioka. He had taken the night train on the tenth and had arrived at about six o'clock the next morning. He had an old friend in Morioka who had taken over his family's business, and he went there with the intention of swallowing his pride and asking for a loan to tide the company over.

"I will say it again: Kōsuke had not meant to escape when he left Tokyo."

Sako sounded so much like Kōsuke that in the dark Kinumura couldn't help feeling that it was Kōsuke himself that he was talking to.

"When he arrived in Morioka, he went to a coffee bar to wait until about eight o'clock when he could phone his friend. While he was there, he watched the news on the television, and you can imagine his surprise when he saw his own face appear and learned that while he had been sleeping on the train, a warrant had been taken out on him for the murder of Seiji Nasuno.

"From what he could gather from the news, the 'evidence' had been handed in to the police at about nine o'clock the previous evening and Shimako had said she had no idea about his whereabouts. Later his car had been found near Ueno station and the police had decided that he had gone on the run and took out a warrant for his arrest. However, he couldn't understand why things had come to this; he had explained the whole situation to Shimako and asked her not to tell the police until he contacted her. Why hadn't she listened? Even if Naitō had telephoned the police without telling her, she only had to tell the police that he had gone to try to raise the money to keep his company solvent and surely they would have held off on the warrant. It was from this moment that he started to suspect Shimako.''

Sako's voice took on a hard edge.

''Now that he had become a wanted man, everything had changed. He couldn't very well meet a friend he had not seen for ten years. Who knows—he might turn him over to the police. He spent the day in Morioka, thinking it over, and after staying the night in a business hotel there, he phoned me the next day. Of course I urged him to go straight to the nearest police station and turn himself in. There was still time, and if he went to the police, things would go much easier on him, but the longer he delayed, the worse it would become, and there was always the chance that he would be arrested first. However, we were cut off and he obviously thought that as the police had already decided that he was a fugitive, he might as well become one for real. Maybe my warning that it would be the end if he went on the run had the opposite effect and convinced him that it was too late to step forward.''

Kinumura listened in silence.

''After he spoke to me on the phone he made his way to Tazawa, where he tried to fake his suicide. But when the police realized it was a fake, things became even worse than before: the case had caught the imagination of the public and no matter where he went he was notorious. I don't know what happened after that; I only had the one call, but it was enough to give me an important clue— namely, that there was a good chance that Shimako was involved in the murder. If you look at it that way, everything makes sense. It would be easy for her to slip one of his golf clubs out of the trunk of his car and plant the evidence under the shed, then make it look like a dog had accidentally dug it up. However, she couldn't have done it all on her own; there had to be a strong-willed, ruthless person behind her telling her what to do. In other words, a man.''

The giant shadow of a man took a pace forward and Kinumura stepped back until his legs hit the bumper of the car.

"I told you that I didn't threaten Shimako without reason, but even though my voice may resemble Kōsuke's, her reaction was excessive. Nobody would want to receive a call from a person they thought dead, but surely if it was someone that they loved, they'd find some comfort in the sound. Shimako, however, reacted so violently that I was convinced that I was right. I phoned again, and on the third time she couldn't stand it anymore and panicked. I daresay you told her not to see you until the whole affair had blown over, but you had forgotten to take human emotion into account. I think that it's safe to say that most plans that fail do so because of human frailty."

It was true that Kinumura's main worry from the beginning had been whether Shimako could bear the strain. But in the end he had come here himself, despite the inner voice that told him to stay away. He could sense that defeat was not far away, but still he struggled against it.

"I think it's fairly certain that you and Shimako planned it all so Kōsuke would become wanted by the police, but the only part I didn't understand was the telephone call. However, the woman who made it came to see me tonight and said she wanted to see you, but I thought it might be best if I saw you first and we talked it over."

This was the second time he mentioned talking it over and Kinumura thought furiously to try to understand exactly what he meant by it.

"How about it? That's more or less how it happened, isn't it? Of course it's all supposition, so I can't be quite sure of the details. I'll leave them for you to fill in, but if you want to cooperate, I'd be willing to help you."

"What do you mean? Do you want to make a deal?"

"Take it any way you like."

"But I've got nothing to discuss."

"Are you sure you can afford to say that? Shimako will be questioned by the police soon and I don't think she'll be able to hold out very long. It's only a matter of time before the police find out that you were in it with her."

"Don't be ridiculous, I had nothing—"

"Of course, I might be able to make sure that she didn't say anything. And then again, I could have her testify that it was all your doing and that you made her help you."

"You're mad!"

"So what do you want to do? Do you want to make a deal? At the moment I'm the only one who knows about you and Shimako; the same goes for the telephone caller. She has told me the whole story in detail and wants you to go to the police with her. That's why I thought I should talk to you first—to make sure that your stories match. But if you're sure that you have nothing to say . . . ?"

"Yes, it has nothing to do with me."

"In that case, you leave me no choice. I'll call the police and have them come and question her at my house." He stared at Kinumura for a moment and then turned and strode off into the dark again. Kinumura took two or three steps forward, then stopped and took a deep breath.

"Wait," he called out without meaning to. "What . . . what does she say?"

The black hood turned to him again, then after a moment's pause he replied. "She says that you ordered her to do everything."

"Ordered . . . ? But that's—"

"Isn't that how it was?"

"No."

"Then how was it?"

"I don't know, I haven't done anything."

"So we have nothing more to say then."

He turned away again, but as he did so, Kinumura found himself gripped by an overpowering emotion, and giving a slight moan, he grabbed the other's arm.

"Wait, let me see her, let me see Shimako!"

The man in the windbreaker was taller and heavier than Kinumura. He turned and looked down at him, a slight smile playing on his lips. " 'Let me see Shimako'? That is what you just said, isn't it?"

Kinumura didn't reply.

"That means that it was Shimako all along. It was she who telephoned Kōsuke and pretended that it was a wrong number in order to get him out of the house."

"No, I meant . . ."

"You meant what? Why should I know where Shimako is? I merely said that the woman who made the phone call was at my house. I never said that it was Shimako."

Kinumura could not speak.

"Yes, now I see it all. I guessed that you and Shimako had worked to ensure that the blame for Nasuno's murder fell on Kōsuke, but I couldn't be sure if that was only after the murder or not. However, you were both in it together from the beginning. First Shimako made the phone call to get Kōsuke out of the house and into the vicinity of the murder while you committed the actual deed."

Halfway through the other's speech, Kinumura had found himself unable to listen. He was staring at the other man's face. It was dark, but he could make out the thick lips, a strong chin, a sloping forehead, and a pale complexion. Did Sako look like this? He struggled to remember, but no, he was a red-faced man with thin lips. But if this was not Sako, then who was it?

"You killed Nasuno, didn't you, Kinumura? No doubt Kawai found out about it and so you killed him, too. You tried to put the blame for that on Kōsuke, too, didn't you? You wore the kind of clothes that I am now and used that golf club you have in your hand."

Who could this man be?

The next moment Kinumura took a deep breath and let it out in a horrible, howling scream that was filled with fear and despair. Then raising the club in his right hand, he swung it down toward the other's head.

The other man dodged and ran off to one side. Kinumura followed and raised the club for another swing. They moved into the light of the headlights, and at that moment there was a woman's scream from the direction of the bamboo grove. Two men ran out from the shadow of the restaurant and grabbed Kinumura's arms.

"Kinumura! Calm down! We're the police!" Wakura's voice echoed through the night. "We want to ask you some questions, so please come with us to the station."

By the time that Kinumura realized what was happening to him, the man in the black windbreaker had disappeared into the night.

* * *

Chiharu ran blindly through the bamboo grove in the opposite direction to the road. No matter how many times she tripped on the roots of the bamboo, she continued to run as fast as her legs would carry her.

Where has he gone? she thought.

Since Kōsuke had disappeared she had started to receive phone calls from a man who sounded identical to him. The first one had come while she was staying in Nagoya. He had said that he was Sako, the lawyer, and he had telephoned her at her home, but her mother had given him the number of her hotel there. He said that now that Kōsuke was dead, he wanted to find the real murderer of her father and Kawai and asked for her help. She could still remember her shock at meeting him in his office at Nihonbashi and his seeming indifference to Kōsuke's fate, but now he sounded so sincere and desperate that she found herself agreeing to help.

This was not her only reason; she also wanted an ally in her search and was willing to accept help from any source. She told him about her meeting with Professor Akiyoshi at Tōmei University, and after thinking about it for a few moments, he asked if there were any detectives at Himonya that she felt she could trust; if so, she should give them her information.

"If they think it's your idea, they might well give it their unbiased attention."

Chiharu had already thought of telling Momozaki, and hearing it from Sako convinced her. She was also willing to accept his advice because of his voice; she couldn't help feeling that Kōsuke himself was asking her. She even found herself thinking that it might really be Kōsuke, and that he was keeping his identity secret from her because he didn't want to surprise her and risk her telling someone else. She knew this was illogical, but still, she couldn't shake the belief that it was Kōsuke. The fourth time he had rung her had been the previous night.

"I'm going to call Kinumura over to Ekoda tomorrow to have a confrontation with him and I wondered if you could come to act as a witness in case he admits to the murder."

He told her the place and time.

"Excuse me for asking, but are you really Mr. Sako?" she asked before she could stop herself.

"Please think of me as such, at least for a little longer."

Chiharu went to the designated spot and listened to the two men arguing on the road, but it appeared that she was not needed as a witness after all. The police obviously already suspected Kinumura and had been keeping him under surveillance. This was probably the work of Momozaki, which meant that he had listened to her when she had told him her theory about the phone call.

All these thoughts rushed through her mind as she hurried through the bamboo grove, and finally she came out on the other side. She found herself on a much wider road, with many more houses on both sides, interspersed with fields and small woods. She looked left and right, but there was nobody in sight. She turned to the left and started to run again.

Maybe it was Sako after all she thought with a shock of disappointment. He had achieved his aim and probably didn't want to get caught up with the police, so he had taken the opportunity to slip away.

She came to a junction and saw the high wall of the temple she had first seen on her way there. She turned right and headed toward her car, which she had left some way from the bamboo grove to ensure that Kinumura did not see it and become suspicious.

The temple wall came to an end, and turning left, she could see the rear of her BMW parked at the roadside. She was out of breath and slowed to a walk.

The rear of the temple lay on her left and on the opposite side of the road was an area of wasteland with a large camphor tree standing on it. Chiharu reached the car and gave a deep sigh. A wave of disappointment swept over her and she felt as if she could just collapse where she was standing.

She looked around one more time, but nobody was in sight. There was a large stone memorial or something under the tree in the wasteland, but as she watched, it started to move toward her and she was able to make out a tall man with a hood. She watched as he approached and found herself moving toward him.

When they were standing face-to-face, he raised a gloved hand and removed first the hood, then the sunglasses. She stood and looked at his thick eyebrows, his delicate nose, and his determined mouth and then spoke with a calm that amazed even her.

"Hello, Kōsuke."

# 19

# A Dawn Journey

MOMOZAKI WAS WAITING AT THE HIMONYA station when Wakura and his colleague brought Kinumura in for questioning. While watching Shimako's house, they had seen her go to his apartment in the middle of the night, and from what they saw of their actions when he brought her home in his car, they guessed that the two of them had a more than casual relationship. After that, they also kept a watch on Kinumura as they guessed that the two of them would meet in private again, and when they did, they would pick them up for questioning. They intended to cross-examine them both separately and see what they could learn.

Obviously, before they decided on this course, they checked Kinumura's alibi and motives again and found that he was not necessarily as blameless as they had originally thought. The detectives at the Ogikubo station found that after Nasuno's death, Kinumura had had several arguments with Kawai and Kawai had told his mistress that he intended to use his stock to force Kinumura out of the company and gain control of the capital for himself. Nasuno had left Kinumura in control of the firm's assets for many years and it was quite possible that he had been murdered in a dispute over this money.

When Kinumura left his apartment at 10:30, Wakura and his colleague had followed him and kept Momozaki up-to-date on developments over the radio. When they got him to the station, he seemed to be deep in thought and refused to answer any of their questions. They contacted Commissioner Yamane at Central HQ and he hurried over to take charge of the questioning, but he didn't get any further than the others.

They held a brief conference and decided to bring Shimako in and try questioning her first. They had originally meant to leave her until afterward, but as things now stood, they had little choice. From what Wakura had heard at Ekoda, they knew that the man who had called Kinumura had been a lawyer called Sako, and although they had wanted him to come with them when they picked Kinumura up, by the time they managed to get Kinumura to settle down and stop swinging the golf club around, he had disappeared. They telephoned Sako and asked him to come to the station, but when he heard why, he seemed at a loss and told them he hadn't set foot out of the house at all that night. This made no sense, but two detectives went out to see him to get his story anyway.

Two detectives were sent to Shimako's house to bring her in for questioning and it was 1:45 in the morning by the time they arrived. They rang the front bell and Tome eventually came to the door, then went off to wake Shimako. Shimako's bedroom was at the back of the house, far from the front door, but the night was quiet and the detectives could hear Tome's voice. They waited for three or four minutes, and although they could hear Tome calling out in a high voice, they didn't hear any sound of Shimako getting up. Surely, if she were getting up, Tome would stop calling out like that. The two detectives exchanged a glance and at the same moment heard Tome running back.

"Please come quickly, something's wrong with her!" she gasped, halfway down the hall toward them.

"What do you mean?"

"She's asleep, but no matter how much I call or shake her, she won't wake up."

The two detectives exchanged another look and, as they did so, slipped their shoes off.

They hurried down the hall and through the open door at the end into a dressing room *cum* lounge. On the other side of the room was another half-open door that led them into the master bedroom. There were two beds, one with the covers still drawn, and in the other they saw Shimako sleeping. She was lying on her back with the covers drawn up close under her chin. There was a lamp on the bedside table and in its light she looked as if she was just asleep.

"No matter how I shake her or call out, she won't wake up and she's generally such a light sleeper."

One of the detectives checked her breathing, then he stretched out a hand to grasp her shoulder and shook it. "Hello . . . Mrs. Ōkita . . . Shimako."

She made no answer and her head lolled lifelessly on the pillow. Even when he put his mouth to her ear and called out in a loud voice, there was no reaction.

The detective looked over to the table; there was a clock that said two minutes past two and a water pitcher with a glass, but there was very little water left. "Did Mrs. Ōkita ever take sleeping pills?"

"Yes, occasionally; she got them from the local doctor."

The detective telephoned for an ambulance and then called through to the station to tell them what had happened.

"What time did she go to bed tonight?"

"A little after eleven o'clock. Recently she's been telephoning someone at eleven every night and usually talks for a long time, but tonight it appears that she couldn't get through."

She told them that when Shimako dialed the number, the phone in the kitchen would make a noise, so she always knew. Shimako had been making the calls for four days now, but during that interval she refused to answer any other calls and wouldn't let Tome touch the phone either. However, she never missed her call in the evening;

she seemed to be looking forward to it all day and would take her bath and get ready for bed in plenty of time.

"For some reason, the person on the other end of the line didn't answer tonight, and after she'd tried the number about four times she seemed to give up, and I assumed that she'd gone to bed."

While they were waiting for the ambulance to arrive, the detectives searched the bedroom and the room next to it, and in the wastepaper basket they found seven empty plastic sheets that had held pills. In one of the drawers they found an envelope with a local doctor's name on the outside and four pills inside in the same sheet as the ones in the waste bin, and they guessed that it was same medicine. Shimako had obviously saved up the pills she received from the doctor and then swallowed them all at once.

"Did she ever say anything about wanting to commit suicide? Not just today, anytime recently."

"I'm not sure, but she's been behaving very strangely since we started getting those phone calls I told you about from someone who sounded like the boss." She blinked several times. "She used to say the strangest things at times, too. Last night at dinner, she suddenly looked at me and said in a serious voice, 'It was me who rang Kōsuke on the night that Nasuno was murdered, you know.'"

She had then given a sad laugh, but Tome had not taken what she said seriously.

The news of Shimako's attempted suicide was transmitted to Yamane and Momozaki right away.

"Ever since she went to visit you in your apartment the other night," Momozaki said to Kinumura, "Shimako has been phoning someone every night at eleven o'clock. It was you she was calling, wasn't it? When you went out to Ekoda tonight, nobody was there to answer her call."

As soon as the detective said this, Kinumura's face was filled with dismay. He had been so busy wondering what he should do about Sako's call that he forgot all about Shimako's.

"She thought even you had deserted her and she was so upset that she tried to commit suicide."

"How is she?"

"She's been taken to the hospital and is undergoing treatment, but it's still too early to say."

Kinumura held his head in his hands and collapsed over the desk. He had kept himself under control until then, but now he started to tremble and groan as he swayed to and fro. "If she dies, it will be me who killed her. She was against it from the beginning and she has regretted it ever since."

Once he heard about Shimako's suicide, all the fight seemed to go out of him. He no longer tried resist their questioning and finally started to recount all the events leading up to the murders.

"I first started to work for Nasuno before the Uchibō club opened. I'd been the site foreman for one of the companies involved in building the course and I met Mr. Nasuno when he came to view the progress. We got along well and he soon offered me a job with the club, working on the sales. Shortly afterward, he started Camellia and put me in charge.

"Although the company was officially responsible for the sales, the actual work was done by other companies and we were just there to keep everything under control. There wasn't very much real work to do and I did virtually all of it myself. Looking back on it now, I realize that Nasuno just wanted someone he could control completely to look after the capital."

When asked how much capital Camellia had, he resisted them again, but after repeated questioning he finally came clean.

"There were actually nearly eight thousand memberships sold for the Uchibō club, and of these, Kawai and Nasuno sold three thousand directly. That's where the three billion yen that the members are all claiming disappeared came from, but Camellia didn't have anything to do with that; our profits all came from the forty-eight-hundred official sales."

Camellia managed to skim fourteen hundred million yen off the sales, and after they had paid all their taxes and overhead they were still left with eight hundred million. Acting on Nasuno's orders, Kinumura invested this in various stocks and land deals, and at the end of seven years the capital had grown to twelve hundred million yen. When Nasuno decided to start the Tanzawa club, he had withdrawn five hundred million, but that still left seven hundred million in Camellia's name, or at least, so he thought.

"Nasuno first thought of the Tanzawa club in the summer of seventy-eight, and although I opposed it bitterly he wouldn't listen. He didn't seem to realize that things had changed after the oil crisis and that what with the drop in memberships and the increase in land prices and running costs, numerous clubs would go bankrupt or change hands every year. However, neither he nor Kawai could forget how much they'd been able to make out of the Uchibō club and they wouldn't listen to me."

No sooner had they started, however, than they found that Kinumura had been correct. The contractor's estimate was much higher than either of them had anticipated.

"That was when Nasuno first thought of giving the landscaping to another company. Not only would a small company be willing to do the job cheaper, but it would also be easier to cheat. I knew him well enough to guess what he had in mind, so I suggested that he use Kōsuke's company."

When asked whether he had some sort of a grudge against Kōsuke, he frowned and stared at the desk for a few minutes.

"Ōkita was three years my senior at college, but we were both members of the ski club, so we still met occasionally at the meetings and it was at one of these, four years ago, that I met Shimako. I married when I was twenty-seven, but it only lasted for two years and I've been living alone ever since."

His wife had left him because his business left him no time for her, and when he had met Shimako, she was in the same position. He felt sorry for her, and at the same time he also felt himself irresistibly attracted by her cold beauty.

Three months after they were first introduced, they began meeting in secret. He would leave work early and pick her up in Shinjuku or Shibuya, then they'd go to a hotel or to the condominium he'd bought around the same time.

Sometimes she'd pretend to visit her mother and sister, but in fact she would stay with him at his apartment.

Three years ago Shimako had become pregnant.

"I don't know if Kōsuke realized she was being unfaithful. I think he guessed something was afoot, but he never knew that it was me that she was having her affair with or that I was the father of her child."

"Is it because he found out that they had the argument that led to him hitting her?"

"No, not exactly. She had told him she was going to her mother's for the night when actually she came over to see me. She often went to stay with them, and when she was gone for some while he would sometimes phone her, but if she was only going for one night he very rarely bothered. That night, however, he called, and although Shimako had told her mother and her sister to make up some excuse, something went wrong and he found out she wasn't there."

When she returned home he asked where she had been and she couldn't think up an excuse on the spur of the moment, so she panicked and insisted that she had been at her parents' home. Kōsuke lost his temper and struck her, but unfortunately, she hit her waist on a table as she fell. That was the cause of her miscarriage."

"Did Ōkita know that she was pregnant at the time?"

"Apparently, but anyway it destroyed their relationship altogether, and at the same time it gave me cause to hate him."

He closed his eyes and an expression of pain crossed his face. Momozaki gave a heavy sigh. Even if it was partly Kōsuke's fault for neglecting her, Shimako had wronged him by having an affair with Kinumura. However, Shimako would only remember that it was due to her husband's violence that she had lost her only child and Kinumura would feel the same way, too. The result was all too predictable; husband and wife would draw even farther apart, Kōsuke absorbing himself even more in his work and Shimako driven by her loneliness to see even more of Kinumura.

"When I heard that Nasuno was looking for a landscape gardener, I thought it would be the perfect way to get revenge for both of us.'' For the first time Kinumura's expression brightened.

"So you mean that the designer's complaints about Kō-suke's work had been planned from the beginning as a way of lowering the price?''

"It's the only possible explanation. The design office is connected to Nasuno and also Kawai used the same technique with the suppliers of furniture and fittings for the clubhouse in order to get them cheap.''

Kawai and Nasuno had used every trick they could think of in order to lower costs, but even though they were able to swindle a lot of people, it was not enough. The one hundred and twenty million owed to Kōsuke was a drop in the bucket compared with the three billion yen they owed elsewhere, and of this, one and a half billion was due to the landowners and couldn't be delayed any longer.

"Kawai and Nasuno met on the twentieth of September and agreed that they would both invest a further seven hundred and fifty million each to pay for the land. Nasuno called me into his office and told me about it on the twenty-second—'' He broke off and sat gazing into space as he thought back to the meeting.

"He told you he was going to use Camellia's money for that, didn't he?'' Yamane asked quietly; their investigation of his background had been quite thorough. "However, Camellia didn't have as much capital as he thought it did; he had left you to invest the capital, but you had used a lot of it on yourself instead. You bought your condominium four years ago for six million yen, and then there was the land you bought in Karuizawa and the membership in the famous golf club, all bought with Camellia's money—but without Mr. Nasuno's knowledge.''

"Of course you intended to pay it back,'' Momozaki said, taking up the story. "No doubt that's why in 1980 you started to act as a moneylender. You began by lending only to friends, but recently it has reached the point where you'll lend to anyone who has an introduction. You charge a lot of interest, but the risk is also great.''

There was nothing Kinumura could say; they obviously knew everything. The company ledgers that he had presented to Nasuno had listed seven hundred million yen in assets, when in fact he had used two hundred and fifty million of them on himself.

"When he told you he wanted to use the seven hundred million for the Tanzawa club, you realized that your misuse of the money would come to light and so you decided to kill him. Am I wrong?"

"No, that's not the whole story," Kinumura said in an anguished voice. "I admit that when Mr. Nasuno told me he wanted to use Camellia's seven hundred million for the Tanzawa club I was very worried, as I knew he would find out what I had done, but that wasn't all. He was going to take away everything and leave the company with nothing at all; Camellia would cease to exist in all but name, and if that happened, the ten years I spent building the company would have been completely meaningless. I know that the original capital for the company came from the Uchibō club and that Mr. Nasuno probably thought of it all as being his, but it was me who struggled to make the company a success, it was me who managed to almost double the capital in ten years.

"That's why I did my best to make him change his mind when he first thought of starting the Tanzawa club. I told him that Camellia was a separate company and that it should be kept that way, but he wouldn't listen. When he first took five hundred million from the company, he promised that would be all, but I realize now that I was becoming too much of a nuisance for him and he thought this would be a good time to get rid of me. He wanted an obedient robot who would do what he was told—that's why he first gave me the job—but when I started to make demands of my own, he probably decided to do away with Camellia altogether and, by so doing, rid himself of me, too. However, it's only because I thought of it as my own company that I was able to devote myself to it for the last ten years."

"Not to mention all the money you embezzled," Momozaki said with a bitter laugh. "Well, I suppose that after you had been left in charge of the money for ten years, it must have felt as if it were your own, but it wasn't only the fear of discovery that drove you to murder." His voice took on a hard edge. "There were still four hundred and fifty million yen left in the company. You and Nasuno were the only people who knew what happened to the money since it was siphoned off from the Uchibō club. Even Nasuno's partner Kawai had nothing to do with it, so if you were just to say that it had all been used up in the last ten years, nobody would be able to call you a liar—at any rate, you must have thought so.''

Kinumura had sat listening to this in silence, but gradually his face grew red and he finally said in an angry voice, ''But he was going to get rid of me, just like that. It didn't matter how many years I had been working for him, I was still nothing more to him than a disposable robot!''

After Nasuno had told him to make the necessary arrangements to withdraw seven hundred million yen from Camellia for use in the Tanzawa club, Kinumura went back to his apartment in shock. He spent the next three days trying to decide what to do, and the only way he could see out of his predicament was to murder Nasuno. One of the main factors that brought him to this extreme course of action was the bad blood between Kōsuke and Nasuno, and when he heard about the fight they had had in Nasuno's office on the first of October, he realized he would never have another chance like this.

He knew that without another suspect the police would find their way back to him in the end, but after the fight Kōsuke would be the obvious suspect. But to set Kōsuke up, he had to make sure he didn't have an alibi and then plant some false evidence. This, coupled with his quick temper and strong motive, would leave nobody in doubt about his guilt.

''That's when I realized I couldn't do it without Shimako. She may look very cool, but in fact she's a very passionate woman and will do anything for her man. I didn't really want to involve her and she was scared when I told her what I wanted, but we didn't have any choice. It was only a matter of time before Nasuno sued me for breach of trust and embezzlement, and once that happened we'd be finished anyway. The thing that really decided it for her, though, was her hatred for Kōsuke. As far as she was concerned, he had killed her child, and when she thought of that, she forgot everything else."

Kinumura drove around the Himonya area and checked out all the likely phone booths and coffee bars, and then on October 3 Shimako came to stay at his apartment, bringing the spare key to Kōsuke's car with her. She had told Kōsuke that she was feeling poorly and would be staying at her mother's house.

The two of them finalized their plan and decided to carry it out on the sixth. Kinumura and Nasuno would be taking some customers out for a meal that day, so Kinumura could attack him on the way home. All they had to do was lure Kōsuke out of the house.

He was finally getting to the details of the crime.

"That night Nasuno and I took the customers out to a restaurant in Akasaka and after that we went drinking in Ginza. We went to two bars and left the second one a little before eleven."

Kinumura often went drinking with Nasuno, so he knew that the other always sent his car home first and that he generally liked to call it a day around eleven o'clock.

"Nasuno called for three cars to take them home around ten-forty, and a few minutes later I telephoned a coffee bar in Himonya called Sharon and asked for a customer called Okamura. Of course there was nobody of that name there, but it was the signal for Shimako to put her part of the plan in action. Immediately after she heard the waiter calling for Okamura, she left the coffee bar and hurried up to the phone booth by the church."

Nasuno's car arrived at 10:50, but it couldn't stop near the bar, and when he heard that it had arrived, Nasuno and the clients had started to walk toward it while Kinumura said his good-byes at the club and then hurried to his own car, which he had left nearby, and drove straight onto the expressway.

"I knew it would be ten past eleven before his car left Ginza and it wouldn't be going as fast as me, so I'd arrive at his house at Oh-okayama at least ten minutes before him."

While this was going on, Shimako had arrived at the phone booth about three minutes after leaving the coffee bar, and after connecting a hearing aid to the mike of the phone as she had practiced at the apartment, she proceeded to dial her home number. She set the hearing aid at the lowest setting and spoke in as deep a voice as she could manage. This alone would make it very difficult for anyone to recognize her voice, but at the same time she also mimicked her mother's Okayama accent and panted as if she were sick or in pain.

"I remembered reading about using a hearing aid to disguise one's voice in a magazine somewhere. A professor who had helped analyze a kidnapper's voice for the police had mentioned it in an interview and it just stuck in my mind ever since."

Momozaki felt a shock when he realized that Chiharu had been one hundred percent right in her reasoning and wished that he had listened to her earlier.

"Personally I thought it was taking things a bit too far to use the hearing aid, but Shimako was terrified that Kōsuke would guess who it was. Even though he had killed her child, they had once felt something for each other and she didn't want him to know that it was her who had betrayed him."

Shimako was convinced that Kōsuke would not be able to ignore her request if he thought it came from a blind person. Not only was there his cousin's accident, but the weather had been very cold and wet for three days and he knew that Himonya was very deserted at night.

She made her call at 10:37; it lasted for exactly three minutes. If everything went according to plan, Kōsuke would spend some minutes trying to pass on her message, and even after he discovered that he couldn't get through, they guessed that it would take him at least thirty minutes before he made up his mind to do anything else.

Shimako went back to Meguro Avenue and entered another coffee bar, this one called Nana. There were any number of coffee bars on the main road, but this one was particularly quiet and didn't even have any music playing. Thirty-five minutes after the first call she dialed her home again, this time as herself. Tome answered and told her that Kōsuke had gone out five minutes earlier; Shimako told her she was feeling much better and would be coming home the next day. Of course if Kōsuke had answered the phone, she planned to say the same thing, but now she knew that their plan had worked. Kōsuke had left the house by 11:15; it took twenty minutes to get to Himonya, and even if it took him a while to find the church, he should be there by 11:40.

Soon after she had hung up, Kinumura telephoned the coffee bar asking for someone called Yamada, and this time she took the call. He had already left the expressway and was near Nasuno's house. She told him that everything was going according to plan and gave him the go-ahead.

After she hung up, she left the coffee bar and hurried back to the phone booth. The streets were still deserted and she could see the light from the phone booth spilling out over the road. She opened the door and put the handkerchief and the note on the shelf next to the phone. She had two ready, one directing him to the coffee bar Eri, and the other to a different one that was farther away and harder to find, just in case he had left the house earlier. If he had left soon after her call and driven directly to the phone booth, he could have arrived by 11:20, and if he were then to go straight to the coffee bar and spend about twenty minutes there, it would have given him a perfect alibi.

"Not that we thought there was much chance of him staying in the coffee bar once he knew that the mystery woman was no longer there, but we chose a dark one where it would be difficult for anyone to remember his face, just in case," Kinumura said, his eyes blank as he thought back over the time when they plotted the murder.

"But Shimako really did go to Eri, didn't she?" Momozaki asked.

"Yes, after she left the message in the phone booth, she went there and used the phone at the counter but pretended that she couldn't get through."

Momozaki remembered the waitress saying that a thin woman in a dark raincoat had sat in a corner seat and drunk a hot lemon juice. She also remembered seeing someone who looked like Kōsuke, but she couldn't swear to it, and anyway, even if she could, he had only been there for two or three minutes, so it wouldn't provide him with much of an alibi. The way the police looked at it, the coffee bar was only about a five minutes' drive from Nasuno's house and he could always have just stopped in after the murder in an effort to make an alibi. No, once they lured Kōsuke away from his house in Kinuta and over to Himonya, they had already succeeded in their aim.

"And what were you doing all this while?" Momozaki asked quietly.

Kinumura dropped his eyes to the desk and sat in silence while he gathered his thoughts together. The room in which they were sitting was becoming quite cold, but he didn't seem to notice and a sweat stood out on his forehead. An hour and a half had passed since he had started his confession, and during that period his face had lost all its color and his cheeks seemed to become gaunt.

"I got to Nasuno's house at eleven-twenty-five," he said in a low voice, realizing that he couldn't avoid it any longer. "The driveway had been under repair since the end of September, and when I arrived, some new concrete had just been laid and it was covered with tarpaulins."

After he had checked that it could not be driven on, he drove his car some way off and parked it in a dark side street. He put on a dark windbreaker and gloves, then made his way back to the house with a number-five golf club in his hand.

"That was Kōsuke's club, wasn't it?"

"Yes . . ."

"When did you take it?"

"The night before, I sneaked into his garage. . . ."

To be more precise, it had been at two o'clock on the morning of the sixth. Kinumura had opened the trunk of Kōsuke's car with the key that Shimako had given him and slipped out one club; then at eleven o'clock on the night of the same day, he had been crouching in the bushes by Nasuno's front gate with the same club in his hand.

The car that had brought Nasuno home arrived at 11:42 or 11:43. A light drizzle was falling and the driver had come around to Nasuno's door with an umbrella and offered to see him up to his front door, but Nasuno had waved him away, saying that he would be okay. The trees over the drive kept away most of the rain, and anyway,

Nasuno never bothered with an umbrella unless the rain was very heavy.

As soon as the car drove off Kinumura ran up the driveway after Nasuno, who was striding quickly up to the house. Kinumura was wearing sneakers, so Nasuno didn't hear him until he was almost on him.

"Nasuno!" he called out, and the older man swung around in surprise. He guessed instinctively that something was wrong and took a step back.

"Who is it?"

"Kōsuke Ōkita."

It was dark and Nasuno couldn't see the other's face, but he obviously believed it was indeed Kōsuke and his whole body tensed, but it didn't save him. The next moment Kinumura swung the golf club at his head.

"I hit him in the head twice and he fell to the ground. I checked for his pulse, but I couldn't find one and he seemed to have stopped breathing. . . ."

Kinumura finally managed to get the story out, although his voice failed him several times.

"Was it you who dragged him into the bushes?"

"Yes."

"And why did you cover his head with a handkerchief?"

"I don't really know, I wasn't thinking straight. Maybe I was trying to hide the wound, but when I went through his pockets, I came across a white handkerchief and it just seemed the natural thing to do."

"And why did you use Ōkita's name?"

"I thought it would be safer in case anyone interrupted me or I didn't manage to kill him. Then he'd think it was Kōsuke who did it, but it's strange, you know, when I did it I really did feel as if I was Kōsuke."

Things went more or less according to plan after that. Kinumura made a big show of trying to defend Kōsuke, but the police soon found out about the trouble between Kōsuke and Nasuno from Kawai and the others, and two days later he was asked down to the station for questioning. He had the motive and the opportunity; all that was needed to push for a conviction was some evidence.

"I wanted the evidence to come to light in as natural a

way as possible and that was when I remembered Shimako complaining about a local dog that sometimes came and dug up their garden."

"Were you responsible for all of that?"

"Yes. I slipped into their garden at about three o'clock on the morning of the tenth with the club, the gloves, and the towels I had used to clean off the blood after the . . . after I did it."

He had dug a hole under the shed and half buried the evidence. He had told Shimako what he intended to do the day before and she just waited until Naitō or Tome went to fill in the hole and discovered them.

"That night at about eight o'clock I had a call from Shimako. She told me that Kōsuke had been at work when the things were found, and when she phoned and told him about it, he hurried home to see them for himself. He knew that once you saw them it would be the end for him, but before he was arrested he wanted to try to gather enough capital to keep his company solvent until everything was sorted out. He told Shimako that he was going to go out and that she was not to call you until he phoned and told her it was all right to do so, but that had been the morning and she had heard nothing more from him since then and didn't know what to do.

"When I heard this, I knew it was perfect. If nobody knew where he was when the evidence was handed over, you'd automatically assume he had gone on the run and wouldn't hesitate to take out a warrant for his arrest."

"That night Naitō phoned and said that he was phoning on behalf of Mrs. Ōkita," Momozaki said, watching Kinumura's face closely. "He was telling the truth, but do you mean that you were telling her what to do all the time?"

"Yes, she was already losing control of herself and was completely unable to make any decisions. I had no choice but to tell her what to do."

"Just a minute. There's one point I'd like to make quite clear before we proceed any further. Do you mean to say that Ōkita had no intention of going on the run when he first disappeared?"

"Not as far as I know."

"But it was Shimako who led us to believe that he had?"

"Yes."

Momozaki had felt all along that there was something strange about Kōsuke's escape attempt and he nodded to himself, understanding everything at last.

While it was true that it was Kinumura and Shimako who had driven Kōsuke to go on the run, Kinumura insisted that neither of them had any idea what happened to him after that.

"I had told Shimako that under no circumstances should we meet until after the whole affair had died down, but when she phoned me on October twentieth, I could hear right away that something was wrong, so I hurried over to see her. When she showed me the letter and the finger, I was shocked and couldn't think what to do, but finally I decided that it would be best if we just told you everything and let you handle it."

"I decided I had better stay with her; she was so upset that I had no idea what she might say if she was left on her own. I had absolutely no idea what was going to happen; the whole thing came as a complete surprise to me."

He continued to deny any knowledge of the kidnapping and Momozaki tended to believe him. They had checked out his movements and he had an alibi for the time when the parcel and letter were mailed, and there appeared to be no sign of his having left Tokyo during the five days prior to their delivery.

"Okay, we'll leave that for the time being," Momozaki said. "But by staying at the house with us, you were able to learn a very valuable piece of information. You were able to learn of Kōsuke's death two hours before even the press were told and you used this information in a very clever way to provide yourself with a brilliant alibi. You had some of us completely fooled for a while, but as soon as we realized what you had done, it was obvious that it was you. You were responsible for Risaburō Kawai's murder, too, weren't you?"

"I'm one of the people you managed to fool," Yamane added with a wry laugh.

"A man wearing a black windbreaker with the hood up

and carrying a golf club was seen hanging around in the vicinity of Kawai's house between ten-twenty-five and ten-fifty. He went into a bar and a Laundromat to use the telephones there and made a point of being overheard when he announced that his name was Kōsuke Ōkita. It then seems likely that he went to the Kawai house and waited for Kawai's return—the timing is just right. He left a footprint at the scene of the murder of approximately the same size as Ōkita's and it seemed obvious from the first that he was trying to lay the blame for the murder at his doorstep. We might have been fooled into believing that it was him except for one thing—two hours before the crime we had heard that Ōkita was already dead.''

Kinumura sat with his head bowed, his face as white as a sheet.

''We may have known that Ōkita was dead, but nobody else did. The press was told at ten-thirty and it first appeared on the news at eleven o'clock, so we automatically assumed that whoever it was who made the attack either believed that Ōkita was still alive or thought that we still didn't know he was dead and considered it the perfect chance to have the blame placed on him.''

When Yamane had said this at the conference on the night after Kawai's body had been found, Momozaki had felt there was something wrong. He probably already suspected Kinumura instinctively, but what Yamane had to say had sounded so logical that even he had found himself believing it for a while.

''The only people apart from the police who knew about Ōkita's death were those who heard the report at his house—namely, you, Shimako, and Tome—so you were automatically struck off the list of suspects. You couldn't be expected to try to lay the blame on a dead man as the truth was sure to come to light soon, but that was where you were very clever.''

''I have to admit, you acted very fast indeed.'' Yamane picked up the story. ''You left the Ōkitas' house with me at a little after nine o'clock, and as you had your car parked nearby, you could have gotten back to your apartment in about twenty minutes. You picked up the black windbreaker, sunglasses, and golf club there before going back to your car. I guess you bought a pair of sneakers the same size as Ōkita's for the Nasuno murder and you wore them, too.''

"At that time of night it would only take you about fifteen minutes to get from your apartment in Eifukuchō to Ogikubo," said Momozaki. "You then put on the windbreaker and sunglasses and walked into the Pico bar at ten-twenty-five. It would have been quite feasible for you to have arrived there at that time. After behaving in a suspicious manner and gathering as many witnesses as possible, you went to Kawai's house and lay in wait for his return. You had picked up an old tricycle from a nearby rubbish dump and put it in the middle of the road so Kawai's car couldn't pass and he was forced to get out. That was when you attacked him. Did you say your name was Ōkita that time, too?

"Why was it necessary for you to kill Kawai? Was it because of what he had told his mistress before he left her that night? He had said that since Nasuno's death you were behaving as if Camellia's money was your own but that he wasn't going to let you get away with it. He also owned stock in the company and he intended to pressure the other stockholders into forcing you out. Was that the reason for this murder, too? Camellia's money?''

"Had he begun to suspect your embezzlement? Were you worried that he would make it public and that by so doing would show your motive for killing Nasuno, too?

"Was Shimako an accomplice in this murder, too?''

Kinumura just sat and listened as they both accused him. Sweat dripped from his face and his shoulders shook. "I'm sorry, it was exactly as you say. I killed Kawai and tried to lay the blame on Kōsuke. When I heard the news about his death, I knew it was the perfect opportunity to commit the murder without anyone suspecting me, but I had to act quickly and had no time to think over what I was about to do." He looked at them both pleadingly. "But I did it all on my own. Shimako had absolutely nothing to do with it.''

They both regarded him in silence.

"It's the truth; I didn't need her help to kill Kawai, and anyway she was in no condition to do anything.''

"Did she know what you were doing?"

"No. I told her it was the work of the Kuretani gang and I think she believed me. But even though she didn't know it herself, she was one of the main reasons why I felt forced to kill Kawai. It was all my fault; I should never have asked a sensitive woman like her to help me in murder to begin with."

Kawai and Nasuno had been partners for more than ten years, but they avoided discussing each other's personal finances. However, Nasuno had gone to Kawai's office on September 20 and told him all about Camellia's financial state and then suggested that they both invest an additional seven hundred and fifty million in the Tanzawa club. Camellia had seven hundred million on the books and he would get the other fifty million from somewhere else. He asked Kawai to do the same.

"It was the first time he had ever talked about his financial position so openly and Kawai later guessed that he had sensed his imminent death somehow."

After Nasuno's death Kawai told Kinumura everything that he had said.

Kinumura had thought that only he and Nasuno knew about Camellia's financial situation and he was shocked to discover that Kawai knew so much. Once he found out that almost forty percent of the money was missing, Kawai wouldn't hesitate to sue him, as he was even stricter about such things than Nasuno had been.

"That was half the reason why I felt I had to kill him but also . . . well, you see, Shimako had suddenly turned up at Nasuno's funeral service on October fourteenth. She had been wearing a smart black suit; she signed the register in her maiden name and just sat quietly in a chair before going home again. . . ."

Momozaki had heard about this at the time from the detective who had followed her there. "What did she go there for?"

Kinumura sat looking at the desk for a moment, then he pushed his glasses up and said in a quiet voice, "When I asked her afterward, she said she wanted to see me, even if only for a moment, and she just couldn't stop herself."

Kinumura had told her repeatedly that they mustn't be

seen together until everything had died down. If people knew of their affair, they'd soon start to put two and two together. Shimako, however, couldn't stand it any longer and thought that there couldn't be any harm in just watching him in the crowded funeral parlor. Acting on the spur of the moment, she had grabbed a taxi and hurried over. When she saw Kinumura, she realized what a mistake she'd made and hurried out, but the harm had already been done.

Later, when Shimako ran to Kinumura's apartment in the middle of the night, Wakura finally realized why she had gone to the funeral, but he wasn't the only one who had noticed their relationship. The other person had been Kawai.

"I heard from him later that he had seen us coming out of a hotel together once and immediately realized that our relationship was more than casual, although at that time he had no idea who I was with and didn't take much notice of it. He was always interested in women, though, and never forgot a beautiful woman's face."

That was six months before the funeral and Kawai had almost forgotten about it when he saw Shimako in the funeral parlor. She seemed to be trying to be inconspicuous, but when Kinumura walked down the aisle toward her, they had exchanged a look and hers had contained a terrible sadness and pain. She had sat like that for a few moments, then suddenly hurried out of the parlor, almost as if she were trying to escape from something.

"Who was that woman?" Kawai had asked. "I think we've met, but I can't remember her name."

After pretending to think about it for a short while, Kinumura finally answered that he believed it was Kōsuke's wife.

"I had a nasty feeling about it when he asked me. He seemed to be laughing at me, but what could I say? If he found out later, my inability to answer would seem suspicious, so I thought the safest thing was to tell him."

His premonition had been correct: when he visited the Tanzawa club three days later, he bumped into Kawai in one of the corridors there.

"I never knew that you and Ōkita's wife were so intimate. I can see that I'll have to keep an eye on you, but now that I know, it's given me all kinds of interesting ideas."

It was then that he told Kinumura that he had heard from Nasuno about Camellia's capital and that Kinumura had better hurry up and arrange for its transfer to the Tanzawa club. He even gave detailed procedure instructions and hinted that if Kinumura failed to cooperate, he would use his stock to force him out of the company altogether.

"He even hinted that if I didn't want my relationship with Shimako made public, I should do as he said. However, I realized that no matter what I did, it was only a matter of time before he drove me out of the company and tipped you off about Shimako and me. Since Mr. Nasuno was dead, he tried to blame him for the missing money and he wanted to get rid of everyone who knew the truth before he took complete control of both clubs." Kinumura showed his resentment for the first time and ground his teeth in anger.

"I wanted to avoid killing him at all costs—after all, even if he revealed the truth about Shimako and me, it wouldn't mean we had killed Nasuno. There was no proof, but I could see that Shimako wouldn't be able to stand the strain of an investigation.

"She was obviously heading for a breakdown. I could see that if Kawai tipped you off and you questioned her, she'd soon fall apart and confess everything. He may not have any evidence, but he didn't need any; all he had to do was contact you and that would be the end. So I decided to shut him up permanently before he could do anything else."

Kinumura then told them in detail how he had proceeded. It was exactly as they had thought, right down to the child's tricycle that he had found at a nearby dump.

"There was an unusually thick fog that night, and when I suddenly appeared in front of him and said that my name was Kōsuke, I think he really believed me. In a strange way I also felt that I was Kōsuke exacting my vengeance on him."

"Are you quite sure Shimako had nothing to do with this?"

"Yes, absolutely. Apart from anything else, I knew that

the knowledge would be too much for her and she'd probably attempt suicide or something. As it turned out she did so anyway. How is she—have you had any news?''

The news arrived at dawn that day. Shimako had arrived at the hospital at 2:15, and seeing the pills and the empty containers that the detectives had found at her house, the doctors guessed that she had taken seventy sleeping pills. They immediately pumped her stomach and inserted a tube in her throat to help her breathe, but from what the housekeeper told them, more than two hours had passed since she took the pills and most of them had already been absorbed into her system.

Even after the doctors had done all they could for her, she showed no sign of recovering consciousness. Her pulse grew weaker, her blood pressure dropped, and at 4:20 that morning, she finally stopped breathing. The cause of death was listed as barbiturate poisoning brought on by an overdose of sleeping pills.

In death Shimako's face was even paler than it had been in life, but gone were the fear and the loneliness, and she looked stunningly beautiful.

Kinumura had virtually finished his confession when the news reached the police station; when he heard, he collapsed onto the desk in front of him.

''The poor thing, she couldn't stand it any longer. It's as if I killed her myself.''

He burst into tears that seemed to be endless, and even Momozaki felt moved by his anguish and sat in silence with his eyes closed.

In this way the mystery of the Nasuno and Kawai murders was finally solved; all that remained was the kidnapping and murder of Kōsuke. But the time had come for this, too, to be cleared up. That morning, November 26, the six o'clock news on the television and the radio led off with the story of Shimako's death and Kinumura's confession, and soon after that, Kōsuke appeared at the Himonya police station in person.

# 20

# A Twilight Meeting

Tuesday November 30 was a fine day that found Chiharu at home. Usually Thursday was her day off from the golf club, but today she had a feeling that something was going to happen and so she took the day off.

Five days earlier, in the middle of the night, she had met Kōsuke on a starlit piece of wasteland. He had not been out of her mind for a minute since he first disappeared and she had resigned herself to never seeing his handsome, masculine features again.

"Is that you, Kōsuke?"

"Yes, it's me. I've been wanting to see you so much."

That was all they said before she led him back to her car. She guessed that the detectives who had appeared and arrested Kinumura would also want to see Kōsuke, and she still feared being arrested herself. Kōsuke also seemed to want to spend a little more time with her, just the two of them.

"I had almost given up hope of ever seeing you again," Kōsuke said. "Would you like to hear what happened to me after we last separated? I'd like to tell you before I go to the police and my story gets splashed all over the papers. All the time I was on the run, I thought of the time

289

when I'd be able to sit down with you and tell you every-thing.''

He told her that he had been staying in a hotel near the fun fair at Toshima since he had come back to Tokyo at the beginning of the month, and she drove slowly in that direction while he spoke. He tried to keep the story as simple as possible, without getting worked up, but it pierced her to the heart to hear of the life he had spent as a fugitive.

"Still, I had better go and turn myself over to the police now," he said with a strained expression when they had arrived at the park at Toshima. "If I wait too long, I'll only make trouble for Mr. Sako. I used his name, but he knows absolutely nothing about any of this. Anyway, I want to get everything sorted out as soon as possible. I'm sick and tired of living like this."

"But will you be all right?"

"I think so. Those two detectives heard everything Kin-umura and I said to each other, and if I give myself up, he won't be able to deny it."

"But don't you think it might be better to wait until he admits everything and you're not a suspect any longer?"

The hotel he was staying in was surrounded by tall zel-kova trees, most of which had lost their leaves by now. It was an old, three-story building with a blue neon sign on the roof, and here and there Chiharu could see where the tiles had fallen off the façade. She found herself thinking about the hotel she'd seen in the residential area of Nagoya and realized that they were both very similar.

Kōsuke told her to pull up a ways from the hotel and then he turned and looked at her. He was much thinner than he had been and she could see numerous emotions struggling in his eyes. He wanted to stay and talk to her, but at the same time he didn't want her to know just how bad it had been while he was on the run. Chiharu was not scared, though, and thought that if it were necessary, she'd stay with him until his name was cleared. But before she could articulate her thoughts, he placed his gloved hand over hers on the steering wheel.

"You're right; I'll wait a little longer. Kinumura's in-terrogation should be finished by morning. Believe me, once everything has been cleared up and I'm really free again, you're the first person I'll tell.''

"You promise you won't go anywhere else?"

He smiled at her. His face seemed to have forgotten how to smile for a moment, but suddenly his cheeks softened and he gave her a beautiful smile. He then got out of the car and walked toward the neon sign. Chiharu wanted to get out and follow him, but she felt unable to. It was just like the last time they had met; he had forced her to stand and wait while he disappeared into the darkness.

She arrived home late, but the next morning she was up in time to hear the first news about Shimako's suicide and Kinumura's confession. A short while later, on the next news, she heard that Kōsuke had given himself up.

Even though his innocence no longer needed to be proved, Chiharu expected it to be several days before he'd be able to call her. After he finished with the police, he'd then have to organize Shimako's funeral.

She went to work every day, and after work was finished she stayed behind to practice on her own. She felt that physical exertion would take her mind off Kōsuke, but thinking of him disappearing into the seedy hotel that night, she sometimes found herself just staring at the ball and worrying that it had all been a dream.

The thirtieth dawned bright and clear, but Chiharu telephoned the club to say she wouldn't be coming in. She had a strange sense of expectancy and was quite happy to stay in and talk to her mother in front of the family shrine where her father's memorial plaque was on display.

The phone was in the hall. When it finally rang at around four o'clock, she ran to it and took it into the reception room before answering.

"Hello?"

"Hello, is that the Nasuno residence?"

"Yes."

"Is that Chiharu?"

"Yes."

"Hello, this is Kōsuke speaking."

Chiharu felt a shock run through her. It was the first time she had heard him pronounce his name on the phone for what seemed like months, and it meant that the nightmare was finally over.

"Yes, it is me," she said in a bright voice.

"Thank you for everything you did."

"Not at all. You know, I had a feeling you were going to call me today."

"If you're free, I wondered if you could come out and meet me."

"Yes . . ."

"I'm on my way to Kokubunji to visit one of my suppliers; he did a lot for my company when I was . . . away, and I want to thank him. I should be finished in about an hour and I wondered if I could see you after that?"

Kōsuke spoke in a slightly formal way, the same he had when he called her in October. She guessed that he had become so used to being on his guard while he was on the run that it had become a habit.

"Okay," she answered brightly, "I'll get ready right away."

She had half expected him to suggest that they meet in the same coffee bar as before, but instead he asked her to come to the place in the fields where they had separated. She explained to her mother where she was going and then hurried out to her car. As she drove up the ring road she was able to accelerate, the roads still being fairly empty before rush hour.

He's finally come home, she thought. This time he's here to stay.

She felt an emotion too powerful for words, but the sense of relief that she had first felt when she met him again still overwhelmed her.

As she drove onto the expressway the surrounding scenery was full of the colors of autumn, and in the distance she could see the peaks of the Chichibu mountains silhouetted against the reds of sunset.

Driving along the same route as before, she found her thoughts going back to that day. Kōsuke had said on the phone that he might not be able to see her again for some time, and later, when she heard about the evidence that had been found in his garden, she thought he had already decided to go on the run, but she had been wrong. He had realized that it was only a matter of time before he was arrested, and even though he was confident that his innocence would triumph in the end, he knew it might take some time. He wanted to see Chiharu once more before they were separated. Chiharu had also felt sure that his innocence would be proven in the end; she just wanted him to remain healthy until then. She didn't care if he was arrested, as long as he was alive.

He came back in the end, she thought to herself again, still only half believing it.

Just past the red gateway to a shrine the road climbed suddenly and she soon came to the Coral Tree coffee bar where she had met Kōsuke the last time, but she drove straight past without stopping. She turned into a small track leading into the fields, and passing a grove of black pine, she came to an open area and stopped the car. She stepped out and felt a refreshing chill and smelled a faint trace of woodsmoke in the air. The shadows were deepening, and in the west there was only a faint reminder left of the golden sunset.

She started to walk along the same path she had trod with Kōsuke in October. There were small bushes planted at regular intervals among the pine and boxwood and here and there she noticed a flaming maple tree. The evening air was becoming chilly and no one was in sight.

She came at last to a crossroads and paused for a minute, remembering how the last time there had been a wind soughing in the trees when she passed this spot. She continued for several yards until she became aware of the silhouette of a man standing among the trees, facing her. It was the figure of a tall man with a coat over his shoulders.

It was so long since she had seen Kōsuke that she stood watching him for a short while, drinking in the sight of him. They walked toward each other and then came to a halt. His face was still rather gaunt, but he looked much healthier than he had the last time they had met, although she couldn't say whether this was due to his new haircut or the laughter that seemed to flow from his eyes. He reached out and drew her toward him with both hands. He

held her as he would hold something precious that he never
wanted to lose again, then hugged her even tighter to him.
Their lips met for what seemed an eternity and Chiharu's
mind went completely blank until she felt him loosen his
grip slightly. Tears started to flow down her cheeks.

"You came back . . . you really came back."

"Because you were waiting."

"You won't go away again, will you?" Chiharu asked,
looking at him pleadingly. "There's nothing more to be
frightened of?"

"I was never frightened. I always knew that no matter
what happened, you would still believe in me."

"Yes, I never doubted you for a minute."

Now that she thought about it, she realized it was true;
she had always been convinced that he would come back
to her in the end.

He put his arm around her shoulders and they started to
walk. Chiharu smelled his after-shave lotion and realized
that from now on she would always be able to smell it.

"How is your golf these days?" he asked after an interval.

"Well, I've been practicing, but since my father died
things have been so upset that I haven't been able to concentrate properly."

The investigation by the public prosecutor's office and
the tax people proved that Nasuno and Kawai had indeed
appropriated three billion yen. The tax people decided that
it was to be paid back from the dead men's estates and
they also demanded a huge amount in unpaid tax. Chiharu's mother had even said that they might have to move
out of their house in Oh-okayama in order to pay it all
back. Although she knew it was very unfair on her mother,
Chiharu found that she couldn't worry about it any longer.

"How's your company doing? It must be very difficult
for you still."

"Yes, it was a miracle that it didn't go bankrupt in my
absence. Everyone was remarkably kind and I don't think
I'll ever be able to repay them. But you can't believe how
good it feels to move around freely." His voice sounded
really happy. "I hope to be able to keep solvent until the
contractor's takeover of the club becomes official and I can

get them to pay me what is owed, but it'll be okay, I think.''

Chiharu had heard the story of his travels the other night as she drove him back to his hotel. He had been sitting in a coffee bar in Morioka watching the news on the television when he was shocked to see his picture appear on the screen and learn that he was a wanted man. He felt that everyone was watching him, and he remembered Sako telling him that if he tried to escape that would be the end. As the police already thought he had gone on the run, there was nothing left for him to do but try to escape, and he decided to make his way to Lake Tazawa. Luckily, he had withdrawn all the available money from the company the day before in order to pay as many of his creditors as possible, so he wasn't hard up for cash.

"I knew the area as I had been there skiing when I was in college, but when I arrived I saw that my picture had appeared in all the local papers and I realized I'd never be able to escape unless I managed to convince the police that I had in fact died. That night in my room at the hotel I made my plans and tried to fake a suicide."

The fact that bodies were seldom found at Lake Tazawa gave him the idea.

"It was about four in the morning when I left the note and sneaked out via the fire escape. I was wearing the shoes I had bought in Morioka as part of my disguise, so I left the other pair by the lake. I went and hid in the shrine at Gozanoishi, then took the first bus back to the station. Now I realize that I stood little chance of getting away with it, but I wasn't thinking logically at the time.''

He had told her how he had made his way west toward Nagoya, sticking mainly to local trains all the way, but there was still one thing he had yet to tell her about.

The sky had turned a deep blue and the stars were already beginning to shine weakly as they walked through the fallen leaves together. Their silhouettes merged and they felt cut off from the world around them. Chiharu had her arm around Kōsuke's back, and holding his gloved hand, she could feel that the end of his little finger was missing. She thought back over what he had told her.

"I tried hiding in Nagoya, but my position was getting

worse day by day and I knew that if things were left as they were, it would only be a matter of time before I was caught. So I decided to try one more gamble.''

He had left the hotel Excel and moved to one on the other side of the city, and that night, in the bathroom, he had amputated his little finger. He had then packed the finger in a pen case and sent it and the ransom note to Shimako.

''I had two reasons for doing this: first it would put the police off my track. They would be busy looking for my body, not a living person, and even if someone saw me walking around and thought I looked like the Kōsuke Ōkita who was wanted for murder, they'd remember I was dead and wouldn't bother to tell the police.

''Second, I knew that Shimako would be very shocked when she received my finger, and then later when she got a phone call from someone she thought was dead, it would frighten her so much that she was sure to run straight to her accomplice. I knew from the minute I was put on the wanted list that Shimako was *somehow* connected with the plot to frame me.'' When he mentioned Shimako's name, a look of pain passed over his face.

''All the same, it must have been very difficult for you to bring yourself to cut off your own finger,'' Chiharu said, looking at him wide-eyed. ''I suppose that people can do anything if they're strong enough.''

''When I used to be a skier, I noticed that if I injured myself when I was cold, I didn't feel anything and that gave me the idea. . . .''

He had wrapped a rubber band around the base of his finger and then put it into a glass of iced water. When he had lost all feeling, he put a carving knife against it and hit the back of the knife as hard as he could with a hammer. He had done it in the bathroom of his room, so it had been quite easy for him to clean up the blood afterward.

When Chiharu heard this, the mere thought of cutting off her own finger was enough to make her feel queasy and she wasn't brave enough to ask any more.

They kept walking until they came out on the other side

of the field and could see the lights of a housing estate shining coldly in the night sky.

"I'd never given it a thought until all this happened, but now I realize just how valuable freedom is."

Kōsuke took a deep breath of the cold night air, which still smelled of smoke and of green things growing. He turned back toward the way they had just come, but then he noticed for the first time that Chiharu had been stroking his hand gently through his glove. He looked down at her and she met his gaze.

"Is the wound on your finger all right now?"

"Yes, I didn't go to a doctor, so it took about a month to heal, but it seems to be fine now."

She hadn't had the nerve to ask to see it, but now he brought his hand up in front of her face and said, "Would you like to see it?"

He gave a little laugh and pulled off the glove to reveal a strong male hand with the little finger cut off from the base. The place where the finger had been removed was covered with skin, and in the dim light it didn't look nearly as bad as Chiharu had imagined. She took his hand in both of hers and tears started to run from her eyes as if the pain had been transmitted to her own little finger.

"Don't cry; it wasn't as bad as all that. It didn't hurt as much as I thought it would, and although I spent a day in bed afterward, I was able to go to the post office myself the day after that to mail it.

"I had written the ransom note beforehand. I used a ruler in order to fool any handwriting experts who might see it, then all I had to do was pop the finger in the plastic case and take it down to the post office."

They both started to make their way back to the car.

"There's still something I don't understand," Chiharu said, trying to keep her voice as light as possible. "When your finger arrived, the police checked the fingerprint to make sure that it was yours and then they sent it to a university hospital, where it was discovered that it had been amputated after death. How did they make such a mistake?"

Kōsuke looked up at the stars for a moment before answering. "It was quite simple really. First I cut off my finger at the base, which meant that my finger was no longer alive. After that I cut it again just below the second joint, which meant that it was, without a doubt, removed after death.''

# About the Author

The bestselling mystery writer in Japan, Shizuko Natsuki has written over eighty novels, short stories and serials, forty of which have been made into Japanese television movies. Several of her short stories have been published in *Ellery Queen's Mystery Magazine*. She is also the author of *Murder at Mt. Fuji* and *The Third Lady*. Ms. Natsuki lives in Nagoya, Japan.

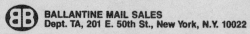